Also by Jay Crownover

Rule
Jet
Rome
Nash
Rowdy

JAY CROWNOVER

Asa

HARPER

This novel is entirely a work of fiction.
The names, characters and incidents portrayed in it are
the work of the author's imagination. Any resemblance to
actual persons, living or dead, events or localities is
entirely coincidental.

Harper
An imprint of HarperCollins*Publishers*
1 London Bridge Street
London SE1 9GF

www.harpercollins.co.uk

A Paperback Original 2015
1

A catalogue record for this book
is available from the British Library

ISBN: 978-0-00-757909-9

Set in Meridien by FMG using Atomik ePublisher from Easypress

Printed by RR Donnelley at Glasgow, UK.

Dedicated to everyone living and experiencing this moment right now with me. This is for the readers, the book lovers, the bibliophiles, the word junkies … my peeps that understand nothing is better than a new book and the escape into a new story. I love that we get to share this world together and I am and always will be proud to be one of you.

INTRODUCTION

We made it! The end. Oh, my word—or many, many words, to be more accurate—I don't know how, but six books in and we're finally here. It's unbelievable and sort of fitting that Asa closes this particular circle. He wasn't supposed to be part of the group—wasn't supposed to be family—wasn't supposed to get a book or an HEA, and yet fate had other plans for him. Sort of like it did for me. He had to fight to get where he belonged, and a couple of times along the way I've felt like I had to do that, too. I tell ya what: this southern boy undid me on a lot of levels, and not just because he's closing the chapter on this series that forever changed my life.

It's unbelievable to me when I think about the fact that Asa's book will be number eight in a little over two years, and that's just insane and superexciting. I never thought I'd have even one book published in my entire life! So the fact that we are all here at the end together is pretty damn amazing.

Initially, I had written a very different intro for this book. It was long and drawn out and outlined all the things I struggled with to get to this place where I am now … the end … and the beginning. It hasn't always been a smooth journey for me, but I realized somewhere along the way that this wasn't what I should be focusing on as we close this chapter together.

No, what I needed to focus on was this moment. This exact second, when I am able to say good-bye along with my readers, and when I hopefully entice them with me into starting the new series. I needed to be present in the here and now and not looking over my shoulder at all the would'ves and could'ves and should'ves … that's something I struggle with on a daily basis. I sometimes forget I'm not the boss of the entire world and letting go of the want and need to control particular outcomes and situations is very hard for me.

But I'm doing it NOW.

Right now, I'm sitting here being overwhelmed with gratitude that I got to give each of these men and women a story. I'm overcome with emotion for the support and love my stories and ideas have found along the way. I am humbled by the amount of people that are willing to take a chance on me time and time again. And mostly I am filled to the brim with so much love for these books and the people that love them as much as I do that I can't even stand it. Readers bring such joy and excitement into my life, and any struggle, any complaint, any gripe I have pales in comparison to that.

Thank you for being here. Thank you for letting me be here …

As always Love & Ink
Jay

Happiness, not in another place but this place … not for another hour, but this hour.

—*Walt Whitman*

You must live in the present, launch yourself on every wave, find your eternity in each moment. Fools stand on their island of opportunities and look toward another land. There is no other land; there is no other life but this.

—*Henry David Thoreau*

CHAPTER 1

Asa

Not too long ago when I watched a girl purposely get as drunk as this pretty one did, I would've moved in for the kill. I would have taken her home, taken her to bed, and not felt guilty at all about knowing that she was making choices without all her cylinders firing. I used to never let an easy opportunity pass me by, and I never felt bad that my actions weren't exactly going to win me any awards for morality. I used to like it when things were handed to me with no effort on my part, and I liked it that when I walked away, I could always brush off any kind of responsibility for wrongdoing and put it on someone else. Accountability was a foreign thing, and back in the day I avoided it like I owed it money.

But times had changed and somewhere between dying on a hospital bed and coming back to life and seeing the last chance I had at any kind of normality flicker in and out of my little sister's eyes, the barest hint of a conscience had woken up inside of me. Now, when I watched this very pretty drunk girl, obviously out of control, obviously looking for trouble, I wanted her to know how heavy an anchor regret could be. I still wanted to take her home and take her to bed, only I understood the connotation was different. Now that sliver of conscience was poking at me to do something I had never done and pretend that I was chivalrous and save her from herself.

No one would ever call me altruistic or considerate, but if I didn't step in, the beautiful redhead was going to get herself into a whole world of hurt. I knew from first-hand experience that some hurt and some mistakes could weigh you down forever. Carrying the load was exhausting and she deserved better than that, even if at the moment she seemed to have forgotten it.

I wiped my hands on the bar towel that was hanging loosely from my belt in the back and lifted an eyebrow at my cocktail waitress, Dixie, who was watching the same show on the dance floor that I was, with wide eyes. It was a Saturday night, so the bar was pretty full and there was a live band playing on the tiny stage, but pretty much every pair of eyes in the place was trained on the way the redhead was moving across the dance floor. I knew I should have cut her off, she was a lightweight as it was, but her big, chocolate-colored eyes were so sad, so tormented, I had a hard time telling her no. Now that I could actually feel shit like empathy and compassion, I knew that I had overserved her, which led up to the virtual striptease that was now happening in the middle of the dance floor.

"You think all those guys trying to grind on her would flip out if they knew she's more than likely armed?"

Dixie's voice was laced with dry humor as she took the Jack and Coke I mixed for her order from me.

"When a girl is clearly intoxicated, looking for a good time, and just happens to look like her, a bullet isn't very much of a deterrent. I'm gonna go pull her out of there. After you drop that off, will you watch the bar for a second?"

She lifted her own eyebrows back at me with a grin. "Are you sure you want to do that? That's like a pack of jackals circling a fallen gazelle. It might get ugly if you go and ruin all the fun."

The band that was the live entertainment for the night switched to a cover of Tom Petty's "You Got Lucky," and the girl in the center of the storm suddenly turned and locked her eyes on mine. Somewhere in the middle of all her bumping and grinding, she had lost her shirt, so all she had on was a skintight tank top that wasn't doing much to cover her up. Her rich auburn hair had fallen out of its ponytail and was sticking to the sweat on her chest and neck, while her eye makeup was smeared under her dark eyes. Her chest was rising and falling from exertion as all her flawless, exposed skin gleamed with a sheen of perspiration. She looked like something out every wet dream any guy had ever had or a real-life Victoria's Secret model using this no-name bar to strut her stuff instead of a catwalk. She was going to cause a riot, and I think somewhere under all the kamikazes fueling her blood at the moment she knew it. I could see it as she stared defiantly at me across the space that separated us.

"I'm okay with ugly; I'm not okay with her being in the middle of the carnage." I shouldn't care. Shouldn't be concerned. The redhead was more than capable of taking care of herself, and like Dixie had mentioned, she was probably packing, but I couldn't stop the surge of protectiveness that floated to the surface when a clumsy frat guy put his hands on her tiny waist and drew her back to his chest.

She didn't struggle at first, her senses and reflexes obviously dampened by the steady stream of alcohol she had been swimming in all night.

Dixie left to deliver the drink and came back around the bar with a sigh. "I can't wait until Rome hires his friend to hang around and do security stuff on the weekends. I love this place, I love my job, but watching you guys have to tangle with drunken hotheads all the time is getting old."

I shrugged and moved past her so that I could go put a stop to the impending disaster. The redhead had finally gotten her sluggish wits in gear and was now actively struggling in the frat boy's hold.

"It's just part of the job."

Though I had to admit that when the boss, Rome Archer, mentioned he had an old platoon buddy that was getting ready to come back home and was gonna need something to do until he got his feet under him, I was relieved that my time banging heads together when the crowd got rowdy on the weekends was going to come to an end. I had a criminal record. A long, colorful criminal record, and anytime I put my hands on another human being in any kind of violent way, I automatically saw pages and pages getting tacked onto it. Like so much from my life before I had died on that hospital table, it was something from my past that would always define me and hold me down.

Dixie called to me over the bar as I started to weave my way through the crowd: "You're too pretty to put that face in front of a flying fist, Asa. Be careful."

Frat Boy was holding his face while blood rushed out between his fingers as he covered his nose. The redhead was being held by two other guys, one with each wrist locked down as she glared at the group of men surrounding her. She was tall and in ridiculously good shape, but none of these inebriated guys would have any clue as to why. All they saw was a feisty girl that was wasted and had been enticing them all night long, whether it had been intentional or not. And of course, now that she had made one of them bleed, had unmanned him in front of an entire barful of spectators, it was clearly about to get nasty. It was one thing to get your ass handed to you by a girl. It was an entirely different thing to get your ass handed to you by a girl that looked like she should be walking a runway wearing fuck-me stilettos. It also didn't help save face for the guy that she had on bright yellow pants that hugged her curves just right and breasts that it should be illegal to ever cover up.

In half of a heartbeat she was in the middle of a tug-of-war between the two guys holding her arms and I could see the anger building in the watery eyes of the guy whose nose she had probably broken.

I gave him a warning look. Dixie was right: I was pretty, too pretty to be as ugly as I was on the inside, but to counteract the deceptive beauty of my face, I was also big and had been in trouble since the day I took my first breath. So I generally had a way of letting an opponent know they were going to be on the losing end of a confrontation with me. The bleeder took a step back as I manhandled the guy closest to me off of the redhead's arm. He grunted and swore at me, mostly because as soon as she was free and had enough leverage, she rammed her knee right into the guy's unprotected balls, doubling him over.

I shook my head at her as she turned and sloppily swung at the remaining guy clutching her wrist.

"Royal. Knock it off."

She ignored me as the band picked up a quick tempo cover of Shooter Jennings's "A Hard Lesson to Learn," and went into full-on attack mode.

Now, I fully believed there was nothing wrong with a woman defending herself against unwanted advances, and it was obvious she didn't want this guy's hands on her anymore. But this particular girl, this surprising young woman that just happened to look like a supermodel, was actually a member of the Denver police force, and I knew she could cause serious damage even in her less than sober state. I couldn't allow that. Not just because the Bar would be liable, but also because I didn't want her to do something that could ultimately end up costing her her job.

I reached around Royal and got my hand on the fingers locked on her wrist as she wiggled and swung wildly at her captor. Prying his fingers free was a task made even more difficult by the fact I kept having to duck to avoid an elbow in the face or the back of her fist on the backswing. She was quick and strong, something that the guy holding her finally realized as she landed a solid punch to one of his temples. He suddenly let go and stumbled back as I trapped her flailing arms to her sides and pulled her back to my chest. I bent just a little so I could whisper in her ear, "Calm down, Red."

We both stared at the guy that had grabbed her, and I tried not to notice the way her really spectacular rack was rising and falling right above the arm I had locked across her rib cage. Even when I tried to help out, all those old instincts burned bright and hot right under the surface. I wanted to touch her in an entirely unhelpful way.

"She assaulted me." He sounded like a disgruntled toddler that had lost his favorite toy to a bigger kid on the playground.

I nodded and made sure the hills of Kentucky were thick in my voice when I told him, "She sure did. But not until you put your hands on her." Good-ol'-boy charm worked wonders to calm down a volatile situation. I think it made people think I didn't have enough smarts to be any kind of real threat despite my size.

The band was still playing but I don't think anyone was paying attention. Everyone was watching the chaos Royal had created unfold.

"She punched Bobby in the face and all he was trying to do was dance with her. She broke his nose."

Again I nodded and tried not to think about the way that Royal's absolutely perfect backside lined up just right with my fly. She turned her head just enough that I could see a hint of awareness and panic working through her dark gaze. Her tongue darted out to slick across her bottom lip and I had to remind myself I wasn't a guy that took advantage of drunk girls anymore. At least I didn't want to be that guy, but I never really figured I had much of a choice in the matter.

"Bobby needs to learn to ask if he wants a girl to dance with him. Look, everybody can just go to their separate corners, we can all forget this happened—"

I was cut off as he pointed at me and then narrowed his eyes at Royal. "I'm gonna call the cops."

I felt Royal start to shake in my grasp. That was exactly the outcome I was trying to avoid. I lifted an eyebrow, shifted my hold on her so that she was behind me, and crossed my arms over my chest. I figured I looked a lot more intimidating not covered by a too-sexy-for-her-own-good redhead.

"You can do that, but it's gonna shut the party down. The band is gonna have to stop, all these other folks in here are going to have to stop drinking, and it's gonna make them mad since they had to pay a cover to get in and hear the music. Plus I'm gonna have to call the bar owner and let him know what's going down, and that's like waking Godzilla up from a nap." I rubbed my thumb along the side of my mouth and gave him my best "country boy" smile. It had disarmed more than one person who was out for blood, usually mine, but I didn't mind using it to prevent any of Royal's from spilling. "Plus, between you and me, she has friends on the force."

The other guy was trying to vet if I was serious or not, so I inclined my chin. "Her best friend is a cop. If you call the DPD, chances are they're going to send him in since he knows this is where she likes to hang out, and then she's going to tell him you and your buddies put your hands all over her without her permission and the cameras will back that up." I pointed to one of the surveillance cameras Rome had installed all over the place. "You think that's going to end well for you?"

He looked like he was considering how to answer when the lead singer of the band suddenly called out over the mic so that the entire bar had no choice but to listen: "You guys suck. Take your bleeding friend out of here and let everyone go back to having a good time."

That rallied the rest of the bar-goers and suddenly a chant of "You suck!" went up and the grabby-hands bunch really had no choice but to leave. There was no way left for them to save face and they didn't want to risk the chance that Royal did in fact know a cop.

They slunk toward the front door as I hauled Royal toward the bar and plopped her fine ass in a seat right in the middle, where I could keep an eye on her. I caged her in between my arms and leaned in close so that our noses were almost touching.

Through clenched teeth I told her, "Sit. Now I can either call Saint to come get you, or you can sit here, drink water, and eat something greasy and terrible until you sober up enough to get yourself home. Those are your only two options, Red."

She blinked criminally long lashes at me and I could swear she looked like she was going to cry. I saw her gulp and she gave her head a little nod of agreement.

When she spoke it was only a hint of sound. "Don't call Saint. I'll wait it out."

Saint was her closest girl friend, and also my friend Nash's lady. She was a sweet and shy young woman that somehow managed to balance out all of Royal Hastings's bold and brash attitude. They were an odd pair, but I knew Saint would drop whatever she was doing in a heartbeat to make sure Royal was taken care of. I didn't blame Royal for not wanting her friend to have to come collect her in her current state. She was a mess. She was still beautiful, kind of wild and untamed looking, but under it all she was a disaster, courting trouble as well as danger and other bad things, which is what she had been actively doing for the last two weeks. This wasn't the first disaster I had been forced to avert because of her antics, and the time had come to tell her it had to stop.

I pushed off the bar, walked around the open end, and glowered at Dixie as she smacked my ass on her way back to the floor.

"My hero."

I grunted at her in response. I was not hero material. I fell more along the lines of arch-nemesis or supervillain. I poured Royal a glass of water in one of the giant beer steins I had behind the bar and thumped it down in front of her without a word. She jumped a little and I could see the regret and remorse starting to work its way into her face. A pink flush was blooming over the exposed crests of her cleavage and filling her cheeks.

I made my way across the entire length of the bar, stopping to refill a couple of drinks, closing a tab, clearing some empty plates until I got to the kitchen entrance that took up the entire back part of the bar. We typically only served food until midnight, but I knew Avett Walker, the new girl Rome had agreed to hire to work in the kitchen as a favor to an old friend, was still lurking somewhere around. I hadn't seen her hot-pink hair dart out of the front door as soon as her shift ended like it normally did.

She was a mouthy little thing that had nothing but poison and attitude running in her veins as far as I could tell. She clearly didn't want to be working here. Her mom, Darcy, was the kitchen manager and her father was the guy that had sold Rome the bar originally, but Avett didn't seem to have any kind of fondness for the place. In fact she didn't seem to have any kind of fondness for anything at all. She acted like coming to work each day was a prison sentence, which by default made me her jailer since I was her boss. We didn't exactly get along. I think I saw too much of my old careless and thoughtless ways reflected back at me when I interacted with her.

I called Avett's name, and when I didn't get an answer I prowled through the empty kitchen until I got to the massive walk-in fridge. I didn't have time to screw around, so I found some cheese, some bread, and some random pieces of fruit and figured that would have to do. I needed to shove something into Royal that would soak the booze up so I could tell her to get her head out of her ass and have the command stick.

I was kicking the door closed with the heel of my boot since my hands were full when the door to the beer cooler suddenly popped open and Avett came strolling out, fiddling with the zipper on her obviously stuffed-full messenger bag. She stopped dead in her tracks when she saw me, her eyes widening and then narrowing in defiance.

"What are you doing back here? The kitchen is closed." Like she had any right to question where I went in this place. It was a diversionary tactic I knew all too well.

I just stared at her and didn't say anything. I looked pointedly at her bag and then back up to her chilly hazel gaze.

"What's in the bag?"

She shifted her weight, and there was no mistaking the sound of bottles clanking together. She was trying to smuggle beer out of the cooler. It figured. My night needed one more complicated female I had to straighten out to make it more of a headache.

"Nothing." She went to move past me and the sound of bottles clanging together got even louder.

My hands were full, so I just moved my entire body into her path to stop her. Avett took after Darcy way more than Brite, her dad. Brite was a giant of a man with a beard that I was sure had folk songs written in its honor. Avett was petite and barely came up to the center of my chest, and she had to tilt her head back in order to keep glaring up at me. What she lacked in height, she sure as hell made up for in bad attitude.

"Put it back. Don't do it again and this is the last you'll hear about it." When I was irritated, the South tended to be heavy and thick in my voice, and not in the same way it was when I used my drawl to get something I wanted or to make someone think I was nicer and stupider than I really was.

"Get out of my way, Asa."

"No. You don't get to steal from Rome. I don't care what your beef with Brite is and I don't care that you obviously would rather be out wrestling wild mountain lions than working here. I'm not letting you take advantage of Rome. He's a good guy and he deserves better than that."

We had a glare-off and for a second I thought she was going to try and step around me knowing my hands were occupied, but I think there was some kind of invisible thread, some kind of aura that we shared that made her instinctively know that she could get away, but not for very long.

She huffed out a breath that sent her pink bangs dancing across her forehead. She would be a really cute girl if she wasn't such a pain in the ass and practically a decade younger than me. She was just a kid really and she sure as shit acted like it.

"I'm going to a party and I don't have any money for beer. I didn't think it would be a big deal to take a twelve-pack from the cooler. After all, my dad practically handed this bar over to the soldier for free. A few beers seems like a fair trade."

I rolled my eyes. "It wouldn't be a big deal. You know that Rome wouldn't care if you asked him. But walking around like you're owed something for some unknown reason isn't all right with me, and I'm not going to let you do it." I furrowed my eyebrows at her and shifted my weight. "How can you be broke? You just got paid on Friday." Since she worked in the kitchen, I knew Rome paid her an hourly wage. It wasn't enough to retire on but it was enough that it shouldn't be gone in less than twenty-four hours unless she was up to no good.

Instead of answering me, she whirled around and went to put the beers back in the cooler. I waited until she came back out, and made her lead the way out of the kitchen back to the bar. I had been gone long enough that the band was done with their set and that meant a crowd had gathered and Dixie was standing behind the bar trying to catch orders up. I nudged Avett with my elbow and deposited my haul into her hands. I pointed to Royal, who was sitting stoic in the middle of the rush, her head bent down and her gaze locked on the bar top.

"Feed the redhead. Make sure she eats it, and if I ever catch you trying to steal again you're out of here. I don't care what I promised Brite or how much it would break Darcy's heart."

She gave me a baleful look and muttered just loud enough that I could hear it, "Funny coming from you."

She wasn't wrong. It was ridiculous coming from me, so I ignored her and dove into the mess of trying to sort the rush out. It was only half an hour until last call, so it proved to be a little trickier than usual. The weekends at the Bar were getting busy enough since Rome's remodel that I thought maybe I was going to have to ask him about hiring another server as well as a bouncer. Business was good, and in order to keep it that way we needed to make sure the crowds got service just as good as the battered old veterans that littered the place during the daytime hours.

I tried to keep an eye on Royal. I was worried she was going to try and leave before I could talk to her and before I could judge if she was sober enough to drive, but she was in the same spot, head bent down, eyes focused on the bar, and her water was gone. She had also put a good-sized dent in the food in front of her, so that made me breathe a little easier. She was abnormally quiet and I wished I had thought to grab her shirt for her when I pulled her out of the crowd earlier. She looked rumpled, like she had just climbed out of bed, and that wasn't doing a thing to help me remember why I needed to get her out of the tailspin she had been in ever since the week before Christmas.

I got last call done. I paid the band and thanked the lead singer for helping me out with the frat kids, and he in turn asked me if I thought Royal would be interested in going on the road with them as a backup dancer. I had to laugh and broke the news to him that she already had a full-time job. I didn't bother explaining what it was because I doubted he would believe me anyway. I helped Dixie clear the floor, and when we started to move people toward the front doors, I stopped next to Royal's side and told her, "Hang out for a minute."

She didn't respond but she pushed some of her hair out her face, tucked it behind her ear, and looked at me out of the corner of her eye.

I took that as silent assent and helped Dixie get everyone outside and gave her a hand putting all the chairs up so that the cleaning crew Rome hired could spit-shine the place before we opened again tomorrow. Dixie and I had a system since we did this together six nights a week, so it was work that went by pretty quickly. When I was done I went behind the bar, poured myself a Dalwhinnie on the rocks, and took myself and my drink back around the other side of the bar so I could sit on a stool next to Royal. Everyone teased me that I should drink bourbon or whiskey, being as I was from Kentucky, but I preferred the smooth and dirty taste of scotch. It sort of fit since I was both those things myself.

I took a swig of the drink and set it down with a thunk on the bar. I ran my hand through my dirty-blond hair and looked at Royal out of the corner of my eye.

"So this is what you do now? Get drunk, rile up the natives, take half your clothes off in public, and just generally act the fool? 'Cause I gotta tell you, after two weekends in a row of it, I think it's probably time you find another bar to haunt."

I saw her shoulders slump and she matched my side-eye look.

"Why didn't you tell those guys I was a cop?"

I sighed and turned to face her. I really wished she wasn't such a looker. It made trying to be level-headed and rational around her that much harder.

"Because even though you can carry concealed legally because of your badge, you still can't be drinking while carrying a loaded weapon. That's illegal and a headache you really don't need."

"All of a sudden you're concerned with others being law-abiding." A little bit of her sass was coming back and that was a nice change from her maudlin moping that had settled around her since I pulled her off the dance floor.

"No. I don't give a flying fuck about others being law-abiding, but you've got a job you like, friends that care about you, and you're way too young to be flushing it all down the toilet. Even if that seems to be your new mission in life. You need to get your shit together, Royal, before you're too far gone to fix the mess you seem so eager to make." She was barely twenty-three. That seemed a lifetime younger than me, even though I had a couple more years ahead of me before I hit the big three-oh.

"That's funny coming from you."

Second time I had heard that in less than an hour. Maybe I just needed to keep my nose out of it and let everyone learn their own hard lessons just like I had been forced to do. I picked up my drink and took another slug.

"Get it together or don't, but this is the final warning about bringing that nonsense into my bar. You want to go down in flames, I guess that's your call, but I'm not going to watch you burn."

Something flashed across her eyes, something so sad and lost it really made me want to reach out and comfort her, but touching Royal was like touching a live wire and I already had a hard enough time keeping my mind out of my pants and my hands to myself when I was around her. She blinked those long-ass lashes at me, stuck her tongue out to flick it across her bottom lip, and I forgot how to breathe for a second. She did it on purpose. I had no doubt.

"One of these days you'll come home with me when I ask, Asa." She leaned over on the bar stool a little and put her hand on my thigh. My fingers tightened around the tumbler in my hand so hard I was shocked the glass didn't break.

"Is that why you're here? Is that what the show is all about? You really want to make that kind of mistake?" My drawl was thick enough that the words were languid and heavy sounding. I felt blood start to race under my skin and I had no doubt that my eyes were probably glowing bright gold in my face. It wasn't often someone made me uneasy, threw me off my game, but Royal had done it more than once in our short acquaintance.

She pressed her weight forward and stopped when her mouth was just a fraction away from mine. I could almost taste her. In fact, if I stuck out just the tip of my tongue, I *would be* tasting her. I clenched my teeth to stop that from happening, even though I was pretty sure she would taste like candy and fire.

"It seems like all I make anymore are mistakes. At least making that kind of one with you would be fun."

She used her leverage on my leg to push herself upright as she slithered off the bar stool in one seamlessly sexy move. It made me bite back a groan.

"If you don't want me here, I won't come back." She tossed her heavy hair over her shoulder and gave me a steady look out of her dark brown eyes. "I really thought you would make this easier."

I didn't say anything as she walked away, steady on those killer shoes and missing her shirt even though it was winter in Colorado. She was obviously sober enough to drive, but I had no idea where her head was at otherwise.

Dixie locked the door behind the redhead and wandered over to the bar. She grabbed herself a bottle of Bud Light, which of course was sacrilegious in this Coors Light–dominated bar, and refilled my scotch.

"I don't know how you've managed to turn her down more than once." She shook her own strawberry-blond curls and grinned at me. "I'm not even into chicks and I think I would do her if she asked. She's pretty amazing."

I muttered a few swearwords under my breath and tossed the second round back in one swallow. It burned a little and I had to blink.

"She's a cop, a cop that has arrested me. I have better self-preservation instincts than that." In my experience, cops were not my biggest fans, and I really couldn't blame them. I set the empty glass down on the bar and climbed to my feet. It was late and I needed a hundred cold showers. "Besides, she doesn't actually wanna fuck, she just thinks she does."

Dixie snorted. "That's not what it looks like to me."

It might look pretty cut-and-dried from the outside. Royal was pretty, I was pretty, and we definitely had a spark, but I hadn't lasted as long as I had screwing over everyone whose path I crossed without learning how to look deeper, how to see the danger looming, and it was obvious to me that Royal was dangerous in more ways than one.

"That's a very pretty girl with a very ugly hurt, and somehow she got it in her head that she deserves to be punished, to hurt even more."

"So she's trying to drag you to bed to punish her? That sounds kinky and fun."

I tossed my bar towel at her and pushed up from the bar so I could do the nightly cash-out and go home. Now the idea of Royal in her handcuffs and nothing else was going to be running around in my head for the rest of the night. Like she needed any help being unforgettable.

"She feels bad and she's doing everything in her power to make herself feel worse." I didn't know all the details of what had started Royal's recent decline, but I did know her partner on the force, who really was her best friend and had been for most of her life, had been injured pretty badly in the line of duty and that Royal was currently on administrative leave while the department investigated the circumstances that had led to two cops being shot. One of the officers hadn't made it and the other was still in the hospital. The other being Dominic, Royal's partner. "I'm not looking to be any part of that."

I had used enough people in my life, even those that loved me unconditionally, to know what being a means to an end for someone else looked like. I wasn't going to help Royal self-destruct.

Dixie gave me a soft little grin that reminded me that even though she was tough as nails when she needed to be, she was really a romantic sweetheart at her center.

"Maybe you should give it a shot and you could make her feel better, and maybe she could make you finally see that you have changed over the last year or so."

I just gave my head a shake and told her flatly, "That's not what I do." Nope; I destroyed things not repaired them.

I never lied about the man I had been for most of my life or the things I had done. There were so many kinds of really ugly, twisted, and dark things I was capable of and yet everyone that knew me now seemed to be under the impression that I had undergone some kind of transformation after coming out of the coma I had been in after I died and came back. The truth of the matter was I was never going to be a good guy. I was never going to be the type of man that made things better. Regardless of what anyone wanted to believe or how desperately it seemed Royal needed someone to wade in and pull her out of the mire, I wasn't made to be a hero or a savior. I was already so far under the thumb of the specters of my past mistakes there was no way I could pull anyone else to safety.

The old saying was true, a leopard never changed its spots; and just like the lurking jungle cat, I was a predator through and through even if others wanted to think I had somehow become a house cat.

CHAPTER 2

Royal

When my phone, which I had left lying right next to my head the night before, went off the next afternoon shrieking Britney Spears's "Toxic," I almost rolled out of bed onto the floor in my haste to turn it off. I felt terrible. Partly because I was hardly sleeping anymore, so slipping into a restless catnap in the middle of the day was all that was sustaining me, but mostly because the number on the phone was the one I had been waiting for week after agonizing week to show up.

I silenced the bubblegum-pop song with a swipe of my finger across the screen and tried to sound more alert than I actually was when I gasped out a shaky greeting. I didn't care what anyone thought of my awful taste in music. I slummed in the gutter all day long. I tangled with junkies, and wife beaters, and parents that neglected their kids every single day. I refused to listen to anything that wasn't upbeat and full of infectious pop. My job wasn't always fun, so I tried really hard to make sure the rest of the things in my life were.

"You do know I'm busting out of here today, right?"

I shoved a tangled hank of dark red hair out of my face and scrambled up to the edge of my bed. I chomped down on my bottom lip and tried to regulate my breathing. Of course I knew he was getting out of the hospital today. What I hadn't known was if he was going to want me anywhere around him when he finally got the green light to go home. I squeezed my eyes shut and was so grateful that we weren't face-to-face. Dominic Voss knew me better than any living soul on this planet, and if we were in the same room he would be able to feel the guilt and self-loathing I had been drowning in lately. Hell, if my current state of distress was apparent to someone as disconnected as Asa Cross, there was no way my best friend and partner could miss it. Dom being Dom, he would know it all came from what had happened to him on that callout from hell.

"I know. I wasn't sure if you wanted me to come or not. I know your sisters are coming to stay with you until you get back on your feet and I didn't want to get in the way."

I sounded pathetic and ridiculous to my own ears.

Dom and I had been inseparable since we were five years old. There had never been a time when he didn't want me around. There had never been a single moment in our friendship where I was ever in his way, and his entire family thought of me as one of their own. I think that made what had happened weigh even more heavily on my shoulders.

I heard Dom sigh and then he swore. His deep voice sounded strained as he gently scolded me. "Get your cute ass here, Royal. I've let you sulk for two goddamn weeks.

Get over it. Shit happens and it's gonna keep happening because that's what being a cop is about. I'm in a fucking cast from my ankle to my junk. I have a broken shoulder and I can't breathe without it feeling like I'm drinking acid. I look and feel like hammered dog shit, and my best friend hasn't been around for any of it. Can you maybe knock it off now?" I couldn't stop the tears that were starting to leak out of my eyes. I used a knuckle to swipe at them as I climbed to my feet. His next words stabbed through me like I was sure he intended for them to do. "I need you here, girly."

We had always needed each other, both in our day-to-day lives and on the job. That was why I felt so bad. It was why I couldn't get my head around how badly I had let him down. I was supposed to have his back like he had always had mine, and instead I had almost gotten him killed.

"I'm on my way."

I hung up the phone after he barked at me that it was about time, and rushed around my apartment trying to make myself look presentable. After a hard night of drinking I never exactly looked great, but throw in a sleepless night and yet another rejection from an outrageously sexy, southern bartender and I probably could match Dom in the looking-like-crap department. I had dark shadows under each eye, I was way paler than normal, fine red veins threaded through the white in each eye, and I had really ugly bruises surrounding each of my wrists, which made shame and regret battle the guilt for the top spot in the flood of emotions I was choking on.

I knew better, I really did. I wasn't the type to go out and lose control. I rarely drank, and when I did I always acted responsibly because I had a big picture to think about. Only lately that big picture had narrowed to tunnel vision and all I could see was Dom getting hit by bullet after bullet and falling over the edge of the fire escape on the side of the building. When I wasn't seeing that, I was seeing the wife of the officer that hadn't survived the shootout collapsing in the hall of the ER as another officer told her that her husband hadn't made it. If that wasn't enough to eat at my soul, the memory of my lieutenant telling me I had to turn in my gun and badge and go on administrative leave while the department conducted an investigation danced around in my head every second of every day.

In order to shake some of those awful thoughts loose, I was determined to do things I never did, things that made me feel free, so that's why I was hanging out at the Bar. That's why I was drinking like a fish, and really that was why I was unabashedly throwing myself at Asa Cross. I had never had to chase a guy. I had never been interested in the kind of guy that oozed charm and trouble the way Asa did. And I most definitely had never been one to mix business and pleasure. I knew Asa was bad news, barely tiptoeing on the right side of the law, and it was a firm rule that I never got involved with anyone that had been in the back of a police cruiser. Well, Asa had not only been in the back of my cruiser, but he had also been in and out of jail since before he was old enough to drive. The guy liked to make up his own rules and he didn't have a very pretty past. Cops shouldn't be romantically interested in criminals, even reformed criminals. But I was. In fact I was more than interested, but every time I made a move on him and he turned me down, it made me wonder if he could see the failure that was haunting me. I wondered if that was why he kept saying no.

I mean, I knew what I looked like. I knew that when we stared at each other there was interest and attraction glinting dark in his bronze eyes, and I knew he was the kind of guy that liked a sure thing. I was a sure thing. I needed something that felt good. I was searching desperately for something that would help me forget, even if it was for only a second, and I wasn't afraid to admit that I wanted him. I made it so easy for him to say yes and yet he kept turning the other way. I didn't understand it, so it only made me feel even more lost and adrift than I already did.

If he really wanted me to find another bar, I would. I only went to the dive he worked at because I wanted him to take me home. I wanted him to pull me across the bar and kiss away all the hurt and ugliness that was filling me up. I knew I was going about it the wrong way, knew that a guy like Asa had no use for someone that enforced the law and tried to keep the peace. Plus it was a long shot considering I had been forced by circumstance to arrest him for assault not too long ago. Asa might think I was pretty, and he might be trying to save me from myself since we had mutual friends, but I seriously doubted he was ever going to be able to look at me the same way I looked at him after I had snapped cuffs around his wrists and dragged him to the police station.

I pulled my hair into a messy ponytail, shoved my feet into a pair of battered motorcycle boots, and hit the front door. I was about to slam it closed behind me when I remembered to grab my keys. I was forever locking myself out of places—my car, my apartment, and even my patrol car on several occasions. It was a bad habit that was a pain in the ass for more than just me, but I couldn't seem to shake it even after a mishap had almost led to the breakup of my neighbor and his lovely girlfriend.

I dashed back inside, frazzled and frustrated. I scooped the keys up off the spot they lived in by the door and rushed back out. This time the hallway wasn't empty, and the neighbor's girlfriend, who also happened to be my one and only female friend on the planet, was exiting their apartment across the hall. Saint was a sweetheart. Soft-spoken and serene, she just had something about her that had instantly called out to me. It was like the chaotic pace and often dangerous parts of my day-to-day died down and mellowed out when I was around her. I had forced her to be my friend even though she had fought me and the friendship at first. Now she was almost as close to me as Dom was, and just as concerned about my recent behavior.

She was dressed in scrubs under her heavy winter coat, so obviously she was on her way to work at the hospital where she was an ER nurse. Her coppery hair, which was several shades more orange in color than mine, was piled on her head in a messy bun and her face was scrubbed clean. Saint was a doll and could work the whole fresh-faced-girl-next-door thing. Unfortunately

I wasn't lucky enough to be able to rock the less-is-more look successfully, so the darkness under my eyes told the entire story of my wild night without me uttering a single word.

"Dom's getting out of the hospital today," I told her in a rush.

She blinked her soft gray eyes at me and the corner of her mouth tilted in a half smile.

"I know. I've been checking up on him."

I sighed. Of course she had, because she was an awesome friend.

"Thank you."

She nodded slightly and we silently headed for the front door of the converted Victorian we lived in.

"He asked about you every time I stopped by his room."

I gulped a little. Not because she was passing judgment or being mean, but because we both knew I should have been by the hospital to see him. I squeezed my keys in my hand so hard the metal dug into my skin deep enough that it hurt.

"I just couldn't. I stayed until they came out and told us that he was stable after surgery, but it was too much." I shook my head and shivered as the frigid Denver air snaked down the collar of the hoodie I had thrown on. The reason Dom was in the hospital for so long wasn't the shattered ankle and broken femur but because one of the bullets that had hit him had sliced clean through one of his kidneys. He had almost bled to death before making it to the hospital. "His mom was there watching me without saying a word. I could see her wondering how I had let Dom get hurt. I could see his sisters thinking, 'Why Dom and not her?' I knew I was going to have a breakdown and I didn't want to do it where anyone could see."

She reached out and squeezed my elbow. "No one blames you for anything, Royal. That is not what Dominic's family was thinking and you know it."

Dammit. When had she started to see me so clearly? This is why having friends was hard for me.

"I blame me, Saint."

She sighed and let go of my arm. "That's what I figured, but eventually you'll have to get over that. How's the investigation going?"

That was a topic I wanted to talk about almost as little as I wanted to talk about how Dom had ended up in his current, broken state.

"It's going. Internal investigations are always complicated when there's an officer death involved." And it was complicated because I was actively avoiding all the things I was supposed to be doing to help myself out. There had been other officers on the scene. There were witnesses from the neighborhood. Dom had given his statement and so had the partner of the officer that hadn't made it. All the stories matched and laid out the facts that I had done nothing wrong, that there was no fault on my part, and that the kid I had been forced to shoot was going to keep pulling the trigger until everyone in a uniform was out of his way, but I didn't feel cleared. I felt dirty and unqualified. Not because I had pulled the trigger, but because I had pulled it too late.

"I'm sure everything will work out for you in the end. Is the department making you talk to someone? That's a pretty intense situation to work through on your own."

Saint was big on processing feelings. I think that's why she was so good in the crisis situations she handled every day. She powered through all the tragedy and stress while she was at work, compartmentalized it all, then came home and let it all out so it never had the chance to fill her up and take her over. I wasn't that great at letting it all go. In fact, as of late, I was holding on to everything that affected me on the streets in a death grip. I guess I thought if I held on to it, no one else would have to deal with the yuck of it all.

"I'm supposed to go tomorrow." *Supposed to* being the key. If I could find any excuse to skip hearing a shrink tell me I was just suffering from survivor's guilt, I was going to latch on to it. I had screwed up. I knew it and I didn't need anyone to lead me to that conclusion, but if I wanted back on the job I was going to have to bite the bullet and force myself to go lie on some stiff leather couch and get my head shrunk.

Saint stopped when we got to my 4Runner and tilted her head as she regarded me solemnly. I stared back at her because I valued her and the honest friendship she offered too much to just dismiss her concern.

"Go. Listen to what the psychologist has to say. You don't have to go through whatever this is alone, Royal."

She reached out and gave me a one-armed hug, which I returned stiffly. Whatever *this* was, it was clearly not only affecting me at this point.

When we pulled apart I gave her a lopsided grin and told her, "I tried to get Asa to go home with me again last night."

She lifted one of her rust-colored eyebrows at me. "Again?"

I wrinkled up my nose and pulled open the door to my old SUV. "He keeps telling me he's not interested. Maybe he just doesn't like me."

She gave a delicate snort and moved to zip up her coat as the wind picked up and turned the winter air into something hovering on the edge of unbearable.

"Of course he likes you. Maybe he can just tell that you don't like you very much right now."

I scowled at her but didn't argue. I didn't like myself so much at the moment. I lifted up the sleeve of the hoodie on one arm and showed her my wrist, which made her gasp in shock. "I had too much to drink and got myself into something I shouldn't have. Asa pulled me out of it and then took care of me until I was sober enough to get myself home."

"Nash says even with all the stuff from his past, Asa really is a pretty decent guy." Saint sounded unsure of the truth in that though.

I just shrugged and turned on the car. It was freezing and the motor took forever to heat up enough to do any good.

"Decent is boring if it means I can't even get to first base with him." I sounded petulant and frustrated, which made her shake her head at me.

"I think you're looking for trouble on purpose."

Her warning fell on deaf ears. I *was* looking for trouble, but trouble wouldn't look back, so it was a moot point anyway.

"I'm looking for something, and I don't think there's anything wrong with that."

"No, there's not, but when you have your shield back and you're in uniform again the game changes, Royal. You might want to consider that."

I didn't want to think that far ahead. I didn't want to think about any of it at all. I grumbled under my breath as Saint took a step back so I could close the door.

"I'll call you Monday after I talk to the shrink, if I do, and I'll tell Dom you said hello."

"Dominic loves you no matter what, you know."

I nodded, and for the second time that afternoon I felt tears well up in my eyes. "That's what makes all of this so much worse. I'll talk to you later."

She gave a little wave and headed over to her own little Jetta that would heat up and defrost a million times faster than my old tank. I could afford something newer and sleeker but the 4Runner had been with me since I was a teenager and there were so many good memories tied to it I couldn't stomach the idea of letting it go.

Dom did love me and I loved him. He was everything to me. He was my guiding light, my voice of reason, Dom was without a doubt my hero, and more than that he was the one that always was there to remind me that I had a purpose beyond being a pretty face. If it hadn't been for Dom, there was a good chance I would have bought into my own hype early on when it became clear that the genetic gods had been giving with both hands when it came to my physical attributes. Dom was always the one that reminded me I was worth so much more than being a piece of arm candy or mindless fluff. I was smart, I was capable, and I wanted to make a difference. If I hadn't had Dom to believe in me, to push me, I never would have reached the goals I set for myself. If it wasn't for Dom reminding me of my worth, there was a good chance I could have ended up just like my mother.

The very thought made me shiver.

I loved my mom, I really did, but I had zero patience for her deplorable choices and the way she burned through men like it was a competitive sport. My mom had always been more like a best friend than a parent. She loved me unconditionally, I was her whole world, but I wasn't enough to fill up the hole that was left when my father didn't leave his wife to be a family with us. My mom never got over the rejection, and as a result was constantly chasing down true love and looking for validation from men in all the wrong places.

My mother was a stunner, so I came by my good looks naturally. She was also an habitual adulterer and had been through so many marriages and relationships that I stopped counting before I got out of my teens. When I was younger I thought it was embarrassing and it made me uncomfortable. As I got older I realized she simply wasn't happy, had never been happy, and as much as she loved me and doted on me, I was never going to be enough to fill the void she had in her heart. I learned to accept the relationship we had, not ask questions, and just tried to support her like she had always supported me. Even if the majority of her decisions when it came to the opposite sex made me squirm in my seat, I loved the mom I had, every flighty, flirty inch of her.

It was because of Dom and not my mother that I excelled. I strove for greatness and I had reached every goal I had ever set for myself. And now, because of me, he was laid up, full of holes and broken. It was absolutely unfair to him and I had no clue how I was supposed to ever make it up to him.

The hospital parking lot felt like it was a million miles wide as I trudged across it in the cold. By the time I hit the sliding doors my fingers were numb and my uncovered ears were burning from the wind. I felt like an idiot because I didn't even know what floor Dom was on or what room he was in. Some best friend I turned out to be. Shame settled heavy and thick on my shoulders and I really had to fight the urge to turn around and go back home and bury my head under the covers.

The person at the reception desk found Dom's information for me and I took the elevator up to the correct floor. I didn't have to worry about finding his room because both of his sisters were lingering in the hallway as if they were waiting specifically for me.

All the Vosses had beautiful dark hair and eyes in various shades of green. Ariella was the youngest of the three siblings and she was a firecracker. Greer, the oldest and the most reserved of the group, snatched me up in a hug that shocked me into stillness as soon as I reached them.

"We've been so worried about you. You haven't called or shown your face. No one knew what happened to you or how you were handling the investigation. I thought Ari was going to have to sit on Dom to keep him in that hospital bed after the first week when you were a no-show."

I groaned and hugged her back. I couldn't believe how selfish and thoughtless I was behaving.

"I just ..." I trailed off as Ari rolled her eyes at me.

"You were being an asshole."

Greer snapped her sister's name, but I squeezed her hand and nodded at Ari. "I was. I've never let Dom down before and I was having a hard time with it." *Was* implied I had moved past it, but they didn't need to know that was a big fat lie.

Ari gave me a hard look but inclined her head toward the open door a few steps down the hallway. "He's been waiting to see you for forever. We're going run to his apartment and make sure it's all ready for him. He's gonna be wheelchair-bound for the next three or four weeks. Greer and I are going to alternate weeks with him until he's okay to be on his own."

I blinked dumbly. Dom was a big hunk of beefcake. He was tall and powerful, in amazing shape, and had always been the most capable man I had ever known. The idea of him in a wheelchair and needing help with day-to-day living made the cement block that lived in my guts now get five times heavier.

"I can help. Just let me know what you need." I sounded kind of strangled and strained to my own ears.

"You'll be back to work soon. Ari and I got it. Besides it's payback for all the times he took care of us growing up."

Dom's dad had been on the job when they were growing up. He was a patrol cop until a confrontation with an armed robber had gone awry and the Vosses had suddenly found themselves burying the patriarch of the family well before his time. Dom had instantly stepped in to fill his old man's shoes like any good son was bound to do. The fact that he had taken it as far as going into law enforcement just like his dad was still a sore spot for his mom.

I cleared my throat and fought the urge to fiddle with my hair nervously. "Dom has always taken care of me, too."

Greer sighed, grabbed my shoulders, and turned me so I was facing the room.

"Right, he has, and we both know what he wants is for you to go back to work. He's not going to be able to for Lord knows how long, so he's going to have to live vicariously through you for a while, Royal. What he's always wanted for you is for you to live up to your full potential. Don't let this knock you down after how hard you've worked to build yourself up."

If only it was that easy. I inhaled deeply and took the step I had been avoiding for two weeks.

He was propped up in the bed, dark hair mussed all over his head. His green eyes were locked on the doorway, obviously watching for me. His big body was all wrapped up in plaster and bandages. His handsome face was dark with irritation and a scruff of beard that was pretty impressive. He looked terrible and wonderful all at the same time. I was so lucky that he was still alive and I wasn't the one having to tell his family that they had lost another person they loved to the job.

I couldn't help it, the waterworks started up. I really wasn't much of a crier, but something inside of me was wrong, off, or not working right. The tears leaked out and Dom reached out his uninjured arm slowly, the small movement obviously hurting him.

I bolted to the side of the bed and let him tug me softly to his side. I felt his lips touch the top of my head and his broad chest rumbled as he told me, "'Bout damn time."

All I could do was whisper back, "I know."

I should have been here all along, or even more accurately, I should have been the one lying in this hospital bed all along. How was Dom ever going to forgive me if I knew there was never going to be a time when I could forgive myself?

CHAPTER 3

Asa

The following weekend came and went without any kind of incident. I wasn't sure if that was because Royal had taken my warning to heart and stayed home, or because Rome's friend Dashel—Dash—Churchill was officially on the payroll. There was no way anyone would be stupid enough to tangle with the massive wall of muscle that hardly spoke but glowered like a pro. The guy's scowl was enough to shut down even the slightest bit of misbehavior, and while the break in having to be the bad guy was nice, I was worried the guy's dark and brooding demeanor could scare off potential customers.

Rome was fairly hulking, and on the quiet side as well, but there was something about this other ex-soldier that indicated, loud and clear, that at some point in time not too long ago, the man had been a stone-cold killer and was not to be messed with. Even Dixie, who could get along with anyone and everyone, was giving the new recruit a wide berth, even if she was also giving the brute an interested side eye when she thought he wasn't paying attention. All the ladies in the bar seemed to think the caramel-skinned behemoth with his mixed ancestry and impenetrable dark gaze was easy on the eyes—not that he seemed to give a rat's ass about the female attention.

It was slow for a Monday night, so I had sent both of them home early and let Avett close down the kitchen. There was no sense in paying them to hang around when there was only one person at the bar. I knew Zeb Fuller pretty well. He was friends with my brother-in-law and the rest of the crew I spent most of my time with, and he was a regular at the Bar. He was another beast of a man that emanated a whole lot of don't-fuck-with-me. It must be something about the clean mountain air that allowed the men in the state to grow into giants. I wasn't small by any stretch of the imagination, but more often than not, I found myself eye to eye or having to look up at most of the guys that made up my social circle. It was just one more incentive to keep my ass in line. There were way too many guys around that were very capable of kicking my ass six ways to Sunday if I screwed up again.

Zeb had a pensive look on his face and was absently stroking his beard. Since moving to Denver, I had learned quickly that the three B's ruled all—beards, beer, and babes. The mile-high had a plethora of all those things, and when in doubt a conversation could always be started by picking one of the holy trinity. In a pinch, the Broncos always worked as a substitute B as well. Zeb had the beard, he didn't drink beer, and I knew, since he was at the Bar spilling his guts all the time, that his current babe situation was stuck in neutral because the girl he was hung up on seemed clueless to how he felt about her. She was also the older sister of one of his best friends, Rowdy, who wasn't exactly thrilled with Zeb's interest in his sibling.

I was finishing wiping down the bar and restocking the cooler while Zeb sulked into his almost empty glass of Jack and Coke. I never thought I would be the guy that others went to with their problems. I wasn't exactly sympathetic or patient with things that I thought were obvious, but ever since I stepped foot behind that bar, I felt more like a therapist than a drink slinger. What was even more shocking was that I liked it. I liked being able to see the situation from the outside and point out things from my own unique perspective. After all, I had screwed up enough for an entire army of people, so I figured I might as well put those hard lessons learned to good use.

"Why don't you just ask her out on a date?" I tossed the bar towel onto the dirty-rag pile and picked up the remote to turn off the TVs. I was going to shut it all down at midnight since Zeb was the only customer and I knew enough to know he just wanted to talk, not to drink.

He looked up at me and frowned. "You've met Sayer. Does she strike you as the type to go on a date with a guy like me?"

Sayer Cole was a bit of a mystery. She was a lawyer, beautiful in a really elegant and refined way, and she had surprised our little group of misfits by coming to Denver and claiming one of us as her own blood. Rowdy never knew he had a sister after growing up in foster care, so the reunion had been rocky at best. Only now she fit in seamlessly with the rest of the wayward souls that made up the tight-knit unit my little sister, Ayden, had been so fortunate to marry into. I was also lucky that they all took me into the fold based entirely on the fact that Ayden wasn't going to give me up. She might not like me very much all of the time, but she loved me unconditionally, and that was enough for the rest of the group to welcome me with open arms.

"She's nice. She seems pretty cool with whatever comes her way."

Zeb pushed his empty glass at me and ran his hands through his unruly hair. The guy was a contractor, built things for a living, so it kind of fit that he reminded me of a modern-day lumberjack.

"I've been flirting with her, teasing her and dropping hints since the day we met. She's smart. If she was interested she would pick up on what I'm laying down."

"Maybe." I braced my arms on the bar and leaned across from him. I gave him a steady look and asked seriously, "But don't you think she's probably a little more used to formal invitations from someone that wants to take her out? Everything about Sayer screams country club and formality. Maybe she just doesn't get what you're after."

He blinked at me for a second and then leaned back on his stool. "You think?"

I shrugged. "I don't know. She hired you to work on her house even after you told her you served time. She let you be around Salem's sister when we all know she's protecting that girl like a mama bear, so she obviously trusts you and is comfortable around you. Maybe she's waiting for you to up your game. Not all ladies are gonna start pulling off their clothes and crawl between the covers because you smile at them. I heard you tell Rowdy once that you weren't afraid of doing the work if the lady is worth it. Sayer is worth it."

She really was. She had helped me out of a hard spot not too long ago, and when Rowdy's girlfriend had needed a safe place for her little sister to recover from a really terrible situation, Sayer hadn't hesitated to take the girl in. She was as kind and generous as she was lovely. She deserved a guy that was willing to go the extra mile for her even if that guy kinda resembled a tattooed Paul Bunyan.

Zeb pushed up off the bar and lifted both of his dark eyebrows at me. "I question taking romantic advice from a guy that's repeatedly turning down the hottest piece of ass I've ever seen. That's just wasteful, man."

I rolled my eyes and crossed my arms over my chest. "That's the whole point: she's not a piece of ass, and I don't know why she's suddenly acting like she is. Besides, any chick that can throw me in jail when I piss her off is off the table." What I really meant but didn't say was that I knew I was bound to screw up and piss her off. That was just what I did.

Zeb grunted. "I think I'd risk a night in lockup for her. Saying no to all of that is like a Herculean feat. Someone should nominate you for sainthood."

I laughed drily and followed him to the front door so I could lock it behind him. "The halo would burst into flames if they got it anywhere near my head."

He gave me a hard look. "You know I don't think you're half as bad as you seem to think you are, Asa. Trust me, I know better than most about screwing up on an epic level, but I've never let that define who I was going to be for the rest of my life."

I might have bounced in and out of jail since I was a teenager, but I had never had to spend more than a few weeks at a time locked down. Zeb, though, had served several years behind bars for his mistake. The difference between us was that Zeb had broken the law because he felt like he didn't have any other choice. I broke the law because I wanted to. The law got in my way, prevented me from getting what I wanted or what I thought I needed, so I ignored it and pretended like it didn't matter.

"Some people screw up, and then some people *are* screw-ups. I fall firmly into the second category."

There was no other explanation as to how Ayden and I could have half of the same genetic makeup and be so vastly different. Granted there was a good chance I absolutely took after my scumbag of a father, a father we didn't share. Yet we were so opposite I often had to wonder how we had been brought up in the same house and lived the same hard-knock childhood. I had no clue how she could be as together, as composed and steady, as she was. I don't know how she had found a space in her new life for me or how she had stayed by my side when I was dying. I knew she had every reason to walk away from me, but instead she had done everything in her power to save me and she had given me a new life of my own. One I was terrified I was going to rip to shreds any second now.

Zeb shook his head a little and yanked the door open. "I think you need to cut yourself some slack."

I shrugged. "Maybe."

I shoved him on his shoulder out the door and closed it in his face. I liked Zeb. We had a lot in common, but he didn't know the whole story, didn't know some of the really terrible things I had done. He didn't know that when I died, when everything went black and I knew I wasn't coming back to rejoin the mortal coil, every single, terrible, awful, horrible thing I had ever done in my life floated before me live in vivid color.

The way I used Ayden. The way I had never stopped her from doing what she was doing, which I did so that I could get what I wanted. The sex, the drugs, all of it a kaleidoscope of regret so hard and heavy I was sure it was dragging me to hell. I loved my sister more than anything in the world and yet I hadn't ever been able to stop myself from treating her like a pawn in one of my games. Watching what I did to Ayden, what I allowed her to do for me, was worse than every blow from the baseball bats the bikers had wielded. Seeing the heartbreak in her whiskey-colored eyes when I finally caught up to her after years apart was enough to make me glad I wouldn't ever be opening my own eyes again.

On top of that, there were the old ladies I scammed and the bikers I ripped off. There were the cars I stole and the men I knew my mom was sleeping with to pay our rent while I did nothing to stop it or help the family out. There was the debutante I had charmed into giving me her college fund, which I promptly wasted on a back-room poker game. There was the elderly gentleman looking for a companion that I had convinced not only that I was gay, but that I was interested in him, convinced him just enough to get him to write me a check so I could pursue my passion for photography; needless to say, I wasn't gay or a photographer, but his ten grand had gone a long way in funding my next scam. The number of people I had screwed over was endless, and as their faces rolled like a movie behind my eyes as life leached out of me, I knew I was getting what I deserved.

When I had woken up, had seen Ayden looking down at me while I struggled to realize that even the devil in hell didn't want me, I realized something bright, sharp, and clear. I was an asshole. I was a bad man that had done bad things and I was always going to be that guy, but I never, never wanted to hurt my sister again. I never wanted her to have to worry about me, never wanted her to have to suffer for me or lose anything because of me ever again. I was always going to be a screw-up, but I was going to actively try to avoid causing any more damage, and so far it had been going pretty well. I just had to hold on to those memories, those regrets and that remorse, tight enough that my hands would be too full to ever do the devil's work again.

I pulled the cash drawer out and put it and the sales receipts in the safe that was in Rome's office. I made sure all the cameras were on, especially the ones in the parking lot that he had recently installed. I got jumped one night after work by a bunch of kids with a vendetta that had actually led to my arrest and a legal headache that had taken longer to deal with than it should have because of my past. So now I was hypervigilant and always made sure the eye in the sky was watching my every move.

It was a little after one in the morning. The parking lot was mostly empty except for a few cars that were left over from people that hadn't wanted to drive home after drinking or local neighborhood cars that Rome let borrow a slot. The Bar wasn't in a terrible part of town and I was now pretty used to keeping odd hours since I didn't get out of work until well after most of the world went to bed. I kind of liked the quiet of it all.

It was cold out. Being from the South like me, it had taken a couple of winters to get used to the frigid mountain air. I didn't love the chill. My dislike of winter was enough that I was seriously considering buying a car even though the studio apartment I rented was barely two blocks away from the Bar. That was another thing that had changed after I came back to life. Now I could care less about things. I used to want the best of it all. The nicest clothes, the flashiest ride, the biggest house, and of course the prettiest girl. I wanted everything I had never had growing up and I wanted to show it all off and prove my worth. Now I wanted nothing. The less I had, the less there was to lose.

I was rubbing my hands together briskly and blowing into them to try and warm them up when headlights suddenly illuminated me and a vehicle rolled into the parking lot and didn't stop until it almost reached me. The lights cut out and the driver's-side door swung open. I would've worried, tensed up and walked the other way, if I didn't recognize the ancient SUV and the female driver. Royal was always going to be prettier than any of the other trophies I used to flash around back in my heyday ... prettier even when it was obvious she hadn't been sleeping well.

I pulled the collar of my shearling coat up around my jaw and stepped around the door to where she was sliding out of her seat to the ground. She looked like she had just come from the gym. She had on some kind of stretchy skintight pants and a big sweatshirt. Her hair was tangled in a messy knot on the top of her head and her eyes looked a few shades darker than their normal sweet chocolate color. She also had on running shoes instead of her typical sexy footwear, and she was shivering in the night air.

"You're out and about late." I tried to keep my tone even. She was unpredictable and I never knew which way she was going to go with things. I was used to being able to read people like an open book, but she kept turning the page on me. It was always surprising and unexpected.

She pulled the sleeves of her sweatshirt down over her fingers and looked up at me in a way that made my dick twitch hard behind my zipper. It should be legally prohibited for anyone to be that effortlessly sexy.

"I was at the gym because I haven't been sleeping well. The powers that be cleared me to go back to work at the end of the week as long as I keep seeing the department shrink for the next three months."

I thought she would sound happier about that fact than she did. "That's good news ... isn't it?"

Her shivering turned to outright shaking, and I knew it didn't have anything to do with the cold outside. Against my better judgment I reached out and hooked an arm around her neck and pulled her against my chest. I pulled open the sides of my coat and let her burrow into me while she shook uncontrollably. I felt her hands snake around my sides and search for warm skin below the edge of my shirt on my lower back. I jolted and I wanted to tell myself it was because her hands were like ice, but that wasn't it. Her touch made my skin ripple in excitement.

"I've never worked a shift without Dom. He's like my other half. They're assigning me a temporary partner to work with until Dom comes back." She pulled away so she could look up at me through her silky lashes. "Only they didn't say *when* Dom comes back, they said *if*. I don't know if I can do what I do without him."

I felt her fingers dig into the hollow right at the top of my ass and I had to fight down a full-body shiver.

"You love your job." I knew it was true. Even though she was acting wild and off the tracks lately, she was so much of what she did for a living. "You don't need your partner in order to be a good cop, Royal."

We stared at each other silently for a long moment and then the corner of her mouth kicked up in a grin that made my gut tighten and turned my blood thick. I needed to let go of her and get to getting before I did something stupid.

"Did you miss me this weekend, Asa?"

That was a loaded question if there ever was one. Of course I had noticed she wasn't around, but I had steadfastly refused to acknowledge how her absence made me feel, so I sighed and asked her, "What are you doing here so late?"

She cocked her head to the side and her eyes narrowed just a fraction. Her fingers dipped below the waistband at the back of my jeans, and I had to suck in a breath through my teeth, which hurt because the night air was freezing.

"I don't know. Every time I can't seem to figure out where I'm going lately I always end up wherever you are."

I swore and went to take a step away from her, but her hands just dipped lower and tugged me closer. "You need to get your compass fixed, then. It's pointing you in the wrong direction, Red."

Suddenly it went from being below zero to feeling like we were standing on the surface of the sun. My breathing went shallow and a little erratic as her gaze went all liquid and melty.

"The more you tell me that, the more determined I am to prove you wrong."

Then she stood up on her toes so that she could put her mouth on mine, and it was all over. I knew it was coming. We had been dancing around each other for months. She was too pretty and too persistent for this not to happen at some point in time. She was also too kind, and far too good, to let someone like me put my hands on her. I wasn't really what she wanted, but I was getting tired of trying to tell her that. Despite my best intentions, this inferno that raged between us was going to burn out of control and she had just lit the match and tossed it carelessly on the tinder.

Her hands found their way to my sides as her soft lips did their best to render me mindless and stupid with lust. I could inhale her. It would be so simple to just get lost in all the soft and sweet that made her delectable, but somewhere in the back of my mind all the ways in which this was going to go horribly wrong were poking at me. I raised my hands and gently cupped her jaw. I ran my thumb back and forth across skin that couldn't possibly be that soft, and tried my damnedest not to let her lead me to a place I would never find my way back from. I pulled away from the exquisite brush of her mouth along mine just as her tongue darted out to trace along the sealed seam of my lips. It made me groan out loud. I was going to put a stop to it, I needed to end it now, but she was quick and took advantage of my reaction by slipping her tongue inside my barely parted lips, and then it was hopeless to stop the avalanche of desire that engulfed me.

After all, I never claimed to be an angel and even the devil could only play with fire for so long before he gave in to unholy temptation and danced in the flames.

I backed her into the open doorway of the car. I tunneled my fingers into her hair where it was tight against her head and I inserted a leg between hers so that our pelvises were flush against each other. I wasn't nice. I kissed her like she had been after me to kiss her from the beginning of this game. I used my tongue. I used my teeth. I didn't let her breathe and I didn't give her any kind of space to move away from me as I crowded in on her. I reached around her and grabbed her very spectacular ass in one hand in a really classless move and made sure to manhandle it and her in a very obvious way.

If she wanted me how I really was, then she was going to get it. I had no problem letting the pretense fall away, especially when she was writhing and whimpering against me. I twisted my tongue around hers. I sucked hard on her lower lip until she gasped. I pressed my chest into hers until I could feel the rigid points of her nipples even through all the layers of clothes that separated the two of us.

I felt her fingernails dig harder into my skin where her hands were still trapped under my shirt. I thought maybe she was getting the point, that this was bound to be a train wreck and that her common sense was finally waking back up. But just as I was about to let her go, to pull back and get some much-needed breathing room so I could get my whirling thoughts back in line, one of those dangerous hands suddenly detoured drastically south and the next thing I knew she had her palm wrapped fully around the rock-hard erection that was straining the front of my jeans.

The contact was enough of a shock that I automatically reared back and moved to grab her wrist. She just grinned devilishly up at me and fluttered her eyelashes with false innocence.

"We're in a parking lot, out in the open. You really want to go there with me, Red?"

Not to mention this little fiasco was being recorded for all of eternity and it wasn't exactly a show I wanted prying eyes to see. I don't think Royal was an exhibitionist either, but whatever was working in her complicated mind had her acting out in all kinds of hazardous and surprising ways. I growled her name when she slid her palm up and down, making my dick jump like a well-trained animal at her touch. One of her auburn eyebrows shot straight up and she stuck just the tip of her tongue out to taste her still-damp bottom lip. Goddamn if every single thing she did didn't make me think of darkened rooms and lots and lots of naked skin.

"Why not? It's the closest you've ever let me get." She gave the turgid shaft a hearty squeeze, and that made my eyes roll back in my head. I was on the verge, right on the cusp of picking her up and throwing her into the SUV and just giving her what she had been asking for, when my phone rang.

Considering it was well past the middle of the night and the ring tone was the specific one assigned to my little sister, I had a mild panic attack and pried Royal loose from my junk and finally stumbled a few steps away from her.

"Ayd?" I couldn't help the harshness of tone as I barked out her name.

"Oh my God, Asa, Shaw just went into labor!" My sister was screaming, so I had to hold the phone away from my ear.

"Okay ... and ...?" Shaw was Ayden's best friend. The two of them were beyond tight and I knew it had been really rough for Ayden to move to Austin so that she could be closer to her husband when her best friend was expecting her first child. I calmed down when I realized Shaw was okay and there was no crazy emergency.

"You better get your ass to that hospital and be there in my place until I can get to Denver. Jet is booking a flight for us right now, but I still won't be there until the morning. You need to be there for me, Asa."

Jet was Ayden's husband and also a really good friend of the baby's dad. He would move mountains to make sure Ayden didn't miss this major moment in Rule and Shaw's life. I rubbed my hands through my hair and blew out a breath that fogged up in front of me.

"Shaw isn't going to want me there, Ayd. She'll want you."

"I know that, but I might not make it in time, so you're going to go to the hospital and substitute for me!" She was screaming and almost hysterical, so I knew there would be no reasoning with her. "You need to keep me updated on everything that's happening while I'm on my way there. You have to do this for me, Asa."

Rule was Rome's younger brother. The entire Archer clan was bound to be on hand, not to mention all the other various members of the gang that worked with Rule at the tattoo shop he owned with Nash. The maternity-ward waiting room was going to be full of the Marked family and they really didn't need me in the way, but I had promised myself I was never going to let Ayden down again, so I grumbled my agreement to go and hung up on her before she could keep screaming at me.

I looked at Royal, who was texting on her phone and chewing on her lower lip not at all like a mere moment ago she had had her hand in my pants. She looked back up at me with a crooked grin.

"Saint just texted that Shaw's in labor." I nodded and then frowned when my phone buzzed in my hand with a text. I thought it was going to be Ayden, so I was surprised when the message was from Rome instead.

Another Archer is on the way. Get your ass to the hospital.

It took me a minute to understand that I was actually wanted there for this big event. I looked up at Royal in confusion. "Rome wants me there."

"Of course he does."

I frowned at her. "What do you mean, 'of course he does'?"

She made a face at me and moved to climb into the driver's seat of the 4Runner. "You're friends and practically business partners. Rule has Nash, Jet has Rowdy, and Rome has you. Everyone needs someone to lean on, and bringing a new life into the world is most definitely a big deal. Now come on, I'll give you a lift down there."

I was stunned speechless, so I just moved around the car and climbed in the passenger side. I slumped down once I was situated and stared straight ahead.

I liked Rome. I respected the hell out of him. He was also on my newly formed list of people I never wanted to disappoint. He had given me a shot when everyone else in the world seemed like they were just waiting for me to fuck everything up. I owed him a lot, but it had never occurred to me that somewhere along the line that had morphed into him relying on me and respecting me as well. It was kind of a foreign concept to me and I wasn't sure what to do with it.

"One of these days you're going to let me finish what I'm always trying to start with you, Asa."

Royal's voice was low and there was a needy thread in it that twisted and twined around my heart. That couldn't happen. I couldn't let her get to me; that would be bad news for both of us. It was time to stop pretending and let her see my true colors.

I leered at her and told her flatly, "Any guy that gets your hands around his dick is gonna finish, Red." It was crude and unnecessary, but it made her be quiet for the rest of the ride to the hospital and I spent that time convincing myself it was for the best ...

... Wasn't it?

CHAPTER 4

Royal

My adrenaline was crashing. Partly from the lack of sleep and the excessive workout in the gym, but mostly from being burned alive from the inside out by Asa. I knew that once he let me get close enough to touch, I wasn't going to be able to stop. There was just something about him, some kind of lure that pulled at me when I was around him that was too hard to fight against.

I wasn't exactly shy, but I also wasn't the type to just stick my hand in a guy's pants and go for the gold either. Asa pushed me against all of my boundaries, made me forget that there were consequences to my actions, and I loved every single thing about it. I loved that when I was close enough to breathe him in, he was all I could feel, and I loved the way his glimmering amber eyes seemed to see everything I was trying so hard to hide. They were hot enough to melt the hardest metal and I was far from being forged out of steel and iron at the moment. I felt like I was made of paper and fluff.

I had every intention of just dropping him off at the hospital and going home to try and pretend to sleep. The ride to the hospital passed in absolute silence and I could see the way the muscles in his chiseled jaw were clenching and unclenching as we got closer. I wasn't sure if it had to do with me or with the impending new addition, but it was clear he was lost in his own head and I wasn't allowed inside. Whatever he was musing on it wasn't making him too happy. I could tell even in the dark of the car as his eyes shifted from their normally burnished gold color to a much darker and heavier brown.

I pulled to a stop in front of the massive medical building and waited for him to climb out. I wasn't going to say anything, figuring I had gotten myself into enough trouble for one night, but he cocked his head to the side and turned in his seat a little to look at me questioningly.

"Aren't you coming in?"

My hands curled around the steering wheel involuntarily and I blinked at him in confusion.

"Why would I?"

I was tight with Saint and I really liked Nash, he was pretty much the nicest guy ever, but I hardly knew Shaw, and Rome's wife, Cora, kind of scared the crap out of me. I got along fine with Salem, her no-bullshit attitude was awesome, and I liked that she always spoke her mind. Plus, when her sister had been abducted, I was the first person she turned to and that created a lasting bond between the two of us. But I was pretty sure Ayden was going to show up in no time flat, and I really didn't want to be around when she did. Yes, she had apologized for losing her shit and being a stone-cold bitch to me when she found out I was the one that had arrested Asa, and I believe she meant it, but I had no plans on hanging out and making a happy situation awkward. I hadn't seen Ayden since the day she bailed Asa out of jail, and I was in no hurry to have a reunion. Especially if I couldn't manage to keep the way I felt about her troublesome brother on lockdown.

I knew instinctively she wouldn't approve.

"Why wouldn't you?" His drawl was so smooth, so velvet soft, as it wrapped around me. I just wanted him to whisper things to me in the dark forever.

"I'm friends with Saint and I adore Nash, but this is a big deal, something you share with family. I'm not part of that."

He just stared at me and then grunted. "Go park. We're going up together."

I shook my head. "No, we're not."

I watched as the fire lit back up in his eyes and they switched back to their intoxicating whiskey color. "Fine." He settled back in the seat, crossed his arms over his chest, and lifted a sandy-blond eyebrow at me. "If you don't have to go up, then neither do I. You can drop me off back at the Bar."

I gasped at him a little and narrowed my eyes at him. "Rome asked you to come. You should be inside right now, not arguing with me. You're wanted up there."

His mouth kicked up on the side, and I saw just how easy it was for him to charm people out of common sense. He was pretty day in and day out, but that grin had the devil and temptation in it, and it turned him into something otherworldly. No mere human looked that good after a full day of work and a bout of unfulfilled groping and fondling. It was obvious the path to every decadent sin led right through Asa Cross, and man oh man, did I want to race down it. I would never understand why he insisted on putting so many roadblocks in my way.

"Saint got in touch with you, so obviously someone wants you here. She's shy and there is a lot of commotion to handle when this group gets excited about something. You ever stop and think maybe she needs you as her buffer?"

I cringed because I did know that. Saint loved Nash's friends, was deeply immersed in their world and definitely accepted as part of the ramshackle family, but it was easy for her to get lost in the sea of strong, dominant personalities and she did like having me around to be her port in the storm. Only instead of wanting to be there for my friend, I wanted to run because I didn't know if I could stand any more judgment coming my way. I had only been doing my job. I hadn't wanted to be the one to put Asa in cuffs and take him in, but it had to be done and I unfortunately had to be the one to do it. I respected all of those ladies so much; seeing disappointment in their eyes when they looked at me might very well be the thing that tipped me over the edge of the cliff I was precariously holding on to at the moment.

I sighed because I could see that Asa was serious in his threat. Calling him every bad name in my head that I could think of, I wheeled the 4Runner into a parking spot and turned the engine off.

"You're a manipulative jerk, you know that?"

He finally threw the door open and climbed out. The blast of winter air almost knocked me over and I remembered belatedly that all I had on was my gym clothes.

He walked around the front of the car and stopped when he reached my door. Without a word he pulled it open and put a hand on my arm and practically dragged me out. He shook his head when he saw how I was shivering, and took his big, heavy coat off and put it around my shoulders. It smelled like him and I wanted to cuddle into it and rub my face in the leather, but I was too busy glaring at him as he told me, "Now you're catching on, Red."

All he had on was a long-sleeved thermal, so I tried to hand the coat back to him, but he just grunted and put a hand on my lower back and guided me to the front doors. I blew out a breath that fogged up the air in front of us and told him quietly, "Your sister hates me. She's gonna lose her mind when she shows up and sees me here with everyone."

He chuckled and the sound sent chills racing all across my skin.

"Ayden is protective ... of her friends, of her man, of me. She sometimes goes off before she thinks things all the way through. She doesn't hate you. She hates that I've lived the kind of life that I have. In fact the only person she's ever actually hated is me. That wasn't the first time she's had to come get me out of jail, and Lord only knows if it'll be the last. She knows you were just doing your job, Royal. She just wants to save me. She's always wanted to save me."

I cut him a hard look out of the corner of my eye. "Why didn't you say anything that day? Those kids jumped you, hurt you, and yet you just let us take you in with no complaint. Why?" I had wondered since the day Dom and I had been sent to the Bar to pick him up.

The hospital was busy. I was here enough that I knew the way to the labor and delivery unit without having to ask for directions. Asa followed along beside me without responding to my question. I thought he was just going to ignore me, until we got in the elevator and the doors swished closed. He turned and faced me, and that grin that turned his face into something I would dream about forever flashed at me.

"What's the point? I'm always going to be the bad guy even when I'm not."

I frowned. "You could have defended yourself. You were innocent. Those kids set you up."

There was video proof of the fact, which had ultimately led to him being cleared of all the charges that were filed against him.

I started a little when he reached out and very gently ran the tip of his index finger over the line that had furrowed between my eyebrows as I scowled up at him.

"I'm not defending myself ever again. Not to my sister. Not to the police. Not to anyone. People are going to think what they want, and sadly most of those things that they think are going to be right about me. I'm guilty of a lot of bad shit, Royal. Most of it I never got caught for. Karma has a way of catching up with you, especially when you laughed in her face one too many times."

I was baffled by his response and sort of stunned by the care in that simple touch.

"Are you telling me you would've been willing to go to jail for something you didn't do as some sort of penance for all the other bad stuff you did in the past? That's crazy, Asa."

He just shrugged a shoulder and the doors swished open and we walked into a waiting room full of anxious and excited family and friends. I knew he was carrying around a barrel stuffed full of shame and remorse from his misdeeds of the past. What I hadn't realized up until that very moment was that he was willing to let that barrel crush him rather than set it down and sort through its contents.

Saint was at the desk talking to the lady behind it. Rome was pacing back and forth in front of an older couple that I assumed had to be his and Rule's parents since Shaw had almost no contact with her family; Salem was curled up in a ball on one of the chairs with her head on Rowdy's shoulder; Nash was leaning against the wall with a baseball hat pulled low over his eyes; and Cora was nowhere to be seen.

I faltered a little bit when all eyes turned to us as we approached. At first I thought they were all wondering why I was there, but quickly realized that they were all wondering why Asa and I had shown up at the exact same time and that they were all probably curious as to why I was still wrapped up in his coat. I shrugged out of it even though it felt like I was handing over a security blanket and cleared my throat.

"Hey."

Asa echoed the greeting and shook Rome's hand as the gigantic retired soldier walked over. I squeaked a little when the big man scooped me up in a tight hug that I couldn't help but return. When he put me back on my feet I just gaped up at him in surprise. He smiled down at me and I couldn't help but smile back.

"I was going to have Cora ask you to go get him if he didn't show. I was gonna tell you to use force if necessary."

Asa made a noise and lifted an eyebrow at his boss. "Where's Cora? This doesn't seem like something she would miss."

We wandered farther into the waiting room and I let out a sigh of relief when Saint made her way over to my side. She linked her arm through mine and gave me a knowing look. I just shook my head and told her, "Later. We can talk about it later."

She just smiled at me and propped herself up next to Nash, who tilted his head down at me in greeting.

Rome ran his hands over his head and his massive chest expanded as he huffed out a frustrated breath.

"She's in the bathroom." Something shifted across his handsome face. "She's not feeling well at the moment."

Rome and Cora had recently gotten engaged and they had a daughter who was just starting to walk, which constantly kept them on their toes. She was full of her mother's fiery personality and her dad's stubbornness, which meant keeping up with little RJ was a full-time job. They were a rock-solid family unit and it made me have hope for my own future. I wanted to believe that something like what Rome and Cora had could exist without infidelity, without jealousy and drama, in my life at some point. In fact all of these people had relationships I envied and admired. They were all determined to make them work. No matter what the cost. They wanted to be together and they all did whatever it took to make that happen. I really wanted someone to feel that way about me.

Nash pushed the brim of his hat up and his periwinkle-colored eyes shone at me with unbridled amusement.

"Any particular reason you showed up at the exact same time as Asa?" I was pretty sure Saint had told him about my current infatuation, but I wasn't in the mood to share or be teased, so I just shrugged.

"Good timing, I guess." Nash was Rule's best friend, so punching him in the gut to get that cocky grin off of his face wouldn't be in good form considering the situation.

I let go of Saint's arm and found a seat that was off to the side. I kicked my feet up on the one across from me and settled in to wait. Having babies took a long time and it wasn't like I was going to sleep anyway.

I was drifting in my own thoughts. Thinking about Asa's startling revelations that he was willing to go to jail to pay for past crimes, thinking about the way he tasted, the way he felt so hot and hard in my hand. I was thinking about the idea of going back to work without Dom at my back and how that was almost impossible to get my head around. I also couldn't get my mind off the fact that all I wanted when I couldn't sleep and the gym wasn't enough was to go toe-to-toe with the southern bartender I couldn't get out of my head. My crush was turning into an obsession.

I jolted a little when a tiny body landed in the chair next to me. Cora looked at my sprawled-out form and kicked her much shorter legs out in front of her with a grin. "Not even close." There was still a foot beyond the toe of her combat boot and the opposite chair.

I rolled my head to the side so I could look at her as she settled in next to me. Cora was the unofficial guardian angel of this group. She was a petite powerhouse of a woman, and when I wasn't sort of terrified of her, I really liked and respected her. Tonight she looked a little pale and she had obvious bags under her two different-colored eyes.

"How's it going?" I figured if anyone would know it would be her.

"Fine. Rule's actually handling all of it better than Rome did. Rome had the nurses and my OB-GYN scared to come near me. Rule's taking it all in stride. As long as Shaw is cool, he seems cool, but the real contractions haven't started yet. We might have to send in the reinforcements if he flips out like his brother did."

I laughed. I had no doubt Rome was extra scary when he was stressed and freaking out. He looked like he could win a war all by himself with no weapons, just standing off to the side chatting with Asa.

"Well, that's good. It's nice you're all here to support them. Ayden called Asa. She's on her way already."

Cora tilted her head back on the chair, put a hand over her tummy, and squeezed her eyes shut. She looked a little green all of a sudden and I sat up straighter. I was going to ask her if she was okay when she breathed deep and then turned her head to look at me as whatever was wrong with her apparently passed.

"She's going to be devastated if that baby comes before she gets here. Moving to Austin with Jet was the best choice, but it's hard on them with all of us still here."

"She told Asa he had to be here just in case she couldn't make it."

Cora nodded and smiled at me. "He needs to be here regardless, and so do you."

It was uncanny how she always seemed to see everything. "I'm here." I said it begrudgingly.

"Yeah. But you had to think about it first. You belong here, Royal. Don't doubt it."

But I did—doubt it, that is. I just didn't know how I fit. "Things just felt off and a little strained after I had to take Asa in. I wasn't really sure how to handle that, and making friends has never been all that easy for me."

Most girls didn't like me or didn't trust me and boys only wanted to pretend to be my friend in the hopes it would lead to more. Aside from my tight bond with my mom, my relationship with Dom and his sisters, and now Saint, I had lived a pretty solitary life.

"Shit happens. What happened with Asa wasn't your fault and we all know that." She gave me a very pointed look, her brown eye hard and her blue eye sharp. "Do you?"

I wanted to tell her everything felt like it was my fault. It felt like all I could do anymore was make mistake after mistake. I never got the chance, though, because panic crossed her pretty face and in a heartbeat she was up out of the chair and darting across the waiting room to where the bathrooms were located. Rome's deep voice rumbled with a litany of swearwords as his mom scolded him, which he blatantly ignored as he followed his tiny fiancée into the ladies' room. He ignored the nurse that called out to him as well, which had all the guys gathered around laughing.

I was pondering Cora's words about fault when her now-vacant seat was filled with a much bigger, masculine body. Whenever I was within touching distance of him, all my senses seemed to go into overload. He draped one of his long arms across the back of my chair and looked at me out of the corner of his eye.

"You okay?" His voice was softer than usual and way too close to my ear. I gulped a little and nodded.

It was the fact he asked, the fact that I think he really cared whether I was okay or not, that overshadowed all the red flags he liked to wave in my face warning me away from him.

"Yeah. I'm glad I came up with you. It's nice to see this."

"See what?"

I waved a hand vaguely around the room indicating where Salem and Rowdy were cuddled together, where Nash had wrapped Saint up in his arms and was holding her, where Rome had disappeared after Cora, and even where the older Archers were sitting huddled together.

"Happiness. Togetherness. Unity. It was just me and my mom when I was growing up and she jumped from man to man always looking for something she couldn't seem to find. It's pretty cool to see couples that actually want to be together. Stability is kind of a foreign concept to me."

He kicked his long legs up like mine were and adopted a similar pose. I shivered a little when his side pressed along my own. He grinned at me when he noticed my reaction.

"You can have all the stability you want when you stop looking for trouble."

He was probably right, although trouble sounded like so much more fun right now, and what I wanted and what I needed were absolutely not the same thing.

I didn't reply; instead I tried really hard not to move as I felt the tips of his fingers start to play with the end of my long ponytail where it hung over the back of the chair. I don't think he was even aware that he was doing it. That is, until I glanced at him and noticed the golden glow shining out of his eyes. This was not a guy that ever did anything without being very aware of the effect it was having on the people around him. He wasn't just trouble, he was potent and more dangerous than most of the stuff I saw on the streets every day.

At some point the monotony of waiting for endless hours long into the night, the quiet murmur of voices, the squeak of rubber shoes on the linoleum floor, all worked together to lull me to sleep. One minute I was thinking about how odd my night had turned out. About how when I felt my absolute worst there was this remarkable foundation of wonderful people to catch me. I wasn't used to having any kind of safety net aside from Dom, and I had to admit it was really nice to have a soft landing instead of a brutal crash for once in my life.

But of course, like everything in my world lately, drifting off into a little catnap couldn't just be easy and rejuvenating. As soon as the darkness descended, it was there. The day everything changed forever.

I heard the gunshots. Heard the cops that had been on the scene before us shouting. Heard the people in the neighborhood chattering next to the dilapidated building that had been converted into a monster meth lab. I heard the sirens. I heard my radio squawk that there were several officers down. It was a bad situation all around, but Dom and I were trained. It was our job to go into bad situations and make them better.

I heard Dom telling me we should go into the alley and I blindly agreed. I heard his boots rattle on the metal as he found a fire escape and started to climb up. I told him I was right behind him, we always had each other's back. Dom barked at me to stay put, to cover him from the group. We had no idea how many shooters there were, had no idea if the building was clear or not, but again, we were trained and this was our job.

I had my gun out. I was watching, staring hard at the space above Dom's head, making sure no one could get the drop on him. There were more shots fired, I had no idea if they were our guys or the bad guys, and I didn't care as long as my partner was okay. I heard Dom make a noise as he reached the top of the fire escape. I could swear I heard every single snowflake that was falling that night as it hit the dirty ground around my booted feet.

I heard Dom call an all-clear, saw him move to go through a shattered window, and then I heard it ... nothing more than a whisper. A faint sound of a can or some other piece of trash rolling on the asphalt. I moved my attention away from Dom for a split second, half of a heartbeat, not even a full blink, and then hell was unleashed.

A kid, a boy that was barely out of puberty, popped up over the edge of the roof, opened fire from his higher position, and hit Dom. He took two shots in the vest, one ripped through his arm. The force and surprise sent him stumbling backward until he hit the waist-high railing of the fire escape and started to tumble over it. One last bullet had caught him just right in the side, but it was the fall that did the most damage.

Then all I could hear was screaming, my own and Dom's as he fell. I returned fire, caught the kid dead center in his chest. It didn't matter. I thought Dom was dead and I couldn't stop screaming.

I woke up with a jerk. I was covered in a light sheen of sweat and noticeably shaking. Luckily this time I wasn't making any noise and no one seemed to notice my disheveled state, mostly because Ayden and Jet had arrived and everyone was gathered around saying hello. I watched as Asa pulled his strikingly beautiful little sister into a warm embrace.

And then it was like Shaw and the baby knew, like her and Rule's baby boy had been waiting for just the right minute to make his grand entrance into the world. He seemed to know the exact moment that his whole family was there to meet him because it wasn't until the entire gang was present that Reyer Remington Archer made his debut.

I had to say it was the best thing that had ever been waiting for me on the end of the nightmarish visions of that horrible night, and I would forever be grateful I was allowed to be part of it.

CHAPTER 5

Asa

About two weeks after the night at the hospital, I walked into the Bar full of trepidation. Rome had called and asked me to come in an hour early because he wanted to talk to me about something. I couldn't for the life of me figure out if I had screwed something up or done something wrong, but his grave tone was more serious than usual and it made my long-honed self-preservation instincts kick in. If he was going to can me, tell me to get lost, I told myself it was no big deal. I could hit the road, I could figure out something else to do, but the Bar had really sort of become the first place that felt like it was solid under my feet, and I didn't want to admit that losing that scared the hell out of me. Not having this place really would set me adrift, and when I was adrift I got into trouble ... lots of trouble.

Ayden and Jet had stayed for a week. My sister wanted to be there when Shaw took baby Ry home and got settled. The nickname was cute and Shaw loved it because she was a huge J. D, Salinger fan, plus knowing who the kid's dad was, he was bound to have a little Holden Caulfield rebellion in him. It wasn't enough time with my sister, and even though I could see she was happy, really happy with her choice to move in order to get more time with her man, I missed her and I could see that she was still worrying too much about me. I tried to tell her that I was fine. I tried to explain that if I was going to fuck up, it wouldn't matter if she was here in Denver or in Austin, but that just made her tawny eyes spark at me in anger. I loved Ayden more than I ever knew I was capable of, but I wasn't going to try and fool her into believing that I was never going to screw up again. All I could do was try. Try and be better, try and be honest, try staying on the right side of the law and not running when things got hard. Trying was just going to have to be enough. For Ayden and for me.

During the day the Bar was fairly quiet. There was a whole slew of retired veterans that liked to hang out and share old war stories. It never ceased to amaze me how many of them had to do with ex-wives and old lovers rather than any actual war. Rome typically opened the bar up and hung out until I got there in the early evening to run the night shift. He wanted to be home with his family during the evening and I couldn't say I blamed him for that. Being a retired soldier himself, Rome had an easy way with the grizzled clientele and preferred to leave the more lively and rambunctious party crowd to me.

When I walked in the front doors, he wasn't around, and Brite, the guy who had sold Rome the Bar in the first place, was standing in my usual spot behind the long wooden bar. Darcy, the Bar's cook and Brite's ex-wife, had her head poking out of the kitchen and the two of them appeared to be arguing in low voices.

I don't think either of them copped to the fact that they might be exes but were still practically married. Wife number three was long gone, and Darcy wasn't just his only child's mother, but really the love of his life. I had asked Rome about it once and he just shrugged and told me that good women were complicated and hard to hold on to. I didn't understand it until I walked into the liquor storeroom unannounced one day between shifts and found Darcy with her legs in the air and Brite's giant form hovering over her in an unmistakable way. There might not be rings, but there was love and passion still there. Too bad their daughter was a grade-A pain in the ass.

Brite cut off whatever he was saying to Darcy, and she ducked back into the kitchen. His teeth flashed at me through the miles of beard that covered his face and he crossed his arms over his barrel-like chest. Brite had so much don't-fuck-with-me pouring off of him it always surprised me how soft-spoken and insightful he really was. He looked like a Hell's Angel not a savior, but he was. He had saved this bar. He had saved Rome. He had given all those vets a place to feel secure, and now he was trying his hardest to save his obviously wayward daughter even though she absolutely didn't seem to appreciate the fact.

"How's it going, son?" His voice rumbled like thunder over the Rockies.

I shrugged off my coat and ran my hands through my hair. "It's going. You have any idea why Rome called me in early?"

He shook his head and lifted a bushy eyebrow at me. "How is Avett doing? Tell me the truth, Asa. Rome doesn't want me to worry, says he can handle her, but I raised that girl. I know all the kinds of headaches she can be."

I sighed under my breath. "Her attitude sucks. She doesn't listen. She fights with Darcy. She hates it here, which is a shame because she's one hell of a good cook." She really was. When she wasn't just throwing together the bar food the joint specialized in, when she made something for herself or was playing around, the girl was obviously talented. I told Darcy once that someone should tell Avett to go to culinary school, to which Darcy had sighed and looked like she was going to cry. Turned out Avett had just flunked out of regular college, so any kind of expensive specialty school clearly wasn't in the cards. The girl was on a downward spiral. I could see it clear as day, mostly because it was a ride I was all too familiar with.

Brite swore under his breath and raised a hand to stroke his beard. "You feel comfortable firing her if she crosses a line?"

I dipped my chin down, thinking about the beer in her purse. "I will do what I have to in order to keep the Bar and Rome safe."

He nodded grimly at me. "That's what I wanted to hear. She's driving Darce nuts. The girl is going to be the death of us both."

I made a noise of agreement. "Rome in the office?"

Brite nodded and again flashed me a grin that had to fight through his facial hair. "You look nervous, son. Don't be."

I was annoyed that my typical mask of indifference and carelessness had slipped, so I struggled to put it back in place as I walked down the hallway where the restrooms, storage, and tiny back office were located. I knocked on the door before pushing it open and noticed Rome was on the phone when I walked in. I sat in one of the ratty chairs that was up against the wall while he continued to grunt and reply in one-word sentences to whomever he was talking to. There was paperwork on the desk, cases of alcohol were piled up on the floor, and Rome's gym bag took up the space on the other available chair. His chair squeaked as he leaned back heavily in it, said, "I love you more," meaning the person on the end of the call had to be Cora, and finally hung up and looked at me.

I wanted to grin at him, to play it all off like whatever was about to go down didn't mean shit to me, but instead I felt my spine stiffen and my eyes narrow. "What's up?" I didn't really know what to do with the fact that this somehow mattered so much to me. The only things I had ever cared about before were materialistic and my sister; this was so foreign, and I hated how uneasy it made me. I wanted to squirm but I forced myself to stay still.

He rubbed his palms into his eyes and pressed down on the scar that bisected his eyebrow.

"Cora's pregnant."

I rolled my eyes and crossed my leg so that my ankle was resting on my knee. "You don't say?" Sarcasm was as thick as Kentucky grass in my tone.

He blinked at me for a second and then blew out a breath. "What do you mean?"

I snorted. "I saw her at the hospital. I saw you at the hospital. If it was the flu or just a cold, you wouldn't have been all over her like a mother hen, and I doubt Cora would've looked so happy."

His blue eyes widened a fraction and then a grin split his stern expression. "Yeah. She just hit a little over two months. She wasn't as sick with RJ, but she was a hell of a lot moodier."

"I didn't know you were trying to have another baby."

His big shoulders rose and fell. "We weren't. But we weren't not trying either. I got a fiancée and a new baby all within a few months of each other and that makes a man start to think about what's next."

That made me laugh. I was genuinely happy for him. "Congratulations."

"We wanted to wait until Rule and Shaw got to take Ry home and had a little while to bask in the new-baby awesomeness before we said anything. Rule as a daddy is a miracle that needs to be appreciated fully for a while, and I don't think my mom can handle any more Archer good news without exploding. So you and Brite are the only ones that know for now."

"Got it. Is that what this little powwow was about?" If so, all my muscles could unclench and the breath I was holding could finally escape my frozen lungs.

I gritted my teeth when he shook his head in the negative.

"No. I need to talk to you about the Bar."

I didn't want to give away the fact I was sort of falling apart on the inside, so I just stayed silent and waited for him to keep talking.

He just stared at me for a minute and then rocked back in the chair and put his hands behind his head.

"Brite sold me this bar for a hundred bucks. I thought he was crazy." I agreed. "I didn't get it at the time, but I do get it now. It wasn't about the bar or about giving me something to do, it was about taking something beaten, something that had adapted and survived, and breathing new life into it. Did you know that even with the expense of adding Dixie and Avett to the payroll, we still turned a profit last year? And not just a few bucks; an actual, decent-sized profit."

We were busier and busier and the crowd was getting more and more diverse. The live music helped and so did the fact that Rome's friends and family were gorgeous and liked to hang out here. The Bar was hip now, so I really wasn't surprised.

"That's good news."

"Yes, it is, and it has a shit ton to do with you, Asa. You work your ass off. You're here more hours than is healthy. You take care of the staff. You take care of the customers, no matter who they might be, and goddamn, you're good behind that bar. People fucking love you."

That's because I spent most of my life tricking people into thinking I was lovable when the opposite was true.

He dropped his arms and got to his feet and walked around the desk so he could perch on the corner closest to me. It was a small space and Rome was an intimidating guy, but there was a gleam in his gaze that was all about excitement and expectation.

"I want you to hire some more staff. I want Dixie to have help on the floor and I want you to hire a full-time day bartender that's good with the military guys and a night guy to give you a break."

"I don't know that a break is the best thing for me. You know what they say about idle hands."

I lifted both my eyebrows up at him as he scowled down at me from where he was most definitely looming.

"This bar gave both of us a crutch to lean on when we were trying to figure out what we were doing with our lives. It's helped us both out by keeping us busy and given us something to focus on. You more so than me because I had my Half-Pint and the baby to worry about. I think it's also offered me the insight into what happens next." He looked at me to see if I was still with him and I was. I couldn't disagree that the Bar was a safe haven when I was trying to leave behind a life and turn into something, someone, more respectable. "There are a lot of businesses that could use a little revitalization, a second chance, if you will. The gym I go to is falling apart. It needs some new equipment, some new blood, to bring it into this century. I like that the place feels like an old gym from the 1930s or something, but it needs some help. I want to invest in it."

I blinked in surprise and just stared at him. He cocked the eyebrow with the scar in it at me and kept going.

"Nash has a buddy with a garage. He does killer restoration projects but is pretty small-time. I've seen his work and met the guy a few times. I think I want to funnel some cash into his enterprise as well."

I hissed out a whistle between my teeth. "Man, you weren't kidding about a decent profit, were you, Boss?"

Rome grunted at me. "I also want to help Nash and Rule out if they do decide to expand and open a third shop somewhere. What I don't want to do is sit on my ass anymore and wait on whatever it is that's going to happen next to find me. I'm buying a house. I'm having another kid, and when all that's said and done I'm marrying the most perfect girl in the world."

I didn't really think "perfect" and "Cora" went together in the same sentence, but to him she was absolutely the perfect choice and there was something to be said for feeling that way about the mother of your kids.

"Those are all good plans, Rome, and I gotta say I'm a little shocked you decided that being an entrepreneur and investor was your calling, but I can get behind you wanting to help out struggling businesses. That's pretty noble of you."

He gave me a hard look. "Second chances matter. You and I both know that."

"They do." I worked hard every day to make sure my second chance wasn't wasted. I owed myself and the people that loved me at least that much.

"I want you to consider being my business partner. You do a good job here—fuck, a great job. You're way better with people than I'll ever be and I think you're the only other person that can understand why I want to invest in the businesses I do."

Well, shit. That was unexpected.

I scooted forward on the chair a little and raised my hand to rub vigorously at the back of my neck. Old shame and bitter regret surged to the surface and I had to try really hard to fight it back down.

"I don't have that kind of money floating around, big guy."

He paid me a fair salary and my cost of living was practically nil, but when you died on an operating table and they brought you back to life, it cost a fortune. With no insurance, that meant every extra cent I had went back to paying the medical bills that were astronomical. Ayden and Jet had offered to help, but as soon I settled into my job at the Bar, I refused to let them. It was the first time in my life I was actually owning up to the consequences of my actions.

His mouth quirked and he pushed off the desk so that he was on his feet. "So give me a hundred bucks. It'll be the best money you ever spent."

I swore at him and got to my feet. I still had to look up at him, but he seemed less imposing now that I wasn't sitting down.

"Look, I appreciate the offer and I would jump at the chance, but I can't, and I can't let you give me a free pass like that."

He opened his mouth to argue with me but I cut him off by putting a hand on his massive shoulder and shaking my head.

"I've always taken any shortcut I could find. When I didn't get shit handed to me, I took it because I thought I was entitled to it. I can't do that with you. Not after everything you've done for me, Rome. If I ever get in a place where I can legitimately buy my way into a partnership with you, and the offer is still there I'll jump on board. Until then, you just let me know if you need help with anything. I can be your go-to guy."

"You've been that since the first day you started work here."

I cleared my throat as heavy gratitude pressed in on me from all directions. "Thanks for trusting me enough to even consider getting into some kind of business with me."

He grunted and we both left the office. "You've never given me a reason *not* to trust you. I know there was ugly shit before, but that doesn't have anything to do with now. I've had to learn to leave the past where it belongs or it really fucks up the good stuff happening in the here and now."

We were both pretty solemn as we walked back into the front of the Bar. Brite was gone and Dixie was standing behind the bar watching Dash, who insisted we all just call him Church like Rome did, as he walked around straightening tables. Rome gave the cocktail waitress a one-armed hug and stuck his head in the kitchen to let Darcy know he was leaving. He also gave Church a fist bump as the other dark-skinned ex-military man walked up to the bar and then looked at me with lifted eyebrows as he turned to go. "Lemme know if you change your mind, Opie."

"Will do." The nickname was ridiculous. I was so far from being the innocent southern kid in overalls at the water hole it was laughable, but a drunk kid had once lobbed the name as an insult, and not surprisingly it stuck.

Since it was a Saturday night I ran through what we were looking at business-wise for the night and told both Dixie and Church that Rome wanted to look for some more staff. I told them if they had any recommendations to send them my way and then went into the kitchen to make sure Avett had at least showed up for her shift. She was standing by the big walk-in cooler and Darcy was in front of her.

The older woman had her daughter's chin in her hand and was screaming at her, "I know goddamn well you did not trip and fall and give yourself that black eye, Avett."

Avett's gaze darted anywhere but at her infuriated mother and landed on me. I saw her bottom lip tremble and I frowned at her over the top of Darcy's head.

"If he's putting marks on you that other people can see, it's only gonna get worse. Not only does that mean he doesn't give a shit about you, it means he doesn't give a shit that you actually have people that might not want to see you hurt. That's dangerous. You should cut ties and run like a rabbit with its tail on fire."

Avett's swirly eyes narrowed at me and she jerked away from her mom. "You don't know anything. Neither one of you do. Jared was drunk. It was an accident. Leave me alone or I'll walk out and you won't have anyone to work the busiest night of the week."

She was shaking and I knew she didn't believe her own words. I could see it as she bit the inside of her cheek. You had to be able to lie to yourself before you could lie expertly to other people. Avett wasn't quite there yet, and maybe there was time to stop her before she got there. I was done playing babysitter; it was time to let the bad guy out and maybe he could get results where coddling this troubled girl had failed.

I told her flatly, "You walk out, you aren't walking back in. I'm done playing your spoiled-brat games. You don't wanna be here, well, guess what, I really fucking don't want you here either, but I owe your dad and your mom is a good lady, so I endure working with you. This"—I waved a hand around the kitchen to encompass the dramatic scene I had interrupted—"is the threshold for my bullshit tolerance." I made sure I looked at Darcy so she could see how dead serious I was before I walked back out of the kitchen.

It was a busy Saturday night even without a band, but all the patrons seemed to be on their best behavior. There was one little squabble among some girls, but as soon as they saw Church making his way over to where they were causing a ruckus, they quieted down and went immediately into flirt mode. I stayed busy until midnight, when a scraggly-looking dude walked in looking strung out and shifty. I had the sinking suspicion he was here for Avett. He totally looked like the kind of scumbag that had no issue hitting women or asking them to steal from work.

He stayed just inside the front door and was twitchy enough that Church hovered close by. I was getting ready to round the bar and ask him what his deal was when Avett came barreling out of the kitchen and rushed to the guy's side. He scowled at her and shrugged her off, all while hauling her body out the front door. I saw Church's eyebrows snap down in a fierce V, and without me saying anything, he followed the young couple into the parking lot. At least we could stop the idiot from pounding on her while she was at work. I made a mental note to mention something to Brite. He was the baddest of the bad and anything he would have to say to his daughter's loser boyfriend would be far more effective and terrifying than anything I came up with.

"Can I have another lemon drop, please?"

My attention shifted back to the smiling lady that had been sitting at the bar since ten. She was a tad bit older, probably in her midforties, but she was a looker. I wasn't sure how much was natural versus how much was man-made, but she had an amazing face and sleek blond hair, and a look in her dark eyes that let me know she would like me to serve her more than a martini. I thought it was funny since she was with a guy that looked younger than me and he was bending over backward to keep not only her attention but her obvious wealth focused on him. He was glaring at me every time she tried to engage me in conversation, so of course I had played it up all night.

I smiled back, made sure to flex when I shook her drink, and kissed the back of her fingers when she handed me a twenty for a tip. I laughed under my breath when the guy turned beet red and looked like he was going to explode. She was a classy-looking chick, but I wasn't into being man-candy, so I took her money and fucked with her boy toy for my own amusement. They weren't our normal type of customer and I wondered where in the world they had wandered in from. I was going to ask but got distracted by a blown keg I needed to change and by a couple that thought they could walk out on Dixie without paying their tab.

I was tired by the time the bar was shut down and Church was getting ready to walk Dixie to her car. They asked if I wanted them to wait for me but I needed a minute to decompress. I had so much stuff floating around in my head: Rome's offer, Avett's crappy boyfriend, where my life really was going, and of course Royal. I hadn't seen her since the hospital, but she was back at work now, so maybe that was enough to have her acting right instead of acting out. I didn't want her to be all tangled up in my mind and my confusion, but when I closed my eyes to go to bed at night, I still tasted her winter-cold lips against my own.

It was after three by the time I hit the lights and locked everything up. I drank a couple fingers of scotch while listening to the Raconteurs on the digital jukebox before hitting the back door, then I shrugged into my coat for the walk home. I was lucky it was close because I really didn't love Colorado winter weather. How February managed to be so much colder than either December or January still amazed my inherently southern bones. With my hands in my pockets I put my head down against the bitter wind and started across the parking lot. A soft feminine voice dropping really ugly swearwords brought me up short.

I blinked because I couldn't believe she was back at my bar in the middle of the night. Once again in gym clothes and looking all too delectable. She was pacing in a very agitated manner and stopping to alternately kick the tire of her SUV and thunk her forehead on the driver's window.

"Royal?"

She jerked around when I said her name and gazed at me with dark and hypnotic eyes.

"I'm not stalking you." She stiffened as I made my way over to her. She seemed automatically defensive.

"I didn't think you were."

She sighed and let her head roll back to hit the window. "I couldn't sleep, so I went to the gym. That didn't help, so I thought I'd stop and have a drink, then I remembered you don't want me here. So then I had to sit in the car for a few minutes and decide what I wanted to do, but while I was doing that a really drunk girl came out of the convenience store over there." She pointed to the little corner store across the street. "She was going to drive, so I had to go over and say something." Her pretty mouth quirked up in a tiny grin. "I took her keys and waited until she got a cab, only as usual I left my purse inside the 4Runner along with my keys and phone." She thunked her head back again and I wanted to reach out to pull her into a hug. "I locked myself out of my car."

I blew out a breath and it fogged in the air between us. It was much like the last time we had been here, only her hand wasn't around my dick and I wasn't pawing at her like a crazy person.

"You don't keep a spare?"

She rolled her eyes. "Of course I do. But not on the car. I'm a cop. That would just be asking for trouble or a pissed-off perp waiting for me in my backseat after a shift. Saint has one, Dom has one, Nash even has one, but it's three in the morning and I don't exactly want to make that call and piss everyone off. Besides Dom is the one I would call and he can't exactly ride to my rescue right now." I saw her gulp as she said it and her eyes darted away from mine.

I groaned and I knew she heard it. "Come on. You can come crash at my place and call the cavalry in the morning. It's cold and I'm too tired to try and figure out a smarter solution."

She cocked her head to the side and considered me for a long moment before asking, "Smarter solution?"

I took her by the elbow and felt her shiver. I took my coat off again and wrapped her up in it. Someone needed to explain to her that it was fucking freezing outside and she needed to wear more than skintight workout gear if she was going to wander the streets at night.

"You and me alone is the dumbest idea I ever had, Red. Don't say I didn't warn you."

CHAPTER 6

Royal

I knew I could just ask him for his phone to call a cab and get a ride back to Capitol Hill. I also knew Nash would be happy to get up and come collect me even if it was well past the middle of the night. But I had been angling for Asa to take me home for weeks, and if this was the only opportunity I was going to get, then I was going to roll with it, even if he looked more annoyed and agitated than amorous. Besides, he had given me his coat again when the temperature was freezing cold and I knew somehow that meant something even if he wasn't aware of it.

"How was going back to work?" His drawl was honeyed and warm as he guided me along the silent streets. I don't think I knew anyone else that was a grown-up yet didn't own a car. It was just one more piece of the puzzle that was Asa Cross.

"It's been tricky. I've never partnered with anyone but Dominic, so it's strange being on patrol with someone new."

My temporary partner was a guy named Barrett. He was quite a bit older than me and most definitely the strong, silent type. I was used to letting Dom take the lead, to following his moves, so it was strange trying to adjust to being the more vocal partner. So far my shifts without Dom had been pretty uneventful and I hadn't had to pull my gun or really wade into any danger. I was dreading the day it happened, even though the department shrink told me that was normal. She was convinced I was suffering from some low-grade PTSD symptoms and that my guilt at being distracted and seeing Dom almost die was tied to the fact that I had escaped the shootout unscathed.

I leaned into Asa's side when I noticed that he was shivering in the cold. A thrill raced through me when he wrapped his arm around my shoulder and huddled into me. Sure, it was probably for warmth, but my libido didn't care.

"How is your partner doing?"

I hated to think about Dom being laid up and healing. He was a guy that liked action, that liked to be hands-on, but in his current state all he could do was lie in bed and watch endless hours of Netflix while his sisters hovered over him. It also rankled me every time I put my uniform on that I was the one that got to go to work, that I was the one who ended up all right, while Dom was the one stuck not knowing what his future was going to look like. The unfairness of it all grated across my skin and sat heavy in my gut every single shift.

"He's getting there. He's going to need a lot of physical therapy once he's back in fighting form. That broken femur is no joke."

"If you need a name, I know a guy."

I looked up at him from under my eyelashes. "You know a guy?"

We reached a very nondescript and frankly crappy apartment complex and I followed him up a few flights of stairs. This isn't ever where I'd picture him living.

"Well, Rome knows a guy. He used to date Rome's younger brother, Rule's twin, Remy. His name is Orlando Fredrick and he's some big-shot sports physical therapist. I've met him a few times when he popped into the Bar to talk to Rome. He seems like a pretty cool guy, and according to Rome, he knows his shit."

Rome didn't strike me as the type that handed out praise or respect lightly, so I made a mental note of the name to pass along to Dom and followed Asa into the apartment. It was tiny, really tiny, and there wasn't much in it. I mean it was a studio, so there wasn't a lot of space to keep stuff, but beyond the bed, a decent-sized flat-screen TV, the little bistro set, and a well-worn recliner, there didn't seem to be any part of him in the apartment.

If he was concerned or interested in my slightly startled reaction to his place, he didn't show it. He flipped on the lights, tossed his keys and his cell on the itty-bitty little table, and shoved his hands through his thick, blond hair.

"Let me dig out some clean sheets and you can change the bed while I take a shower." He inclined his head toward the chair. "I'll crash in the recliner since I can sleep anywhere and you can take the bed."

I opened my mouth to argue. It wasn't a king-sized bed but it was definitely big enough for both of us to share. Yet there was a glow in his gold eyes, a warning light that had me clicking my teeth together in frustrated silence. I always felt like he was trying to say something to me without words, like he had an unspoken message for me I was just too thick to pick up on. Something was working behind those jungle-cat eyes and there was a coiled tension in him that I could feel vibrating and waiting to spring loose. I shrugged out of his coat and hung it on the back of one of the chairs that sat at the table. I took the sheets and blanket he shoved at me before he turned and headed to what I assumed was the bathroom.

I sank to the edge of the bed and stared blankly at the cracked-open door. I set the bundle in my arms down next to me and tried to get my head around what was happening. This was absolutely not what I had pictured coming home with the sexy southerner to be like. I was sure once it was just the two of us, alone, the undeniable heat and chemistry that popped and sizzled between us would reach a bursting point. Then I would finally get all that I knew Asa had to offer directed at me. I wanted that smooth charm, that effortless sexiness, and all the turbulent desire I knew was lurking just below the surface of his good-ol'-boy façade. I sighed and looked at his abandoned cell phone, wondering if I really should call someone to rescue me. It was starting to seem like Asa's desire to save me from what he clearly thought was going to be a mistake was far stronger than my desire to make that mistake.

I got up and went to crack open the door to the bathroom enough that I could tell him I was going to call a cab and head home. I wasn't going to kick him out of his bed when he obviously didn't want me here. I already had enough things in my life making me feel bad about myself; I didn't need to chase after more rejection from Asa.

"Hey, I'm just gonna …" I trailed off as my tongue suddenly forgot how to work and all thought fled.

Of course there wouldn't be a full-sized bath and shower in this tiny apartment. Just a shower stall enclosed in barely frosted glass that hid nothing. The steam from the shower wasn't enough to obscure the sight before me, and my hand pushed the door open the rest of the way like it was operating independently from the rest of me.

He had one arm bent above his head with his forehead resting on it as the water cascaded down around him. He turned to look at me as the door opened. Even with the shower steam and the hazy glass between us, I could see his brilliant gaze lock on mine as his other arm moved to work his fist up and down an impressive erection that was obviously meant for me.

I knew I should shut the door and turn away. It was his space, his private moment, but I couldn't do it and I was equal parts turned on and furious watching him as he worked himself over all while he watched me unblinkingly. He was beautiful; it was beautiful. Yet I was so mad that after all the ways in which I had made it clear to him that he could have me, he would rather self-gratify than take me to bed, that I was having a hard time appreciating all that beauty even if I was transfixed by the sight. He was wasting something that was rightfully mine and I wanted to scream at him to stop, to ask me to join him under the water and put that throbbing evidence of his arousal to better use, but I was stunned into silence, rooted to the spot by twin spikes of passion and fury.

He was all long, lean lines and taut golden skin. His blond hair was slick, shades darker from the water, and his eyes shone out of his face like something was lighting them up from deep within him. The muscles in his arm and across his broad shoulders flexed and danced as his hand moved over the thick, impatient-looking arousal that hung prominently between his legs. His defined abs contracted then released as he let out a long groan after a few more purposeful strokes brought him to completion. His entire body jerked just a little and I could swear he mouthed my name as he came, but that might have been wishful thinking on my part. His fist relaxed and he blinked slowly at me while reaching out with a hand to push open the shower door. We stared at each other for a long silent moment and I put a hand up to my throat because I felt like everything I wanted to say to him was stuck there.

"You suck and I kind of hate you a lot right now." My words were raspy and rough as I turned on my heel and stormed out of the bathroom, making sure to slam the door behind me.

I wanted to choke him and fuck him, not sure which desire was stronger. I stalked to the table and snatched up the phone with every intention of getting out of this apartment. Away from him. It was an emotional overload that I didn't want to make me do something I would end up regretting later when I was thinking more clearly. The fact of the matter was I knew he had set me up, had wanted me to walk in on him and see what he was doing. The door was left open for a reason; he had left me to stew as soon as we walked in the front door on purpose. He was a calculating son of a bitch and I was really starting to see who he was under all the gloss and charm he hid behind most of the time.

Asa wanted me to know that even though he wanted me, he wasn't ever going to go there even when it was just us, alone in his apartment. His point had been made in a startlingly clear and vivid way, and now I had to get away even if I would never, ever forget the images he had imprinted on my mind forever.

Of course the phone had a password on it, which just amped up my frustration even further. I stared at it blankly, trying to figure out my next move, when his fingers wrapped around my wrist and he pulled the useless device out of my hand. He spun me around and absently tossed the phone back onto the table. He was glaring down at me, which maybe would have been intimidating—after all, I didn't really know Asa that well—but he hadn't bothered to put anything on, not even a towel. He was standing way too close and was way too naked for me to feel anything other than the damn lust he seemed to own as it rushed back to the surface.

We glowered at each other, his fingers wrapped around my pulse where it thundered under his touch. His mouth was in a hard line and water was running down his temples and across the smooth plane of his chest. Asa was a beautiful man when he was wearing worn jeans and an old T-shirt; naked and angry, he looked like an ancient Greek god visiting amongst us mere humans.

I jolted in surprise when he used his other hand to reach up and pull out the tie that was holding all my hair on top of my head in a messy knot. The tangled strands fell haphazardly around my shoulders and I tilted my head back to look at him.

"You have no idea what you're getting into with me, Royal." His voice was always so rich and full of warm southern tones. Right now he sounded gruff and there was a tremor in it that made my heart stumble over itself.

"Yeah, well, I'm a big girl, Asa. I should get the option to figure that out without you deciding it for me."

His fingers fluttered over my wrist, then moved up to my elbow, traveling farther up so that his palm smothered my shoulder, and then he was cupping my jaw in his hand while rubbing his thumb along my bottom lip.

"You're a cop." Like that was reason enough for him to keep fighting against this vortex of want and need that pulled at both of us.

I blew out a breath and lifted my own hand to wrap around his wrist. "I know, but that's not all that I am." The surrealness of having this conversation, finally, while he was naked and while I was still pretty pissed off at him, made me dizzy. Maybe he was right. Maybe I didn't really understand what I was trying to get into with him.

A smirk kicked up the corner of his mouth and he took a step back from me. He looked devilish and far too tempting. "You're mad at me."

I nodded in agreement. "I am. That stunt in the shower was a dirty trick. I know you planned it out. You wanted me to see you. You wanted me to know that even though I've been chasing you, have made it clear that I want you ... that you aren't going to cross that line with me. That was a total dick move."

At first I wanted him because he seemed like the perfect distraction to all the other stuff going wrong in my life. Then I had wanted him more because he was making it impossible to get him. Now I just wanted. That was a whole lot of sexy, naked man standing in front of me, and any reason I might once have had for wanting to be with him seemed frivolous when faced with all his ridiculous masculine beauty.

He tilted his chin down just a hint, just enough to let me know that I had hit his motivations right on the mark. He held his arms out to the side, lifted up both of his blond eyebrows in challenge, and told me in a silky and seductive tone, "It should've been enough. Too bad it wasn't, because I was thinking about you the entire time. I don't know if we're lucky or doomed that I never seem to be able to do the right thing for very long. You've been after me for a minute, Red. I'm not gonna cross the line, but if you want to, I'm not going to stop you anymore."

I bit my bottom lip and watched his reaction flare in his eyes. "What happens after I do?" There were threads of hesitation in my voice and I knew he could hear them. He let his arms fall and he turned back to the unmade bed.

I hadn't really thought very far ahead when I had my hands down his pants in the parking lot or when I was purposely pulling my clothes off in front of him on the dance floor at the Bar. All I knew was that he was the first guy to ever make me want, really want, and he was the first man to ever make me chase him. I never stopped to consider what was going to happen if I actually caught him.

"I can't answer that, but if I had to guess I'd say it's probably going to end in destruction and heartbreak. That's usually what happens when I get something good in my life."

He crawled up on the bed and then turned on his back and stacked his hands behind his head. "If you want the code on my phone, I'll give it to you so you can leave. If you want to stay, hit the lights and crawl up here. I promise to behave ... for now."

I looked at him, looked at the phone on the table, and sighed. Really there was only one option and it had nothing to do with him behaving or me leaving. He told me the line was mine to cross and that's exactly what I intended to do even if it did indeed lead to destruction and heartbreak.

I ran my fingers through my hair trying to untangle it, kicked off my sneakers, and hit the lights. The tiny apartment was immediately lost in pitch blackness and the only thing I could see was the glint of Asa's blond hair, and I could swear his eyes shimmered in the dark even though I knew that was impossible. Maybe because there was no light, maybe because I knew I had to be all in this time with him or I would never get another chance, but instinct told me that if I wanted to prove to him that the line didn't exist for either of us anymore, being as naked as he was when I crawled into bed with him was a surefire way to do it.

I pulled my Under Armour shirt off over my head, wiggled out of my sports bra, and left my pants and underwear in a pile on the floor. It was oddly liberating, I thought as I moved toward the bed. I wasn't shy or reserved, but this was bolder than anything I had ever done. Everything where this guy was concerned had forced me to be the aggressor, the pursuer, and I kind of liked the idea of finally winning the reward for not being afraid of going after something forbidden and oh so enticing.

His long legs shifted as I hit the edge of the bed and reached out a hand to feel my way in the blackness. I felt his calf muscles contract at the first brush of my fingertips and I couldn't help but grin at the reaction. The bed wasn't big enough for me to slither up alongside him, so I had to literally crawl up and over him, which had naked skin dragging and brushing against both of us. There was no way he was going to miss the invitation. It also had my hands shaking, my nipples getting hard, and I didn't miss the way his breathing hitched and shuddered at the contact. His hands landed on my waist as I straddled him in the dark. His thighs tensed under my bare backside and his cock was stirring and rising between us. His thumbs ran along the ridge of my rib cage and he told me gruffly, "This might be the worst crime I ever committed."

He couldn't see my expression, but I scowled and leaned forward with my hands on his chest. I liked how smooth and hard his sculpted muscles felt under my palms. He really was like an artfully carved statue created for generations to enjoy and admire.

"What do you mean?"

His hands moved up farther until he was cupping each of my full breasts in his hands. I jerked at the sensation and then gasped when he ran his thumbs over the distended peaks on each side. It felt so good I started to quiver from the inside out. He wasn't exactly gentle or reverent in the way he touched me and I think that made it even better.

"When a girl that looks like you takes her clothes off, it should be a crime to have the lights out. The idea of you naked is enough to get most guys off, Royal. Having the reality right in front of me and not being able to see it should be illegal." It was a crude compliment, but it was a sweet sentiment nonetheless. I had heard similar things before, but coming from him, they didn't seem like throwaway words meant simply as a way to get into my pants. Not like he needed words to do that anyways; my pants were clear across the room already.

I was going to tell him that I felt the same way, he was too beautiful to go to bed with in the dark, but all thought spiraled into nothingness when his stroking thumbs suddenly turned into a light pinching grasp that had my back bowing and my head falling back as sharp pleasure worked from the point of his touch to my core. He hadn't even kissed me, hadn't done anything romantic or passionate, and I was already wanting to climb onto the jutting erection that had come to life between us and assuage the ache that was building low in my belly.

He let go of one nipple and reached up to tunnel his fingers in the thick hair at the back of my head. He pulled me down over him until our lips touched. I sighed when his trapped dick twitched eagerly against my belly as he devoured my mouth, a skill that should be considered a weapon. No one kissed like Asa. At least no one I had ever kissed before. He kissed in a way that really felt like he was trying to make it the best kiss I ever had. He kissed like he wanted to make sure I knew whoever I kissed after him would never compare. He kissed me like he wanted to tell me things with his lips and tongue that he couldn't say with words. It made my head fuzzy and my heart start to pound. It was also enough to have me unconsciously moving against him in need.

Sex wasn't exactly something I had sought out before Asa. I mean, I was by no means a virgin, but I had learned pretty early on that sex tended to be way more about the guy than it ever was about me, and that never made me overly eager to strip down to get busy. I had dated a really nice guy for almost a full year while I was at the Police Academy, but somewhere along the line it had occurred to me that nice wasn't enough to keep a relationship together, and even with him, sex had been pleasant at best. This wasn't pleasant. This was hot, shiver-inducing, body-breaking levels of feeling, and not just the reactions from my body. My heart was racing. My mind was frantically trying to take in every single sensation and my lungs were burning from lack of oxygen as Asa continued to bite and suck at my mouth. He was trying to get me off just by kissing me and he was talented enough that he just might make it happen, but I had waited too long for this, had been thinking about being with him like this for too long, to not have him inside of me.

I pulled back, leaving us both panting and gasping in the dark. I reached out and found the edge of his nose and ran my finger along it, then up across one of his arched brows. "You were thinking about me in the shower?" My voice sounded wistful to my own ears.

He made a noise low in his throat, wrapped his arm around my back, and flipped us over so that I was sprawled out underneath his big body. He reached over me, which drove our hips together and had his cock pressing right where I wanted it between my legs. I heard a drawer open and then slam closed and the crinkle of foil as he tossed what had to be a condom on the pillow next to my head. He couldn't really be as bad as he kept trying to tell me. Protection hadn't even crossed my mind, and yet there he was once again looking out for my best interests without me asking him to.

"I've been thinking about you since the first time I saw you. I think about your eyes and your hair. I think about those long-ass legs and the fact that you have the nicest rack I have ever seen in my life." I snorted at him but he wasn't done. "I think about the way your ass looks in those tight skinny jeans you wear when you're trying to get my attention. Then I remind myself that all of that comes with a badge and a gun, and remember why jerking off in the shower instead of taking you to bed is a far safer course of action for both of us."

I stiffened automatically but he took one of the condoms, handing it to me while dropping his head so he could lick all across my collarbone. He nuzzled his nose against my cheek and then put his lips to my ear and whispered, "And yet here we are."

I gulped a little as he lifted himself off of me by bracing his forearms on either side of my head. I opened the condom packet with my teeth and somehow managed to get it where it was supposed to go even though my hands were shaking like crazy. Suddenly I was wondering what I was going to do if this ended up being as lackluster as all the other times I had done it. It seemed really stupid to walk into the lion's cage and tug on his tail without knowing the risk was worth it. Where was all that clarity up to this point?

I wrapped an arm across the broad expanse of his shoulder and another one right above his sculpted backside and whispered back, "Here we are."

He left one arm arched over my head and lowered his other one until his fingers curled tightly around my thigh.

He pulled my leg up high along his side and I felt just the tip of him prod at my entrance.

I saw his teeth flash in the dark right before he lowered his mouth back to mine. Against my lips he muttered, "Let's hope we both make it out alive," and then he kissed me in that soul-stealing way he had as he sank all the way into my welcoming body.

It was anything but lackluster.

I felt him everywhere, inside and out. His fingers dug into my flesh as his mouth moved, insistent and demanding against mine. It was almost too much. Too many sensations, too much feeling, too much anticipation. I felt my body respond with minimal effort on his part. All he had to do was touch me, slide in and out in the steady, strong rhythm he had set. I was already writhing, already feeling my insides quake as they tightened with contractions around him. I dropped a hand to one of the firm globes of his ass and dug my fingers in just to get a good grasp on something because reality was spinning away. This was most assuredly sex that was all about me. He was kissing me everywhere. My mouth, my neck, behind my ear, and all along where my pulse was racing at the curve of my neck. His hand that had been holding my leg up where he wanted it, left when it was clear I was going to stay splayed and arched just where he wanted me. It detoured to that hot spot right between my legs. At the first press of his fingertips on that sensitive nub I screamed his name. It was so loud it hurt my head, but it just made him chuckle into my damp skin, where he was nibbling hard enough to leave marks.

His fingers wiggled and brought me dangerously close to going over the edge. I could feel my reaction to his touch and to his thrusts get all liquid and hot between us. There was no hiding how effectively he knew how to touch me in order to get the most dynamic reaction. I pressed up even harder against him. I wanted closer and that wasn't even possible. It all felt so good that it almost hurt. I felt the brink of an orgasm racing up and over me. I wanted to tell him to slow down, that it was going to be over too fast after such a long wait, but then his mouth was by my ear again and that voice that was all honey and smoke whispered, "I can't see you but I can feel you, Royal, and you feel beautiful."

Holy shit he was good. Between his words and what he was doing with his fingers, along with the relentless drag and pull of his body inside mine, I was done for. I tossed my head to the side and he kissed me on the cheek as I broke apart underneath him. It was unlike anything I had ever experienced before and definitely worth the work I had put into getting it. My eyes slid closed. His breath hitched and he said my name on a sigh. Then his body jerked against mine and his chest settled down against my own as he collapsed on top of me. His heart was just as unsteady as mine where they beat wildly against each other. I was feeling too much, exposed in a way I hadn't anticipated, and I wasn't sure I could handle whatever it was that would be looking back at me in his amber gaze. I was suddenly really glad there were no lights on.

He shifted so he could pull out of my limp and spent body. He squeezed my butt and rolled off the side of the bed. I heard him banging around in the bathroom, rolled to my side, and put my hands under my cheek. For some reason I really felt like I was going to cry. Destruction and heartbreak really didn't sound as fun as they had before I had gone to bed with him.

The mattress dipped under his weight when he returned and I thought he was going to just roll to the opposite side and go to sleep. Asa didn't strike me as a cuddler, and in all honesty I could've used a minute to get my shit together, only he didn't give it to me. Instead he curled around my back, wrapped one of his strong arms around my front, and pulled me into his chest so that we were pressed tightly together. His voice was all thick southern drawl and sleepy, warning me, "Trouble is always a whole lot of fun ... until it isn't anymore."

I was finally starting to believe him. All I could do was close my eyes and let his even breathing lull me to sleep even though I felt like I hadn't just crossed the line. I had blown it up and tap-danced all over it.

CHAPTER 7

Asa

Waking up wrapped around a warm body was nothing new. Waking up wrapped around a body that I wanted to snuggle into, lose myself in over and over again, and not let go of ever—well, that was a first.

We were facing each other in the narrow bed, and Royal had her head tucked under my chin and her breath was tickling my throat. Her arm was resting across my ribs and one of her long legs had situated itself between my own. We were pressed as tightly together as two people could be without having sex, and my morning erection was pretty much insisting that I take advantage of the situation. It throbbed between us where her hips were practically locked against my own. It was entirely too intimate for my peace of mind.

I liked sex—a lot—and I wasn't averse to having whoever shared my bed for the night sleep over. I was a pro at getting my own way and defusing awkward situations with pretty words and a clever grin, so I typically never had to worry about morning-after catastrophes. In fact, I usually could look forward to a repeat performance when the sun came up, but somehow I knew if I went there with Royal in the bright light of day, it would change things.

I already felt it in the way my hands wanted to linger at the delicate curve of her waist. In the way my skin tingled and felt alive where it touched hers. In the way I wanted to simply look at her in all her naked and fiery beauty while she held on to me. I absolutely couldn't get serious about this girl, we were beyond wrong for each other … not that I was ever going to be right for anyone, but especially not right for her. Too bad my body and my mind didn't agree on that fact.

Everything inside of me tightened and coiled, ready to strike when she muttered my name in her sleep and wiggled her body even closer to mine. She was seriously going to make me come just by breathing on me, so I sighed and extracted myself from her sleepy hands as delicately as I could. I needed some space, both physically and mentally. She was far too easy to get lost in, and the fact that she was strong enough, secure enough, to come after what she wanted even though I told her what the inevitable outcome was going to be was a turn-on like no other. I had been chased by women before, often because I led them on for my own reasons. But I had never been chased and then caught by a woman that knew all the rules going in. I both loved and loathed her fearlessness. It made it impossible to say no to her.

I had no clue if she needed to be up for work or not, so I decided to take a quick shower and then call Nash to see if he could rescue her trapped purse from her car. That was a call I wasn't eager to make. I could already see the wild fire of concern and worry that would burn through our group of friends when it was made clear that Royal and I had spent the night together.

Sure, we were consenting adults and it was no secret she had been after me for more than a minute, but now that I had broken the seal, taken what was offered, it would be a whole different ball game of subtle hints and more obvious warnings that I better treat her right and better not do anything to hurt her. Of course I didn't want to hurt her, that's why I had avoided this inevitable hookup for as long as was humanly possible. But now there was no choice. The line had officially been crossed and I knew there was a crash-and-burn hovering somewhere down the line for both of us on this side of it. That's just the way things in my world worked and it was better to accept them than be blindsided and devastated by it when the crash happened.

I took a second to brush my teeth, then turned the water in the shower on as hot as it would go and stepped underneath the spray. This was early for me to be up and about, but my insistent dick and whirling mind weren't going to let me crawl back into my occupied bed without either a fuck or a fight. The water was enough to jar me fully awake and aware as I bit back a groan when I realized every time I stepped into this shower stall I was now going to have the image of Royal watching me, with those wide, chocolate-colored eyes forever imprinted on my brain.

She should have been offended and embarrassed. Instead she was pissed, and rightfully so. I had known all along what I was doing, had felt the burn and want for her pressing hard at the base of my spine. I also knew she wasn't going to sit idly by while I disappeared into the bathroom. Her nature was to be curious and a problem solver, so I'd known she was going to get a show when she eventually came looking for me. What I hadn't planned on was her staying to watch, or how ridiculously hot her doing so had made me. I was just trying to prove a point, trying to get her to see what I was really all about and how little regard I could have for her feelings. Only she had turned the tables, made it about something more; between her melted-candy-colored eyes and her furious pout, she had made it something more. Of course I said her name on a curse when I came and I also knew she wasn't leaving the apartment until I took her to bed. But then she had curled so innocently and so trustingly into me while she slept, and just like that she had turned sex into something more as well. She was making all of it into something more, including me, and that felt beyond dangerous.

The water almost scalded as it poured over the top of my head and down across my shoulders, but it felt good and released some of the tension that was riding me hard. I turned my head and couldn't say I was surprised when she stepped between me and the spray. The water turned her hair from burnished mahogany to almost jet black and her eyebrows nearly touched her hairline as she gazed up at me.

"Everything okay?"

I should be asking her that. Instead I reached out and caged her in between my arms and the tiled wall while the hot water continued to cascade down around us.

"I was just envisioning the lecture that is bound to be headed my way when we call Nash to get you into your car."

Her slick hands moved up and down my ribs in a caress that I'm sure was designed to soothe but instead made my already hard cock even harder. She couldn't miss it the way it was pointed straight up between the two of us.

"It won't be any worse than the one I'm sure Saint is going to give me." Her voice was still soft with sleep and heavy with something I didn't want to try and dissect.

I bent my head down just a little and the water ran off my nose and dripped across her parted lips, and told her quietly, "You should listen to her. Whatever she has to say."

I was going to kiss her, because I had to. She was just too much temptation all wet and shiny before me. She looked better than most when she was dressed down and without makeup. Dripping wet and naked as she was, there was nothing more beautiful than this woman. It was impossible not to feel incredibly lucky she was here with me for no other reason than she wanted to be. Not because there had been tricks or subterfuge on my end. I scowled at her when she turned her head away at the last minute and leaned forward to press her lips against the center of my chest.

"Listen to her tell me to be careful, to watch my step with you, because you're unpredictable? You've been telling me that yourself for weeks. I've heard the warnings and I've decided to proceed at my own risk." She lifted her head up to look at me, and I think I might have loved her just a little bit when she blinked water out of her eyes and smiled up at me. "But I didn't brush my teeth this morning and I don't think I'm willing to scare you off with morning breath after I finally got you where I want you."

That made me laugh. There was no way something like morning breath could ever distract me from her overall amazingness, but it was cute that she had basic insecurities like everyone else. She could so easily be one of those girls that knew she could get away with murder based on her looks alone, so it was refreshing and adorable that she wasn't like that at all.

"I think it would take more than some funky breath to scare anyone off of you, Red." My voice got all husky against my will. She just did something to me that made me want to fight against all the normal asshole tendencies that I had.

She laughed a little and then her tongue was licking over my nipple, which made me gasp, while her fingers were tracing the lines of my abs where they tensed and flexed under her touch. I really wanted to kiss her, but before I could snatch her up, she was on her knees in front of me and my cock was in her mouth. There was no way in hell I was able to form a coherent thought after that.

Between the hot water, her even hotter mouth, and the way she looked all sexy and wet on her knees in front of me, this wasn't going to last very long. I threaded my fingers through her heavy hair, closed my eyes, and tried to remember anything in my life ever being as good as this. The way she rolled her tongue over the tip and across every single ridge had my heart thundering in my ears. When she added her hands and sent them exploring between my legs, I had to really concentrate to stay upright because the pleasure was so much it nearly knocked me down. She made a satisfied sound at the back of her throat that vibrated all along my entire length where it was trapped between her plump lips.

I pulled lightly on the long tresses that I had wrapped around my fingers and told her gruffly, "You need to let up if you want a turn with that."

I felt her mouth quirk around my dick and then she was using her hands along with her mouth in a way that was meant to render a man absolutely useless. My knees shook because I came with her name on my lips once again. She rose to her feet in one elegant move, the water running down her naked form making her look like some kind of satisfied sea siren that knew good and well how thoroughly she had just ruined me. I was struggling to breathe, to get my head out of the clouds, when she turned her back to me and picked up the shampoo bottle I had resting on a caddy under the showerhead.

"I have to get my car and head home. I have to work tonight and I want to go see Dom before my shift. I don't have time for a turn, but I'll take a rain check." Her point was clear. Last night had been all about her, this morning was all about me. "You should consider that some games are always more fun when they are played with two people."

She lathered up her long hair either unaware of or purposely ignoring the fact that I was a boneless, shaking mess behind her. I had never had anyone offer something up without expecting something, usually more, in return. I couldn't get my erratic heartbeat under control so I could put all that emotion her selfless actions had awoken in someplace safe.

I rallied enough to help her scrub her extraordinary head of hair. I almost shored up the reserves enough to help her soap up, which really just meant I ran my hands over every slippery inch of her until she was breathing heavy and looking at me with desire-glazed eyes. I was all for moving her to the bed and returning her early-morning attention and then some, but she just shook her head at me and stepped out of the shower. She snagged the only towel I had hanging on the rod and gave me a pointed look.

"Next time you're in there and thinking about me, think of that instead."

She swept out of the bathroom with far more dignity than a girl that was clad in only a threadbare towel should be able to muster.

Now that the water had turned lukewarm and my raging lust had been quelled, I actually showered. She hollered across the tiny apartment asking for the unlock code on my cell. I didn't even hesitate to shout out the numbers to her. I was long since past the point where I had things to hide in my life and I had never been stupid enough to keep incriminating evidence on something that was as easy to misplace as a cell phone. I heard her talking to whomever it was she called for rescue, and sighed, as I had to stand on the bathroom rug to drip dry for a few minutes before making my way over to the single closet in the room to find something to wear.

She was perched on the arm of the recliner, back in her gym clothes with her hair in a long braid. She looked so fresh and so clean if I hadn't just been there I never would've believed all the dirty, sexy things she could do with her mouth.

I pulled on a pair of jeans sans underwear. I never wore them. I didn't see the need even though it was cold in Denver and I often cursed myself for not having a layer of something between my dick and the chilly metal of my zipper. I found a black thermal and a hoodie that I tossed to her after I pulled my shirt on over my head. She caught it with a smirk and tossed the phone at me as I sat on the edge of the bed to pull on my black boots.

"You call Nash?" She nodded in answer to my question as she glanced around the bedraggled apartment that looked a hundred times worse during the day.

"This isn't where I would've pictured you living."

It wasn't where I ever thought I was going to live either, but shit happened. "I stayed with Cora and Ayden when I first moved here. It was cool for a little while because Jet was gone so much, but then Ayden was on my ass about everything. Then she thought I had something to do with the Bar getting robbed and I knew I had to move out or we would kill each other."

I rubbed my hands over my damp hair, making it stick straight up and sending water dancing every direction.

"I was laid up, couldn't work because I had a broken leg and all kinds of other broken junk inside of me. All I could do was limp around the house and mess around on the Internet. I'm dangerous when I don't have something to focus on." I couldn't believe I was about to disclose this to her, not because I was worried about how it would make her think about me, but because she was a cop and I was about to admit to some straight-up illegal activity.

"I started gambling online. I was messing around on Internet poker sites, winning and losing money like crazy. I had no idea how I was going to support myself now that I was determined to stay on the straight and narrow, and at the time it felt like an easy score that wouldn't hurt anyone."

I let out a bitter laugh and climbed to my feet as she watched me carefully. "Cora walked in on me more than once and asked what I was up to. I always just shut the computer down or shuffled away before she could see what I was doing, but I think she knew I was up to no good. I made enough to pay off a huge chunk of my medical bills, but instead of doing that ..." I made sure she was paying attention, that she really understood how seriously fucked up I was. "Instead of doing that, I bet it all on one hand because I was on a hot streak. I lost it all." I waved a hand around the barren room and lackluster decor. "I think that's why I lost it when Ayden thought I had something to do with the robbery at the Bar. Weeks before I was actually fucking shit up, but as soon as Rome threw me a lifeline, I took it and realized the only way to stop drowning in my own mistakes was to start living within my actual means."

I scowled and looked down at the tips of my boots. "All my life, even when I try to help myself or someone else, I screw it up. The day Rome offered me the job at the Bar, I told myself I would live on what I made and that's it. No more get-rich-quick schemes. No more high-risk endeavors that may or may not pay off. I live here because it's cheap and close to work. I don't have a car because I pay off my debt with anything extra I have a month. For once I'm living the life I'm supposed to have instead of doing whatever it takes to try and live the life I always thought I *should* have. Do you understand?"

It was important that she did. Having the evidence of the kind of man I really was staring her in the face might open her eyes to how risky this thing that dragged and pulled between us could be if she kept chasing after it just so she could feel good for a fleeting moment.

She shrugged into the hoodie and turned to the door. At first I thought she was repulsed or angry at my honesty, but as she shifted to pull her long hair out of her collar, she told me quietly, "I think it's odd you thought you would just automatically turn into a choirboy after a lifetime of doing whatever you wanted. People aren't born either good or bad, they have to be taught how to be one way or the other. No one ever took the time to teach you how to be good, Asa." She walked to the front door and turned to look at me over her shoulder as she pulled it open. Her dark eyes were steady on my own. "It might take some trial and error along the way, but for the most part you seem to be doing okay now."

I followed her out the door and locked it behind us. I put my hand on her lower back as we walked down the stairs and started to walk the short distance to her car, and I didn't respond to the faint hint of hope that laced her last words. That was the thing: everyone that cared about me wanted to think I was doing fine, and I was, for now. I wasn't as sure of myself as the people that cared about me seemed to be and I wasn't so sure that I hadn't actually been born bad. The temptation not to do fine was thick and heavy around my shoulders every day, so much that, sometimes, not letting it cover me up and sink me back down to the bottom where I had always been was more work than I would ever openly admit to.

When we reached the Bar's parking lot, Nash already had her SUV running and warming up. I didn't say anything as Royal moved away from me without so much as a good-bye hug and went willingly into Nash's tattooed embrace. She kissed him on the cheek and rubbed her hands along the flames that decorated the sides of his head over his ears. She threw a wave out the window and took off without a word about anything I had disclosed to her or about the fact that we had just screwed each other stupid.

I shifted uneasily as Nash walked over to me, questions swirling bright and clear in his unusual-colored eyes. I thought I could cut him off at the pass by changing the obvious topic before he started in on me.

"How's your partner in crime doing with the new baby?" I hadn't seen Rule or Shaw since their newest family member had come along.

A grin split Nash's face and he shoved his hands in the pockets of the peacoat he was wearing.

"He's adjusting. More to the fact that he now has two people in the world he has to take care of and love forever than anything else, I think. Rule was always sort of a lone wolf, and now his life just has so many important things in it he's trying to figure out how to balance it all."

"He'll figure it out." I didn't know Rule before he was with his wife, but I had heard the stories, and none of them were exactly flattering. If he could turn it around for the girl, I had no doubt he would quickly find his footing in fatherhood.

"Yeah, in the meantime he's just crankier than usual, which of course means that we give him as much shit as possible."

I shared a grin with him and was thinking I was going to be lucky enough to escape without getting a lecture when he inclined his chin at me and narrowed his eyes. "So you and Royal?"

I sighed and rocked back on my heels a little. Of course I wouldn't be that lucky. "Anything you think you're going to say to me about her I've already told myself and told her. She chose not to listen and I'm sick and tired of turning her down."

He chuckled which surprised me. "Asa, I know Royal well enough to know she's going to do whatever the hell she wants, no matter what anyone has to say to her about it. All I was going to tell you is that you need to be careful because she's been off and not acting like herself since her partner got hurt. I don't know what's up with her, but she's being reckless and anything she's doing right now might just be a reaction to Dom getting injured. I don't want you to be a casualty of her overreaction." He lifted a black eyebrow at me and muttered, "Plus Dom is a big-ass dude that gets to legally carry a weapon and he loves that girl like crazy. He won't care why it ends or who ends it if Royal goes crying to him with a broken heart."

I rolled my shoulders and lifted a hand to rub the back of my neck. I knew how big Royal's partner was. He had been there the night she arrested me. He was scary as hell and not just because he had a badge of authority. He exuded a seriousness and determination that left no doubt he would take more than bullets for Royal and in order to get his job done.

"She and Dom … have they ever …?" I hoped the question was obvious without having to actually ask it. Nash shrugged at me and pulled out his phone as it dinged in his pocket.

"I don't know. They're close, really close, and I know that he would gladly rip the face off of anyone that hurts her. They grew up together and went into the Police Academy together, but I don't know if they ever had a romantic relationship. Royal never mentioned it and Saint has never said anything about it, but who knows? I don't know how a guy could be that tight with a chick that looks like Royal and not at least try to get some." He tapped in a message on the keypad and then looked up at me with a smirk. "Saint wants me to ask you how far along Cora is."

I let out a startled laugh. "What?"

He held out his phone and showed me the text that his lady had just fired off. Indeed it said:

> Ask Asa how far along Cora is. I know she's knocked up and I bet Rome told him!

"I'm not supposed to say. Rome didn't want to take any attention off of baby Ry just yet. Tell Saint she'll have to bug Cora about it." If Rome didn't want the info out in the world yet, there was no way I was going to be the one to leak it.

His phone pinged again and apparently this message wasn't one for sharing because his gaze sharpened and I saw him suck in a quick breath.

"All right, I gotta go. Saint doesn't have to work until tonight, and I don't have to be at the shop until noon." Apparently whatever she had sent him had him eager to get back home to her. I couldn't blame him. The redheaded nurse was a stunner and as sweet as could be. Nash was another lucky man as far as finding his perfect match was concerned. "Just remember that no one wants to see either you or Royal end up hurt, so try and tread carefully. Something I know you aren't used to."

I grunted and turned without saying good-bye so that I could stick my head inside the Bar and say hello to Rome and see if I could charm Darcy into cooking up some breakfast. I had been treading carefully for months. There was no going back now that I knew how beautiful everything was on the other side of the line Royal had willfully crossed. Now all I could do was hold on to it until it fell apart.

CHAPTER 8

Royal

"Do you think if the situation had been reversed and Officer Voss had been the one in the alley while you went up the fire escape, he would be beating himself up as violently as you've been doing?"

I looked at the department shrink and tried not to roll my eyes. She had been asking me variations of this same question every week when I went in for my appointment with her. I think she was tired of me giving her the same answer, but it wasn't going to change.

"Dom wouldn't have been distracted. A herd of elephants could've run through that alleyway and Dom wouldn't have blinked."

The doctor looked at me over the rim of her stylish glasses and sighed. She was frustrated with me. It was obvious. I wanted to tell her to join the club. Dom was also over my pity party and mountains of regret about what had happened to him. He flat-out told me to get lost and not come back until my head was screwed on right. He was sick of me moping around, and done with the constant apologies racing off my tongue. He kept telling me shit happened and I just needed to deal with it. Then he lectured me for an hour on how stupid it was to purposely place myself in bed with a known criminal. He didn't want to hear at all that being with Asa was the only thing that made all the bad things churning in my gut settle down.

He took all my focus, all my energy, every single bit of emotion I had to keep up with him. He switched so quick from charming and flirty to challenging and brutally honest that if I didn't stay on my toes I would miss all the little hints that slipped through his artfully constructed mask. But I had seen enough, peeked at the naked core of who Asa Cross really was, and I had figured a few things out. One of the most important realities I had come to terms with was that he wasn't lying when he claimed to be a bad man. He might not actively be hurting anyone anymore or doing anything to break the law, but it was there bold and brilliant every time he warned me away from him ... danger lurked under the surface, and not too far down. He was a guy that had done bad things and was convinced that he would continue to do bad things. Maybe he was right. Another thing I was certain of was that it didn't matter to me. Good or bad and anything he might be in the middle, I was drawn to him, attracted to him, fascinated by him in ways no one had ever pulled at me before. I saw enough kindness in him, enough drive to be a better person and live a better life now that he had something to lose, and because of this, the threat of the badness wasn't enough to keep me away. In fact it drew me to him. I liked the bad in him even if I was starting to understand that he hated it and that it made him not like himself very much.

The shrink leaned forward on her fancy leather chair, put her elbow on her knee, and propped her chin on her hand as she stared pointedly at me.

"Do you think you're a good police officer, Royal?"

I was slumped back on her requisite leather couch but her question had my spine snapping straight. "I always wanted to be a cop."

She just stared at me until I shifted uneasily under her probing gaze. "That's not what I asked. We're supposed to be talking about you, about why you can't sleep, about why you can't accept that what happened on that callout could've happened to any set of partners on patrol. But all I hear from you is, Dom is this, Dom said that, Dom did this ... to hear it from you, your partner runs the show and you just follow along like his sidekick. That's not what makes a good police officer, and it definitely isn't enough for a bright, talented young woman like yourself. Have you even considered what happens if Dom doesn't get medically cleared to return? Is your very promising future over just because his is in question?"

I gasped involuntarily and squeezed my eyes shut. That was my worst fear. How could I carry on if I was the reason Dom might not be able to return to his dream job? I felt my hands curl into fists as I whispered to her, "I can't answer that."

She sighed again and I forced my eyes open just as she was sitting back in her chair. "You need to. If you're just going through the motions because this isn't what you *really* want to do, then you run the risk of putting not only yourself in danger but whoever is out there on the streets with you as well. You need to figure out if being a cop is what you're supposed to be or if you were just living Dominic's dream with him instead of having your own. Getting through the academy takes dedication and perseverance, so I know that a part of you really wants to be on the force, but this is a dangerous job that requires all of you."

I felt scalding-hot tears start to burn at the back of my eyes. I bit down on the very tip of my tongue to keep them at bay. Apparently the feel-good part of therapy was over and now it was time for real talk. I really wanted to call the woman some immature names and get up and storm out of the office, but I couldn't do that if I wanted to keep my job … which I did … didn't I?

"I'm not going to put anyone else at risk." My voice sounded broken.

"You can't predict that. All you can do is go out and do your job, use your best judgment, rely on your training and your fellow officers to keep you safe. Which is exactly what you did the night Officer Voss got injured. I have looked at your jacket, Royal. I can answer the question for you …" She lifted an eyebrow at me. "Yes. Yes, you *are* a good cop. A very good cop, and yes, the margin for error in your job is minuscule, but errors do happen. If you can't accept that, then this isn't the job for you."

Luckily I saw her look down at the elegant watch on her wrist indicating the hour was up. It was my turn to sigh in relief. I got to my feet and reached out for my hat, which was part of my patrol uniform. She stuck her hand out to shake like she always did, only this time she gave my hand a little squeeze.

"Next week we really need to address why you can't sleep. Those bags under your eyes make you look like a perp got in a lucky shot."

Great; not only was I mentally a mess, but I looked like crap as well. I just nodded absently and hauled ass out of her office.

The night I spent with Asa at his terrible little apartment was the most sleep I had gotten in over a month. It was only a few hours and I was worn out from the seriously intense sex. Still, the dreams had left me alone, making the anxiety that was crawling along my insides take a backseat to all the other exhilarating and complicated things he made me feel. I hadn't stopped by the Bar or called him in over a week. I didn't really know what to say to him or how to approach him after our intense night together. I understood he thought I was just after him for a thrill, that I was just trying to let off steam and play around with something that should be forbidden, but that wasn't the case. I more than wanted him. I was pretty sure I needed him and I was pretty sure he needed me, too. As much as his life had changed, as much as *he* had changed, he needed someone he could let the leash off with. I wasn't scared of the Asa that lurked behind the veil. In fact I craved him. I wanted to be a safe place for him, but given my career choice, I didn't know if that was even a possibility.

The shrink's office was in LoDo and the police station was up in Capitol Hill, so I had to drive. If it wasn't winter I would've just walked, since the station was so close to the Victorian, but it was cold and I didn't want to be late. My new partner was pretty laid-back, a rock-steady cop, but he was a huge stickler about punctuality. I was just getting out into the midday traffic and humming along to One Direction on the radio when my phone rang from where I'd tossed it on the passenger's seat. I loved some Justin Timberlake and I loved that when he sang to me it meant my mom was calling me. She seemed to have an uncanny ability to know right when I was on the brink and at my most raw. She was checking up on me and I needed her to after that visit with the shrink. My mother had always just accepted me for whatever and whoever I was. She had never pushed, never tried to guide me one way or the other, and I kind of needed that cushion after that soul-stripping session with the psychiatrist.

"Hey, Mom."

"Royal! I haven't talked to you in forever. How are you? How is Dominic doing?"

Forever was only four or five days, but she liked to keep tabs on me. I grumbled a little, fished my sunglasses out of the cup holder, and slapped them on my face. "I've been busy. Sorry I didn't call. Going back to work as well as adjusting to a new partner has been keeping me on my toes, and Dom is fine. He's going stir-crazy and I think he's lost about twenty pounds of muscle and gained five pounds of facial hair. His sisters are taking good care of him."

She made a high-pitched noise of sympathy and I could almost see her clutching her throat in a dramatic way. My mom was nothing if not over-the-top.

"That's wonderful news that you're settling back in work, honey. What's the new partner like? Is he handsome?"

Ultimately, as much as she loved me, that was what it always came down to with my mom, a man. She never would understand how I was okay being single. How finding someone to be with had never been a priority for me like it had been for her.

"He's married."

"So?"

I groaned out loud. "Mom, that right there is why you have to keep a divorce attorney on retainer. Married is off-limits." Sometimes I felt like I was talking to someone my own age and not a grown-ass woman that should know better. If she had simply followed the rules in the first place, she wouldn't have ever thought my father was going to leave his wife and kids for us.

She laughed a little. "I think married and happily married are two different things. Besides, I haven't been fishing in that river for some time and you know it."

She didn't need to remind me. Her last catch had been a wealthy real-estate magnate that believed in true love and had been foolish enough not to make my mother sign a prenup. After a quickie wedding and an even quicker divorce, my mom was rolling in the greenbacks and dating young studs that were closer to my age than her own. She had drifted firmly into cougar territory, and in her typical careless fashion didn't care about how that made her look or how it might make me feel. Sometimes I wondered if she was acting so outlandishly just for the attention. I couldn't see her as much or spend as much time with her now that I was working full-time and had actually gone out in the world and made a friend or two. My mother didn't do well when she was lonely.

"With you I never know." I never wanted her near a married man again.

"So with the new partner being off-limits, I don't suppose you're out there meeting anyone. You know I worry that you're going to end up all alone and not find anyone to make me beautiful grandchildren with."

I swore at her and she laughed. "Mom, seriously?"

"I mean it. You aren't getting any younger and your job is very dangerous, young lady. You need to find a husband before you get old or injured. I want you to be happy and have what I never did."

"You know you're crazy, right?" I didn't need a man to be happy, not that I would run the other way if a certain blond sex god suddenly declared his undying love for me, but still I had plenty of time to worry about stuff like forever after. She would never understand that, though.

"That isn't how you should talk to your mother."

I groaned again and pulled into the parking lot for the police station. I settled my hat on my head and looked at myself in the rearview mirror. The shrink was right. I looked like I had twin black eyes and my pallor was straight-up waxy and gross.

"There's this guy." I was going to regret telling her anything, I just knew it. "He's different. I like him a lot but he makes it hard." He really did. Having feelings for someone shouldn't feel like so much of a battle.

She squealed loudly and I had to hold the phone away from my ear. "What's he like? What's he do? Does he come from money?"

I made sure I had my keys and everything I was going to need before hopping out of the SUV and slamming the door shut behind me with more force than necessary.

"He's tricky and smart. He's prettier than me and he knows it. He's charming when he wants to be. He's southern and—" She cut me off before I could tell her that he also had the most wonderful whiskey-colored eyes, which were richer than all the money in the world, and that he was a bartender.

"Ohhhhh ... southern boys are the best. All they need to do is say your name with that drawl and it's love. Maybe he comes from old money."

Who said things like that in this day and age? I rolled my eyes and pulled open the front doors of the station. "Mom, I'm at work, so I gotta go. I'll talk to you later, okay?"

"Love you. Stay safe."

"Love you, too."

I waved to Barrett as I walked in. I still had to put my vest on and grab my radio and utility belt from my locker. It took a few minutes to get ready to go and Barrett was already out in our patrol car when I was finished. I grabbed some coffee and made my way to where he was waiting. He never really cared who drove, which was a major change from riding with Dom. My best friend always wanted to be behind the wheel and I never argued. The shrink's words about being Dom's sidekick sort of slammed into my brain and rattled loudly around. I didn't like the truth that was obviously embedded in them, and it made me quiet and surly for the entire first part of our shift.

Barrett was mellow, liked to talk about his wife and his kids. He was a third-generation cop and had aspirations of making sergeant soon. He had enough years on the force and his record was spotless, so I was pretty sure his goal was entirely reachable. It was actually similar to listening to Dom talk about his future; the passion was there, and the drive, which made me wonder if I sounded the same when I talked about my future on the force.

We had an early dinner since we were working swing shift, which was two in the afternoon until ten or midnight depending on how the shift went. Scarfing down burgers and shoving fries into our faces got interrupted by a call about domestic violence from dispatch. We were by far the closest unit to the address, so we ditched dinner and rolled out. So far, since I'd been teamed up with Barrett, we hadn't really had any kind of call that made my nerves ratchet up or my doubts grab hold. But domestic violence calls were so unpredictable that I was starting to sweat and breathe a little harder than normal.

The call was for a neighborhood that was on Colfax up past Colorado. Not quite into Five Points but close enough that it made my skin feel all tingly and had all my senses going on high alert.

Apparently the neighbors had called because the couple could be heard screaming through the walls of the apartment complex they lived in. Sadly, most people try to stay out of it when private business between couples explodes in violence, but apparently this neighbor was concerned because the couple was known to have two small children in the home. Along with raised voices and rattling walls, they had reported hearing the sound of stuff breaking. Barrett and I were going to be the first on the scene for sure and we had no idea what we were walking into. We didn't know if there were weapons involved, if the kids were on site, nothing. All that uncertainty bubbled in my blood and made me hyper-aware of all of my surroundings. Backup was on its way, but according to the dispatcher, they were a solid ten to fifteen minutes out.

I led the way up the stairs. Again thinking that it was weird to be in the front. Out of habit I typically let Dom go into any situation first, maybe because I had been following behind him my entire life, just like the shrink said. I couldn't get distracted with thoughts like that, though, not with the distinct sounds of breaking glass and screams echoing clearly from one of the units. I shot an apprehensive look at Barrett over my shoulder and he just shrugged. It was all part of the job.

I knocked sharply on the door and all noise from inside ceased. No one came to answer right away, so I pounded again and hollered, "Denver police! We got a complaint about the noise."

I heard shuffling from the other side of the doorway and felt Barrett tense with alertness next to me. The door creaked open and a man peeked his eye out to look at me. His eyes dropped to my badge, then to what my badge was sitting above, and I saw his gaze widen. It was a reaction I was used to.

"We didn't call the cops." His voice sounded shaky and I heard a female voice from inside the apartment scream at him, calling him a cheating bastard.

I lifted my eyebrows at him. "No, you didn't, but your neighbors did. They complained about the screaming and said it sounded like *WWE Raw* had moved in upstairs. They also mentioned you have kids, and you must know carrying on like that in front of them isn't okay."

The woman's voice from inside ratcheted up in volume, and behind the man I heard glass shatter. He looked over his shoulder and winced.

"The kids are with my folks. Carla and I are just having a little disagreement is all. It got out of hand. We'll tone it down, I swear."

"Disagreement! You cheating asshole! I caught you in bed with my sister!"

Yowza. It sounded like the woman had a right to be furious with him. I would probably want to break all his stuff, too.

"Look, we just need to make sure everyone calms down and be sure no one is hurt." We also needed to make sure the kids really weren't in the middle of this shit show.

"Look, Officer ..." His gaze skated across my chest again, and I felt Barrett stiffen next to me. I was used to this kind of reaction, so I just brushed it off and kept my eyes glued to the guy. "... Hastings. Carla is a passionate woman. We'll work it all out and be back to making babies in no time. There's no need for you to ..." He trailed off on a curse as the door suddenly fell open and he tumbled out into the entryway at my feet. A big, wooden-handled steak knife was sticking out of his shoulder and a tiny woman stood a few feet away looking down at where he had fallen with unbridled fury and hatred in her eyes. This must be the notorious Carla.

Her free hand was bloody and in her other one she had a much larger knife. It looked like she had raided the kitchen while we were talking to her cheating spouse.

As calm as could be, she pointed the knife in my direction and told me, "I'm going to cut his balls off."

I blinked because she couldn't be serious, but then realized she actually was as she started to advance to where Barrett was taking care of the injured man. He had already called for medical and was looking up at me with huge eyes while he tended to the victim.

I couldn't look away from Carla. I popped open the strap that held my gun in its spot and pulled out the Taser we were all armed with to use in situations like this.

"Carla, you know I can't let you do that." I kept my voice steady and refused to move as she inched closer and closer.

"He's a rat bastard." She was shaking all over and her fury was almost palpable. "My sister! My own goddamn sister! How could they do this to me?"

I didn't have an answer for her other than "people sucked," but that wasn't going to get her to see reason or have her dropping the knife.

"This is bad, Carla. Bad for you and bad for your kids. You don't want to make it worse, do you? You need to put the knife down and just come with me."

I could hear sirens in the distance, which was great, because the idiot cheater had rallied enough to start screaming back at Carla. He was calling her names and telling her that her sister was a hundred times better in bed than she was ever going to be. He was most definitely not helping the situation. Carla was shaking all over and her face went from furious red to sickly pale. She was going to lose it, so I latched on to the only thing that I thought might shift her anger away from her awful spouse.

"Carla, I know you're mad at him, disappointed, and no one can blame you. What he did is terrible and unforgivable, but what about your sister? It takes two to cheat and she's your family, your blood. Don't you want to tell her how you feel about what she did?"

It was like the sun breaking through the clouds on a summer day. I saw awareness dawn, the rage switch from one target to the other and the fresh betrayal slam into this woman's body like a freight train. The knife fell out of her suddenly lax fingers and she crumpled into a hysterical ball on the floor in front of me. I let out a relieved sigh and looked over my shoulder to where the paramedics were loading the victim onto a stretcher and getting ready to haul him off. Barrett was talking to someone that appeared to be a neighbor, probably getting a witness statement, and the backup unit was just hovering in the doorway watching the show.

I walked over to Carla and put a hand on her shoulder. She looked up at me with wrecked eyes. "My sister is a bitch."

I nodded solemnly. "It really sounds like she is."

"What's gonna happen to my kids? They're at his parents' house right now."

Well, that was good. At least they weren't going to have to live with the sight of their mother trying to cleave their father in two with a steak knife.

"I can't answer that, Carla. But maybe they should've been your concern before you picked up the knife."

I helped the woman to her feet and winced as she wiped a gooey mixture of tears and snot across the back of her arm.

"I'm going to jail."

I nodded once again. "I'm afraid so."

She heaved a really deep sigh and looked at me out of the corner of her eye. "I wish I had aimed lower."

It shouldn't be funny and I wasn't going to condone this kind of violence, but I sort of agreed with her.

I read her her rights and put her in the back of the patrol car. I knew we were going to have to charge her with aggravated assault at the very least. It took a few minutes to get everything all situated at the scene and to get all the statements gathered for the report we were going to have to write up.

The ride back to the station was filled with quiet sobbing from the backseat and Barrett muttering to himself as I drove us through early-evening traffic. We got Carla processed in and started on the paperwork when Barrett suddenly stopped what he was typing and looked at me with obvious confusion on his face. I was starving since we had to ditch dinner, and just wanted to finish up the paperwork so we could get back on the street to finish our shift and maybe sneak in some Taco Bell.

I had my hat on the desk next to me and reached up to rub my temples. Paperwork was so boring. I hated it.

"What?"

He shook his head at me and turned to look back at the computer screen. "Nothing."

I snorted. "Obviously something. Spit it out."

"You just surprised me."

I sat back in my chair and narrowed my eyes at him. "How's that?"

He shrugged a shoulder at me. "I didn't expect you to be so unflappable. I mean, you're still pretty new on the force, and it's no secret you and Dom had all kinds of history before coming to work together. I'm not going to lie … I guess I thought maybe you rode on his coattails or something, but nothing could be further from the truth."

I was blinking in mild shock. *Unflappable?* I felt like I was ruffled and flapping all over the place most of the time.

"You don't react when weirdos look at you like you're lunch. You don't lose your temper when losers try intimidating you. You have a really easy time talking to victims, which makes hostile situations less dangerous. You don't freak out or move a muscle when a deranged woman is advancing on you with a knife. And maybe most importantly, you hate sitting at the desk filling out reports almost as much as I do, yet you don't make a single peep about it, you just get it done. I guess I'm just surprised at how really suited you are to do this job. I'm sure you've heard it before, but you really don't look like a cop, let alone a really good cop. You're head and shoulders above every other partner I've been saddled with thus far in my career."

I couldn't respond to him. Barrett was a good cop. He had a stellar reputation on the force and was under no obligation to give me any kind of props or validation. There was absolutely no way he could've known what the shrink had been asking me about before the shift started. All I could do was clear my throat and awkwardly tell him, "Well, you ain't so bad yourself, Barrett."

We finished up the paperwork for the shift. I felt bad for Carla, but people had to consider their actions and how they affected others in the long run. Barrett let me drive and I totally hit Taco Bell as we finished the rest of our mostly quiet shift. All the driving around and little action gave me too much time to think about what the shrink had been poking me with and Barrett's words.

I had never wanted to ride on any kind of coattails. Not for my looks. Not for the fact that I could bat my eyelashes and have the world handed to me. And most certainly not for the fact that Dom loved me and would always look out for me. It had never occurred to me before today that I wasn't being looked at as his partner but more as his shadow or lapdog, and I didn't like that one bit. My biggest fight in life was to prove I had merit, to show I had substance past my face and body, and it sounded like holding on to Dom like a lifeline for so long had hindered my efforts to win that fight.

After my shift I wanted a hot shower and a drink. Well, actually I wanted the guy that was going to serve me the drink, but I still wasn't sure how all that was going to play out. I had enough questions whirling around in my head that I didn't want to tangle with the mystery that was Asa on top of it.

I took a shower and watched some TV. I paced around my apartment and bugged Saint by texting her across the hall. I tried to text Dom as well and pouted when all he texted back was:

Go to bed.

It was after one by the time I crawled between the sheets. I wasn't tired or at least I thought I wasn't, but as soon as my head hit the pillow, I was out. It wasn't until a couple hours later that I woke up. I was panting, I was shaking, and a fine sheen of sweat covered me from head to toe. I wasn't seeing Dom fall. I wasn't back in the alleyway. No, instead I woke up with one hand in my panties with the other squeezing my breast underneath my tank top and Asa's name tumbling from my lips.

I groaned out loud and threw myself back against the pillows. I reached over to the nightstand and found my phone. I had totally called myself from his phone when he gave it to me to call Nash so he could bring me a key the other morning.

I'm ready to collect on my rain check.

I didn't think about the fact that it was really late or that he might not respond. I just sent the text and shifted around on my bed, all keyed up and needing something only Asa could give to me.

The phone sang "Trouble" by P!nk when he texted me back, and that was enough to have my skin tingling all over in expectation. I held my breath as I looked at the phone just in case he was going to tell me to get lost, but the screen glowed bright with the words:

I'll be at my place by 3.

I sighed and held the phone to my chest as everything inside of me heated up and throbbed with want and anticipation. It was so on.

CHAPTER 9

Asa

I put my phone back in my pocket after I sent the text back to Royal and gave my head a little shake to clear it. She had been on my mind a lot this last week, and not just because I could picture every inch of her naked body without any effort. I was wondering how she felt about finally crossing the line, about finally getting what she wanted. I was actually a little worried that I had succeeded in making her feel bad enough about herself and her desire to tangle with a guy like me that I had finally scared her away. The fact that it bothered me on a visceral level spoke volumes about what a bad idea messing around with the pretty redhead really was. Sometimes waking up and entering the land of the living, where all those tenuous emotions lived, really sucked since I was far from being a pro at dealing with them.

On top of being all twisted up over Royal, other weird stuff had been going on all week. The attractive older lady with the arm candy had been back in the Bar twice.

The first time the boy toy was with her, the second time she was alone. She spent the entire evening flirting and obviously trying to get my attention, which I happily gave to her since she was a good tipper. I wasn't interested, not with a sexy cop doing laps in my head nonstop, but the strange part was that I wanted to warn her about what guys like me would do to a woman like her.

She was obviously well off. She was a really good-looking woman and apparently all about a good time. A few years ago I would have moved in on her like she was a gazelle on the plains. I would have inserted myself into her life. I would have lied to her, told her anything she wanted to hear. I would have taken her to bed and let her think she was special, that I loved her ... and then I would've cleaned her out. I would have taken everything she had that wasn't nailed down and I would've done it without a second thought or any remorse. Now I just wanted to tell her not to be a victim, to watch herself, because even her brainless boy toy wasn't with her without wanting something from her.

Instead I just served her martinis and easily flirted back. I knew logically I couldn't stop anyone from being a victim, just like I couldn't stop Royal from courting trouble. When the woman left me her number on a cocktail napkin, I actually fought a little internal battle before chucking it in the trash. It was still really hard for me to let a sure bet go. Easy money, all the dirty and easy things that rested on the bottom, where I was so used to spending time, still had an allure that I couldn't turn a blind eye to. Eventually the reality of the fact that keeping the number meant I would use it and the woman it belonged to hammered hard in my blood. With a curse at my own internal struggle I crumpled up the napkin and tossed it away, disgusted that the battle between the good and bad was still being waged inside of me over something so obviously wrong.

I was also having an issue with Avett.

She hadn't shown up with any more black-and-blue marks, probably because there was no way Darcy hadn't told Brite about the showdown with their daughter. There was nothing like an angry father that looked like an ancient Viking warrior, or a modern-day warrior for that matter, to get a handsy boyfriend to back off. But she was sullen, withdrawn, and acted really skittish and jumpy anytime I spoke to her or one of the other staff approached her. I had hired one of Dixie's friends to work the floor with her and two part-time bartenders to relieve Rome of his shifts during the day. One was a preppy guy still in school that would fit in with the college crowd on the weekends and the other was an older guy that had been around the block a few times. He was a retired Army Ranger and was just as gruff and no-nonsense as Rome, even if he was probably twenty years older. He would be a good fit for the grizzled and grumpy day crew that lingered at the bar. Avett had gone out of her way to be rude to and dismissive of everyone. I was starting to wonder if she needed a good old-fashioned spanking to make her act right instead of getting her ass canned. I just couldn't figure out what her deal was.

On top of her generally piss-poor attitude and penchant for snarling at anyone that got too close to her, she had asked for her paycheck early and then an advance on her check for the following week. Rome was a nice enough guy to cut her one early, but when he told her no way on the advance she had freaked out. I'd never seen a mostly grown woman throw a tantrum like that, but I was used to watching people, used to reading what was really behind their actions, and I could tell it was an overreaction fueled by fear not greed. Something was going on with the pink-haired handful and it was something not good. I would bet good money it all tied into that shithead boyfriend of hers.

Tonight, when I had cashed the bar out and tried to show the new guy what to do, it had taken three tries of counting out the drawer to realize the drop was a couple hundred dollars short. I counted it, counted it again, and then had the new guy count it twice. Two hundred and twenty bucks was gone, and the only way for it to be missing was for someone to have taken it. The new guy was freaking out, swearing he didn't give anyone the wrong change, and it took fifteen minutes to assure him that I wasn't blaming him for the shortage. I also reminded him that there were cameras covering pretty much every single inch of the bar, and that if he ever did want to try something shady, the eye in the sky was watching.

I made the drop short, left a note on Rome's desk for him to call me in the morning, and briefly told him my suspicions without naming names. I couldn't imagine

Avett was stupid enough to take money out of the till knowing she was being watched, but I also knew first-hand just how brazen and bold desperation could make a person.

I only had a few minutes when I got home to make the place look presentable, not that it ever was going to look like anything other than a dump, but I tossed the clothes littering the floor into the hamper, changed the sheets, and made sure there weren't any dirty dishes in the sink. I shouldn't care if Royal thought I lived like a pig, but old habits died hard, and being seen as lacking even if it was simply all I could afford grated on my ego.

I looked at the clock on the microwave and realized I wasn't going to have time to take a shower if she showed up right at three, so I poured some scotch into a plastic cup and tossed it back. I think I was nervous that she wouldn't show. It was stupid. This was Royal. She chased down danger and jumped feetfirst into the fire on purpose. A soft knock hit the door right on time.

I pulled it open and then grunted in surprise when she swept past me with obvious impatience. She had a giant purse on her arm that she threw on the recliner and then turned to look at me with a deliberate toss of her long hair. She had on shiny black heels, and her hair was down and glimmered like a luxurious pelt. All she seemed to have on was a black peacoat that was belted at her waist and hit her right in the middle of her bare thighs. There were endless miles of bare legs on display and that sent every thought I had fleeing and all the blood in my body rushed to the part of me rising in readiness below my belt. I felt my eyebrows shoot up to my hairline as I shut the door behind her dramatic arrival and leaned back against it as my heart slid all the way to my knees and then back up.

"So you finally have a coat on." I couldn't keep the humor out of my voice even if the timbre changed as she turned to look at me with heavy-lidded dark eyes.

The corner of her mouth kicked up in a sexy little smirk and I wondered if she would hurt me if I tackled her to the floor with zero finesse.

"Not for long." She lifted her hands to the top button and watched me as she popped it open. I felt my breath freeze in my lungs, and every single thing in the world hinged on her moving down to the next button on that coat.

"Couldn't sleep again?" I asked. She shook her head slowly from side to side and her fingers moved to the second button. She kept her eyes locked on mine as she slipped it from the hole.

"I was asleep. You woke me up."

I wanted to put my hands in her hair and I wanted to put my mouth on that tantalizing trail of skin that she had bared on the top of her chest. I thought maybe it would hurry her little game along if I narrowed the playing field a bit. I was a master at playing games ... and winning. I reached up and tugged my shirt off over my head in one move. I tossed it on the recliner and felt a swell of masculine pride when I saw the pulse at the base of her throat flutter in response. Her fingers moved on the third button and circled it. She also took a step back toward the bed, which had me automatically moving toward her.

"I woke you up?"

She took another step back on those crazy, sexy shoes and dipped her chin down and looked at me from under her long lashes. She was really the most remarkable thing I had ever seen in my life and I still couldn't figure out why she was here wasting any of herself on me.

The third button pulled free and I really had to fight the urge to pounce on her. The coat split just enough that I caught a hint of pink areola and the curve of plump, high breasts.

"I woke up saying your name and touching myself. I was achy and figured why take care of it myself when you owe me anyways." The spark of humor in her chocolate eyes really undid me. I couldn't keep the space between us anymore.

She was playing with the bottom button on the coat and my patience was lost. Part of the reason I was so good at games was because I made my own rules, and more often than not cheated. I prowled toward her with long steps and had her toppled back on the bed with the coat splayed open behind her and had her laid out like a naked buffet all for me to gorge on in seconds. I braced my hands on either side of her head and gazed down at her with raw longing I could feel filling every part of me.

"What if you had gotten pulled over, or in an accident, or had car trouble on your way over here?" The idea of anyone else seeing those long legs with nothing covering them suddenly had murder seeming totally logical in my caveman mind. Not that I didn't appreciate how easy she made getting into her pants—I mean, when she didn't have any on, it was obvious what was going to go down. Beyond the lust and passion swallowing me up, I was worried about her, and that was a new sensation for me.

She wiggled her arms out of the coat sleeves, which had her breasts doing a shimmy and shake that made me groan out loud. Once she was free, she pulled her legs up where they were bracketing my hips as I leaned over her and curled her arms across my shoulders.

"If I had gotten pulled over I would have explained why I was mostly naked and probably gotten a high five from the cop. If I was in an accident the first responders would have gotten quite a show, but I'm sure they've seen it before. And if I had had car trouble I would've just called a cab." She moved her hand and rubbed the pad of her thumb along the curve of my bottom lip. I snatched the digit between my teeth and caressed it with my tongue, which made her sigh. "With you, the only way to go is high risk, high reward."

I had been a risk a lot of people had taken and lost. I had never been anyone's reward. It made me want to make her promises I knew I could never keep. I wanted to tell her she would never regret taking a chance on me, but that just wasn't the case. I bent my elbows a little so I could reach her mouth and told her, "I better make it worth the risk, then," and then I kissed her like it was the only chance I was ever going to get.

I kissed her like I had to memorize every little taste, every little flick of her tongue, every nip of her teeth, every little whimper that escaped her as our lips pressed together with feverish intensity. One of her hands was in the back of my hair holding me close, the other was scratching across my shoulders, making my skin ripple in anticipation.

I was still dressed from the waist down, but I could feel her heat blazing between us where our hips were locked together as I hovered over her on the bed. Knowing not only that she was here with me, but that she really, really wanted to be here made me kiss her even more desperately. It felt like being with this woman was a once-in-a-lifetime opportunity that I needed to savor like a delicacy.

I let her mouth go when it felt like there wasn't any air left in the room. We both gasped and I moved over to kiss her temple and to nibble on her earlobe. It was a hot spot because she gasped even louder and her hips arched up into mine—hard. I played around with her, kissed her behind her ear, licked across her collarbone, and swept one hand all the way down her side. She was soft and supple everywhere. I liked it that instead of just being pretty, she was also made up of lean muscle and strength. It was an intoxicating combination of beauty and feminine power. I liked that she could not only take care of me in a very delicate and feminine way, but she could also take care of herself.

I brushed my thumb along the curve in her bent leg where it dipped in toward her waiting center. The lights were still on, so this time I could see every pink and pretty part of her. There was something over-the-top sensual about the way she was laid out on the bed with her fuck-me shoes still on as she waited for me to pay up. Like going down on a girl that looked and felt as good as she did was any kind of chore. Sex with Royal was anything but going through the typical motions to get to the main event. I wanted to do every dirty, wicked thing I could think of when it came to taking this girl to bed and getting her off. Then I wanted to do all of those things again until she was screaming my name and tossing all that burnished hair around in mindless pleasure.

I followed the curve of her inner thigh and took a step back so that I could drop to my knees in front of her. I saw her chest heave up and her breath shudder as I used my thumb to lightly trace over her bare opening. She was already hot and wet. It had a hungry sound growling up the back of my throat. I saw her hands tangle in the comforter on either side of her restless hips and her eyes were almost black as she watched me. I picked up her ankles and put one of them on my shoulder. The spike of the heel hurt a little when it stabbed at me, but I was surprised that I liked the sting of it. I used the hand that wasn't dancing playfully around her center to pull her hips closer to the edge of the bed and turned my head so I could kiss her taut thigh that was now resting right next to my face.

"You're torturing me, Asa." Her voice was husky and impatient.

I laughed against her smooth skin because I was playing with her. I was taking my time with her, which is something I never did when it came to sex. Normally it was about instant gratification and scratching a persistent itch. With her, it was about watching her, gauging her reaction, getting her to respond in all the best ways possible. I think the part of me I tried so hard to keep leashed was loose when I got naked with her, and subconsciously, I was trying to ruin her for whoever it was that might come after me.

Without warning, I let my fingers sink inside of her heat and used my thumb to stroke her clit. It had her entire body lifting off the bed; she gasped my name and her other leg automatically lifted to my other shoulder as she arched hard into my touch. She twisted the fabric in her hands, writhing out of control as I stroked in and out of her, my gaze locked on the flurry of emotions racing across her face. A pink flush had worked up into her cheeks and she couldn't keep her eyes open anymore. She was biting on her bottom lip as she ground her hips into my fingers, and I was sure that I had never felt more powerful, more purposeful, in my life. It was like my only reason for being was to bring this spectacular woman pleasure, and that was perfectly fine with me.

I felt her thighs start to quake where they were caging my head. I saw her toned tummy tighten and I knew that I could make her come with just my hands, but that wasn't returning the favor I owed her.

I pressed the pad of my thumb hard on her clit after circling around and around for a long time. "Royal, look at me."

It took a minute and I had to say her name again, but eventually her brown eyes locked on me. She was drunk on desire and so close to the edge I could see her barely hanging on. I wanted to push her over and then be right there at the bottom to catch her.

I tilted my head to indicate her fisted hands. "Put those on your tits."

She blinked at me like I wasn't speaking English, then slowly moved to do what I told her. Pale hands on pale breasts had my dick trying to escape from my jeans all on its own. There was moisture down there that hadn't come from rubbing against her, and that never happened to me.

"I'm going to eat you up, and while I do it I want you to play with your nipples." Her eyes popped wide in her flushed face and a cloud of uncertainty drifted over her gaze, so I pressed against her clit again until she jerked under my touch. "I want you to rub them, squeeze them, and I want you to hold on to them until it almost hurts. I want you to do it until it feels like the pleasure is too much, that it's going to break you in half ... only then can you stop. Do you get me?" I lifted an eyebrow at her and finally let go of her trapped clit. She moaned a little and nodded, just once, to let me know she understood. I grinned at her and I knew it wasn't nice. It was the grin I used when I went in for the kill. "Good, because if you stop, if you let go, then I stop, too."

She swore at me and purposely dug the edge of her heel harder into my shoulder. It made me grin at her even more. Her fight was as much of a turn-on as the rest of her.

She didn't take her eyes off mine as she spread her fingers apart and trapped the turgid flesh between them. The rosy tips peeked out between her fingers and I watched as she squeezed, just like I told her to. That made all the want inside of me ratchet up a hundred degrees. Nothing better than a pretty girl that could get a little dirty when the situation called for it.

I used my thumbs to spread her open and then licked her from top to bottom. It made both of us groan. She was all kinds of liquid goodness that burst in brightness across my tongue. She was better than the most expensive scotch I had ever had, and just as potent. I swirled the tip of my tongue around her clit, went in closer so I could tug the tender flesh between my teeth all while keeping an eye on her to make sure she was still fondling her breasts. Her grip had tightened the more I worked her over and I could see that she was shaking and panting. She stilled one time, just the barest pause in her motion, and I immediately lifted my head and pulled my fingers out of her. She screamed a profanity at me, and I think if I hadn't had her splayed wide open, she would've tried to kick me in the face. I just watched her until she pinched the obviously sensitive peaks, making her gasp and twist in my hands.

I rewarded her by humming in approval against her little center of desire and watched as it forced her higher and higher into the ether of passion. Her hips were all the way off the bed now and I had to slide a hand underneath her backside to keep her level with my mouth. I licked and nibbled. I stroked in and out. I petted her and did exactly what I told her I was going to do—I ate her up like she was my last meal. Her legs quivered alongside my head, her hands moved frantically over her own flesh, and she watched me like she was hypnotized by what we were doing.

I could see the instant it all became too much for her to handle. I saw her mouth drop open in a silent scream. I watched as her hands lost their grip on her firm flesh falling uselessly to her sides as she suddenly crested and broke into a million pieces of pleasure on my tongue. Her inner walls pulled at my fingers as she vibrated and shattered against me. Her legs clamped around my ears in a desperate bid to hold on to the sensation, and all I could think as she whispered my name over and over again was that she was the sweetest victory I had ever tasted. This was one debt I would never, ever complain about paying off.

I smoothed my hands along the outsides of her legs and gently set them back down on the edge of the bed and rose back to my feet. She was breathing shallow but her eyes were open and locked on me, slightly dazed but full of contentment and residual passion. I worked my belt open and motioned to the nightstand.

"My turn." She reached out an arm and I heard things clattering around in the drawer until she returned with a foil packet.

She pushed herself up so that she was sitting right in front of me and eye level with the instant erection that was now popping out of the open fly of my jeans. She worked the fabric down over my ass and then fisted my cock and rubbed her hand up and down. It made me grunt and thrust into her grip unconsciously. I liked that she wasn't afraid to be a little handsy and rough. She let go and rolled the latex down the shaft with quick and efficient motions. Then she leaned forward and kissed me right above the light dusting of blond hair that led to my groin.

"I love taking turns." She rubbed her cheek against my hip, which had her silky hair twining around my dick. It was an unbelievable sensation. I threaded my fingers through her hair and bent down so I could kiss her again. We tasted like sex and always.

When I pulled back she was smiling up at me and tugging me down as she scooted back just enough to give me room to fall into her. Now those spiked heels were digging into my lower back and her breasts were flat against my chest as I buried myself as deeply inside of her as I could go. I kissed her one more time and started to move. She was already slick and supple, so I didn't bother to take it easy on her. I pounded into her, I rode her hard, and between the way she responded and the bite of her shoes into my back, it didn't take long until I was ready to release all the coiled-up pleasure inside of me into her. I hitched one of her legs up higher on my side, buried my face in the side of her neck, and drove into her welcoming heat over and over again. Her hands were in my hair and her breath was uneven in my ear. As soon as I felt the tiniest flutter race along the sides of my dick, I was done. I felt my fingers bite into her hips hard enough to bruise and muttered incoherently as she followed me into utter bliss a second later. In a true dickhead move I hadn't even worried about getting her there again, because once I was inside her, all I could do was chase down all the amazing things she made me feel. She made me sex stupid just by being her.

I lay limply on top of her for a long minute knowing I should get up and take care of the condom, but she felt so good and her hands were stroking up and down my spine in such a soothing way that all I wanted to do was lean into her touch. I rubbed my cheek on her shoulder and asked her, "You wanna spend some time with me when we aren't naked and in bed, Red?"

She shifted under my weight a little and her hands stilled on my shoulders. I knew she liked fucking me. I needed to know if she wanted any part of me outside of the bedroom.

"Like on a date?" She asked the question quietly and it made my back teeth click together.

"It can be whatever you want it to be." I went to roll off of her but she moved her arms up around my shoulders and kept me pinned to her.

"Yeah, Asa, I wanna spend time with you. I don't care if it's in bed or out." She laughed a little and wiggled under me, which had the part of me still nestled inside of her twitching. "Though I am a pretty big fan of what happens when we spend time in bed together."

I snorted and pushed off of her so I could clean up. I shoved my hands through my hair and looked down at her. All those pretty promises I wanted to make to her were screaming at me, trying to force their way out of my mouth.

"I don't know why you're here, but I feel like I need to thank any God that might exist that you are."

She blinked at me once and then again and I saw her blush. She moved so that she was on the bed the right way and stared at me with wide eyes.

"I'm here because you finally let me be here." Her hair fanned out behind her on the pillows and I wished I could paint so I could capture her beauty for future ages to appreciate. "And I'll stay as long as you let me."

If only that was the case. She would stay until something happened or I did something that forced her to have to go. I needed a minute to get my thoughts back in order after the way she had just owned me, so I didn't respond to her and disappeared into the bathroom to take care of business. If only figuring out what I was going to do about this girl and all the ways she made me feel was as easy as cleaning up after the best sex I had ever had.

CHAPTER 10

Royal

When Asa's phone went off the next morning, it felt like it was the crack of dawn instead of nine. Granted we had kept each other tangled up and very occupied until the sun was just starting to come up, so there hadn't been a whole lot of sleeping going on. He groaned and reached over me to silence the noise with a flick of his finger. His amber eyes were sleepy and the dust of golden scruff on his face made him look even more rakish than usual.

I stretched out lazily under him and lifted my arms up over my head, which had his whiskey-tinted eyes turning from lethargic to hot and glowing in seconds. I was going to ask him why he had to get up so early since I thought most bartenders slept until noon, but my drowsy movements under him were clearly causing other thoughts to enter his mind. I was totally on board with the plan until I was right on the edge of an orgasm that I just knew was going to turn me inside out when he suddenly froze, went absolutely still, and stared down at me with wide, heated eyes.

I had my hand wrapped around his biceps and I felt the muscles lock rigidly into place. He was breathing hard and barked at me not to move when I went to lift up to get him back in the groove of things. I scowled up at him and dug my fingernails into his tense arms as he gritted out between his teeth, "If you move it's all gonna be over and I don't have a condom on." His eyebrows furrowed even farther over his nose. "I've never had sex without protection before. No wonder condoms get a bad rap. I'm about to lose my fucking mind."

His teeth were clenched and his nostrils flared as he torturously started to pull back from my body. I was too close, and even with his stilted movements it still felt too good, and so even though I forced myself not to move an outer muscle, my inner muscles were having none of it and dragged and pulled all along his length, which meant we were both left with a sticky passionate mess to contend with when it was all said and done. I thought it was funny; he didn't seem nearly as amused as he dragged me into the shower to clean both of us off.

I tried to tell him it was no big deal, but I realized he wasn't upset about the situation, he was mad at himself for getting so carried away that he forgot something as basic as protection. He was used to being the one running the games and I don't think he liked it that I got to him just as effectively as he got to me. I had never been on birth control in my life. My sexual partners were too few and far between, and even with the guy I dated long term I had never been into the sex enough to really warrant it. There was no getting caught up in the moment with him. For Asa I would totally do it, but not without a guarantee that it was just the two of us from this point on, and I didn't think he was ready for that conversation just yet.

"Why are we up so early?" He was scrubbing my hair and obviously a thousand miles away in his own head.

"I need to talk to Rome about work stuff. We're having an issue with Brite's daughter."

I sighed as his fingers massaged my scalp. "Rome really looks up to Brite. That's got to be tough."

He moved behind me and I sucked in a breath as our slick skins rubbed together. He sounded frustrated when he replied, "Yeah. I don't get why she's such a brat. I mean, I was a nightmare, but I didn't have two parents that obviously cared about me or anyone trying to give me a helping hand up from the bottom. She has this loser boyfriend that is obviously strung out and I'm positive he's used his hands on her more than once. She has lifelines trying to pull her out of shitty situations and she just keeps turning a blind eye to them."

His big hands worked around the front of me as the soap cascaded out of my hair and down my shoulders. He wasn't so much cleaning my chest as he was playing with my boobs and making me pant.

"Do you think you would've taken the hand if one was offered to you when you were younger?"

One of his hands flattened on my stomach and I felt his lips land softly on the back of my neck. He reached past me to turn off the water.

"No. I was destined to be a screw-up from the start." He shoved his hands through his wet hair, stepped out of the shower stall, and found a towel that he handed over to me. "My dad was in jail before I was born, my mom had a ninth-grade education and no desire to live beyond the trailer park. I was always the poor kid, the white-trash kid, and instead of being ashamed of it, I used people's pity, their sympathy, to get what I wanted."

I watched him carefully as he wrapped a towel around his waist and leaned back against the tiny vanity. He watched me just as closely as I rubbed the excess water out of my long hair. He crossed his arms over his broad chest and went on.

"When I started school and I realized all the other kids brought lunch or had meal plans and I didn't, at first it made me sad." He shook his head and his mouth pulled tight. "Then it made me mad that all those kids had something I didn't, that I had a mom that couldn't get her act together enough to feed me. I found a girl in my class. She was quiet, didn't really have any friends because she was shy and kind of weird, and I spent all my time convincing her we were the best of friends." His eyes flashed from gold to bronze and I could literally see him falling into the decades-old memory. It obviously didn't sit right with him now if the way his shoulders tightened was an indication. "She was a sweet kid, a little slow, but she had a huge heart and came from a lot of money. She brought me lunch every single day until fifth grade."

I wrapped the towel turban style around my head and went to move past him. But his fingers locked onto my wrist and he pulled me to a stop in front of him. He wanted me to hear this, he was always trying to pull the curtain back and show me the darkness that swirled inside of him. It didn't seem to matter to him that I already knew he was made up of black marks and misdeeds and I just didn't care about them.

"In fifth grade I started to understand that the other girls in class besides her thought I was cute, that if I gave more than one girl attention I could get more than just lunch. I told one she was the prettiest girl in class so she would do my homework, told another I would be her boyfriend so she would buy me clothes, let another sneak kisses so that she would take me out to eat at restaurants, not even fancy ones because there aren't any in Woodward, Kentucky. Then was another girl, she was awful. Stuck up, mean and horrible to anyone that crossed her path but because her family had a pool and she would invite me over to swim I decided to start walking her home from school. I loathed her but I did it every day because she had something I wanted. I did all of that after coldly and callously ditching the first girl that had been so nice to me and so sweet to me for *years*. I just unceremoniously ditched her and didn't care when other kids teased her or made fun of her even after she made sure I never went hungry. I wasn't even a teenager yet and I was already that kind of guy."

I shook his hold off and went into the living area so I could put on the clothes I had stuffed in my purse. I wiggled into a pair of skinny jeans and pulled on a cute, off-the-shoulder sweater over a tank top. I took the towel off and shook out my tangled hair as I dug around for my brush. Asa came out of the bathroom scowling at me, so I lifted an eyebrow in his direction and worked on making my hair manageable.

"What?" I made sure to keep my voice light because I could see he was just waiting for me to unleash a torrent of disgust and judgment at him and was unsure what to do with my indifference.

"That's all you have to say about what I just told you?" He dropped the towel in jerky moves and walked naked to his closet. He really was perfect. Every long, lean line of his back, every flex and dimpled indent in his backside, the broad expanse of his toned shoulders ... there was nothing about him that had any hint of imperfection. It was an interesting juxtaposition that such a beautifully crafted shell held so much ugliness and self-loathing on the inside.

"What do you want me to say? That you suck? That you were a total jerk and deserved what you eventually got? Do you want me to tell you that was a totally douche move not just to the first girl that gotten taken in by you, but even to the mean one because you were just using her, too? You know all of that, Asa. You might not have known it then, or not cared, but now you do, so me telling you what you already know is pointless." Once my hair was mostly tangle-free, I pulled it into a loose ponytail at the base of my neck and dug around in my purse for my makeup kit. "Someone should have been around to take care of that little boy so he didn't have to resort to that behavior in the first place."

He pulled a faded black T-shirt on over his head and plopped down heavily on the bed so he could pull on his boots.

"No one made me do those things, no one taught me. I figured it out on my own, and by the time I was a teenager, I had learned every dirty trick there was in the book."

I sighed at him and slicked a coat of lip gloss across my mouth. I crossed my arms across my chest and met his predatory look with one of my own. "Do you want to confess every single sin you've ever committed to me? Do you think it will scare me away or absolve you of past misdeeds? Because I have to tell you, neither of those things is going to happen." I furrowed my brow at him and made my voice hard so he would know I was serious and told him pointedly, "I'm never going to dislike you as much as you dislike yourself, Asa."

He got to his feet and moved toward me. He really did look like a big, wild cat stalking its prey as he prowled closer and closer. He stopped when we were almost touching but I refused to look or flinch away from him.

"You have no idea what you're talking about, Red."

I reached out a hand and put it right over the place in his chest where his heart was thundering. He was upset, but like usual I knew it was directed more inwardly than it was at me.

"Yes, I do, because I've been having a really hard time liking myself ever since Dom got hurt. I know how it feels and exactly what it looks like. Why do you think I was chasing after you so hard? I needed someone that wouldn't tell me it was just an accident, that it wasn't my fault. I needed someone that it was okay to feel bad with, and so do you. We aren't always going to do the right things, make the right choices, and somehow you're the only one I feel safe with coming to terms with that. You don't judge me, you don't try and make it better. You just let me feel bad while making me feel really good … I want to do that for you, too."

His unusual-colored eyes flashed from gold to bronze as the truth and depth of my words sank in. He muttered something under his breath I couldn't hear and then he tilted his head to the side a little and told me, "I'm the opposite of safe. I fucked you without a condom on this morning because you make me stupid with want. That isn't exactly looking out for your best interests."

I fisted his shirt in my hand and tugged him down so that we were almost eye to eye. I appreciated that he felt like he had to keep warning me about all the ways in which this volatile thing between us could go wrong, but at some point he was just going to have to man up, get on board with what was happening, and stop waiting for it to implode all around us.

"There were two of us in that bed this morning. I'm just as responsible as you are for what happens there. I can protect myself and am more than willing to do so if you're willing to be honest with me and tell me if this thing between us is important enough, interesting enough, to give a shot. If the answer is no, then that's fine, but I won't be back and we'll just chalk it up to raging hormones and lust."

He curled his fingers around my wrist and let his fingers rest over my erratic pulse. I wondered if anything with him was ever going to be simple.

"I'm not taking anyone else to bed as long as you're in it, Royal."

That was as much of an agreement to stop being a naysayer where we were concerned as I was going to get. I would take it. I pressed up on my toes and kissed him lightly on the mouth.

"Good. Now, how about you let me drive you to the Bar so you can meet with Rome and then we go grab something to eat at the Breakfast King after? I'm starving." It seemed like such a simple, couply thing to do and I needed that. I craved it with him.

He ran his hand over the length of my still-damp ponytail and lightly tapped me on the ass. "Sounds good."

Why couldn't everything between us be that cut-and-dried?

George Thorogood was on the jukebox when Asa and I walked into the Bar. It was early enough that the doors weren't open for customers yet but Cora was sitting at the bar talking to a guy standing behind it that I didn't recognize. Asa deposited me next to her and introduced the new bartender as Danny before disappearing off toward the back office. I told Cora good morning and then spent five minutes staring at her trying to figure out why I thought she looked different from the last time I saw her.

Her blond hair was still short and styled in an artful disarray and her two-toned eyes were still bright and glittery with mischief. She was swinging her short legs back and forth watching me scope her out with obvious amusement. She had on tight black pants and a flowy top that had a bunch of flowers on it. She was colorful and fun just like every time I saw her, but as she turned to fully face me, I felt my eyes widen when I noticed a certain part of her that seemingly had grown out of proportion to the rest of her tiny frame.

"Did you get a boob job?" I realized how rude that sounded and went to apologize when she started laughing so hard her eyes began to water.

"No, I didn't, but I think half the reason Rome likes to knock me up is because of this particular side effect."

I gaped at her for a second. "You're pregnant? Wow, congratulations." I let my gaze slide up and down her still-petite figure. Aside from the craziness happening in her bra, she still looked like a little pixie. "I had no idea."

She nodded. "We've been keeping it pretty quiet. I wanted Shaw and her new baby to get all the same love and attention we got when Remy came into the world, but we're going for the ultrasound today to see if we're bringing RJ home a brother or sister, so it won't stay secret much longer."

I reached out to give her a one-armed hug. "Ugh, I can't believe I missed it. I'm going to make a terrible detective."

She laughed again and patted me on the knee. "You don't spend enough time around me to pick up on all the subtle little clues—something you should change, by the way." She gave me a look and cocked her head to the side. "You know Ayden and Jet are coming back to town for spring break in a few weeks. We should all get together for a girls' night like we used to. I bet Shaw could use a night away from the baby … and Rule."

She grinned at me as I involuntarily flinched at the idea of hanging out with Asa's sister. I had been to their girls' nights before, but ever since Ayden moved and the babies started coming around, they had been few and far between. Now I usually just had coffee with Saint in the morning or grabbed a drink with Salem if she asked. We hadn't all gotten together in longer than I could remember and it for sure had been before I locked Asa up.

"Uhhh …"

She rolled her eyes at me. "If you and Asa are going to be a thing, then you understand Ayden is part of that package, right?"

"I really wish someone else had answered that call. I hated having to take him in when he was hurt and obviously innocent. If I was his sister, I wouldn't be happy with me either."

She didn't get a chance to say anything else because both the guys came out of the back room looking grim and unhappy. Rome was scowling pretty hard and Asa's mouth was pulling tight in a straight line.

Cora swung around on the bar stool and went to her hulking man. She wrapped her arms around his waist and he automatically returned the embrace and bent to drop a kiss on the top of her head. It was so easy, so effortless, how they leaned on each other that I felt a sudden ball of emotion lodge in my throat as I watched them.

"Not good?" She asked the question softly and Asa was the one who answered. He leaned on the end of the bar and shook his head.

"Not good." He sounded frustrated and disappointed. All I wanted to do was hug him and make it better like Cora was doing for Rome, only we were nowhere near there yet. His eyes shifted from me to Rome and then back. "The big guy doesn't want to press charges, but we're going to have to fire her and we need to talk to Brite and Darcy."

Cora made a sympathetic noise. "It's gonna break Brite's heart."

Asa pushed off the bar and walked over to where I was sitting. I hopped off the stool and he wrapped an arm around my shoulders and tugged me to his side. A full-body shiver worked its way from the top of my scalp to the tips of my toes as I responded by putting an arm around his lean waist. I wanted to be able to hold him up. I just wasn't sure I was strong enough.

"He's not going to give up on her. He loves her too much." Asa's voice had hints of guilt laced with penitence in it and I wondered if he was talking about the employee or something far closer to home.

Rome grunted and squeezed Cora hard enough that she squeaked. "We have to go. I wanna see my new baby."

We followed them out of the bar and Cora looked at me over her shoulder before Rome hefted her up into his big truck and told me, "No escaping girls' night, Royal. I'm making it happen."

I groaned and agreed with a shrug. Asa gave me a questioning look as we headed the couple blocks from the Bar over to where the diner was located. After we were seated and had steaming cups of coffee sitting in front of us, I wanted to ask him exactly what was going on with the employee, but he beat me to it and questioned why I seemed less than thrilled to hang out with the girls.

I stirred copious amounts of sugar into my coffee and stared down at the table while I thought about how to answer that.

"I've never had a lot of friends. It's always just been me and Dom. I like all those girls and I love Saint to death, but hanging out like that isn't something I'm used to, and frankly I'm still slightly terrified your sister wants to kick my ass."

He gave me an exasperated look that indicated how ridiculous he thought my fears where Ayden was concerned were, and picked up his own mug. His golden eyes gleamed at me over the rim as he asked, "Always just you and Dom, huh? There ever been anything there that's gonna have a pissed-off cop on my ass if he finds out where you've been going when you can't sleep?"

I had to blink for a second because what he was asking was so ridiculous it took a second for it to compute. "NO! God no. Dom has been my best friend my entire life and now he's my partner. Nothing romantic has ever been between us, and he doesn't get a say in who I choose to spend my time with just like I don't get a vote in his personal life. We love each other but we aren't in love with each other and never have been."

Asa stared at me unblinkingly for a long moment before setting his coffee cup down and leaning a little closer to me with a smirk on his face. "How's that possible? How does he spend endless hours around you, stuck in a patrol car with you day in and day out, and not try and get some? Doesn't add up."

I flushed under the scrutiny and gave the same response I did whenever anyone questioned how Dom and I could have a strictly platonic relationship over all these years.

"I'm not Dom's type, and I know him too well to ever think we could work out."

Asa leaned back in the booth and I could see the pieces of the word puzzle clicking into place in his head. He really was as smart as he was pretty. "Not his type?"

I shrugged a shoulder. "Nope. Not at all."

"I see." He sounded amused, and maybe it was wishful thinking but I think there was a hint of relief in his tone as well.

I copied his pose in the booth and asked, "Do you?"

"Red, there are only a handful of reasons any guy would consider you 'not his type' and it doesn't take a rocket scientist to know what the main one might be."

I let out a little breath of relief and didn't say anything else as the waitress set down our food in front of us.

It was a question I had fielded a lot over the years, especially as Dom and I had gotten older and both of us went into law enforcement. In high school, we were even voted prom king and queen regardless of the fact that we were not, and had never been, a couple. Sure, maybe in a different world where Dominic liked girls instead of boys we could have fallen in love and lived happily ever after. As it was, I was absolutely NOT Dom's type and we were just going to be best friends forever and I was simply grateful that I got to have him in my life in whatever form that happened to be. I never felt like it was my place to speak for Dom about why there was nothing romantic between us, so I was relieved Asa picked up on what I wasn't saying and let the subject drop.

He was watching me in obvious amusement as I shov-eled breakfast into my face with no delicacy. I didn't care. I was hungry and he had already taken me to bed, so appearing ladylike and demure had no place here. After I polished off my entire plate and what was left on his, I sat back with a satisfied sigh and put my hands on my full tummy. He was still watching me and now his eyes were glowing like they were lit up from somewhere deep inside of him.

"You're cute." He sounded amused, so I wrinkled my nose at him.

"That doesn't sound like a compliment." I told the waitress no when she asked if we wanted anything else even though I totally could have gone for a chocolate milk shake. Asa asked for the bill and pulled his phone out to look at it. When he spoke it was with sincerity and honesty even though he wasn't looking at me.

"It is. You surprise me. The way you look doesn't always match up with the things you do … I'm never sure what to expect."

I pushed my ponytail over my shoulder and slid out of the booth. He followed my lead after throwing a wad of bills on the table to cover the check. I melted a little on the inside when he took my hand. It seemed like such a normal thing for a guy to do for a girl he liked and so against the way he had behaved toward me up until this point.

"I get that a lot, you know? Like the way I look should have anything to do with anything—ever." He rubbed his thumb along my wrist and my pulse jumped in response to the simple caress. "My mom is really beautiful and it's never brought her anything but trouble."

"If she looks like you, I can see that."

I scoffed at him as we stepped off the curb. "People thought she was my sister or my friend when I got older. The guys in high school used to hit on her all the time, and I wanted to die. She just laughed it off. She was good at handling the attention; she was also really good at letting me find my own way when it became clear I wasn't going to follow in her glamorous footsteps."

He was watching me like every word I said held parts of my soul in it. Maybe it did. Sometimes it was easy to forget about all my mom's wonderful attributes and get lost in her overzealous quest for Mr. Right.

"What do you mean?"

I smiled a little thinking about my mom showing up at soccer games in six-inch heels and in full hair and makeup. I shrugged a shoulder and told him, "She just let me be me and never questioned it. When I told her I wanted to follow Dom to the Police Academy, she didn't miss a beat. She was worried about my safety but she never questioned whether or not I could do it. She just told me to go and be the best cop I could be and look fabulous while doing it. She's always been supportive of anything I wanted to take on, and since it was always just me and her, having her approval was important to me. It still is."

"I like the way you look." He said it like it was obvious, and maybe it was. But coming from him it made my insides flutter and tiny pieces of my heart want to burst out of my chest and put themselves in his very dangerous hands. "But I like the things you do, the way you act, the things you say, and the way you are even more. You could have mousy hair, acne, and crossed eyes and still be completely beautiful by just being you. Your mom knew that, that's why she just let you be."

I had to stop, even though we were in the middle of crossing the street, to look at him to see if he was serious. He was good with words, had a way of saying things that I think he knew I wanted to hear—hell, that *any* woman would die to hear—but it was there, stamped on his too-handsome face, that he meant everything he had just said. I had to clear my throat before I could respond.

"That might be the nicest thing anyone has ever said to me, Asa. Especially since I haven't been very fond of myself lately." He shrugged it off like it was no big deal, like he hadn't just given me more than enough reason to throw common sense out the door and go ahead and fall completely in love with him. He always had exactly the right words to use. No wonder he had been such a good con man. Pretty words out of that too-pretty face made you want to believe they were the truth.

"It's true." His voice was a little gruff and he shifted uneasily from foot to foot as we got back to the Bar and stopped in front of the 4Runner.

I tilted my head back so I could look up at him. "I like who you are, too, even if you don't."

"Not much to like, Royal. I keep telling you that and you just don't want to listen."

"You're wrong." I knew he was. He bent down and pressed a light kiss to my lips. He tasted like pancake syrup and coffee, and when I kissed him there were so many things I liked about him I could literally drown in them. When his lips touched mine it was the only thing that felt certain and real in my otherwise unsteady life. I wanted to tell him that watching him torture himself over things he couldn't ever change had given me the perspective I so desperately needed, but I knew enough to know we weren't there yet. I put a hand up on his bristly cheek and stepped up on my tiptoes so I could put my lips next to his ear. "But if you want, we can go back to your apartment for a little while and I can show you what I like the very *best* about you."

Since I was stretched out all along his tall form, there was no missing the way his cock reacted to my words behind the fly of his jeans. I was going to have to figure out a way to get him to see that even though he had all kinds of broken parts that were ugly and misshapen on the inside, there was enough of him that was salvageable and really beautiful to make this thing between us work and for it to flourish into something solid and lasting. He might have been a criminal in the past, but now I was the one that wanted to steal something from him and keep it for my own … he was going to put up a fight once he realized I was after his heart. After all, it was my job to capture the bad guy … only this one I wasn't planning on letting go of.

CHAPTER 11

Asa

"The outside isn't much to look at and the interior is trashed, but the engine is solid, and with a little love and care she could be a beauty."

I pulled my head out of the window of the 1971 Chevy Nova I was considering buying and looked at Wheeler. I didn't know him really well but Nash assured me he was a good guy and wouldn't screw me over. Plus Rome had agreed to tag along with me while I looked at cars, and even with a squealing, blond toddler running around his legs, he still didn't come across as a guy anyone wanted to mess with. Especially since he was considering sinking a healthy amount of cash into this garage in the near future. He was watching the baby like a hawk to make sure she didn't grab anything off the greasy ground and put it into her mouth and texting on his phone. He wasn't paying very much attention to me or the mechanic.

"I like it. She's a classic." Even with the rust on the body and the totally trashed interior.

Wheeler nodded and leaned against the fender. He was a little bit shorter than me, had shaggy auburn hair and wild ink on either side of his neck. He hadn't said much but it was obvious he loved his cars and wouldn't just let any Joe in off the street to take a gander at his inventory.

"I was going to save it for a project car, but I just got in an old Plymouth Wayfarer and that's going to take some major work. I'd rather let the Nova go and sink the money into that."

I nodded like I understood and appreciated his dilemma. I liked a nice car as much as the next guy, but really I just needed something that would run and get me from one place to the next. It was a far cry from how I used to look at a ride. Before the coma all I had cared about was the flash, the expense, and how I looked to others driving around in a car that cost more than some houses.

"How much do you want for it?" The engine was in good shape but in no way restored or souped up, so I was hoping he would be reasonable. Before he could answer, I was hit in the shins by a giggling little body that gazed up at me with gigantic blue eyes. RJ stuck her plump little arms up and stared at me until I hoisted her up off the ground. She laughed at me and reached out to poke my nose. She was the perfect mix of Rome and Cora. Now that she was mobile and talking, she was a complete handful.

Wheeler grinned at us and told me, "Five grand."

It was more than I wanted to spend. I had it—I mean, I had practically zero expenses but buying the car meant less money to pay off my medical debt. RJ laughed again and used her tiny hands to pat my cheeks. She was singing some little baby song, and I couldn't help but smile at her.

"Is that the best you can do?"

His light blue gaze shifted between me and the baby. A tiny smile pulled at his mouth and he dipped his chin down. "Normally I would stick hard and fast. But since you're friends with Nash and the crew from the Marked, and the fact that RJ seems to dig you obviously means you're a good guy, I'll drop it down to forty-two hundred."

RJ was too little to know any better, but I wasn't about to tell Wheeler that. I shifted the little girl to the other side so he and I could shake on the price and looked at Rome as he suddenly appeared at my side. The baby instantly stuck her hands out and started chanting, "Da-Da-Da-Da," as the large man relieved me of my fluffy bundle.

"You make a deal?" I nodded and so did Wheeler. Rome grunted his approval and turned to look at me. "I need to make a stop before we head back to the Bar. Is that all right?"

I couldn't really argue. I hadn't been sure if I was going to buy a car today or not, so it wasn't like I was ready to take the Nova home this minute and I needed a ride back downtown. Wheeler and I exchanged information and I told him I would be in touch in the next couple of days. I really wanted to have a set of wheels locked down before Ayden showed up the following week for spring break.

I climbed up into Rome's massive truck while he locked RJ down in her car seat, and asked him where we were going. He had been even more brooding and withdrawn than normal ever since we had watched the video of Avett taking the money out of the cash register behind the bar. I don't know what she had said to the new bartender to make him think it was okay, but it was there in irrefutable proof that she had stolen the missing money right from under our noses. Rome had had a long talk with Brite about the situation, but Avett hadn't shown back up at the Bar, so both of us had been spared the awkwardness of having to actually fire her. According to Rome, Brite was all for him filing charges against Avett, but Rome just couldn't do it.

"Where are we headed?" I felt like it was a fair question to ask since he was glowering out the windshield and not saying much as he pulled out into the city traffic and headed toward Capitol Hill.

"We need to swing by Rule's." He cut me a sideways look and the edge of his mouth quirked up in a grin. "Shaw left him alone with the baby while she went to the college to try and figure out when she can go back, and he's freaking out."

That startled a laugh out of me. "Oh yeah?"

Rome chuckled. "Yeah. It's the first time he's been alone with him and he says Ry won't stop crying. He doesn't want to call Shaw and worry her, so he called me."

"Big brother to the rescue." I might be teasing him a little but really I admired him. In a different world I would have been a better man and been there to save my sister instead of the other way around. I didn't regret much, just accepted that I was born to be a loser and fuckup, but that was something that burned deep in my gut every time I thought about it. That was something that I would change if I ever got the opportunity to do over again.

"Rule hasn't ever been really big on asking for help, so when he does I know he really needs it."

"He's lucky he knows he can always count on you." I could hear it in my voice. Under the soft little twang was the regret that ran bone-deep about the things I had let Ayden do, the way I had allowed us both to suffer and to sacrifice in order to barely get by.

Rome cut me a look and then glanced in the rearview mirror when Remy called to him. An unwitting grin tugged at his otherwise stern face as his daughter talked to him from the back of the crew cab.

"Are you gonna try and tell me that if Ayden called you right this minute and told you that she needed you that you wouldn't have your ass on a plane headed to Texas before she could hang up?"

I shifted uneasily in the seat and turned my head to look out the window as we rolled up into the area of Capitol Hill where Rule and Shaw lived.

"Now I would; before ..." I trailed off because it was almost impossible to put words to how truly heartless and callous I had been toward my little sister. It made places deep down inside of me fester and burn with something ugly and dark. "Before, I really had myself convinced she could take care of herself. I knew better. I knew she was doing dangerous things, risking her neck to keep me out of trouble, doing things she didn't want to do because people wanted her more than they wanted to punish me. I let it happen because that's what served me best."

Now it was his turn to shift uncomfortably. Ayden was a strong, brilliant young woman with a quick tongue and a rock-hard exterior. Rome knew her well enough now to be aware that all her iron armor hid a very soft and delicate center. To hear in no uncertain terms about some of the more unsavory parts of her past had to be unpleasant for him. It made me feel like a monster every day when I woke up, living with the knowledge of what Ayden had risked and suffered through for me.

"That was then. Now you would give up anything to make her happy. I know you were sad when she moved with Jet, but you kept your trap shut because you want her to have a good life and the only way she can do that is with him. If you had asked her to stay, she would've, for you, just like she always did. What you do now for her matters just as much as what you didn't do for her then."

I didn't need to respond because we pulled up in front of the Craftsman Rule had bought for Shaw a few years ago, and as soon as we got out of the car, the sound of a very upset baby could be heard from the inside of the house. RJ wrinkled her fair eyebrows in concern as Rome hefted her out of the truck and settled her on his hip.

"Let's go see what has your cousin so upset." She nodded her head like she understood what he was saying to her and I followed them inside since Rome didn't bother knocking.

Rome had to actually shout for Rule over the racket, and when we went into the living room, I had to really try hard not to laugh. RJ threw her tiny hands up over her ears and looked at the very small person making more noise than I had ever heard in my life. Rule was holding the naked little boy and pacing back and forth across the floor. His normally wild and spiky hair looked like it had spots of both baby powder and baby throw-up in it, and I was stunned that all the crazy and wild colors of the rainbow that usually tinted it were missing and it was just a normal, dark brown very much like Rome's.

Rule's very pale blue eyes snapped to his brother in clear desperation as Rome set Remy down and reached out for the squalling infant.

"How long has he been screaming at you for?"

Rule shoved both his hands through his hair in obvious frustration and bent down to hug his niece as she toddled over to him. He was messing with his lip ring and practically vibrating with nervous energy. She tapped her fingers on the snake that decorated the back of his hand and laughed when he wiggled his fingers at her to make the forked tongue dance. She seemed oblivious to his distress.

"Longer than a half hour. I don't know what's wrong. I changed his diaper. I tried to lay him down for a nap. I tried to feed him the bottle Shaw left. Shit, she's never going to leave me alone with him again."

He rose to his full height and started to pace again, this time minus the little boy Rome was jiggling up and down. Ry wasn't a happy camper and all of us could tell.

I wanted to just go wait outside but figured that would be rude, so I wandered over to the fireplace and dodged Remy as she tried to tackle my knees. There were a bunch of pictures on the mantel—a few of Rule and his twin, Remy, before Remy had passed away, a bunch of the brothers and the rest of the gang from the tattoo shop. It made me happy to see that Ayden was smiling and looked really happy in every single shot she was in. There were also wedding photos and pictures of Rule and Shaw with their new baby. It was a lifetime displayed for anyone to see.

"You've never had a baby before. There's a lot to learn and Shaw knows that. You and the little fella will be fine once you both start to figure things out." Slipping into bartender advice mode was second nature and I didn't even realize I was doing it until Rule stopped his frantic movement to stare at me.

There was some banging around in the kitchen and a few loud swearwords, then suddenly blissful silence filled the home. RJ looked up at her uncle, then to me, and clapped her little hands. She spun in a little circle and told Rule something that sounded like "all better."

Rome came out of the kitchen with the baby. He was balancing a bottle and cooing in a deep and grumbly way that shouldn't be soothing but apparently was to babies.

"The hole in the nipple on the bottle wasn't big enough. He was hungry and not getting any food. He's gonna be big and strong like all the rest of us Archers, so he needs to eat." Rome grinned at his brother and went to hand the baby back. For a split second Rule looked like he wanted to refuse, but the emotion came and went so fast I was pretty sure I was the only one that caught it. I understood that fear.

Rule took the naked baby and settled him in the crook of his arm with a sigh. "I suck at this."

Rome crossed his arms over his chest and leveled his brother a hard look. "No, you don't. You need to cut yourself some slack. There is no guidebook on how to raise a kid right. It's mostly trial and error."

The infant gurgled up at his dad and I could swear it was Ry trying to tell his dad everything was all right. Rule lifted one of his tattooed hands and used it to softly rub over the baby's cap of dark hair.

"I feel like I don't get a second chance if I screw shit up." He sounded so torn up about it that it really spoke to how much this life and this little person meant to him.

Rome walked over to where RJ was banging the remote to the TV against the floor and picked her up high over his head, making her laugh out of control.

"When we love someone there's an endless amount of times we forgive them when they screw up. Shaw did it with you and with me. You had to figure out your issue with Mom and Dad. Thank God Cora never walked out on me when I gave her every reason to." Rome switched his attention to me and I heard what he was saying even if he didn't bring up Ayden's name. "You're gonna screw up, Rule, and so is he. You'll both just forgive each other, keep on loving one another, and move on." The baby let out a yawn and blinked like he was agreeing with his uncle.

Rule popped the now-empty bottle out of the baby's mouth and shifted him to his shoulder, where he patted his back softly until a little baby belch found its way out. The baby sighed and closed his eyes.

"Thank you for coming by and not making me feel even worse than I already did."

Rome nodded and RJ waved as we headed toward the door. I trailed behind, still caught up on the time line of love and happiness stretched out on that mantel. I don't think Ayden and I had a single picture from our childhood. In fact the first time I could remember being in front of a camera outside of class photos in elementary school was when I got picked up for shoplifting at a gas station when I was fourteen and instead of calling the cops the store owner had snapped his own mug shot to display in a window with *Do Not Serve* written under it. There weren't any snapshots of joy or happiness, which made that dark place that lurked inside me gape open even wider.

"Anytime. You know it."

Rule rubbed a hand up and down the baby's back and lifted his pierced eyebrow. "By the way, congratulations on the new baby ..." He trailed off, leaving the "asshole" part of his statement implied in deference to the sensitive ears hovering between them.

Rome paused in pulling open the front door. "Cora told you?"

"Dude, I worked with her last time you knocked her up. I know what those mood swings and overnight double D's mean. I've known for months. I was just waiting for one of you to come clean."

Remy looked between the Archer men and widened her bright blue eyes that looked so much like her father's. "Baby?" At least that was what I think she was saying in her own little-baby way.

Rome nodded and groaned while Rule and I laughed. "Yeah, honey, a baby."

She just giggled and repeated the word over and over again. Rome shook his head in exasperation. "We just found out it's a boy. Cora really wanted you and Shaw to have your moment in the new-baby sun before saying anything."

Rule grunted and followed us out into the driveway, Ry now fully asleep and content against his chest.

"There's enough excitement for the good things in life in this group to handle Ry and your new addition, you both shoulda known that. A boy, huh? We're gonna run out of *R* names at this rate."

Rome chuckled. "I think maybe this go around we're gonna go with a *C* after Half-Pint. We'll just have to see."

Rome moved around the truck to get Remy situated and I moved toward the passenger side when Rule stopped me by saying my name softly.

I looked at him and was surprised at how intent and serious his icy gaze was. "You're quick with some really good words for other people, Opie. You know just what to say and exactly how to say it. So when do you start giving yourself some of that advice?"

I frowned a little because I wasn't following. "What do you mean?"

"I heard you finally let Royal catch you, but now that you're on the hook, you're flailing around like a fish out of water."

I didn't love how that image made me look but it was pretty damn accurate. I rubbed a hand across the back of my neck and looked down at the ground. "To be fair, I wasn't running too far out ahead of her in the first place."

"Doesn't matter. Think about what you just told me. You've never had anything good in life before, it's new to you, so maybe you just need to allow your own learning curve like me and the little man here. We all need a break every now and then."

"The difference is you earned your break. I haven't earned anything." Especially a shot at something lasting with a knockout redhead that blew my mind and made me feel like with every breath I took that had her in it, I was finally, truly waking up from that coma I had been caught in. I didn't want to think about it, so I just nodded a good-bye and climbed up into the truck.

It was a pretty quiet ride back to the Bar. RJ fell asleep and Rome seemed lost in thought. He offered to drop me back off at Wheeler's so I could pick up the Nova, but I told him I would find my own way there. I had work in less than an hour, so I hung out and asked Darcy to feed me until my shift started.

She was mopey, had been since Avett vanished. I knew she was worried about her daughter and at a loss about what to do in order to help her. Plus we were now down a cook and hadn't been able to find anyone to fill the spot. Darcy couldn't work day and night, so Brite had called in an old Marine buddy to fill in the slot until Rome and I could come up with a more permanent solution. I was surprised at how much I was worried about the pink-haired menace myself. I knew she wasn't taking money or beer for herself. I knew she wasn't making excuses for an abusive boyfriend because she was stupid. There was deeper trouble there. The kind I used to be intimately acquainted with, and I hated that Avett had found herself down in that gutter. No one should have to experience that, not even someone as young and foolish as Avett.

The shift started out pretty slow and then picked up when a bachelorette party wandered in. Dixie was frustrated that all the girls wanted to do was flirt with me and make sexy eyes at Church, so she pretty much hung out behind the bar while I handled the group. They were pretty tipsy and extra handsy, but I knew a killer tip was at the end of it, so I didn't mind throwing on the drawl extra thick and making sure I smiled at each and every one of them individually a lot.

At some point in the night the older woman that had become a regular fixture found her way inside, and when she noticed I wasn't locked back behind the bar, she took a seat at one of the tables. She was watching me like I was a steak and she was starving for some red meat. I saw Dixie give me a jaunty wave from behind the bar as I sauntered over to my admirer and asked her what I could get for her. She smiled at me and again I was struck by how easy it would be for me to fall back into my old habits. Easy was so long ago I almost forgot what a golden opportunity looked like.

"You never call me Roslyn." She had mentioned her name several times during her visits since she ditched the boy toy, but I stuck with "ma'am" since I didn't want to give her the wrong idea. I propped a hip on the chair opposite her and gazed down at her steadily.

"Nope. I sure don't."

She batted her eyelashes at me and lifted her fingers to play with the fancy and obviously expensive necklace at her neck.

"You should. I would love for us to be friends."

I tossed my head back and laughed. If her forehead hadn't been chemically pumped with Botox, I bet she would have frowned at me. Instead her mouth went flat.

"You don't want to be friends, Roslyn. You want something I told you isn't on the menu. I'm not interested." For bigger reasons than Royal. There was no way I was even going to crack that door open a little bit. Easy was addictive and I had gone cold turkey. I wasn't going back.

She reached out and clasped my hand as I pushed off the table when one of the bachelorette party started to pull off her clothes. Church caught my eye, shook his head, and moved toward the noise and revelry. I looked down at the woman and her desperate hold on my hand. I didn't remember easy feeling so suffocating. There was something wrong here. There was a level of anxiety and want pouring off of this woman that felt toxic and dangerous. It was like she was throwing down this gauntlet not because she wanted to, but because something was telling her she *had* to. I didn't like anything about it or how uneasy it was making me feel.

"Anything is on the menu for the right price. Do you want to bartend for the rest of your life, Asa? Isn't there something more out there? Don't you want more for yourself?"

I had. I had wanted more than more, I wanted it all, and it had nearly killed me and almost destroyed my only family. Now I just wanted what little I could do for myself and a brief minute of blinding perfection that was Royal Hastings. It was more than enough.

"No, more is an inescapable trap because it's never enough. I'm not sure you're really suggesting what I think you are, but I have to say I'm not exactly thrilled that you think I would be into that."

She let go of my wrist, pushed her chair back, and rose elegantly to her feet. She considered me thoughtfully for a second before picking up her purse. "I like pretty things. Men are complicated and more of a headache than I can endure. My dating days are long past, but I still like to have a good time and be treated well. I've learned one surefire way to make that happen is to offer something most men want, lots of available sex and money. I like to take care of people that take care of me. You're beautiful, Asa. I would make any time we spent together very much worth your while."

I just bet she would and I hated that there was a greedy, snapping buzz under my skin just popping at me to take her up on her seedy and scandalous offer.

"I don't have sex for money and I don't take advantage of lonely women no matter how attractive they may be." At least I didn't do any of those things anymore.

She was a couple years and a near-death experience too late. "I'm not in the market for a sugar mama, Roslyn, and frankly you need to be more careful who you invite to keep you company."

She pursed her lips and moved past me with a haughty air of offense, like I had somehow been the one in the wrong. "I won't be back."

I nodded at her. "That's probably a good idea."

Her gaze skimmed over me one last time. "What a waste." And then she was gone. Church walked over to where I was staring after her with an obviously disturbed look on my face. He lifted a pitch-black eyebrow at me and I wished I could read what was going on in the fathomless dark of his calculating gaze.

"Everything okay?" Church was from somewhere deep in Mississippi, so his drawl was far more pronounced than mine. He even had a really deep and gravelly growl that was kind of similar to Johnny Cash's unmistakable tone. With the voice and the sandy hair that contrasted with his darker complexion, it was no wonder he was constantly fending off overly zealous female admirers. Ladies loved a good brooder and I don't think I had ever met anyone that brooded better than Church.

I lifted a hand and rubbed it over my face. "I just got propositioned to be a gigolo."

"Shit. No kidding?" He turned to look in the direction Roslyn had disappeared in. "That's pretty fucked."

I looked at him and dug my phone out of my back pocket. "I guess no matter how far you come, how far you go, once you've been on the bottom long enough, it just sticks to you. It identifies who you're always going to be. She obviously thought I was the kind of guy that would be up for fucking for a few bucks."

I pulled up Royal's contact info and started to text her. After the weirdness of today something was shifting inside of all that darkness that weighted me down, something reaching desperately for the brightness she brought around with her.

Wanna do something with me tomorrow night?

The new guy needed a shot at shutting down the place on his own and I needed a breather. I just hoped she wasn't working.

He cocked his head to the side and scowled at me. "That's bullshit and you know it. Some chick thinks you're for sale? That's on her not you. I've worked with you for almost a month and I haven't seen a single thing that indicates you're on the take. The bottom is all about perspective. You should see some of the things I've seen, the poverty, the ravages of a lifetime spent fighting a war no one asked for, the loss of everything ..." His mouth pulled tight. "And yet there's joy, happiness, and love in places where there really shouldn't be any. There is life on the bottom if you know where to look, and the only thing that can identify who you are is what you do. You told her to get lost." He nodded like his point was made and walked away from me.

Everyone was suddenly full of advice. Too bad I was far better at giving it than I was at taking it. My phone vibrated in my hand and my heart tripped a little at her response.

In bed or out?

I couldn't help the smile that tugged at my mouth. She was just my speed, fast and a little bit wild.

Both.

Count me in. Where are we going?

I had an idea I thought she would like. She was so good, so law-abiding and upstanding all day long, I wanted to see if she liked walking on the dark side just a little bit.

It's a surprise.

It took a minute but she finally sent back a smiley face and the simple words:

So are you.

It made some of that darkness that always wanted to engulf me not just retreat but vanish altogether.

CHAPTER 12

Royal

I winced as I watched Dominic maneuver himself on his crutches to the seat across from me. He had called, telling me he was going crazy cooped up in his apartment, and asked me to meet him for lunch on my day off. Of course I had told him I would and offered to pick him up since he couldn't drive with his immobilized leg. When I got to the apartment it was obvious his sister was going just as stir-crazy as Dom was, and she told me that he was extra grumpy because he needed to get laid. Dom had barked at her to be quiet even though it made me laugh. Dom was pretty quiet about his private life, had always kept his interests and sexual preferences close to the vest, but he was beautiful and single, so I'm sure the fact he was laid up and stuck in an apartment with his sisters had put quite a damper on his social life.

Surprisingly, instead of feeling guilty and blaming myself for yet another thing I had ruined in Dom's life, I just laughed about it with his younger sister, Ari, and hauled my best friend off to get some lunch. Instead of wallowing in blame and regret, I was determined to enjoy spending time with Dom for the first time in too many weeks to count. It looked like my sessions with the department shrink were starting to pay off ... well, those and hanging out with Asa. There was something about watching him be eaten alive from the inside out by the mistakes of his past that really made me question how tightly I wanted to hold on to feeling like I had destroyed Dom's life when my partner clearly didn't agree that I had. Also, working with Barrett, having him appreciate my contributions to our partnership, had made me realize I really was a good cop with or without Dominic at my back.

He grunted and leaned the crutches up against the chair next to him. I couldn't get over how much weight he had lost since being injured. He looked like a different person.

"You're so skinny."

His green eyes glittered at me in humor. "I know. I don't think I've ever been this thin. Not even in high school."

We both got water and told the waitress we would need a minute. Dom was watching me thoughtfully and I could tell he was trying to figure out if I was finally doing all right or not.

"You look good. Really good. Your new partner must be taking pretty good care of you."

I picked up the water and took a sip. I shrugged and pushed some of my hair over my shoulder. "Barrett's a nice guy, a good cop. I could've ended up with someone much worse."

Dom leaned back in the seat and put his arm across the back of the extra chair. "It wouldn't matter who you ended up with. You're great at your job, Royal. You always have been."

I considered him for a second. "I guess I'm really just starting to understand that about myself. Do you think I just followed you blindly into law enforcement? Do you think I just didn't know what to do without you, so I convinced myself that I wanted to do it?"

His mouth tightened just a fraction and his dark eyebrows furrowed over his eyes. "What do you think?"

The waitress came back over and looked a little annoyed we hadn't even cracked open the menu yet. Dom grinned at her and just the flash of his straight white teeth was enough to make her blush and scamper off giggling.

"I think I'm where I'm supposed to be. I might not have gotten there the right way, but it's a destination I'm happy with now. I don't know, honestly. I wasn't sure I could do this job without you when I went back to work, but it turns out I can, and without you to lean on all the time it makes me better at it."

Something dark moved across his emerald gaze and I realized it sounded like I wasn't thinking about what would happen when he healed up and returned to the force. I opened my mouth to tell him that of course I couldn't wait for him to be my partner again, but he held up a hand to silence me and shook his head slowly back and forth.

"Don't. Just don't. I don't want any more platitudes or apologies. We both know that my shoulder is pretty fucked and I lost a kidney. Plus, with the leg, who knows if I'll have a limp or not. My future in law enforcement is uncertain and that's just the way it is. It's not your fault and I want you to keep doing what you're doing with or without me. All I've ever wanted for you is to succeed and for you to be happy."

I bit my tongue to stop the automatic apology for having any part in his uncertainty. He knew I loved him and he knew I was sorry. The shrink was right. We had a risky job and the situations could have easily been reversed and I could be the one trying to figure out what was next, and there was no way I would ever hold Dom accountable for that.

"I'm working on both of those things, success and happiness." Watching Asa struggle all the time really drove home how important it was to find some kind of peace with my life and what was going on in it.

He lifted both of his eyebrows at me and we finally ordered a couple of burgers from the waitress that was now openly flirting with him.

"Oh yeah? Who's making you happy?" That was why I loved Dom with my entire being. He just knew me so well.

I bit on the corner of my lip. His eyes widened at me and his nostrils flared a little as he deciphered my expression.

"It's the guy we arrested a couple months ago, isn't it? I knew something was up when you were so anxious to push his paperwork through when his sister showed up to bail him out."

I nodded a little bit and then rested my elbow on the table so I could put my chin in my hand. "I like him ... more than like him, really."

"He has a pretty nasty record." Of course Dominic would remember that.

"I know. He won't let me forget about it, in fact."

Dom chuckled. "Well, at least he knows he's not good enough for you."

I tapped the edge of my fingernails on the top of the table and narrowed my eyes at my best friend. "Don't say that. He tiptoes around all these ... feelings." I wasn't sure what else to call the currents that dragged the two of us around when we got together. "Because he thinks something tragic is going to happen and I'm going to be forced to walk away from him. I'm trying to pull him closer with both hands and he's fighting me every step of the way."

Dom grunted. "But he'll go to bed with you."

I felt a fiery blush move up my throat. "Yeah, but I was the one that made all the first moves."

"You're chasing heartache, Royal."

I groaned. "I know, but he's a risk I have to take." I was tired of thinking about my own too-hot-to-handle love life, so I switched the focus back to him. "Why does Ari think you need to get laid?" It was hilarious to hear his little sister state the fact so blandly.

He grumbled a nonanswer as the waitress finally brought our food. I didn't miss the way she lingered by his side until he gave her a little wink and told her everything looked great. It was probably a good thing Dom wasn't interested in the ladies, they would never stand a chance against his rugged good looks and rough-and-tumble charisma.

"I was seeing this guy—briefly. After I got home from the hospital, he never even bothered to stop by. It wasn't like we were serious or anything, but a 'hey, glad you didn't die' would've been nice." He chomped on the burger a little angrily, which made me grin. "Ari thinks I need to find a boyfriend and settle down, but I'm pretty sure that's actually Mom talking and not her."

"Isn't that something you want? Someone to come home to at night? Someone that you know is there for you always?"

I had never actually seen it up close and personal until I met Saint and Nash, but now, with that entire group of friends and family, I knew it existed and was beautiful. I had to admit I wanted it for myself. I wanted it with Asa.

Dom made a face and settled back in his chair. He had to shift his body and I stuck my tongue out at him when his cast banged into me.

"I don't know what I want anymore. I wanted to be a cop, to follow in my dad's footsteps and take care of my family." His pitch dropped and his eyes got darker. "But now my sisters are taking care of me and I don't know what I'm going to do if I can't go back to DPD, so yeah ..." He trailed off. "I just don't know. But I do know that if what you're looking for is some easy kind of happy-ever-after, maybe you should consider looking for it with a guy that doesn't have a criminal record as long as my arm. I know he's gorgeous and that southern drawl is hard to resist, but you know better."

I winced because he might as well have been talking about my mom. She had never been one to resist a pretty face and it never worked out well for her or me when I was growing up. Desperation was such an ugly and dangerous emotion.

"When you first got hurt and I couldn't deal with it, couldn't handle that I felt so responsible, I sort of went a little crazy." I pushed my plate out of the way and leaned a little closer so that Dom could tell what I was saying to him was important. "I was acting irresponsible, spinning out of control, and somehow, someway, Asa was the one that kept catching me before I went all the way over the edge. I was hating on myself, my life, every choice I had ever made, and no one could stop me from choking on it except for him."

Dom copied my pose and we were leaning into each other intently, our voices low, and the seriousness of what we were talking about thick between us. I had never felt for a guy what I felt for Asa Cross, and while Dom would never make me justify my choice, it was important that I impart to him just how serious I was about breaking through that cloak of warning and retreat Asa kept throwing up around us. Even as he stuck out a hand to lure me closer every now and again.

"He's done a lot of wrong in his time, and instead of apologizing for it, trying to repent for it, he's holding on to it so tightly that it's suffocating him from the inside out. He tells me all the time he's a bad guy, he tells me over and over that he's capable of really bad things, and I believe him. I really do. But I also believe if he let go, just forgave himself for some of those mistakes and regrets that weigh him down, he could grow, float to the top of the ocean of past misdeeds, and become the guy he is supposed to be now. His self-loathing made me see how dangerous not being able to forgive myself for what happened to you could be."

Dom swore. "What if he never lets it go, Royal? Are you going to sink to the bottom with him? You're telling me you're willing to drown for this guy that you aren't even really dating?"

I couldn't answer that. Every time Asa told me to go away, told me that we were bound to implode, it just made me more determined to hold on to him. When I had first started chasing him, it had been about him trying to save me from myself. Now I wasn't sure who was trying to save who or if we were just destined to destroy each other like he seemed so certain we were.

"I guess it's a good thing I'm a strong swimmer, and hopefully it won't come to that."

The mood was somber after that and Dom decided to fill me in on every single episode of *Veronica Mars* he had been watching on Netflix while he was laid up. It was so nice to have our easy camaraderie back without all my tension and anxiety keeping distance between us. I could tell Dom had missed having the regular old me around. I stopped to get ice cream to take back to Ari and then the three of us spent the rest of the day hanging out like we used to do when we were kids. It was exactly what I needed to gear up for my date or whatever it was that I was going on with Asa later that night.

I was anxious because he wouldn't tell me what he had planned, and beyond going to breakfast or lunch after I spent the night with him, we hadn't really ever done anything alone together. This was our first, actual, out-of-bed spending time together, and I was practically giddy that he had been the one to initiate it. I could talk a big game about being willing to go under for him, but really I needed Asa to do more than tread water if this thing between us was ever going to go anywhere.

My mom called me as I was leaving Dom's apartment and asked me to stop by her town house for dinner. I could tell by her melancholy tone that she was bummed out, which could only mean things with her newest boy toy hadn't panned out. They never did, but I loved her too much to remind her of that.

Since Asa wasn't meeting me at my apartment until much later, I agreed to swing by. I almost immediately wished I hadn't. My mom was dramatic on a good day, but when she was feeling unwanted and undervalued, she was an emotional nightmare. She had a tendency to act like a cheerleader just dumped by the captain of the football team, her emotional state that immature and erratic when her heart had taken a hit. She was going on and on about getting older, about not being attractive anymore, and I had to tell her that she didn't need any more work done like twenty times. She had sucked me dry and left me feeling bad that I couldn't help her. I could never help her when it came to her issues with men. The way she needed them to love her, to worship her, was scary, and I would be forever grateful that I had always had Dom to keep me clear of that way of thinking.

There wasn't time for me to rest, though, as I raced through a shower then worked to dry and straighten my hair. Since I had no idea where we were going, I wasn't sure what to wear, so I settled on a knee-length, gray-and-yellow skirt that had a high waist and a dangerous slit in the back, and a black top that was asymmetrical and left one of my shoulders bare. I made my hair as straight as I could and it nearly touched the small of my back once I was done, which was a little more elegant than my normal ponytail or messy bun. I kept my makeup minimal so that I didn't look like I was trying too hard, and decided on ballet flats instead of heels since I didn't know if walking was part of Asa's mysterious plan. He had mentioned he finally got a car and he was picking me up, but beyond that I had no clue what was in store for me.

I heard a knock on the door a little bit after eleven and had to take a couple deep breaths to stop from reacting like an overeager teenager about to head to prom. When I pulled the door open I felt my heart trip over itself and my breath halt in my lungs. Asa always sort of looked rugged and rough. It was like he avoided any kind of sophistication on purpose, but not tonight. Tonight he was full of polish and shine. It was making me too stupid to function.

He had on tailored black pants with sharp black wing tips instead of boots and a dark gray button-up shirt with the sleeves rolled up his forearms. His blond hair was artfully arranged in a mess and his face was clean-shaven, making his smirk as I openly ogled him even more endearing. He looked sophisticated and dangerous in an entirely different way than he normally did. He was such a chameleon, slipped so easily from one type of guy into another. It made an apprehensive shiver dance up and down my spine.

"You look nice." My voice sounded breathy to my own ears.

"I have my moments, but you"—his eyes skimmed me up and down and landed back on my face with a warm glow—"are perfect. Are you ready to go?"

I nodded numbly and let him guide me out of the apartment. I was thankful that neither Nash nor Saint popped out of the apartment across the hall since I couldn't form words at the moment. He even smelled different tonight, more expensive and exotic than he normally did. It almost felt like I was going out with a stranger and I wasn't sure if that thrilled me or terrified me. We hadn't even reached his car yet and my head was already spinning.

He stopped in front of a beat-up old Nova. The car had obviously seen better days, but the interior was clean and it had a sexy rumble when he started it. I was actively trying not to fidget or twitch, but there was something about all that smoothness and elegance that was wafting off of him that made me feel very unsure of myself and, for once, unsure of him.

"Do I get to know where we're going yet? I wasn't sure what to wear since you were being so secretive."

He looked at me out of the corner of his eye and the edges of his mouth quirked up. "You could go anywhere dressed in garbage bags and wearing a traffic cone on your head and still look better than anyone else in the room. I don't want to tell you where we're going until we get there. Less chance you'll tell me you don't want to go that way."

Well, that didn't do anything for my nerves at all. "If I'm going with you, I want to go."

He turned his head to fully look at me and his teeth flashed white in the darkness of the night surrounding us. "We'll see."

I didn't say anything else and neither did he, which made the vibrating tension coiling all around me seem even more tenuous. He drove us out of the heart of downtown, then took us to a tract of warehouses and industrial complexes off of Santa Fe that didn't seem to have any kind of place for a date. He parked in front of a corrugated building that I was surprised to see was all lit up and had several cars parked in front of it. I opened my mouth to ask where in the hell we were and what was going on, but he slipped out of the car and came around to open my door before I could. That simple act of chivalry was almost enough to make him seem like regular old Asa again, but when he wrapped an arm around my shoulders and pulled me to his chest as he dropped a hard, possessive kiss on my mouth, there was something in it that hadn't been there before. I felt like he was testing me.

"What is this place?" He closed my hand inside of his own and led me to a door that was around the side of the building and well out of sight of any passersby.

He pulled it open and guided me into a gigantic warehouse space that was full of light, music, and people. It was like a carnival trapped inside the metal walls of a warehouse. I turned to look at him with huge eyes while he just stared down at me and asked, "Would it surprise you if I told you I come from a long line of moonshiners and bootleggers? My mom's dad ran a still way up in the backcountry when she was little and got locked up for it before she had me."

A guy that looked like he had dropped out of the 1920s exchanged some kind of greeting with Asa and shook his hand as he passed him some folded-up bills. I continued to shoot him questioning looks as he guided me through the bodies milling about.

"Asa, seriously, what is this place?"

He found a table off to the far side of the floor that was draped in heavy, tacky red velvet and faced a stage that at the moment was dark and slightly ominous looking. He pulled out a chair for me and waited while I decided if I was going to sit down or bolt for the door. Nothing in these walls seemed permanent. It was like some kind of Technicolor fantasy come to life and every hackle I had was raised up and telling me nothing about this was on the up-and-up.

"It's a pop-up speakeasy. The guy that runs them is from out west and they only come this way once a year. I thought it would be fun."

I crossed my arms over my chest and stared at him. "Is any of it legal?" I knew something was going on with him. He felt more on edge tonight, more intense than he had been since I started chasing him around. He was testing me and I was about to fail, because even as much as I wanted him, I wasn't about to corrupt my own morals to be with him.

A young woman dressed like an old-fashioned cigarette girl stopped by and smiled at us both. She was adorable and I felt like I had been dropped onto an old gangster-movie set. Lord only knew Asa could play the part of Bugsy Siegel with hardly any effort.

"Can I get you anything to drink?"

Asa opened his mouth to answer for us but I interrupted with a curt, "I dunno, do you even have a license to sell liquor?" I swore that if I had my badge I would've taken it out and waved it in her face. I was furious that Asa thought he could bring me to an illegal club and that I would just follow along blindly.

She continued to grin at me like I wasn't being rude at all and nodded her head. "Of course we do. We have these events all over the country, and getting shut down would mean most of us don't get a paycheck."

I felt a hot flush work into my face as Asa ordered us a couple of old-fashioneds, and took the seat he had pulled out for me. His gold eyes burned up at me, hot and bright, and all I could do was stare down at him.

"You did it again." My voice was quiet and with the noise of everyone filling up the big, cavernous space, I was surprised he could make out my words. "You set me up again, Asa. You wanted me to think this was all illegal, you wanted me to think that you were trying to get me to do something wrong, and you wanted me to get mad just like you knew I would. Why? Why are you playing these games with me still?" And he had ruined all the excitement and enjoyment I had been harboring about us being out on an actual date.

"It isn't a game, Red." His accent was all honeyed tones and southern appeal. "You jumped to conclusions and they were the wrong ones."

I literally wanted to stamp my foot in frustration. "Because I asked you a hundred times and you wouldn't say anything. You wanted me to jump to the wrong conclusion. You led me there."

He sighed and reached out for me. He caught me around the waist and forcibly hauled me to him until I was standing between his spread legs. I kept my arms crossed even though my fingers itched to thread through the waves of blond hair that were so close. He gazed up at me, and for the first time there was regret in his eyes that didn't seem like it was killing him.

"I thought it would be fun. A little off the beaten path, and something that fit your peculiar sense of fun. I didn't mean to turn it into some kind of challenge. I didn't mean for you to think I was setting you up. I've had a few off days this last week and I think I was just trying to see if you were going to automatically assume the worst about my motivations." His unspoken words at the end of the sentence were there. I had done exactly what he expected me to do, but I refused to take all of the blame.

"I told you if you were there, I would want to be there as well. I wasn't lying, but I'm not going to compromise my own sense of right and wrong for you, Asa. If you had just explained what all this was, I would've been all over it. I would've been more excited than I already was to spend an evening out with you; you wanted me to fail this test." God, he was always so damn slippery and convoluted. I was never going to get ahold of him tightly enough to keep him.

He leaned forward and I had to move my arms when his forehead landed to rest against my middle. I gave up the fight and curled my fingers through the supersoft hair that dusted the back of his head.

"You're absolutely right." I wish those words thrilled me; instead they made me really sad.

I sighed and looked up as the chipper server swung by with our cocktails. She gave me a saucy look when she noticed the way Asa was curled into me and I wanted to tell her it was hardly as romantic or sweet as it looked.

"Have a seat, the show is about to start." She sauntered off and Asa pulled his head up as his hands curled almost desperately around my waist.

"Will you believe me if I tell you I'm sorry?"

I couldn't answer that because I didn't know, and he was so sorry for so many things I wasn't sure I could handle being one more of them. So instead I stayed silent as he pulled me around him and settled me into the seat next to him. I picked up the fancy drink and instead of sipping on it, savoring the quality ingredients and old-school craftsmanship that went into cocktails back in the day, I slammed the entire thing down, gasping as the bourbon burned.

"What kind of show?" I gurgled the words out as Asa leaned over to place a kiss on my bare shoulder. The tension was gone, but now the air between us was filled with something heavier and denser.

"Burlesque. And yes, they have a cabaret license." He nudged a drink toward me and I picked it up gratefully. I was back to not being sure if I wanted to hurt him physically because of how quick he was to toy with my emotions, or if I wanted to drag him to the nearest flat surface and climb all over him because I wanted to show him that no matter what he did, I wanted him. "Actually Salem knows one of the dancers from when she lived in L.A. She was the one that told me they were coming through town."

Salem had led an interesting life before coming to Denver, and I couldn't say it surprised me that she knew someone that was a burlesque dancer.

"I've never seen a burlesque show before." The lights in the warehouse dipped down, and a soft glow from the stage seemed to be the only light as the Killers started to pump through an unseen sound system. It was an oddly perfect modern musical choice for a place that tried hard to create a Prohibition Era vibe.

Asa's hand slid across the back of my neck under the heavy fall of my hair, and I felt his lips at my ear. It was so dark I could only feel him, not see him, and that was erotic and stimulating as hell. He made my breath catch when he whispered in my ear, "I really am sorry."

I watched as a leggy blonde obviously trying to channel Ingrid Bergman in *Casablanca* slithered onto the stage.

"I know you are. I just wish you didn't have to be." And that pretty much summed up how I felt about all the things he was sorry for in his life. I was glad it was so dark because suddenly I felt moisture, hot and pressing in my eyes. It was a date I would never forget and I didn't mean that in any kind of good way.

CHAPTER 13

Asa

If she had merely been mad at me, annoyed that I purposely played her into thinking that we were doing something wrong, doing something illegal, I could have simply kept kissing her neck and rubbing her arm and I knew she would've forgiven me and let it drop. But she was hurt, disappointed that I had ruined our evening out together, and had done it on purpose. I wish I could say I hadn't known what would happen when I took her, with no explanation, to the middle of nowhere to a place that looked like it should be in a movie or a comic book, but I had. Somehow all of the what-I-had-done and the what-I-would-inevitably-do had converged, and it seemed like a good idea to see how far she was really willing to go for me. I wouldn't really ask her to do anything wrong—hell, I had spent a solid month trying to keep her from doing regrettable things—but the way she was under my skin, the way she somehow shined light into my darkest places, made me want to challenge her.

She was sitting stiffly next to me, her arms crossed over her chest while she held herself ramrod straight to avoid leaning into the arm I had thrown across the back of her chair. Her eyes were locked on the stage as half-naked girl after half-naked girl shimmied and shook her stuff. If I hadn't been such an asshole she would probably have enjoyed herself. As it was, her pretty mouth was in a tight, flat line and there was a delicate flutter in her cheek as her teeth clenched. It made it clear to me that we should probably go and I should probably leave her alone—like I had known from the very start. This was what it was going to be like when I finally did end up doing something that was unforgivable. Only then, hearts would be involved and it would feel a thousand times worse.

I moved my fingers so they could brush against her long fall of hair. In the almost dark of the warehouse it looked darker, with none of the pretty red tones in it, but it still felt like silk. I had said I was sorry and I meant it. If she didn't want to forgive me, I would never blame her for it.

Suddenly her head turned and her dark brown eyes locked on mine. They gleamed in the ambient light and I hated myself just a little bit more when I realized that the reason they were sparkling was the light catching the moisture trapped in their depths. I was supposed to be past the point in my life where I made beautiful, strong women cry over me, and the urge to get on my knees and beg her to forgive me, to plead with her to understand that I tried, I really did, almost overwhelmed me.

Suddenly she moved her chair closer to mine so that we were sitting hip pressed to hip. I curled my arm around her shoulders as she burrowed her face into the curve of my neck. Her lips hit right below my ear as she whispered softly, "Is it always going to be like this with you? Never knowing if this is all real or if it's all a game because you are a broken bastard?"

My fingers flexed against her bare shoulder as one of her hands flattened against my stomach, making the muscles there tense at her touch.

"I don't know." I might not be able to give her an answer that she liked but I could be honest with her. I never wanted to lie to her—or anyone, for that matter. "You are the only woman I've ever spent time with without having a hidden agenda. Most of my life all my time was spent trying to convince people I was on the level, a good guy. I lied about who I was and what I was about with every single breath I took. With you, I seem to be doing the opposite and trying to prove to you every chance I get how awful I can be. I keep giving you the worst and you keep taking it."

She sighed into the hollow she was snuggled into and a tremor raced down my spine when the wet tip of her tongue started to trace along the vein that throbbed right there.

"Why can't you just be here with me, right now? Why do you have to try and prove anything, how good or how bad you are? I'm well aware of how things in the past worked with you and I am very aware of what might happen if we keep this up, Asa. What I don't know, what I want to experience, is this moment with you. This exact second in time where it's just you and me together and what has happened and what could happen doesn't exist. Why can't we do that? Just for a little bit."

I wanted to tell her I couldn't do it. I was holding on so tightly to every single thing I had done to keep myself weighted down in order to prevent those same devious deeds from happening again. I was forever stuck between the past and the future. The present drifted by me, which had been fine until she blazed into my life all tragic and resilient, full of a defiant fire. I wanted to take her to the dark places and let her light them up. I couldn't tell her any of that, though. I wasn't ever going to be a burden she had to bear. Instead I was going to ask her if she wanted to go. I could take her back to her place, take her to bed, and not worry about the past, present, or future. I never got the words out because between one pretty naked girl on the stage and the next, Royal had her small hand inside the top of my pants and behind my belt much like it had been the first night I kissed her.

I sucked in a breath, which gave her more room to maneuver, and she tilted her head back to look at me with lingering sadness and mischief in her coffee-colored eyes. "There are amazing things happening right here in the moment with us, Asa. It would be a real bummer for you to miss any of them because you can't let go of the past and because you're too busy trying to sabotage the future."

Unlike the last time she had her hands down my pants, it wasn't cold and we weren't alone outside. No, this time we were surrounded by people, even though it was dark and the velvet covering the table obscured what she was doing. If anyone bothered to stop and take a closer look, there'd be no mistaking the delicate up-and-down glide of her hand under the fabric of my pants or the way my breath was rushing in and out, making my chest rise and fall rapidly.

"Royal?" It was part question, part plea. Her palm glanced over the tip of my dick as it went from interested to rock hard with the sweep of her fingers. I felt my balls tighten up and I shifted in my seat as she continued the little butterfly-light caresses and brushed her lips lightly across the side of my neck.

"Some games can be fun, Asa, but when one person has to lose before we even start playing, there's no point."

Her fingers curled around my thickening shaft as I went still as stone when the cocktail waitress suddenly appeared next to the table. I gulped and fully expected Royal to stop what she was doing but she didn't, and she didn't bother to look up as I strangled out that we were fine and just needed the bill. The girl gave me a look full of knowing and, if I wasn't mistaken, approval before she walked off. I curled my fingers at the back of Royal's head until they were hopelessly tangled in her hair, and lifted her head off of my shoulder enough that I could kiss her. Her hand dipped even lower in my pants and I groaned against her tongue.

"You need to stop." I rasped the words out because I really didn't want to say them. We were in a public place, and while she might have a wild side, I doubted she would let me throw her on the cocktail table and fuck her like everything inside me was screaming to do.

She sank her teeth into my bottom lip hard enough, and when she coupled that with her soft hand squeezing the base of my dick, I was ready to come on the spot. "You need to stop, too."

Her message was clear. She was all for games as long as they were fun and sexy, but she wasn't going to be a pawn, and if I wanted to enjoy her while I had her, I better get my shit together real quick. She withdrew her hand, skating up under the hem of my shirt and letting her fingers run over the ridges of my abs. The scrape of her nails across my skin had me ready to go off like a rocket, so I threw enough money on the table to cover our bill and probably the table next to ours and dragged her out of the warehouse like it was on fire.

She laughed and it did something to the inside of my chest. I had put tears in her eyes first, but somehow she was amazing enough to understand the stuff I did better than I did myself, and now she was laughing about the disaster of it all. It was like the sun coming through the clouds on a stormy day. She was everything bright the darkness tried to swallow and I wanted inside of her so bad that I couldn't see straight.

I pushed her up against the side of the battered car and closed my mouth over hers. I tunneled my fingers through the hair at her temples and kissed her with every bit of urgency I had. The funny thing was, I had to let go of some of the other stuff I was always holding on to in order to get the message across to her, and with the press of her mouth against mine, the brush of her tongue across my own, I couldn't explain it but I suddenly felt lighter.

"I want to take you home and take you to bed." I sounded rough. There was no smoothness in my typically practiced twang. I sounded impatient and needy, two things I don't think I had ever been before this girl.

"I want that, too." Her hands were back under my shirt and running up and down my rib cage. She was breathing hard as well and she kept stroking her tongue over the dip in the center of her top lip like she was tasting me forever and ever. Her dark gaze was softer than the night sky above us, but her eyes glittered with just as many points of light. She angled her head back so that we were looking at each other and some of the heady passion thrumming between us went the way of something more serious.

"Before I go home with you, Asa, you have to do something for me."

I hated ultimatums, but for her, at this moment, there wasn't much I wouldn't agree to do. "I'll do my best. That's all I can do, Red."

She sighed and leaned forward so that her cheek was resting against where my heart was thundering in my chest. It was so sweet, so touching, and so unlike anything that had ever happened to me in my life that I almost pushed her away because I simply didn't know what to do with it.

"I like you, Asa. I like you more than I think is wise for either one of us, but I can't keep this up. I can't keep dodging everything you keep throwing in the way of doing this thing together if you can't tell me one thing, one simple thing, that you like about yourself as well. I get that you did bad things and were a bad man, but part of moving past that is realizing you aren't there anymore. If you can't do that, I can't do this."

She pulled back and I could see the resolve and the seriousness stamped all over her arrestingly perfect face. The gauntlet had been thrown down and she was making me decide what to do with it. I dug my fingers into her hips and tried to smile at her around the bands tightening in my chest.

"I like that you like me more than is wise. Does that count?" She didn't move, didn't blink, didn't do anything but stare at me until I sighed and let my head fall back on my neck so that I was staring up at the night sky. "One thing?"

"Just one." Her voice was quiet and she sounded sad, but not for herself, and I didn't blame her. What she'd asked me to do shouldn't be that difficult of a task to complete, but for me it felt nearly impossible.

I was quiet for a minute. I had to think. Liking or not liking myself wasn't something I invested a lot of time thinking about. I knew what I had done, where I had been, and I knew I was never going back there. That was what I tended to focus on, not what I was doing now that I had my sister back in my life and a whole bunch of other people invested in me. I pulled her back against my chest and rubbed my chin on the crown of her head. Something inside of me fractured off and settled into a warm hot place when she didn't hesitate to wrap her arms back around my waist to hold me in return.

"I like that even though Ayden and I don't see eye to eye on everything, and even when she has really pissed me off, I've never not loved her. Even when I didn't know how to love, when all I was doing was looking out for number one, I still loved her, and I like that I know how to do it right now. I like that I haven't wasted the second chance I was given to be her big brother and ruined it ... at least not yet."

She made a whimpering sound where she was buried into the center of my chest and I felt her fingers curl into the base of my spine right above my ass.

"Have you ever told her that?"

I blinked a little as she pulled back and smoothed a hand over her long hair.

"No. But I've apologized to her more times than I can count."

Her long lashes dipped down over her gaze as she stepped all the way out of my embrace. "When she comes to town next week, tell her that, Asa. Apologizing for what happened or what might happen is a waste of an opportunity to tell her that you like who you are for her now. That's the moment you need to focus on with her."

We stared at each other for a long, intense moment until she reached up and put a hand on each of my cheeks and pulled me down for a smacking kiss. "Now take me home and take me to bed."

Thank fuck. That was something I could do without all the introspection and soul-scraping thought.

I kissed her back and put her hastily in the Nova so we could race back to her apartment on Capitol Hill. When I parked in front of the Victorian, it was a stroke to my ego that she seemed just as eager to get through the front door as I did. She threw her purse absently on the small table by the door and her keys hit the floor with a clatter as I shut the door behind us. She turned around to face me and I felt every predatory instinct I still harbored claw at me to pounce on her to make her submit and give me everything I wanted. I started to prowl toward her, and whatever she saw on my face must have startled her because she took a stumbling step back. Finally she was getting smart and running away from me. Too bad she had nowhere to go and was now trapped in a room with my raging desire and the raw, unsatisfied edge she had sharpened with her little game at the warehouse.

"I might not be able to pick out a whole lot of things that I like about myself, but I sure can pick out about a thousand things I like about you, Red."

She kept backing up as I stalked toward her, her dark eyes wide in her face as her tongue darted out to slick across her bottom lip. "Is that so?"

I nodded and kept advancing on her until the back of her thighs hit the side of her couch that took up most of the available space in her living room. It brought her retreat to a sudden halt and allowed me to trap her between my hips and the arm of the couch as I caged her in.

"Yep. I like that you won't sway your thoughts on right and wrong. I like that you stand your ground and call me on my stupid shit." As I talked to her I snaked my hands down the outsides of her toned thighs until I got to the hem of her skirt where it hit her knees. I heard her suck in a breath as I started to work the fabric up her legs, making sure to drag my fingertips across every smooth inch of her skin that I could reach. "I like that you have no problem watching girls take off their clothes and dance around. I like that you have a penchant for putting your hands down my pants in public." I grunted in surprise when my hands got high enough to grab ahold of the sweet curve of her ass. I was a little surprised that a whole lot of naked skin was what greeted me, but then I remembered that she had shown up at my place in the middle of the night in nothing but a trench coat, and a grin of appreciation pulled at my mouth. "I really like that you seem to detest underwear and that I now know the next time we go on a date I should be the one putting my hands in your pants."

Her eyebrows shot up high and she didn't say anything as she started to work the buttons loose on my shirt. Her eyes were locked on mine and I could tell she was weighing the validity of everything I was saying to her, so I made sure to be as blunt and honest as possible. I squeezed the firm flesh of her backside and put a knee between her legs once I had her skirt all the way up around her waist so that she was naked and exposed where our hips pressed together.

"I like that even though I almost made you cry, you still let me come home with you. I like that you obviously want for me to be better than I am but you're willing to settle for what's right in front of you. And I really, really like that even though we both know you deserve so much better, I'm the one you want."

She flattened her hands on my chest after she had worked all the buttons loose on the front and smoothed her hands up across my pecs, taking the fabric with her. I shrugged it off and reached a hand up under her fancy top so that I could wrap a palm around the heavy weight of her breast. Her nipple immediately puckered and stabbed into my palm as her eyelids drooped a little and she whispered, "I do want you. This you, Asa, not a better you. Only you."

I brushed my thumb back and forth over the turgid peak, pressing hard into my hands until she was grinding her center against the thigh that was pressed high between her legs and she was bending backward trying to get closer.

I leaned closer to her so that I could kiss her throat where the elegant line was bowed in pleasure. Her hands curled around my biceps to keep herself upright while I nibbled and sucked a tantalizing trail all the way up to her ear. Once I reached it, I traced the tender shell with the tip of my tongue and told her, "And I more than like that you're going to let me turn you around and fuck you against this couch."

She gasped just a little and tried to put a little space between us, but her hands tightened reflexively on my skin and I could feel her heartbeat skip under my still-questing lips. I captured the nipple I was still playing with between my fingers and gave it a tweak that was just on the edge of too hard and her mouth fell into a surprised O.

"Remember, you were the one that told me some games are always better with two people." I felt like I should remind her that she started this with her clever hands in the burlesque club.

I think she could feel all the coiled readiness I was harboring because she simply let out a long breath and reached for my belt. She made short work of it and of my zipper, her touch light as her fingers brushed against the rigid erection she released. The chocolate in her eyes was all melted and warm when she told me, "There is no one else, Asa."

I couldn't tell if it was a question or a statement but either way the answer was no. There wasn't anyone else in my bed and there wasn't anyone else that could chase the dark away and cut some of those iron ties to the past so I was light enough to move toward her. "There is no one else, Royal."

She smiled at me and again I felt something inside me break and then fuse together in a better way. "Good, because that means we don't need to use protection."

She turned around, wiggled herself out of her clingy shirt so that she was in front of me in nothing but her bunched-up skirt and miles of mahogany hair cascading down her back. For a split second I wondered if I had died again and this was what my heaven looked like. I reached out a hand to move her long curtain of hair aside so that I could sweep my hand down the flawless curve of her spine. I stepped closer so that I could kiss the back of her neck, which made her mewl softly and rub her naked backside against my throbbing cock. There was no more talking after that. There was no more trying to convince her of anything because she knew I wanted her and she wanted me, too. The time for any kind of games was long over.

I stepped up close behind her and wrapped an arm around her waist so that I could bend her over just enough that I could hold her where I wanted her. I spread her legs farther apart with my own and urged her to brace her hands on the couch cushions in front of her. She gave me a speculative look over her shoulder and I just smiled at her with a lot of teeth. She bit down on her lower lip and I groaned as her hair slid in a sexy fall across one of her shoulders. Everything about her was some kind of perfect, so I needed to focus on doing exactly what she told me to do and appreciate everything about every single moment I got to have with her.

I pressed in close, heard her mumble in pleasure as my dick glided along her slick folds. I was moving fast but she was clearly ready, and nothing was sexier than that. I pressed in, felt her hips tilt back to meet me, and suddenly I was engulfed in all her sweet fire and heat. I let out a litany of swearwords as her body immediately clamped down on mine while I pulled back out and slid back in. I didn't want to rut into her, didn't want to pound against her in a reckless and thoughtless manner. But the combination of being inside of her without anything between her quivering flesh and my own, and the way she kept looking over her shoulder at me and urging me on with her hot gaze, was too much temptation to withstand.

I clamped her to me, thrust against her until the couch moved, and closed my eyes as I was sucked into a vortex of things that felt too good and too powerful to name. At some point I thankfully remembered I had a free hand that wasn't holding her up and let it find its way to that hidden place between her legs. She was slippery and slick. She was hot and tight. She was as close to the edge as I was, so all it took was one swirl with my index finger and one little pinch between my thumb and forefinger to send her over. As soon as she gasped my name and broke across me in a flood of release and ecstasy, I was quick to follow.

It was an orgasm that started at the bottom of my feet and blazed a trail up my legs until it hit my lower spine and nearly had me collapsing on top of her as we both fell forward onto the couch. I had to move so I didn't crush her and that ended up with both of us lying with our legs dangling over the edge, half dressed, her back to my chest as we both panted and tried to catch our breath. I'd never been with anyone so fully before and it felt different. Not just on a physical level, but an emotional level as well. I smoothed my hands over her flat stomach and blinked dumbly up at the ceiling.

"You're right. There are really great things in this moment." I wanted it to be flirty and fun like I usually was after sex, but I could hear the longing in my own voice.

She put her hands on top of mine as we just lay there and absorbed what had changed between us tonight. "Every moment is what you make of it, Asa."

I was starting to wonder if there would ever be enough moments between her and me because so far they were some of my favorites … even the bad moments with her had been better than great moments I had shared with anyone else.

CHAPTER 14

Royal

"So you and my brother, huh?" I had been preparing myself for this conversation all night long. So far I had been lucky, most of the evening was taken up by talk of babies and Ayden catching up with the rest of the girls, but I knew there was no way to avoid this subject all night.

Shaw and Cora had lost themselves in mommy business, Salem was in deep conversation with Sayer, who was her boyfriend Rowdy's sister. She was quizzing the elegant-looking blond woman about the current condition of her own sister, who had bailed on girls' night, which apparently wasn't uncommon, as Poppy rarely left the house for anything other than work, according to Salem. Saint had sent me a text an hour ago that she would try and make it, but there had been an emergency at the hospital, a little boy rushed into the ER with severe burns over most of his body. So even if she did get out of work in time for a drink, she probably wasn't going to want to hang out at the Bar with the rest of us. All of that led to Ayden seeing her opportunity to ask me about what was going on between me and Asa, and moving in for the kill.

Her eyes were the exact same burnt-amber color as Asa's, which was a little disconcerting as she stared steadily at me. I couldn't tell if she asked the question wanting a simple answer or an explanation, or if she was just stating the fact that I was, indeed, sleeping with her brother on an extremely frequent basis. I cleared my throat a little nervously and rolled the beer bottle I was holding between my palms.

"I like him." I winced a little as her black eyebrows danced upward, and gave her an awkward shrug. "I care about him a lot." As it was, I was well on the way to being head over heels in love with him, even if the ride was giving me whiplash. I never knew which Asa I was going to get when I went over to his place after the Bar closed or when he appeared at my door during the night. Sometimes it was the fun and flirty charmer just out for pleasure and good times. Sometimes it was the quiet and brooding boy stuck in the past, obviously choking on regret and remorse but unwilling to move past it. Sometimes it was the rough, demanding man that wanted more than I was ready to give him, the man that still liked to push and play games. Sometimes it was the sharp-minded man that was obviously meant for other things than bartending in a dive.

I tolerated all of those different versions of him because more often than not I got the guy I wanted to be with forever. The witty, too-smart-for-his-own-good, devilishly and effortlessly endearing version of Asa that only made an appearance when he forgot to worry about all the things he had done and ignored all the ways this undeniably significant thing between us could go wrong. That guy made putting up and navigating around all the other ones worth the time and effort even if he only appeared every once in a while.

"Caring about Asa can be a draining task." Ayden's voice was raspy, made even more so by the tequila she had been downing at a steady pace for most of the evening. If I'd had as much to drink as her, I would be on the floor in a fetal position under a table. Ayden didn't even seem buzzed while her eyes were intent on mine. I could feel her weighing and sizing up how she felt about my involvement with her older sibling.

"It can be." But when the Asa I wanted to love was around, it was so worth the exhaustion.

Both of us turned to look at the bar, where Asa was watching our exchange with narrowed eyes. The Bar was pretty busy, so Dixie and the new girl, Becca, had been taking care of us for most of the night. He had stopped by to hug his sister and to plant a hard kiss on my mouth with a warning look at Ayden before he headed back to the bar. It was a statement that couldn't be missed. I knew she was going to want to weigh in on the situation, but so far it hadn't really gone like I expected. Instead of the third degree or blatant disapproval, she seemed oddly curious as she watched me watch him.

"I worry about him all the time still." The corner of her mouth tilted up in a grin. "Every single day I have to fight with myself not to call and check up on him. Leaving him here just when things were starting to fall in place for him was one of the hardest things I have ever done."

I cleared my throat a little and shifted on the chair. "He seems pretty adept at taking care of himself, and one of his biggest fears is that he's going to disappoint you again, so it keeps him on the straight and narrow."

She puffed out a breath and her bangs fluttered over her winged brows. "He's a survivor for sure, but there is a difference between merely getting by and living the life you're supposed to live. I had no idea how love was supposed to look or feel until I met Jet. I wasn't living a full life until he gave me the strength to let go of everything else."

Her eyes flared hot, gold just like Asa's did when he was excited about something. I was a tiny bit jealous that just saying her man's name had that effect on her.

"I want Asa to do more than survive, Royal. I want him to finally be happy for once in his life. I want him to do more than just get by. I want him to have something that is his and his alone that he doesn't ever feel like he has to fight for."

I gulped a little bit as emotion started to clog my throat. I set my almost empty beer down on the table in front of me and twisted my fingers together. "He has all of that within his grasp, but his hands are too busy holding on to the past and reaching for the future to grab on to it."

She opened her mouth and then snapped it closed as she leaned back in her chair. She crossed her arms over her chest, covering up the Valkyrie straddling a flaming guitar and the word ENMITY as she did so. The shirt with the ripped-off sleeves that showed the sides of her black bra seemed out of place with her pointy red cowboy boots, but it was Ayden, so she rocked it and looked perfect doing so.

She shook her dark head. "I know he is. I was hoping that since he can't stop staring at you, and keeps looking at me like he wants to drop-kick me across the bar, maybe you had convinced him to let some of that go. We can't go back in time and we can't predict the future. He's living in suspended animation."

I shifted again as the jukebox switched to an old Christina Aguilera song, which had several middle-aged ladies climbing up from the table they were sharing and doing some serious booty shaking. It made me grin even though the topic of conversation wasn't exactly cheerful.

"Every once in a while he puts it all away, and every now and again I feel like he's reaching for a lifeline to stop himself from sinking. It gives me enough hope that I'm willing to stick around and see how it all plays out."

She ran her finger around the rim of her shot glass and licked the salt off. "What are you going to do if you ever have to lock him up again? He's a trouble magnet. Even when he's trying to keep his nose clean."

I sighed and shoved my hands through the front of my hair. "I keep telling myself I'll cross that bridge if I ever come to it." I leaned closer to her when the dancing women moved a little closer and their laughter got loud enough that I had to talk over it. "Did you know he was willing to do time, to sit in jail for a crime he didn't even commit because he's so twisted up on the inside about everything that happened before? How can someone even function with that kind of guilt filling them up?"

My voice caught and I let out a shuddering breath. I started a little when Ayden's hand reached out and landed on top of the fists I hadn't even been aware I was making. I mean I knew about guilt and the way it could affect a person's thinking. My own guilt had kept me away from Dom when he needed me most, but I let it go when I realized it was poisoning everything in my life. I would always feel bad for what happened that night in the alley and I would never get over seeing Dom fall, but it couldn't be the only moment that defined my life or my career. I needed Asa to realize everything he was missing by refusing to let go.

Ayden's fingers squeezed mine, and I had to squeeze back because she was the only other person alive that could understand how hard caring for a man like Asa could be.

"That's why I worry. All he's done since I brought him to Denver is function. Nothing more and nothing less. That's no way to live. But now he watches you like you matter, like he's worried I'm going to scare you off with all the stories of his past misdeeds. So I have hope, a thin, tiny thread of hope that there is finally something out there in the world that he's going to realize he has to wake up and live for."

I looked over my shoulder toward the bar. He was leaning against the top and talking to a really good-looking man that had a dark beard and colorful tattoos scrolling up the side of his neck. Asa was obviously deep in conversation with the guy, but his eyes were locking on our table and I could tell he was watching me and Ayden intently. I gave him a little grin to let him know everyone was going to make it out alive and I saw his shoulders fall a little as a bit of the tension left him. I turned back to Ayden and tilted my chin up in a defiant manner.

"I want to wake him up."

She laughed, a warm and rough sound that matched her whiskey-tinted gaze. "Atta girl."

Suddenly Cora stood up from the other side of the table and clapped her hands together. It was amazing that just a few extra weeks had led to her looking actually pregnant in other places than her boobs. Her face had rounded out a little and her tiny midsection had the barest hint of an actual baby belly starting to show. She was probably the cutest, most rock-and-roll expectant mom in the world and I didn't miss the way Salem stared at that little bump with open envy.

"We should dance." She hooked a thumb over her shoulder to where the older ladies were still getting their groove on in an uncoordinated and messy show of undiluted joy. "That's going to be us one day, ladies. Escaping the men and children at home so we can have a night out to ourselves." She laughed. "Granted we'll be more colorful and have better haircuts, but that's so going to be us."

Sayer held up her hands and rose to her feet. She was ridiculously classy and looked like she had just left the courtroom. "Sorry, but I don't dance, ever." She pushed some of her perfectly sleek blond hair over her shoulder and looked at the bar. Something in her blue gaze shifted and at first I thought she was looking at Asa, which made me scowl, but when I turned around I noticed the bear of a man at the bar had shifted in his seat and the two of them were locked in an unwavering stare-off. "Um, I'm just going to go tell Zeb hi really fast."

Somehow saying hi had never sounded so much like "strip naked and fuck on the bar." That was a lot of sexual tension happening and it was thick enough to fill the space separating the two of them. With the modern-day-mountain-man look Zeb was sporting and the clearly defined muscles straining against his plain, white T-shirt, I couldn't say I blamed her. There was always something appealing about a man that looked like he could take care of business, no matter what that business might be.

Ayden pulled me to my feet and I suddenly found myself not only in the middle of bumping and grinding but also doing shots. The night faded into a blur of drinks and laughter, more dancing—who knew Ayden was a two-stepping machine?—and a lot of hugging, and hushed talk of what it was like to have sex with a guy that was pierced "down there." It sounded like a whole lot of fun, but I would take a guy that whispered dirty, sexy things to me with a southern drawl over a guy with metal in his junk any day. There was also a lot of gushing about their men and babies, and of course everyone had to grill Cora on when she was actually gonna tie the knot. It was so much fun I couldn't believe I had ever been hesitant to throw myself all in with this entire group. For someone that had never had friends, that had never really been comfortable around other girls like this, I hit it out of the park by being so fortunate to land with this crew.

Since Cora and Shaw couldn't drink because of all the mommy stuff in their lives, they were tasked with getting Ayden and Salem back to their men in one piece. Sayer had slipped out at some point when we were all rocking out to Guns N' Roses without saying good-bye. Though I could have easily hitched a ride with the other girls, Asa sent Dixie over while I was shimmying and shaking to an Eminem song to tell me that he wanted me to hang out until he was done closing the bar and that he fully expected me to go home with him. Uh, yes, please.

I told her to tell him that was fine, but if I was going to stick around he needed to make it worth my while. His response had been to send his bearded friend over with another round of shots and the order to keep me company and keep me out of trouble until he was done working.

Surprisingly, Zeb was really nice and superfunny beneath his intimidating appearance. I liked the way his emerald eyes glittered with easy humor and the way his teeth flashed straight and white in his ruggedly handsome face. Not to mention those muscles he had for days were drool-worthy and totally worth checking out every time they flexed as he brought the beer bottle up to his mouth. I had to give it to Sayer, she had good taste. He seemed fascinated by the fact I was a cop and asked me a hundred questions about my job. At some point in the conversation he mentioned that he had served time, which normally would have made me uncomfortable and turned the conversation awkward, but he was so open about it and so matter-of-fact that I just rolled with it and went on to ask him how he knew Rowdy's sister.

Bringing up the icy-looking blonde shifted the mood of the conversation from mellow to something more intense. He told me Sayer had hired him to fix up her crumbling Victorian. He was obviously interested in the pretty lawyer and seemed slightly annoyed by the fact. It was really cute—well, as cute as a guy that was as masculine and burly as Zeb could be. We chitchatted until Dixie wandered over and told us that she was done and wanted to lock the door on her way out. Zeb told her he would walk her to her car as we all got to our feet.

I looked over to the bar, where Asa had braced his arms wide apart and was watching all of us. I smiled at him a little sloppily and he lifted a hand to crook a finger at me, beckoning me toward him.

I let out a breath and felt my heart flutter. "Holy hell, is that hot."

Dixie snickered next to me and Zeb chuckled. She tugged the big guy's arm. "Yeahhhhh ... and that's our cue to go. Have a good night, Royal."

I absently waved at her and started toward the bar. Asa pushed off the bar rail and grabbed something from the back shelf behind him. When I reached the bar he had turned off most of the lights except for the ones that lit up the actual bar top and the space behind it. He had also come around the other side, so when he got to where I was waiting, he dropped his head and gave me a stinging kiss that made me grab on to the front of his plaid shirt with both hands.

"Everything go okay between you and Ayd?"

His voice was gruff as he pulled out a couple of the bar stools to make space at the bar for us and set down a small, squat bottle of something. I was more than a little bit drunk, so I just nodded and moved easily when he suddenly turned and put his hands on my waist to lift me up. I squeaked in surprise when he turned with me trapped in his grip and set me down on the edge of the bar with my legs dangling over the edge. He put his hands on either side of my hips and looked at me closely since we were eye to eye.

"Seriously. I know you were worried about what she was going to say about us spending time together and she can be pretty fierce when she wants to be."

I leaned forward and shoved my hands into his thick, blond hair and sighed. "She loves you so much. She wants you to have a good life."

I bent just a little bit so I could kiss him on the end of his nose.

"You have to be a good person in order to have a good life, so I think that's a bit of a stretch." His words rumbled out of his chest as he took a step closer to me, which forced my legs apart to make room for him. His words made me so sad that I suddenly wanted to cry, but that also could have been fueled by the copious amounts of tequila I had consumed over the night.

"There is good mixed in with all the bad, Asa. You just refuse to see it or acknowledge it." He grunted at me and then skimmed his hands under the hem of the blousy, off-the-shoulder shirt I had worn over leggings for girls' night. His palms were warm and rough as they traveled over my ribs, taking the fabric with them. My hair poofed up and fell in a static-y mess around my now-naked shoulders. His gaze went molten as it traveled over my bared torso and my breasts encased in a lacy, purple bra.

"I see you, Royal. There is so much good in you that I never really know what to do with it."

His hands snaked around behind me and hit the clasp on my bra. It took my sluggish brain a second to realize what his intent was as I was suddenly topless on top of the bar. I gasped a little and my gaze automatically shot to the series of black orbs secured to the ceiling that hid the surveillance cameras I knew were all over the place. I automatically went to lift my arms to cover myself up but he wouldn't let me.

"Asa, Big Brother is watching." I sounded a little strangled because he had leaned forward and was rubbing the tip of his nose against the puckered peak of one breast.

"I'll take care of it. You don't even want to know what I walked in on Brite and Darcy doing in the storeroom, and I guarantee that I knock whenever Cora is here and the back office door is closed. Not to mention the penchant my sister seems to have for disappearing into bathrooms with Jet. I want to have a drink before I take you home. Just roll with it, Red."

I whimpered a little as he turned his attention to the other nipple and moved his hands to my backside to pull me closer to the edge of the bar, so the ridge in his pants was pressing tightly against my center.

"I need to be topless for you to have a drink?" His hair was like raw silk between my fingers, and now he was doing that swirling thing he did with his tongue around each nipple that made me forget my own name.

"You do." He breathed the words across my now-damp flesh and it made me quiver from head to toe.

He took a slight step back and I felt like I was going to drown in the rivers of whiskey desire that made up his liquid-gold gaze. He put a hand in the center of my chest and nudged me backward until I was braced on my hands and my head was almost hanging over the other side of the bar. I couldn't see his face anymore at this angle but his reflection was clear in the mirror that ran all the way behind the bar. He was looking at me like he wanted to own me. The look on his handsome face was enough to have my core going liquid and clenching in want, aching with a need so sharp it almost hurt.

"Asa?" He shushed me as he traced a random pattern across the taut skin of my stomach with the blunt edge of his fingernail. I stiffened automatically when his fingers hooked under the stretchy top of my leggings. "What exactly are you doing?"

It was a stupid question. I knew what he was doing, I was just having a hard time rationalizing that I was actually allowing him to get me naked on top of the bar. I felt like I should probably be protesting harder, should be using some sort of reasonable argument to prevent this from going down. But I wasn't. It was hot, the sight of him standing between my legs as he worked my pants down my long legs and tossed my heels somewhere over his shoulder. He sighed in pleasure when he encountered nothing underneath, which I knew he would do. I had just anticipated that taking place at his place, not here. I don't think he knew I could see him in the mirror, so it was the first time I actually got to see what others saw when he looked at me. It was beautiful.

His eyes were heavy-lidded and focused only on me. His nostrils flared in excitement and I could see the way he actually licked his lips in appreciation. He looked hungry and almost as needy as I always felt around him. This was the Asa that kept me rooted to the spot. This was the Asa I could have if I got him to let go of everything else he was holding on to. This was the Asa I no longer wanted to deny that I loved.

He dipped his head down and kissed me right above my belly button, and let his tongue dip in and out of the small indent. It made me laugh, and he finally lifted his head and met my upside-down gaze in the mirror. I felt like the heat radiating in that glowing gaze would fuse us together forever.

He smiled at me and my heart tried to fall out of my chest and land at his feet. He straightened and picked up the bottle he had set down on the bar moments ago.

There was a small pop as he slipped the top off of it and the earthy and musky scent of scotch hit my nose. I knew what he was going to do, thought I was prepared for it, but somehow having a gorgeous guy pour a shot down the side of your throat and then chase it all the way down your body just wasn't something anyone could really prepare for.

The booze trickled across the top and down the side of my breast. A little bit of it found its way all the way across my stomach and pooled in my belly button, and there was the trail of liquid that hit the point of my body where it was wrapped around him and ran over the inner curve of my thigh. Asa used his mouth to get every single last drop. The sensation of his mouth moving over every single surface of my skin was electrifying. When he finally got to that sensitive spot where my leg curved in to the parts of me that were all kinds of flutter and greed, I lost my ability to hold myself up anymore and collapsed on the bar with my hair falling into God only knew where on the other side of it. I could see his blond head between my legs, felt the wonderful torture he was subjecting me to with his tongue and teeth. It was when he reached up with his one free hand, the one that wasn't busy teasing and playing with all the wet heat between my legs, and laced our fingers together that I lost it.

It was so sweet, so tender, and so out of character for him that it made me fall apart and burst into a million and one tiny slivers of pleasure and love. In the mirror I watched him as he watched me break for him. His eyes glowed from someplace deep within and I wondered how anything survived inside that kind of fire within him.

I lay there, unable to move at all as he rose to his feet. He put his hands on the bar next to my hips and leaned over me. He placed a light kiss on the center of my breastbone, and then one on each cheek. When his mouth finally settled on mine, I tasted myself and scotch, and it was enough to have my girly parts getting worked back up again. I curled my free arm around his shoulders and threaded my fingers through the back of his hair.

"A good life doesn't seem so far out of reach, looking at you laid out before me with the taste of you all over my tongue, Red."

The words were so quiet I almost thought I had imagined them but when he kissed me again it was so soft, so sweet, and I could swear it had part of his heart in it, and I knew that I would give everything I had in me to give to make him wake up and be right here in this place with me, right now. This was too good to miss and he deserved to experience it even if he didn't think so.

I traced the outside of his ear and felt him shiver. "You better make sure Rome doesn't get more than he bargained for when he comes in tomorrow and looks at the video feed from tonight."

He chuckled and straightened up. He moved away from me to gather my scattered clothes and helped me off the bar so that I could get dressed. He had to hold me up when all the blood rushed back out of my head, which led to some pretty intense kissing and groping since I was still naked. It made us both groan and he reluctantly pulled away, telling me he was going to make sure the video wasn't going to pop up anywhere it could return to haunt either of us. His smile turned from playful to predatory in the blink of an eye as he walked backward and told me:

"My turn when we get back to my place."

My oh my, I really LOVED taking turns.

CHAPTER 15

Asa

"Have you talked to Mom at all lately?" Ayden asked the question from the other side of the Nova where she was fiddling with the old seat belt and staring out of the window. She was getting ready to head back to Austin with Jet on Saturday and had asked to spend the day with me before she left.

I missed her, but sitting around my apartment all day chitchatting sounded like zero amounts of fun, so I picked her up and asked her to come along with me on an errand I had been itching to do for over a month. So far the conversation had been pretty superficial and mellow, but now that she had brought up family, I knew it wasn't going to stay that way for long.

"A couple months ago. She called from somewhere in Nevada. The guy she had hooked up with ditched her at a truck stop and she wanted money to get home." Only I wasn't stupid and I knew money to get home really meant money to stick in a slot machine until the next trucker came along.

"Did you send it to her?" Ayden sounded mad. She always did when our mom came up in conversation. The way we were raised meant we never really had a shot at much. I was so proud of Ayden for clawing her way out of the gutter on her own the way she did.

"No. I told her I would come and get her and she could come stay with me until she got back on her feet. She hung up on me and I haven't heard from her since."

Ayden snorted and turned away from me to look back out the window. "Figures."

I couldn't disagree with her and had nothing to add, so the conversation sort of waned until the neighborhood around us really started to shift to obviously unsavory and rough. Her dark head turned to look at me again and her eyes narrowed just a fraction.

"Why do you want to talk to this girl? She stole money from Rome, she sounds ungrateful and unapologetic. Why are you wasting your time reaching out to her?"

For weeks I had been thinking about Avett. About the way she just disappeared, the way no one had heard from her, including her parents. I couldn't shake the feeling that there was more to her terrible attitude than her being an ungrateful and spoiled brat. I knew all too well that that level of defiance and chilly disregard for the way her actions affected others had to come from someplace deep and dark that was so far down very few people could actually understand or recognize it. I was intimately familiar with self-loathing and could feel it rolling off the younger woman in waves.

I cocked my head toward my sister and lifted a questioning eyebrow. "I think there are those that would question why you wasted not only your time but most of our childhood on me, Ayden. Eventually we all need someone to try and save us; even if they fail, the fact that someone tried might be what matters most in the end."

She blinked eyes that matched mine slowly and crossed her arms over her chest. "You saved yourself. You fought to come out of that coma. You turned your life around when you came to Denver. You have said a million and one times how sorry you are for the things that happened in the past. You were your own savior, Asa. No one did any of the work for you."

I pulled the Nova to a stop in front of a duplex that had clearly seen better days. It wasn't a rusted-out trailer in Kentucky, but it might as well have been. I turned off the ignition and sat back in the seat so I could turn to look at Ayden. She was watching me carefully and I could see how frustrated she was with the entire conversation in the way her shoulders were tensed up and the way her hands had curled into tight balls on her lap. It was the way she used to look whenever I got into trouble and she had to do something desperate and drastic to get me out of it. I reached out a hand and put it on top of her fists.

"I died in that hospital, Ayd. There were no angels playing harps. There was no redemption and repentance. I died and it was very clear that I was going to get exactly the kind of fate I had been courting with all the messed-up shit I had been doing to other people. All I could see was every wrong I had ever committed and every bad decision I had ever made exploding all around me. For once I could see how all of that affected you. I was dying, and I knew what was waiting for me on the other side, yet I couldn't go knowing that was all you were going to have to remember me by. I had to come back and give you something else to hold on to, some kind of good memory to go with the endless miles of bad I laid at your feet. I wanted to have the chance to show you I could be the kind of brother you deserved all along, so no, I didn't save myself—you saved me. Just like you've always done for my entire life."

I saw her bottom lip tremble until she snapped her teeth around it to keep it still. Her fists unclenched below my palm and she curled her shaking fingers around my hand and her already husky voice rasped with even more emotion when she told me what I think I had needed to hear from her all along.

"I have always been proud that you're my brother, Asa. Yes, there have been times in the past I would have gladly fed you to the wolves, and it's no secret that I had to leave home because I didn't know what to do to help you anymore, but we both made it out alive and are better people for it. I know you're sorry for the way things went down when we were younger, but I need you to open your eyes and take some credit for the way you have turned it around to make things the way they are now. I've long since come to terms with the Asa from my childhood. What I want to do is love the Asa that's here with me now. You need to let go of those boulders weighted with all the bad things from the past that are dragging you down before you get crushed under them."

It was eerily similar to what Royal had been telling me the deeper and deeper I sank in with her. I don't think I was ready to let any part of those stones go just yet, but a sexy redhead was slowly and surely eroding bits and pieces of the rock the more and more time I spent with her. By the time she was done, maybe she would be able to carve out something that was worthwhile, something that didn't eviscerate me to look at.

I leaned over enough that I could kiss Ayden right on the center of her forehead between her midnight eyebrows and I felt her let out a shuddering sigh.

"I'm never going to let you down again, Ayd. That is the one and only thing in the entire world that I can promise and know it's a promise I will keep."

We stared at each other for a long and silent moment. The seriousness of the words I had said to her and the fact that I could see that she understood that I really, truly meant them finally worked to absolve me of some of the guilt that seemed to suffocate me whenever I thought about the things she had done to keep me safe.

We both needed a little bit of space and a little bit of air, so we were eager to get out of the car. I told Ayden she could wait on the curb if she wanted, but she just rolled her eyes at me and followed me up to the front door of the duplex. I knocked on the door and winced as it rattled in the frame. Several large flakes of peeling paint landed on the top step next to my boots, and memories of a trailer built like a tin can started to dance behind my eyes. Why Avett would stay here when her parents were so willing to give her a handout was beyond me, but something kept hounding me that there was more to the story than anyone was seeing.

Nothing happened after the first knock or the second and Ayden asked if we could just go. I contemplated actually forcing my way inside the building but figured with my luck someone would call the cops on me and I'd end up back in Royal's squad car, this time for trespassing. It wasn't like I actually had any proof something fishy was going on with Avett, just my gut instinct that the pink-haired hothead had somehow bit off more than she could chew with that tweaker boyfriend of hers.

Ayden had turned and was walking back to the Nova muttering under her breath about little girls not knowing what was best for them when the door suddenly cracked open. One of Avett's hazel eyes peeked out. Even with just the sliver of her showing, I could tell she was a mess. Her dark hair was showing at the crown of her head where the pink typically lived, she looked thin and pale. There was an ugly scratch on her cheek. The hand that was gripping the door had a broken nail on each finger with cracked and scabby wounds healing on each knuckle. The girl looked like she had been in a fight; I wasn't sure, but if she had, she didn't look like the victor.

"What are you doing here, Opie?"

Her voice was strained, scratchy in the way one got after screaming or yelling for a long period of time. The entire picture made me frown and had my hackles rising up.

"People are worried about you. I thought I would come check on you and see if I could put their minds at ease." No way was that happening now. Brite would lose his ever-loving mind if he saw his only child in this condition. "The druggie boyfriend do that to you?"

I crossed my arms over my chest to show her I wasn't going anywhere in a hurry and she pulled the door open another inch. Her bottom lip was split open and it took every ounce of self-control I had not to tense up in rage when I saw the black-and-blue marks that ringed her neck like some kind of horrific necklace.

Avett moved several strands of faded pink hair out of her face and adopted a pose very similar to my own. Even bruised and battered, she was still a defiant little thing, and I had to admire her spark even if it was firing in all the wrong ways.

"I haven't seen him in a few weeks. He said he was in trouble and took off right after I gave him the money I took from the bar. This is from the guys that came looking for him. Apparently he's in bigger trouble than he led me to believe. They thought I was lying when I told them I didn't know where Jared was. This"—she pointed a finger at her battered face—"was their way of persuading me to tell them the truth about his whereabouts."

Her raspy voice wobbled and a chill slid up my spine. I knew all about how bad men tried to use the people in other bad men's lives to try and get information. I would bet all my meager belongings that what I could see was only half of what she had been forced to endure while trying to protect her useless man.

"Why are you still here, Avett? Go home. Let your dad take care of you, let your family help you out. Where do you think this road you're on is going?"

Ayden had taken a few steps back toward the door and Avett shifted her gaze to my sister as she quietly told her, "This road ends up with you hating yourself and walking away from people that love you. It dead-ends with you sitting by the bedside of someone you love praying for them to wake up from a life-threatening injury because there's always more trouble around the corner and eventually it's going to catch up with you and with them."

The young woman shook her head and laced her fingers together as she took a step back toward the open doorway. "You don't understand. Jared isn't a bad guy. He loves me, he just has a problem. He needs me."

Ayden and I exchanged a look. We both knew it was impossible to try and help someone that wasn't willing to help themselves first.

Ayden's voice was hard when she told the younger woman, "His problems don't automatically have to be your problems."

"Rome didn't press charges, your parents bent over backward to give you a shot at a steady and normal life. I'm here because you remind me just a little bit too much of myself right before everything went to shit. How many chances do you think you get before your luck runs out?" I laughed drily and lifted a hand to rub the back of my neck. "Because let me tell you, when the luck runs out it's a really scary thing, and what's waiting for you on the other side isn't something I would wish on my worst enemy."

She just shook her head again, and shoved her mangled fingers through her hair and whispered, "I love him."

She gave me a look that let me know the conversation was over and then turned on her heel and disappeared back inside the doorway.

I stood there in silence for a long moment trying to situate how I felt about what had just happened. Feeling helpless to help someone wasn't something I was used to and I couldn't say that I cared for it very much. Ayden grabbed my elbow and gave me a little tug to get me moving. She bent her head and rested her cheek on my shoulder.

"That kind of love kills." Her voice was quiet and I could hear all kinds of memories and fear twisted through it.

"It's not love."

Ayden murmured her agreement, and we both fell silent as we got into the car and headed back toward downtown.

"So what are you going to do about her? She can't just stay in that place while people are looking for her junkie boyfriend and using her as a bargaining chip." It was all too familiar to my sister and I wished I had refused to let her come with me. She didn't need any kind of reminder about the way things had been for us back in the day.

"I'm going to talk to Brite and my guess is he'll go in there and bodily move her out of that crack den. I know he's frustrated with the choices Avett has been making over the last few years, but there is no way he's going to sit by and let her purposely put herself in danger over some loser with a drug problem."

Ayden let her head flop back on the seat and shifted so she could put her boots up on the dash. If the car had been in pristine condition, I would've had a fit, but considering it was still a work in progress, I figured I could let it slide.

"Brite might not get a choice in the matter." I knew she was talking about me and all the trouble that I used to actively bring right to our doorstep. She turned to look at me and I felt my heart along with several pieces of the soul that I thought had long been lost start to fuse back together when she told me softly, "You're a good man, Asa. You might not see it because you're so used to looking at the man you were before, but you are right here in front of me and I can see the good shining out of you. The fact I can see it means you should be able to as well."

I couldn't say anything to that. There were no words, and even if I'd had them I was too afraid that if I tried to use them it would break this moment, this second that I had been waiting for ever since I had woken up from that coma. I was a good man in Ayden's eyes, and with her saying that I finally felt forgiveness for all the things I had put her through. I could literally feel some of those bricks made of guilt that barricaded me from everything happening around me start to crumble away.

I was taking her back to Rule and Shaw's, where she and Jet were staying, and she was going on and on about how cute the new baby was. I asked her if she thought a little one was in the future for her and Jet, which made her laugh. She told me Jet was all about having kids, but considering our upbringing and our less than stellar example of parenting our mom had left us with, she was less eager to bring a new life into the world. She told me that they had agreed to table the discussion until she was finished with school, but I knew my sister and had seen her with Jet. They would be wonderful parents and I bet he'd convince her to have his baby long before she had a degree in her hand.

I was at a stoplight when my phone rang and Royal's pretty face popped up on the screen. It didn't bode well for me being able to keep any kind of safety zone between us when I felt my pulse kick and my heart trip just at the sight of her name on my cell.

I swiped a finger across the screen and put the phone up to my ear. "What's up, Red?" Without very much effort I could still taste her and scotch all hot and earthy on the tip of my tongue, and it made me shift in the driver's seat while my sister looked at me questioningly out of the corner of her eye.

"What time do you have to work tonight?" It really did something to my insides that she always sounded so happy to talk to me. The fact that I mattered to her was not lost on me. I recognized all of the simple ways she liked to show me.

"I'm supposed to go in around five," I told her, and she sighed and got quiet on the other end of the line. "Royal, if you need me for something, just ask."

I heard Ayden snicker next to me and I turned to glare at her.

"My mom asked me to come over to her place for dinner and I know we aren't really the meet-the-parents kind of couple or anything, but I was really hoping you could come with me. I love her, but she can be exhausting, and she's been in an unpleasant funk lately. I think she would really enjoy meeting you, not to mention you're pretty fun to stare at, even when you have clothes on."

I chuckled. I had met plenty of parents back in the day, but I was usually putting on a show or so deep in a con that it was never actually me that they were getting to know. It was sort of freeing and kind of thrilling to have Royal ask me to spend time with her mother, considering she knew every single one of my faults and failings. Royal had made no secret of the fact she and her mother were extremely tight, so the thought that I actually needed a parent to legitimately like me if I wanted to keep this girl in my life floated around in my head and made my nerves sing.

"I'll call the new guy and see if he can hang out for a little bit longer until I get there. It shouldn't be a problem ... and you know I love it when you owe me one, Red."

She laughed and the warm sound sent bolts of real, honest-to-God happiness shooting throughout my body. She heated me up faster than the best scotch I had ever tasted.

"Paying up is one of my favorite things to do, Asa. I'll come pick you up at your place when I get off of work, if that's okay."

I groaned and told her, "You and those handcuffs. One of these days I'm gonna make good on my threat to use them."

She laughed again. "I can't wait. I'll see you later."

When I hung up the phone Ayden turned herself completely sideways in her seat and was staring at me like she had never seen me before.

"What?" I knew I sounded surly but I wasn't ready to have her pick apart my complicated relationship with Royal. It wasn't like I understood it well enough to offer up an explanation anyways.

"You're in neck-deep with the cop, aren't you? Since when do you agree to meet the parents?"

I was in way past my neck. "Pretty much in all the way over my head at this point, and I meet the parents when it matters."

"Are you scared?" I remembered how hard and fast she had run from Jet when he decided she was the only one for him.

"I'm scared for her. I screw up everything that matters to me, but I've been nothing but honest with her and she's still here. She keeps telling me I'm a risk worth taking." Which meant I had to make a good impression on her mom, even if it meant dipping into my old bag of tricks. "Royal and her mom are really tight. It was just the two of them growing up, so the mom's seal of approval would be nice."

Ayden nodded. "You *are* a risk worth taking … and so is she. If you stop worrying about what *might* happen between the two of you and focus on what *is* happening, you'd be able to see it clear as day. I think you love her but you're so caught up in the then and so worried about the when that you can't even see the now."

"I don't have a clue how to love someone else, Ayd."

She reached out and thumped me on the side of the head, which made me scowl as I pulled to a stop in front of the familiar house on Capitol Hill.

"Stop making excuses. You're too smart for that, Asa. You love me, you love Mom even though she doesn't deserve it, and I think, finally, after way too long, you are starting to love yourself a little bit. You can love Royal if you allow yourself to."

Her eyes brightened as the front door to the house opened and a tall guy with messy dark hair and really tight, black jeans came out on the front steps. Jet Keller and all his rock-and-roll ways was not who I would have ever pictured being my sister's soul mate, but it was there on every feature of her expressive face. He was it for her and always would be. I saw a smile tug at her mouth as she put a hand on the door before she turned back to look at me.

"Allow yourself to love someone fully, Asa. It's what will finally set you free from the past. There's no room for anything else, no space for all that regret and recrimination when you're filled up with that kind of love. I know you said you woke up from that coma for me, but you haven't been living, and I think Royal might be the one to finally give you a reason to start."

She climbed out of the car and Jet started to come down the stairs toward her like the fifteen feet separating them was just too much to bear. I called Ayden's name and she bent down to poke her head back inside the car.

"I miss you. I just want you to know that."

She winked at me and I saw hands covered in heavy silver rings slide around her waist from behind.

"I miss you, too, but I think I'll worry about you less after this trip."

Jet bent down and told me hello, then hauled my sister out of the way and kissed her like he hadn't seen her in weeks instead of hours. If that was what living looked like, I really had been doing it wrong for the last couple of years, and Ayden was right.

CHAPTER 16

Royal

I wasn't really sure what had possessed me to ask Asa to meet my mother. I don't know if it was the need I had to get him to see that this thing working between us was important, more important than anything he was trying to hold on to before, or if I was pulling one of his tricks and trying to see if he could handle my temperamental parent. Either way I knew I had ulterior motives for asking him to go with me, and considering he was smarter than anyone I had ever met, I knew he had to know that as well.

Even so, when I knocked on his apartment door right after work, still dressed in my uniform, he just leered at me and told me never in a million years did he ever think he would find a badge sexy. Then he kissed me hard enough to knock my hat off the top of my head and reminded me again that my handcuffs had more than one use. I just rolled my eyes and followed him to the 4Runner. One of these days I was going to surprise him and let him make good on all the wicked promises I saw in his amber gaze when he teased me about that particular tool of my trade.

On the way to my mom's place in Littleton I gave him a brief rundown of what to expect. I told him how she liked to jump from spouse to spouse. I gave him the glossed-over version of my own origins, which had him lifting a questioning eyebrow in my direction. All I could do was shrug and tell him I had never had a relationship with my father and never wanted one. My mom had worked her ass off to be more than enough for me and I never felt lacking in the parental love and support department. The guy that had contributed the other half of my DNA already had another family when he started fooling around with my mom, so it wasn't like I was missing out on any kind of stellar role model. Asa just snorted and told me that a philanderer was far better than a career convict when it came to father figures, and I had to admit I agreed.

"Mom's been on a bit of an emotional roller coaster lately. She's never liked to be alone, and ever since I went to work full-time, she's been even more prone to looking for love in all the wrong places. I really worry about her, and sometimes I think she's going to cross the line and I won't be able to look the other way. Her men and the way she is with them has always been the one sore spot in our relationship. But nothing I say about it seems to sink in. It would break my heart if a man ever really drove a wedge between us." I gave him an arch look. "So don't flirt back if she starts to lay it on pretty thick. Sometimes I think she actually loses her mind around good-looking men."

He grinned at me and I felt my heart flip over in my chest. Just the fact that he had agreed to go with me meant so much and I doubted he even realized it.

"Stop worrying. If there's one thing you don't have to worry about, it's me being able to handle your mom."

"Handling her isn't what I'm worried about; tolerating her is." My mom was my favorite person in the world, but if she made googly eyes at Asa while I was in the room, I very well might flip out. I had never been the jealous or possessive type before him, but now I was in so deep, so far down in the depths with him, that I wouldn't hesitate to stake my claim even if I logically knew there was no way my mom would ever want to hurt me or upset me like that on purpose.

Asa reached out a hand and put it on the back of my neck, where he could give it a squeeze. It made a shiver race up along my spine. I wanted to pull the SUV over and climb in his lap. To be honest I always wanted to climb all over him, but the fact that he was trying to reassure me, that he was willing to go through the motions of meeting my mom just to make me happy, made me feel even more amorous toward him.

"Moms are a piece of cake. The dads used to take more work, but then again I wouldn't want my daughter anywhere near a guy like me either." His tone was full of self-deprecating humor and I wanted to purr as his fingers stroked along the curve of my neck.

"It's hard to picture you doing the sit-down-and-meet-the-parents thing." It was hard to see him as anything other than this complicated and difficult man that had become the center of everything to me.

"I did whatever I had to do to get me what I wanted, including meeting the parents." There was no humor in his voice now.

I turned to look at him as I pulled in front of the town house and cocked my head to the side as I told him, "And yet here you are doing it for me."

He just stared at me for a long moment and then a tiny grin tugged at his mouth. He bent forward and pressed his lips lightly against my own. "Here I am."

I knew what he was saying to me. Not just was he here to meet my mom for me, he was here with me in this moment. Not because he necessarily wanted to be, not because he was going to gain anything from it, but simply because I had asked him to be and he was making a concentrated effort to be present, for me. There was no question about it any longer, I had handed my heart over to the southern charmer with a criminal past. Probably not the smartest move I had ever made, but I couldn't regret it. Not when he was looking at me with that warm shimmer in his eyes and that knowing smirk on his too-pretty face.

We walked up to the front door and he put his hand on my lower back. I had ditched my hat in the car and pulled my hair out of the coiled-up bun that held it up and out of the way while I was on duty. I actually groaned out loud when Asa raked his fingers through the long locks and rubbed his fingers across my scalp. I gave the door an obligatory knock before walking in and hollering out a hello to my mom. She yelled back that she was in the kitchen, and I headed off in that direction only to be drawn up short when Asa paused at the hallway wall to look at the various pictures that decorated the flat surface. They were all of me, several of me and Dom and his sisters, and a bunch of me and Mom. His eyes seemed glued to the images and all his good humor and gentle handling from moments ago disappeared behind a hard veneer that dulled the typical molten sheen in his gaze. His jaw clenched so hard that I actually heard his teeth grind together and his arm felt like steel when I reached out to touch him.

"Are you okay?"

He jerked like I had electrocuted him, and when he looked down at me it was like he was looking at a stranger. I saw his Adam's apple bob up and down and his hands curled into fists at his sides. His head shook slowly from side to side and he took a step away from me, so that I was no longer touching him. I was baffled by his sudden change in demeanor, so I gave a forced little laugh and asked him, "Did seeing me with braces and knobby knees really scare you that much?"

I was happy in almost every single picture on that wall. It was my life before him laid out in snapshot after snapshot, and I wondered if the reality of coming with me to meet my mom, the seriousness of letting him into every single part of my life, was finally sinking in. He looked like he was struggling for words when I heard shuffling as my mom came around the corner, undoubtedly wondering what was taking us so long. She had a glass of wine in her hand and a welcoming smile on her face as she chirped, "Did you get lost?" I saw her eyes get big and her mouth drop open in a little O of surprise when her gaze locked on Asa. I thought she was probably just stunned by how ridiculously good-looking he was until the wineglass slipped from her fingers and sent red liquid splattering all over her fancy Berber carpet. My mom could be flaky but she typically was as graceful as an old Hollywood starlet.

"Mom!" I yelled at her, and took a step forward as she fluttered a hand in front of her face and jerked her gaze away from Asa to the mess she had just made. She laughed a bit hysterically then turned to run to the kitchen, only to return a moment later with a towel and a bottle of floor cleaner. There was a high flush on her face and I noticed she wouldn't look up at me, which was totally out of character for her.

"I'm so sorry. I don't know what's wrong with me." She got on her hands and knees and I frowned at her and then back at Asa, who looked like he had been carved out of stone. I had never seen him look so hard and so remote. Not even the night I arrested him for something he didn't do.

"Mom, this is Asa Cross. Asa, this is my mom, Roslyn Hastings." My mom looked up from her position and then immediately looked back down to the floor.

"Um ... It's nice to meet you, Asa." She sounded cold and not at all welcoming.

Asa opened his mouth, then snapped it shut again. He lifted a hand to his face and rubbed it across his jaw like he was trying really hard to think of something to say. I scowled at him and crossed my arms over my chest. I was two seconds away from stamping my foot in irritation in a full-on fit.

"What is wrong with you?" I mean I knew my mom was dramatic and that she hadn't made the best first impression, but the stone-man impression seemed a little extreme, especially when he had just assured me he could handle her with very little effort.

Then it was like a switch flipped. Suddenly his stony and hard expression fell away and the harmless good ol' boy underneath was revealed. An easy grin pulled at his mouth and he dipped his chin in a polite nod.

"Nice to meet you, ma'am." I had never heard his drawl so thick or so purposeful. It made goose bumps rise up on my skin and chills race along my spine. He had slipped into a role. Asa was playing a character all of a sudden and it made my stomach hurt to watch the change happen so seamlessly right in front of my eyes. Especially since he was doing it to someone that was so important to me. Something was seriously wrong and I had no idea what it was.

I helped my mom to her feet and was puzzled as to why she was shaking. She gave me a hug and hastily ushered me off to the kitchen with Asa trailing behind us. She started rattling off a hundred questions at me about work, Dom, everything under the sun besides me and Asa, which I thought was superweird. Even if she had enough tact not to openly ogle him in front of me, there was no way she wouldn't at least give him an appreciative once-over. All women did. It was part of the magnetism he exuded so effortlessly. If you were born with a vagina, you were going to check Asa out when you got the opportunity. It was just a fact.

I kept looking back and forth between the two of them, but he was staring at me like he was trying to work out something important to say, and that made me really nervous. I don't know what had happened when we walked in that front door, but I felt like I had entered an alternate dimension.

My mom had us help take dinner to the table, and when we sat down it didn't escape my notice that Asa sat at the very end of the table, as far away from both me and my mother as he could get. It also didn't skip my attention that he didn't touch anything on his plate as my mom chattered on and on about nothing and everything at an alarming speed. She was acting more erratic than I could ever remember seeing her. I set my fork down with a clatter on my plate and narrowed my eyes at her.

"Mom." She closed her mouth with a snap and blinked at me like an owl. "This is the first guy I've brought home to meet you in years and you've spent the last twenty minutes talking about your dry cleaners and a stain in your blouse. Don't you want to know how we met or anything about Asa? You're being very rude."

She balked at me and turned wide eyes to Asa and then looked back at me with a bright red stain on her cheeks.

"Oh ... I'm so sorry. I promise, I usually have better manners than this." Asa grunted as I reached out a foot to kick him under the table. A smile instantly flashed across his face and he shrugged.

"Don't worry about it, ma'am. I appreciate you making dinner for us."

My mom gave a high-pitched laugh and raised a hand to fiddle with her necklace. "So obviously you're from the South. Where would that be?"

"Kentucky." He kept the smile on his face but there was no pleasantness in his voice at all.

"Oh, I bet it's pretty there."

"Not the part I'm from."

I jumped in before it could get any more awkward. "Asa bartends at the bar I told you I was hanging out at."

"A bartender. That sounds like a fun job," she said a little too brightly.

"It has its moments." Asa's deadpan response was the last straw. The tension was as thick as a blanket and so heavy I felt like I couldn't breathe through it anymore.

I pushed away from the table and rose to my feet with my hands on the edge. I swung my head back and forth between the two of them and asked, "What on earth is going on here?" I needed answers as to why he was acting so strange, needed them, like, yesterday.

Asa pushed his chair back.

I turned pleading eyes in his direction as he climbed to his feet. "Asa?" His name came out on a whisper as he made his way over to me. "What exactly am I missing here?"

He put his hand beneath the heavy fall of my hair on the back of my neck and bent down so that he could kiss me on the forehead. It felt like a good-bye, and when I looked up into his face I could see that the affable mask he had been wearing for dinner was gone and the granite stranger was back. All the questions I had about his odd behavior suddenly disappeared under sharp waves of pain as I saw what he was about to do laid out clearly in the depths of his dulled gaze.

"I can't do this, Royal." He brushed his lips along the ridge of my cheek and I saw the light go from dim to completely extinguished in his eyes. "No games, no lying, no more. I told you this was going to self-destruct even if I didn't want it to."

"What are you talking about?" I was so lost, so confused, and I could tell if he walked away from me right now he was doing it for good. "Can't do what anymore?" I didn't know if pressing him to meet my mom had been too much. Maybe it was too far in the realm of serious relationship for him to handle, but I was willing to grab his hand and run out of the town house with him if it would stop him from doing what he was about to do.

I went to grab his arm but he shook me off and headed out of the room toward the front door. I chased after him, angry and baffled beyond belief.

"Asa, what are you doing? Where are you going?" I mean we were in Littleton and I was the one that had driven.

He stopped at the front door and turned around to look at me. If heartbreak had an expression it would be the one that was dancing across his features at that very moment. "I never really thought I'd be able to sacrifice something for the good of someone else ever in my entire life. I guess I really have changed."

I felt like I was going to cry. "I don't understand. Is this because I asked you to meet my mom?" Maybe I had pushed him too far into the territory of what a real relationship looked like and this was his way of pushing back.

"I know you don't understand and I hope you never do. You deserve better, Royal. You always did."

He didn't answer me about my mom, but I saw something hot spark in his eyes. I put a hand to my chest, where I felt like my heart was trying to fly out of my rib cage. I deserved better than what? Him? There was no such thing as far as I was concerned. "I'm in love with you." My voice broke because he still pulled the door open and looked at me over his shoulder as he did it.

"I know you are. That's why I'm walking out this door." With that, he vanished out the front door and left me standing there stunned and dumbfounded.

I stared silently at the door for a solid ten minutes before my mom came to find me. When she did, I was rooted to the spot, shaking, and had fat, hot tears sliding silently down my face.

"Royal?" She put a hand on my shoulder and I jolted. I wrapped my arms tightly around myself because right then I needed a hug like I needed my next breath. When I looked at her, I swore guilt and relief were warring with each other on her face.

"Asa just left." She nodded a little, understanding that I meant he left more than just this disastrous dinner.

"Didn't he ride here with you?"

I turned to look at her, words stuck in my throat as emotion swirled and twisted inside of me so turbulent I felt like it was going to pull me apart. "He left me, Mom." My voice cracked as I said it and she made a noise of sympathy and reached out to put a hand lightly on my shoulder.

"Well, we both know men do that, honey. They leave. Especially men that look like him that have the devil and temptation in their eyes."

I frowned hard at her. I knew "perusing" Asa had a big probability of heartache attached to it, but for some unknown reason I was really starting to think we were going to beat the odds.

I cut my gaze toward my mother and asked her in a voice that was threatening to crack with sadness, "Why were you acting so weird around him tonight?" Everything inside of me was screaming at me to chase after him, to call him, to beg him to explain to me what in the hell was going on.

She harrumphed and patted me awkwardly where her hand rested. "I didn't like the looks of him for you. Something about that face just screams more trouble than he's worth. I've made enough mistakes in the men department for both of us, Royal. Trust me when I say you're better off without a man like that holding on to your heartstrings."

"That's ridiculous and judgmental. You don't even know him." He was so much more than a pretty face. The complexities that lived under his artful façade were anything but attractive and that's what I liked the most about him. His ugliness made him even more beautiful.

"I know men like him and have been victimized by a pretty face more than once in my times, Royal. Your father didn't win me over with sweet words and grand gestures. He was the most beautiful man I had ever seen and that blinded me to the fact he was married and everything else that was wrong with our relationship. You can do so much better for yourself. I wouldn't tell you that if I didn't think it was true, honey. All I've ever wanted is for you to be happy."

I hiccuped on a sob that was trying to force its way out and had to blink to see through the tears that were clinging to my lashes. I hated that both of them had suddenly decided that there was something better out there in the world for me than what I wanted … which was him. "I don't want better. I want him and he does make me happy, mostly because he lets me make *him* happy."

She said my name again, but I was in a daze. There were clues I knew I was missing, a trail of breadcrumbs leading to my broken heart, but I couldn't focus on anything other than the pain I was feeling to try and follow them. I was shattered, and when I wasn't I knew I was going to be absolutely furious with myself for taking such a big risk when I knew the outcome was bound to destroy me.

I opened the door Asa had just exited my life through and walked numbly to my car. I wanted to do this night all over again. I wanted to smack Asa in the face for causing a disastrous end to our union simply because he couldn't help himself. I wanted someone to hold me and tell me this was all a bad dream.

I was going to Dom and then I was going to break down in a blubbering mess to try and figure out how things had gone so horribly wrong in the blink of an eye.

CHAPTER 17

Asa

I had told Rowdy months ago, when he was struggling with putting his feelings for Salem in order, that men who sacrificed, who gave of themselves for others, deserved every bit of happiness the world saw fit to set at their feet. I had only had Royal for a minute, a fraction of a second, but it was time that would matter more to me than all the years and decades I had wasted being a selfish and reckless bastard. What she had created within me was far more powerful and enduring than all the things I had destroyed on my own. For once I had done the right thing without thinking, without latching on to the easy way and just riding out the lie. There was no instinct to pretend—there was only the wish to protect the girl I knew I would love forever. She saw me, all of me, and none of the faces I wore scared her. Because of that, I would never let her know that her mother, the only parent she had, the woman that had raised her and loved her, had also propositioned me for sex. I would be the bad guy in this scenario where I had ultimately done nothing wrong and save Royal the heartache that dealing with that particular revelation would undoubtedly cause. I could be a hero for once even if she didn't know that's what I was doing.

It's funny. It took breaking my own heart and walking away from the one thing I had ever really wanted for me to finally be able to see that I really had moved beyond the guy I had always been before.

Royal had called me every night since I walked out on her at her mom's place. She never left a message, never texted me or showed up at the Bar, but every night when she knew I was off of work, she called and I stared at the phone, fighting with myself not to answer. I knew she was hurting, confused, and lost. Nash had been by to rip me a new asshole. Even quiet and shy Saint had swung by the Bar to let me know she thought I was an idiot and a dipshit. I didn't defend myself, couldn't explain why I had to walk away from Royal even when I had just realized she was what I wanted forever. So I just took the lashes, letting everyone think what they wanted, even Rome, who felt like it was his job to give me the third degree and tell me what an obviously horrible mistake I was making. I put them all off, told them all it was doomed from the beginning, and that I couldn't believe anyone was surprised that my relationship with the beautiful cop had crashed and burned. I told them she wanted too much, that meeting her mom and pretending to be a normal guy in a normal relationship situation was too much for me. I wasn't cut out for it. I maintained to them all that when you had lived a life like mine, good things were not part of the equation, and those words tended to shut everyone up. There were too many questions with answers that I couldn't give, so eventually I just stopped talking about it altogether and the gang got the hint and left me alone about it.

I wasn't at all surprised when I got a visit from a massive fellow in a full leg cast, moving like a ninety-year-old man except he was wearing a glower fierce enough to put the fear of God into any man. I knew he was here for her and I couldn't blame him for the fact that he looked like he wanted to pull my intestines out through my nose.

I had met Dominic Voss one other time, while he was arresting me. The look on his face as he limped his way into the Bar to confront me was a hundred times more ferocious than it had been that night. Even on one leg and in an obviously huge amount of pain, Dom didn't come across as a guy anyone would want to cross. When he propped himself up on the opposite side of the bar from me and stared me down, all I could do was look at him and wait to see what he had to say.

He ran his hands through his dark hair in an aggravated manner and asked me to pour him a shot of Maker's Mark on the rocks. I turned to comply and set it down in front of him with a lifted eyebrow.

"I thought I was going to come in here and threaten to kick your ass ... even with one leg. I thought I was going to tell you what an absolute moron you are for letting her go and that I was going to have to tell you that you have no idea what you're going to miss out on by not letting a girl as wonderful as Royal love you." He picked up the rocks glass and took a swig and then lifted both his eyebrows so that his expression mirrored my own. "But I can look at you and see that you know all of that. So now I want to ask you why you did it."

I hadn't slept in days. I was drinking my weight in scotch every single night. I hadn't bothered to shave, so I was scruffy, and I knew that none of the usual polish that I hid behind could be found. I looked like I had just crawled out of that trailer in Kentucky after a month-long bender and I felt about the same.

Dom continued to stare at me and I continued to stare back. He was just one more person that wanted an explanation I couldn't give.

"You look like shit. She looks like shit. Neither one of you seems to be on board with this breakup, so why don't you do something about it, lover boy?"

I sighed and finally looked away from that penetrating green gaze. I gazed down at the bar and lifted a hand to rub absently at the back of my neck. The knots of tension that were coiled there felt like balls of steel and iron under my skin.

"Nothing can be done about it, cop. If there was a better answer than that, I would give it ... to her, not to you."

He grunted at me and slammed back the rest of his drink. "You broke her fucking heart, which already makes you a piece of shit, but what really makes you a fuck wad is that you broke it after putting it back together for her. Why bother fixing her if you were just going to tear her back to pieces?"

That made my chest contract and my hands clench involuntarily. She was already all together when I got my hands on her. Her pieces were just a little jumbled up and out of order because she cared so much about her partner and seeing him get hurt knocked her a little loose. All I did was straighten those pieces out and tighten her back up. If anyone had put the work in to fix anyone, it was the other way around. I didn't realize how broken I had been until she started tinkering around in all the darkness and shining her light on it. Without Royal, there was no way I would've been able to know that even though I had hurt her like this, it was for the best.

"If there was any other way to do this, I would've found it. Believe me or don't, but I walked away *for* her, not *because* of her."

Dom grunted again and hobbled back onto his crutches. "You better have one hell of a good reason for doing this to her."

Oh, I had a really fucking good reason, but I wasn't going to share it with anyone and run the risk of ripping Royal's small family apart. Sometimes the sins of the parents did not have to be suffered by their children.

"I hope you figure your shit out, lover boy. Royal deserves someone that can stand by her and appreciates her for *all* the amazing things she brings to the table. I don't know how on earth that person managed to be an ex-con with a twang, but stranger things have happened."

I ran my hands over my face as my heart throbbed painfully in my chest. There was no figuring my shit out, and that's what made the situation seem impossible. I called out to Dom as he finally made his way to the door, "Take care of her."

He looked over his shoulder at me with a scowl. "I always have." With that closing salvo he exited the bar and left me feeling even worse than I already was.

I got another visitor at the end of what I swore was the longest week of my life. I just wanted to tell everyone to leave me alone, to shut the world out and mourn for the loss of something I was sure was going to stick with me forever. It was the day after the first night Royal hadn't called, so I was already keyed up and furious at myself and at the circumstances. I had never bemoaned all the crappy things that seemed to find their way to my doorstep, never minded that I had some penance to pay, but this sacrifice felt like it might be what finally took me out, what might make me drown.

I was just a shell. Just a hollow husk of a man going through the motions of the day-to-day because that was what was expected of me. I no longer had to worry or agonize over the good or the bad because there was nothing there. I felt like without her, without her light and her spark, there wasn't this moment or any moment. I was just stuck in neutral while everything carried on and progressed around me.

She came in at the start of my shift. She had on dark sunglasses and a big ol' floppy hat like she didn't want to be recognized by anyone. It was a little late for that. Royal's mother, the woman that had offered to pay me for sex, sat down at the bar and took off her dark glasses so that she was looking at me with wide, terror-filled eyes. Now that I had seen the two of them together, I couldn't believe that I had missed the resemblance. Other than the different-colored hair, Royal was the spitting image of the stunning older woman.

Roslyn cleared her throat delicately and laid her hands on the bar top like she needed something solid to hold her in this reality.

"I had no idea you were seeing Royal when I started coming in here. She told me about the Bar, told me it was fun and that a lot of attractive young men hung out here. She never mentioned you specifically or the fact that she was seeing anyone that worked here." That still wasn't an excuse for the proposition she had laid at my feet. It didn't matter if I was involved with her daughter or not. Now that I had walked away, done the clearly right thing for once in my life with no questions hounding me about my choice, I could see the far-reaching ramifications of that decision as Royal's mother fidgeted nervously in front of me.

I had walked away, but what purpose did that serve if this woman was free to continue to act so irresponsibly with no accountability. Royal would end up hurt anyway, and my sacrifice would be for naught.

I ignored Roslyn and went to fill an order for one of the regulars. Dixie was watching me with careful eyes and I waved her off to let her know I was okay. I needed a second to get a game plan together, a second to pull a few old tricks out of my manipulative hat. I was actually surprised it had taken Roslyn this long to find her way back to the Bar. I held her entire relationship with her daughter in the palm of my hand and she had to know that. If I had been her, this would've been my first stop weeks ago. Maybe if I hadn't been wallowing in my own loss and my own heartache and just generally feeling sorry for myself, I would have gone to her first. The last thing I wanted to do was give up the only woman I ever wanted for my own to have her careless mother hurt her when I wasn't around to make it better for her.

I found my way back to where Royal's mother was sitting after fifteen minutes of purposely making her sweat. When I reached her I braced my hands on the bar and leaned over so that when I spoke it was low and meant only for her to hear.

"The fact that you didn't know about me and Royal doesn't excuse your behavior. You offered me money to take you to bed. Regardless if I was already sleeping with your daughter or not, those kinds of risks are foolish and unnecessary. Put your child ahead of yourself. Put your own well-being above your incessant need for attention from the opposite sex. Even if it wasn't me, how do you think Royal would feel if she found out that's what you were out there doing? Offering strange men money for sex is incredibly risky. You have no idea the devastation I could have brought into your life if I had accepted an offer like that a few years ago. And your daughter's a cop, for God's sake. It could ruin her professionally as well as personally. Did you ever stop to think about that?"

Roslyn recoiled and she started to twist her hands together. "I have never purposely hurt Royal."

I snorted and pushed off the bar. "Exactly. It might not be on purpose, but your selfish and reckless actions do hurt her and have done so even before now. Do you think she likes watching you jump from man to man? Do you think she likes that your loneliness makes you act foolish and thoughtless? Do you think she likes worrying about you and what you're out there doing because you can't manage to take care of yourself? You're lucky to have her and you've never appreciated the fact."

She narrowed her eyes a little at me. "Are you going to tell me you appreciated her while you had her, Asa?"

I lifted a shoulder and let it fall. "I was learning to. I knew from the first minute that I saw her that she was special, that she was too good for me, so I knew I had to take advantage of every single second I had with her."

"Are you in love with my daughter?" It came out as a whisper, and she was the only person that had asked me the question that I was going to give an answer to.

"Yes, I am." And surprisingly, being able to say it was what finally woke me up. Ayden was right. I had been sleepwalking, and allowing myself to love Royal enough to let her go was what had jolted me awake. Only being awake when all I was doing was hurting sucked ass, and I could have totally done without the heartache. Being numb did have its benefits, but I knew I could never go back to that place. The past had to stay behind me. The future had to play out however it was going to play out, and I needed to focus on everything I had right in front of me, right now.

She put a hand to her throat much like she had done at dinner and blinked at me. "So what happens now?"

I gritted my teeth and breathed out hard through my nose. "What happens is you get your act together. You help her through this breakup because I know she's confused and hurting. You convince her that she deserves better than me, and you know that if I ever catch wind of you doing anything as fucking stupid as offer to pay a stranger for sex again, I'll tell Royal everything, and if she won't listen to me, I'll tell Dom. He'll watch you like a hawk and you won't be able to move without him keeping eyes on you to make sure you don't do anything so stupid again. Royal will never forgive you and Dom will never let it go, and we both know it. Your daughter loves you but what you're doing is dangerous and unforgivable. It will be the final straw. She's already over how you behave around the men in your life as it is. Get it together or lose her." It was a threat that I would have no trouble and zero remorse about following through on, and I made sure she could tell that when she finally looked up to meet my gaze.

"Why? Why are you doing this when you could tell her the truth instead? Why give me a second chance when you could throw me under the bus and live happily ever after with her?"

I growled at her because I really just wanted her gone. "I'm doing this because she has loved you longer than she's loved me. I'm doing it because Royal needs her mom more than she needs a boyfriend, and I'm doing it because I never thought I could walk away from the ultimate prize if I had it. I'm doing it because it's the right thing to do." And goddammit, me doing the right thing without hesitation had never been an option before Royal.

And that was all there was to it. I walked away from Roslyn and honestly hoped I never had to see her again. I didn't wait to see if she got up and left. I just went about my business like a zombie for the rest of my shift ... and the shift after that ... and the shift after that.

Another week had passed when Rome finally pulled me into the back office and told me to take a few days off. I told him the last thing I needed was time by myself to think. He told me it wasn't a suggestion, it was an order. I told him to fuck off and things devolved pretty rapidly from there. I didn't really remember him strong-arming out of the Bar and calling me every name he could think of. I didn't recall him knocking me upside the head hard enough that my ears were ringing. What I did remember bright and clear was him telling me to pull my head out of my ass before he really had to hurt me, and that was enough to spur me into action and get me headed back home.

I spent several days wallowing in a drunken haze while lying in my lonely and empty bed. Who would have ever thought doing the right thing felt a hundred times worse than doing the wrong thing ever did?

I was in the shower trying to wash off the vestiges of a stupor and wondering if I was always going to feel so empty when I heard my phone ring from the other room. Considering all my friends and allies were pissed off at me or purposely giving me space, I couldn't stop my traitorous heart from thinking it might be Royal. Even if I wouldn't give in to temptation and answer her call, I'd still look at her pretty face on the screen while my phone sang the Black Angels' "You're Mine" and trashed my heart even more.

I was rubbing water off of my face with another towel when I found the phone and stopped dead in my tracks when the face on the screen wasn't the one I wanted to see but one that I hadn't seen in so long I almost forgot what it looked like. I sat my ass on the edge of the bed and answered the call with a terse "What kind of trouble are you in, Mom?" I had had enough of mothers to last me a lifetime the last month or so.

It sounded like she was at a truck stop. The background noise was full of wind, horns blaring, and engines revving.

"None. Why is that always the first thing you ask me?" Her drawl was twice as thick as my own and I always asked her that question because the only time I heard from her was when she needed something or was in trouble. I guess the apple didn't fall very far from that tree.

"Where are you?" I grumbled out the question and flopped back on the bed so that I was staring at the ceiling. I had spent a lot of lost hours in this exact same position over the last few days.

"Outside of Chicago. Listen, I just got a call from the Kentucky Department of Corrections."

Well, that couldn't amount to anything good. "About what?"

She screamed something that I couldn't make out and then came back on the line. "About your father."

My father was like a ghost story. Something I had heard about my entire life, some specter that existed in theory and used to scare me when I didn't act right, but there was no actual, tangible proof that he was a real, living, breathing human being.

"What about him? Is he finally up for parole and looking for character witnesses?" I said this ironically considering I had never met the man, and if my illustrious past was anything to go by, I got all of my worst character traits from his side of the genetic pool. He could rot behind bars forever as far as I was concerned.

"Asa!" My mom snapped my name and then moved off to somewhere where she wasn't battling the background noise to be heard. "Your dad has been sick for a long time."

I knew I was supposed to feel something at those words, but I couldn't for the life of me figure out what the feeling was supposed to be. "Okay."

She sighed and said my name again. "Your dad passed away in the prison hospital last night. He had a massive heart attack. There was nothing anyone could do for him."

Again I wasn't sure how any of that was supposed to make me feel or what kind of reaction she was looking to get out of me. "Okay."

My mom swore and I actually heard her tapping her foot impatiently on the other end of the phone line.

"Asa, you're his only kin. Your dad never married and his parents passed away years ago. Your dad was an only child, so that means you need to go to Kentucky and settle his affairs."

I groaned and used my free hand to grind it into my eye sockets. "Mom, he was locked up for over thirty years. What kind of affairs could he possibly have? Let the state sort it all out. I'm not interested in going back there." Especially not for a man I had never met. The man I would have turned into if fate and a bunch of pissed-off bikers hadn't turned it all around for me.

"You should know better than that, son. Even the most troubled soul has someone out there to love it. Your father might have made some serious mistakes, but his family never turned their backs on him. They owned a beautiful farm right outside of Woodward that your dad grew up on. Since he's gone, the land and everything on it will pass down to you."

I swore and bolted up into a sitting position. "You have got to be kidding me."

"Do I sound like I'm kidding, Asa?" No, she sounded annoyed that she had to be dealing with any of it at all. "They never cared for my relationship with your dad or the fact you were born right before he got locked up. They thought I was trash and that we ruined his life, but they never gave up hope on your dad."

"Why does it go to me and not to you? If they hated us, why do I get anything?" Maybe that's why she sounded so put out.

"I told you your father never married. That includes me. I was in his contact information on his paperwork when he got arrested because we were living together at the time. The prison called me and his lawyer to pass on the news." She mumbled something under her breath and then all the noise in the background was back. "Go home, Asa. Put your dad to rest. See the farm. Keep it or sell it. Either way you have a way to really start your life over just like your sister did."

She didn't tell me good-bye. she just hung up, leaving me staring at the phone in dumbfounded shock. Suddenly I didn't have to worry about what emotion to feel because I was feeling all of them at once. Happiness, rage, fear, sadness, confusion ... everything surged to the surface. I was no longer hollow, I was no longer empty. I was full of everything that I had been actively avoiding for most of my life, and now all I could do was laugh like a lunatic and throw my phone across the room. I laughed and laughed until tears fell out of the corners of my eyes and my abs hurt from the exertion. I felt like I was losing my mind but I knew the only thing there was for me to do was get on the next plane to Kentucky.

I didn't have to look up when her boots hit the bottom of the porch steps to know my sister had found her way to where I was. She somehow always managed to appear when I needed her the most. Initially I had left Denver without saying a word to anyone. I didn't tell Rome I was leaving, and I didn't call Ayden to let her know what was going on. It only took getting off the plane and taking a cab to my father's lawyer's office for me to have a major change of heart. I was immediately inundated with so much information, given so many decisions to make, that I had to take a second to get my shit together and I realized I couldn't close the door on where and who I had been by myself. I needed Ayden to help me do it once and for all.

I called my baby sister and filled her in, which of course led to her yelling at me for five minutes for trying to handle all of this by myself. I knew as soon as I hung up the phone she would be making an appearance as soon as she could arrange getting herself back to a place neither of us ever wanted to see again.

I called Rome and gave him a brief rundown as well. He took it more stoically and told me to take as much time as I needed. He also reminded me that he was there, they were all there if I needed anything, and told me not to forget that fact. I told him I was long past taking the good things in my life for granted, and I would let him know how everything worked out.

It had taken Ayden two days to get from Austin to Woodward. Two days during which I had given the okay to have the stranger who was my father cremated, and then inherited a hundred-acre tobacco farm that sprawled beautifully across prime Kentucky real estate. The spread was beautiful. Like something off a postcard, complete with a massive white farmhouse and stables for horses. It was like the places I had schemed and conned my way into when I was living in a trailer, and here it had been in my backyard all along. It felt old and important and I couldn't believe it was mine. I couldn't believe something this good had sprung up in the middle of all the bad that permeated this place in my history.

Ayden's boots clattered on the wooden steps that graced the elegant front porch of the house. I didn't look up at her. Instead, I closed my eyes as she sat down next to me on the top step and hooked an arm through mine as she rested her head on my shoulder.

"I'm surprised Jet let you come back here alone." I tilted my head to the side a little so it was resting against hers. We had never been able to do this as kids. Just be. It was always a fight to survive with no quiet time to just take in life and the landscape.

"He doesn't belong here." Her husky voice was quiet and I couldn't agree with her more.

"No, he doesn't."

We sat in silence and took in the enormity of being in a place neither of us ever thought we'd be able to touch in our hometown. It was surreal and I'm sure as overwhelming for her as it was for me.

"So what are you going to do now?" I knew Ayden well enough to know she wasn't asking me about the farm.

I let my eyes drift back closed and took a deep breath. She was the only one I was going to tell, the only one I trusted with the entire sordid story. I knew my sister would keep my secrets and protect the woman I cared so much about, so I laid it all out for her. Royal's mom, the proposition, being stuck between lying to the only girl I was ever going to love in order to be with her or telling her the truth and hurting her, ripping her world apart instead. I knew Ayden would see the impossibility in all of it, and as the tale unfolded I heard her gasp and swear the deeper down the rabbit hole I went. I told her about the games I liked to play mostly because I couldn't stop myself from doing it and how Royal was quick enough and ballsy enough to call me on my shit each and every single time. I told her that I didn't even see the badge anymore and the idea of being in love with a cop didn't even faze me because I knew, just *knew,* that I was never ever going back to that place where I was going to be a danger to myself or others. Loving Royal had given me enough strength to put the past down and to stop trying to predict the future. All I was concerned with was the here and now.

When all the words were done, when everything was purged out of me, I noticed Ayden had silent tears running down her face. She shook her head at me and leaned over to rub her wet cheek on the shoulder of my T-shirt, which made me laugh.

So quiet I almost didn't hear her, she told me, "It shines out of you, Asa."

She was talking about the good and finally I thought maybe she was right.

"I let the state cremate my father. I'm gonna take his ashes out in the field and spread them around. Then I'm going to call the estate lawyer and tell him to get together the offers he has had lined up on this place since Dad's parents passed. Apparently this property is a hot commodity and folks around here have been waiting anxiously for it to go on the market for years."

She made a noise in her throat. "Are you sure you don't want to keep it? It's beautiful."

I laughed drily. "It's not mine. I don't belong here, and we both know beauty isn't everything. Besides, the numbers the lawyer was throwing around weren't too shabby. I can pay off the medical bills I still owe. I can give you enough money to pay off grad school." She lifted her head in surprise and gaped at me. I grinned at her. "I can buy into this new business Rome asked me to partner with him on. I can fix up the Nova. I can look at buying my own bar and moving out of my crappy apartment. It's enough money to really start over with a clean slate."

"Wow ... all that for a bunch of weeds?"

I laughed. "You've been out of the country for too long. You're a bona fide city girl now."

She shrugged. "True enough, but I still wear my boots with pride." We shared a grin and she told me with so much heart that it made my chest ache, "I just want you to do whatever is going to make you happy."

That was exactly what I had told her when she said she was going to leave Denver and move to Austin so she could have more time with Jet.

"I had a shot at happy. It didn't really work out for me."

She sighed again and got to her feet as I rose to my own. I picked up the plain urn that was sitting on the steps next to my feet and lifted an eyebrow at her. She nodded solemnly and followed me as I started walking toward one of the tobacco fields.

"You can't just leave things with Royal the way they are, Asa. You both deserve better than that, and she's smart. Once her heart stops hurting so bad, she's going to start putting the pieces together on her own."

We did deserve better, and maybe Royal would figure it all out in time, but I didn't have an answer on how to fix it while that time passed, so I just looped an arm around Ayden's shoulders as we walked silently into one of the fields to shut the door on the past and all the bad things and demons that lived there in the dark—for good. There was no more before and after. There was only this moment; although it sucked and felt terrible, it was still the only moment I wanted to be in.

CHAPTER 18

Royal

My first instinct was to show up on Asa's doorstep five seconds after he left me and demand answers all while knocking him into next week. My second instinct was to curl up in a ball and cry my eyes out for days, because even if this was just another one of his twisty games, I was done playing with him. So I split the difference and called him every single day for a week, praying he would answer and alternately hoping he would just show up at my door with a brilliant excuse full of pretty words that would set things right. I did all of that while hiding out at Dominic's apartment or sequestered in my bed with Saint at my side trying to talk me off the ledge. None of my emotional upheaval was helped by the fact my mother was suddenly all over me trying to earn a mom-of-the-year award. I couldn't turn around without her asking me how I was, without her telling me there were a million fish in the sea, without her telling me that a guy like Asa wasn't worth a second of my time let alone a single bit of sorrow. She was trying to distract me but all she succeeded in doing was annoying the hell out of me.

I was frantic and furious, mostly because I knew something had happened, something I didn't understand. Something had forced him to walk away from me, and I needed to know what that something was if I was ever going to have a chance to come to terms with the fact that Asa had purposely ripped my heart out of my chest and handed it back to me.

When it became glaringly obvious that Asa wasn't going to answer any of my calls, I cried my last tear and decided I was done. Done worrying about what his reasons were. Done trying to justify his actions for whatever they were. Done hurting over a man that had only ever promised to hurt me from the very start. He had kept his word all right.

I shoved everything I was feeling up into a tiny little ball and did my best to ignore it while I threw myself into work. I forgot to eat. I forgot to keep in touch with Dom. I forgot to go to the gym. All I did was work and go home, work and go home, and then work some more. My new partner asked me a hundred times if I was okay and I just waved him off. Luckily, around the same time that I decided to be an emotionless android, Barrett and I got handpicked by our lieutenant to be on a special task force to investigate a series of break-ins involving all of the different medical marijuana dispensaries that had cropped up in Denver since the drug had been legalized across the state. It was a perfect excuse for me to shut out everything else and brush everyone off when they were checking up on me. I just lost myself in work and pretended like I had never even heard of Asa Cross.

It was all working great … well, aside from the fact that I was giving myself an ulcer, waking up in the middle of the night with tears running down my face, and my heart squeezing so hard that it felt like there was a fist around it. I was faking it well enough that my mom finally backed off and Dom stopped threatening to move onto my couch until I snapped out of my funk. The lie that I was fine fell from my lips as easily as the truth anymore. I told it so much that when I was awake I could almost believe it myself.

I had a rhythm of denial and deflection all in place, resigned to that being how the rest of my existence was going to be, when Saint popped by one night after work with a bottle of wine and some startling news. She told me over the first glass that Nash had paid Asa a visit and reported back that the blond bartender looked and sounded horrible. Over the second glass she informed me that Cora had let it slip that Rome had forced Asa to take a few days off work because he was in such a sorry state, and it was over the third that she let it be known that Asa's dad had died in prison, so he had gone back to Kentucky for a week to settle the man's estate. She also mentioned that tonight was his first night back at the Bar, so a bunch of the guys had headed down that way to check up on him. I had only taken a few sips from my first drink because I was so caught up in any tidbit of information she had about my whiskey-eyed charmer that I forgot I was even holding a full glass in my hand.

I was so stunned by the news about Asa's dad that I almost dropped the glass from my suddenly nerveless fingers. I didn't want to feel for him. I didn't want sympathy and the need to see if he was okay to fill me all the way up on the inside, but it did. We polished off the bottle and Saint gave me a hug and told me it was all right to hurt for someone I still loved, which made me want to break the arctic freeze I had surrounded myself in and start crying and being hysterical all over again. It took about half a minute from the time she walked back across the hall to her own apartment for me to grab my keys, which were thankfully in the right spot for once, and head out to the 4Runner. I was operating on autopilot. Asa had given no indication that he wanted to see me, that he cared one way or the other that we had split up, but everything inside of me was drawing me back to him. It seemed like he was always going to be the magnetic north my compass was pointed at.

It was just after midnight when I pulled into the surprisingly empty parking lot. As I jumped out of my car I noticed Dixie and the new bouncer walking out of the front door. The cute cocktail server stopped when she recognized me and nodded to the massive, imposing man to go ahead. He gave me a once-over and then walked over to a fierce-looking motorcycle that sounded as mean as it looked when he started it up. Dixie twirled one of her strawberry-blond curls around her finger and smiled sweetly at me.

"Everyone has been by to check on him tonight. I can't say I'm surprised you're the last one to filter through."

I bit down on my lip and shifted uneasily on my feet. "How is he?"

She shrugged and lifted her hand to turn it back and forth in a so-so motion. "It's Asa, so it's kind of hard to tell. I think he's glad to be back home, but whatever happened between the two of you is still sitting heavily on his shoulders. He hides it all pretty well, but I've worked with him so closely for so long I can see it. His eyes don't shine anymore."

That made me suck in a hard breath and had my fingers twitching on each hand. "I just wanted to see if he was okay. I knew he wasn't close with his dad at all … but still."

She nodded in agreement. "I think he'll be happy to see you. It was a pretty slow night. Rowdy and Zeb were the last two left at the bar and they took off about ten minutes before Church and I walked out. He's probably getting ready to shut everything down if you want to stick your head in for a minute before he locks the door." She reached out a hand and gave my arm a little squeeze. "I don't know why he did what he did, Royal, but I do know that doing it made him miserable and hurt him just as much as it hurt you."

"I wish that made me feel any kind of better." She made a sympathetic noise and then waved good-bye as she headed off to her own sporty little car. My hand shook when I reached out to pull open the door to the Bar. I didn't know if it was better that he was alone inside or if seeing him for the first time since he demolished me would be easier with the buffer of other people around.

I figured this way if I burst into tears, or made a fool of myself in any other way, at least he would be the only one to witness it and he had already seen me at various stages of my worst.

The lights were still on and blazing bright. The jukebox was on and playing a sad song I didn't recognize. Asa was behind the bar and had turned around to see who was walking in when the doors opened. All I could think was that Dixie was dead wrong. His eyes shone brighter than the sun and hotter than the neon signs on the wall behind him from the distance that separated us. He was a glowing golden beacon of all that I ever wanted, and he was just staring at me while I stood rooted on the spot.

He looked a little rough. He had lost some weight and his normally short, blond hair had encroached on shaggy territory complete with unruly curls that upped his handsome level to devastating. He had more than a scruff of gold fuzz on his face, and where a flirty grin usually lived on his mouth there were fine white lines bracketing a tight frown. I took a deep breath and told myself that even if he had hurt me, even if he was still playing some kind of awful game, I was a big enough person to make sure he was all right. I could live my life without Asa Cross in it even if I didn't want to. When I started walking toward the bar, I saw him tense up as he moved forward and leaned on the opposite side with his arms spread far apart.

"What are you doing here, Red?" He didn't sound upset that I was here, but he didn't sound happy to see me either.

I made my way all the way up to the bar and pushed a couple of the stools out of the way so I could stand directly across from him with the wood of the bar top pressing into my middle.

"I heard about your dad, so I just wanted to see how you were doing."

He just stared at me for a long moment, then pushed off the bar and turned around to grab a couple of rocks glasses that he then proceeded to pour a couple of fingers of amber liquid into. I could tell by the peaty, smoky scent that it was scotch. My cheeks instantly flamed bright red and my breath got choppy when I recalled the last time we had shared a scotch in this bar. He pushed the glass over in front of me and I hesitantly curled my fingers around it.

"I feel like shit every second of every day, but it doesn't have anything to do with my dad passing away."

That much brutal honesty after a full month of silence was almost enough to bring me to my knees. I felt my back teeth clench together and some of the anger that I was surviving on surged to the surface.

"I didn't go anywhere, Asa." God, I wanted him to explain himself more than I wanted anything else in the entire world. I wanted him to open his mouth and make everything better, but he didn't. He just continued to stare at me and I continued to stare at him.

He reached out for his own glass and lifted it until it touched his lips. I could see the memories glittering all along the molten heat in his gaze as he swallowed the liquor down and continued to watch me in silence.

I could see this was going to go nowhere fast. He wasn't going to cave and break his silence. I wasn't going to be able to withstand him licking his lips and looking at me like I was his last meal while he was on death row, without climbing over the bar and either smacking him across the face or sitting on it ... or maybe both. Neither would bring me any peace of mind while he was still being so evasive and secretive. I pushed my untouched drink back toward him and closed my eyes briefly.

"So this is it for us?" I could hear in my voice how much it hurt to say those words.

He made a strangled noise and I opened my eyes as he leaned back up against the bar. Now I could see what Dixie had been talking about. There was no more shimmer, no more glimmer or metallic glow in his gaze. They just looked flat and boring brown like any other guy's ... which Asa definitely wasn't.

"This is it." It sounded like the words had to fight their way past dragons and over cliffs to make their way out of his mouth.

I pushed some of my hair over my shoulder and wrapped my arms around my waist. Once again he left me feeling like I needed a hug.

"You were worth every second of heartbreak. I just want you to know that." I had to let him know that even if he ruined me, my time with him had all been worth it in the end. It was filled with moments I would cherish forever. His eyes flickered away from me for a second and his head dropped down so that he was looking at the top of the bar.

"So were you, Royal." That was it. The finality of it all when a simple explanation I knew he wouldn't give could fix everything.

God he was going to murder my heart and it was a crime he was going to get away with scot-free. I was turning around to leave, and he was turning around so he didn't have to watch me walk away, when the front door slammed open and a disheveled young man came rushing through.

I had been on the streets and on patrol enough to know a strung-out junkie when I saw one, and this guy was higher than a hundred kites. He was twitchy and he was sweaty and his eyes were roaming around the bar in an alarming way. He had on dirty torn jeans and a hoodie that was zipped all the way up even though it was heading into early summer weather and easily sixty-five degrees outside. I shot Asa a look out of the corner of my eye, but he was scowling at the intruder in a threatening and unconcerned way.

"Avett doesn't work here anymore, Jared. She got fired because of you." Asa's voice was calm but his twang was thick in his words, so I knew he was trying to throw the guy off.

The junkie twitched his eyes between the two of us and took a couple of stumbling steps closer to the bar. His skin was an alarming yellow color and his pupils were so dilated that there was no color in his irises, just scary, endless black.

"This is her old man's bar. She has a right to that money. You and that asshole army guy took what was rightfully hers. So her taking that money wasn't stealing."

Asa grunted and moved to cross his arms over his chest. I wanted to tell him that the other guy was way too hyped up to try and reason with or to try and physically intimidate, but I couldn't take my attention off of what I knew was a major threat. A junkie didn't just wander in off the streets in the middle of a high this late at night for a friendly chat.

"Yeah, well, what about the stash you took from your supplier that had guys showing up at your place to work her over? I suppose that wasn't stealing either. They could've killed her because of you."

You couldn't argue or reason with a junkie and I knew Asa had to be aware of that fact. I shifted just a little so I could keep an eye on Jared and still see Asa in the mirror behind the bar. He was jerking his head to the side as he talked, obviously trying to get me to move toward the back office. I narrowed my eyes at him in the reflection and shook my head ever so slightly in the negative. I dealt with guys like Jared for a living and I was armed. I had my off-duty weapon stashed in my purse if the situation called for it.

"That was a mistake. I didn't mean for her to get hurt." The guy moved even farther into the bar and his zealous attention was focused solely on Asa.

"Well, she did, all because of you and your habit."

"She loves me." The junkie rubbed a hand over his face and my spine snapped straight as one of his hands dove into the pocket of his hoodie. I slipped my hand inside the opening of my purse. I wasn't going to leave anything to chance.

"Yeah, and loving you is going to end up with a bullet in her damn head. You want a fix, then leave your girl out of it."

The junkie swore and an ugly flush worked up into his face. He almost frothed at the mouth like a wild dog when he lurched toward the bar screaming, "You don't know anything about it!"

Asa just laughed, and if I had been closer I would have kicked him for antagonizing the unpredictable man. I knew he was doing it on purpose, but still.

"I know more about it than you think." Asa's voice was full of memory and warning.

Jared drew up short and rubbed a hand across his mouth. His eyes flicked to me and then back to Asa, and I let out a long and steadying breath when he pulled a small, black gun out of the pocket of his sweatshirt. He pointed the barrel right at the center of Asa's chest and the entire world stopped moving. Everything narrowed in on the barrel of that gun and what it was pointed at.

I saw Asa's eyebrows twitch up, I saw his mouth pull tight, but other than that, he didn't move a single muscle.

"You're gonna give me every single dime that's in that cash register. I'm gonna take the money and my lady and blow out of town."

Shit. Drugs and desperation were not a good combination. I saw Asa's eyes lift up so that he was looking at me over the top of the junkie's head.

"Avett know you're doing this?" I bet the answer wasn't going to make Asa very happy.

Jared just laughed and waved the gun around with more animation. "Just hand over the money."

Asa slowly turned toward the cash register all the while peppering Jared with questions about his girlfriend. I could see the agitation building and could feel the tension rising. Dealing with someone on drugs was always volatile. Dealing with someone on drugs who was looking for a way out of the trouble they had found themselves in took me right back to that alley and the way things had gone so horribly wrong with Dominic right around Christmastime. I refused to live through a repeat of that night. I refused to watch Asa get hurt like that. Moving at the pace of a glacier, I slowly slipped my off-duty weapon out of my bag, careful not to make any kind of noise or any kind of big motion that would draw Jared's attention to me.

"Are you the one that sent Avett's old man after me or was that the army guy?" I watched as Jared took the gun and aimed it right at the back of Asa's head while he was turned around fiddling the register. The junkie's hands were shaking and the drugs that were fueling him had him all over the place emotionally, but at that close of a distance there was little chance a bullet was going to miss whatever it was pointed at if he pulled the trigger. Asa stopped what he was doing but the register didn't open. He kept his back turned for a few minutes and then twisted his head just a little bit and I saw his eyes widen at the sight of the gun leveled directly at him.

"What difference does it make? Every father should have the right to confront the asshole that hit his little girl. Just wait until he hears you tried to rob his bar. There won't be a hole deep enough for you to hide in when Brite gets word of this."

Asa was antagonizing the unpredictable man to a dangerous level and I didn't want to wait until he crossed the line. I let my purse hit the floor with a clatter and leveled my own weapon at the junkie. Jared's eyes bugged in his face and the weapon swung away from Asa and ended up pointed right at me. I refused to show any reaction or look away even when Asa barked my name like a swearword.

"Jared, you need to listen to me and drop the gun."

"What the fuck!" He sounded scared, which wasn't encouraging.

"Put the gun down, Jared." I made sure I sounded calm and kept his attention on me.

"Who the fuck are you?"

"That's not important. What's important is that we all want to walk out of here without anyone getting hurt."

"Fuck you, lady." I heard Asa growl and saw Jared start to turn in his direction when suddenly sirens could be heard outside the bar. Jared looked from me and back to Asa, who just shrugged and held up his cell phone. Instead of opening the register when he turned around, he had called 911.

"Sorry, dude, I'm not letting you rob this bar."

Jared howled like a wounded animal and swung the gun back toward Asa. I knew he was going to pull the trigger, so I didn't hesitate to pull mine first. The blast of both gunshots simultaneously was deafening and had my ears ringing and my nose twitching from the gunpowder. A bottle shattered behind the bar and I watched as Asa suddenly vaulted over the top of the long bar and took a flying leap through the air to tackle Jared to the ground. I hadn't aimed to kill the young man, just to get him to drop his weapon. The gun was lying on the ground at Jared's feet and he was struggling in Asa's unrelenting hold as he bled from the gunshot wound I had just put in his arm.

I walked over to kick the gun away just as the front doors flew open and several of my coworkers stormed into the building. I laid my own gun on the ground and lifted my hands up in the air, knowing it would take a second to sort out who was who. Luckily one of the guys on scene had gone through the academy with me and Dom, so I got to put my hands down and gave a rundown of the chaotic scene pretty quickly. I knew I was going to have to go through another investigation since it had been an off-duty shooting, but luckily the bar had cameras and there was a viable witness, so I wasn't too concerned about the fallout this time around. I made sure they knew Asa was a victim and not a suspect because if they ran his background it would raise more questions than the situation called for and he had enough of being accused of crimes he didn't commit already.

I was sitting on one of the bar stools recounting the events to one of the detectives and Asa was sitting next to me telling his version to another. I don't know when it happened, but at some point he had reached out and taken one of my hands in his own. His fingers curled around mine and let my fingertips rest against where his pulse was steady and strong. Even if it really was the end of us, I was so grateful for the fact that nothing had happened to him.

"So do either of you know the girl?" The detective that was talking to Asa looked between the two of us as he asked the question. I moved a little closer to Asa so that my side was pressed into his side.

"What girl? Jared came in on his own."

"He might have entered on his own but he didn't arrive on his own. There was a girl waiting in front of the building with the car running when we pulled in. She said she was just waiting on him, that he was running in to apologize for some stink he caused, but that sounds suspicious as hell. What kind of junkie needs to make amends in the middle of the night?"

Asa sighed. "Does she have pink hair?"

The detectives shared a look. "Kind of."

"She's his girlfriend. Her dad used to own this bar. Jared has her all twisted up and acting crazy. She probably had no idea he was planning on robbing the place."

"She was in a running vehicle while an attempted armed robbery was taking place. She's going to get charged as accessory to the crime."

Asa stiffened. "Don't do that. I really doubt she understood what he was up to."

I squeezed the hand I held in mine. "They have to charge her, Asa."

He sucked in a breath. "Jesus. Brite is going to lose his mind."

One of the detectives snorted. "She wouldn't be the first girl to get in trouble for a no-good man. Get her a good lawyer and hope for the best."

Asa swore and the detective rushed through the rest of the questions as the crime-scene tech finished up all their pictures and measurements. It took a few hours and it was almost dawn by the time we were finally alone. Asa looked worn out and even more haggard than he had when I walked in the door what felt like a lifetime ago. I laid my head on his shoulder and asked him, "Are you okay?"

He laughed and it sounded ugly and hard. "Yeah, but I have no idea how to explain any of this to Rome or what I'm going to tell Brite about Avett."

"I think maybe you could worry about that after you take a second to be happy nothing terrible happened. You just had a gun fired at your head, Asa."

He turned his head until his lips touched the center of my forehead. "I know, but that wasn't nearly as terrifying as watching him point that gun at you."

"It's part of my job."

"Your job sucks."

I laughed a little. "Sometimes, but today I was so happy that I got to do it."

We fell into a heavy silence again and I knew I needed to get up and walk away from him once and for all. I just didn't know that I was going to be able to do that.

"Is this really the end, Asa?"

He made a noise in his throat, then climbed off the chair he was sitting in next to me. He walked around the front of me and put his hands on either side of my face. He tilted my head back and bent down so that his lips brushed softly against my own.

"I don't know, Royal. Do you think you can love me enough to let me lie to you for the rest of our lives?"

I jerked back from him just a little bit and blinked at him. "What?"

He kissed me again and this time put some force behind it. His tongue snuck out to touch the center of my lips and I felt the scrape of his teeth when I let him in. He kissed me until neither of us could breathe and I was forced to hold on to him or melt away into nothing.

"I love you, Royal. I love you enough to live for you, to be awake for you, to be here in this moment as long as you are in it with me. I love you enough to let you know every little dirty secret I have and to tell you all the terrible things I have done and how those things left their marks on my soul. I love you in a way that makes me want to be more than I ever have been before, but I also love you enough to want to protect you from things that I know are going to hurt you. If you love me enough and trust me enough to let me keep those things from you for an eternity, then maybe we have a shot. I know it's asking an impossible thing, but that's the only way."

"You've got to be kidding me!" I pushed him away and jumped to my feet. "You love me, but you won't tell me what drove you away in the first place and I'm just supposed to accept that? Is this another one of your games, Asa? Because if it is, you're going to lose big-time."

"No games, Red. Just me, you, and a secret you're going to have to live with if you want us to be together. Believe me, I totally get it if you can't do it."

"Why do you always make me want to love and hate you at the same time?"

"It's part of my charm." A tiny grin pulled at the corner of his mouth and I shoved my hands through my hair in frustration.

"I'm a cop. I don't do secrets."

He reached out and pulled me to his chest. I was finally wrapped in the hug I had been longing for ever since he walked out of the door at my mother's place.

"I know. That's why this situation between us is impossible." He rubbed his cheek against the top of my head and then let me go. "Being with you gave me something I never had before."

"What's that?"

"Something to sacrifice. I never wanted anything or anyone as badly as I want you for my own, Royal. If I have to sacrifice you for your own good, then that's what I'll do."

He was talking in riddles and it was all so frustrating I wanted to scream. "I don't think I can go down this road with you, Asa."

I saw the light in his eyes dim but the tiny smile on his mouth never wavered. "I didn't think you could. I really do love you."

"I love you, too."

We just stared at each other, him silently begging me to accept his terms and me pleading with him to just open the vault and let me know whatever it was he was hiding. It was obvious neither one of us was going to give. After about five minutes I turned on my heel and headed for the front door, all the while praying he was going to call me back.

He didn't.

CHAPTER 19

Asa

Waking Rome up at the crack of dawn to explain the craziness that had gone down my first night back at work proved to be the easy part. Talking to Brite and Darcy about Avett's involvement was much more difficult. Darcy was all for bailing the girl out of jail as quickly as possible, while Brite was so furious with her and her poor judgment he wanted to let her sit and stew. Either direction they finally went in, I gave them the name of the lawyer that had helped me out when I ended up in hot water last year, and wished them luck. The guy cost a small fortune, but he had the reputation of being a ruthless opponent in the Denver court system, and I knew eventually Brite was going to want to wade in to save his little girl. If anyone could sort out the mess Avett had made of her life, it was Quaid Jackson.

Rome decided to shut the Bar down for a few days so that it could get set back to rights and so that I could have a few days to get my head back on right. I needed the time more to handle Royal walking away for good than I did to process having a gun shoved in my face for the second time while working at the Bar. I didn't tell Rome that, though; instead I asked him if I could come over one night. While Cora made dinner and RJ ran around banging pots and pans in the kitchen, I wrote him a check for a hundred grand and told him I wanted to be his business partner.

There was a moment of silence and I could see him debating if he wanted the check or not when Cora leaned out of the kitchen and hollered, "Take the money, Rome."

That shook Rome loose of whatever he was turning over in his head and he took the check and shook my hand. For the first time in my entire adult life I had endless, legitimate opportunities laid out in front of me and I almost didn't know what to do with all that good fortune. The feeling of being satisfied and situated only lasted as long as it took me to go home to an empty apartment and a silent phone.

Weeks passed with no word or no sight of Royal. I went back to work. I asked Wheeler to work on the Nova, and I even started looking for a new place to live. I looked at a few condos and town houses but none of it felt right. It took me a minute to realize I didn't want to move into something temporary. I wanted a home, but I didn't want to live there alone. The more time that passed, the more it solidified the fact that sometimes love really wasn't enough.

Ayden called me once a week to check up on me. It was nice that our calls no longer consisted of her being panicked and worried about what kind of trouble I was going to get myself into. Now she just wanted to make sure I was still moving forward, even with a broken heart. She told me to just cave and tell Royal the truth, to which I answered repeatedly that the only person that benefited from being honest was me. Yeah, I could get my girl back if I spilled the beans about all the ways her mom was fucked up, but I would alienate a mother from her daughter and I refused to put Royal through that kind of turmoil. She didn't need to be up close and personal with the kind of heartache that would follow if she realized just how far off the deep end her mother had gone. Plus I was intimately familiar with the fact that a truly screwed-up person could do really good things with a second chance, if they took it. Maybe Roslyn would be one of them. For Royal's sake I really hoped her mother would take the opportunity she had been given and do something with it. She was another one that my sister would say just needed to let herself be loved and stop purposely sabotaging her own happiness.

Eventually Ayden let it drop and decided to focus on all the good things I had going on instead. When I told her I wanted to look at buying a house in the Baker neighborhood, where the Bar was located, it almost brought her to tears.

"I wasn't going to question anything you decided to do with all that money, Asa. But I have to tell you that it makes me ridiculously happy that you're planting some roots with it."

The idea of roots, of something permanent here in Colorado, was so strange. It felt right and it was a way to show her, to prove to anyone that questioned it, that I was officially awake and making every moment I had right now count.

"I'll make sure I find a place big enough for you and Jet to stay when you come visit."

She snorted at me. "Me, Jet, and this baby we just found out we're having."

I almost dropped the phone because she said it so nonchalantly. "You're pregnant?"

Ayden laughed a little bit and I could almost see her pacing back and forth chewing on her lip as she confirmed the fact. "Yeah. It's still really early on, probably too early to tell anyone, but I can't keep it to myself, ya know?" She was giving me her secret just like I had given her mine.

"I thought you wanted to wait." I couldn't help the pure joy that threaded through my voice. Ayden was going to make a great mom. Both she and Jet deserved to have a happy family and home life after the nightmare of both of their upbringings.

"What can I say? I married a very persuasive man and there is just something about those tight pants that makes it impossible to say no to him." She sighed happily. "And there was something different after I got back from Kentucky. It was like all the bad stuff from there was gone. There were no more cobwebs, no more resentment or what-ifs. It was just all gone. I want to have a family with the man that loved me enough that I had no choice but to love every part of myself, warts and all."

"I know exactly what you mean." I laughed out loud and told her, "You're going to be pregnant at Cora and Rome's wedding."

They had finally decided on a Valentine's Day wedding the following year. Rome couldn't have been happier that his little spitfire was finally going to be legally tied to him for the rest of his life.

"Yeah, well, Cora was superpregnant at Rule and Shaw's wedding, and at the rate we're all going, someone is always going to be knocked up or getting hitched." She wasn't wrong. I had heard through the grapevine that Nash had purchased an engagement ring for Saint, and Rowdy had mentioned more than once that Salem was none too subtly hinting around that she was ready for the baby-having portion of their relationship to start. That was a whole lot of happiness and future building happening around me, and even if I couldn't have it in my own life, I was really happy I got to be around to bear witness to it in the lives of those I loved.

"Congratulations, Ayd. I'm really happy for you and your guitar guy."

"Thank you. I'm scared out of my mind, but I figure if Rule can do it so can I." I laughed, remembering the absolute look of terror on Rule's face when he couldn't fix whatever was wrong with his little boy.

"You'll be fine. I'll absolutely make sure the new house has room for you guys and a baby."

We chatted for a little while longer. I think she desperately needed someone to talk to about the baby besides Jet. I couldn't get enough of hearing the nervous excitement in her voice. Ever since I had woken up in that hospital bed in Louisville, all I had ever wanted was for Ayden to have the best kind of life—just like she wanted for me. I wanted her to be truly and fully happy. It was just one more way in which my entire life felt almost complete to know that she was there. She was happy and where she was always meant to be. It twisted my insides up a little to know that I would never get that with Royal.

It was the following weekend that I finally found my dream house. It was a little farther away from the Bar than I initially wanted, just a few blocks away from Phil Milstein Park and the Platte River. It was totally a family home. Big and sprawling with a massive backyard that had a deck, a hot tub, and a privacy fence. There was a two-car garage and a media room complete with a popcorn machine. The house had an impressive, tricked-out chef's kitchen, which was hilarious considering I didn't own a single pot or pan, and it came equipped with more rooms than a single guy with no family could ever possibly need. But I loved it. It felt right, and the idea of needing to buy a lawn mower to care for grass that was all mine somehow appealed to me on a deeper level more than any of the other places I had looked at closer to the city had.

I told the realtor I was working with, a smoking-hot blonde that was more interested in getting me into bed than she was in getting her commission, to put in an offer at asking price. She balked and told me the place had been on the market long enough to negotiate a better price. I didn't want to gamble or play games. I just wanted the house. I wanted to be present, wide-awake in the here and now. I reiterated my wishes and turned down her offer to go out for a celebratory drink when of course the home-owners accepted. Eventually I was going to have to shake off the haze of Royal that clouded my mind whenever another lady showed some interest in me, but I wasn't ready for that part of moving on with my life just yet.

I went into my shift at the Bar a little stunned. I couldn't believe I had just bought a house. For the very first time since I started working for Rome, I needed a drink before my shift instead of downing one when it was over. Dixie squealed in delight for me and Church just gave me a solemn head nod, which I assumed was his badass seal of approval. Darcy wasn't really talking much ever since the debacle with Avett and Jared, but she managed to scrounge up a smile for me and a hug. She told me Brite would be so proud once he found out, and I had to admit that I liked making the gruff ex-Marine proud of me. He was the closest thing to a father figure I had ever had, so any kind of approval from him was always welcome.

The shift flew by. Mostly because I was thinking about how different my life looked as spring bounced happily into summer this year versus last year. Last year it had been an endless string of pretty girls to keep me company in the dark because I couldn't face them in the harsh light of day. It had been just trying to keep my nose clean and prove to Rome he could trust me. I had been getting shoved in the back of a police cruiser for a crime I didn't commit and I had been willing to sit my ass behind bars because I really thought that was what I deserved.

This year my family was happy, healthy, and growing. I didn't need to wonder if Rome trusted me or about keeping my nose clean. Both of those things were just part of my every day now. I had a home, a job that was both fulfilling and exciting, with all kinds of potential. Quite possibly the biggest change was that I no longer worried about whether I had earned all the good things at my fingertips or not. Regardless if I had changed enough or given up enough in order to be worthy of all this good fortune, it was mine and I wasn't going to squander it away like I had been doing before. I wasn't going to sit my ass in a cell ever again trying to repent. The other big change was of course the fact that only one girl would do. She was the only one I wanted. The only one I couldn't get off of my mind. The only one I dreamed about, obsessed about. She was the only girl that I had ever loved and there wasn't a replacement for that anytime soon. Other girls might come and go, in time, but Royal would always hold my heart, and I knew there wasn't any way to get it back from her. It was probably safer in her hands anyway. I had never taken very good care of it when it was in my possession.

Dixie hollered at me that she had to take a call and disappeared about an hour before it was time to shut the bar down. The new guy was handling business like an old pro and I realized my time spent behind the bar was going to be cut down dramatically. I liked bartending. I liked the flow and freedom. I liked listening to other people's issues and dramas. It always made me feel like my own story wasn't so unusual. I hadn't been kidding when I told Ayden the payout on the farm was enough money for me to not only go into the rehab business with Rome but also for me to look at buying my own bar. I liked the dive that Rome had brought back to life, but I also liked the secretive, exclusive feel of the place I had taken Royal to. There were a lot of options out there and I suddenly wanted to capitalize on all of them.

Dixie came back into the bar laughing and smiling. Church asked her if she had been talking to a guy, to which she just rolled her eyes and told him to mind his own business. I didn't know what was going on between those two other than a whole lot of back-and-forth, but I figured they would either figure it out or they wouldn't. Dixie was a mushy and soft sweetheart. Church came across like he was made of iron and concrete. It was an odd combination, but I had seen stranger things work and lead to happily-ever-after, so I just kept my mouth shut as we closed down the bar.

By the time I climbed into the Nova to drive the few blocks to my crappy apartment, I was drained. The reality of how fast my life was changing, the fact that it was all moving in the right direction but that I was doing it alone, sort of ripped me in half. I was proud of myself for making so many right steps, but still felt broken about the fact that none of those steps were taking me in the direction of the person I wanted.

I shoved my key in the door very aware that my time of coming home to this shit hole of an apartment was very nearly at an end. I chuckled when I realized I was going to have to hijack one of the girls and take her with me to buy an entire house worth of furniture. I didn't own enough to even fill up one of the rooms in the place that was now mine.

It took me a second to recognize that I wasn't alone once the front door was closed. All the lights were off like I had left them, except the light in the bathroom was on and casting a faint beam of light onto my bed, which was very much occupied. I tossed my keys on the bistro table and walked toward the bed. My eyes locked on the chocolate-brown pair that were watching me carefully.

She was naked. Sitting up on her knees and looking at me like I had all the answers. Her auburn hair hung loose all the way to her waist, offering a small amount of coverage for the very pink tips of her breasts, which tightened and peaked as I drew closer to her. It wasn't until my knees were touching the very edge of the mattress that I noticed around her slender wrists shiny metal handcuffs had her hands locked together in front of her. My heart started to race and I had to blink several times to make sure I wasn't dreaming.

We just stared at each other for a long-drawn-out moment. I needed to ask her why she was here after all this time. I needed to know what all of this meant. Instead I reached out a single finger to push some of her hair off of her shoulder so it wasn't covering her up anymore and I could let my eyes feast on all of her. She was so beautiful. I grasped the chain that kept the handcuffs together and gave it a little tug to draw her closer to me. She crawled toward me without a word.

"I bought you a house today." The truth of that statement rang steady in my voice. Her mouth fell open in a little gasp of surprise.

"What are you talking about?" I tugged on the handcuffs again until I had her arms high enough to loop them around my neck. All her plush and naked curves pressed into me and I finally felt finished. She was what I needed to be a complete man. Whole.

"I bought a house today. But I need you to make it a home, Royal." I bent my forehead down so that it was resting against hers. I shouldn't have been pouring my heart out to her until I knew why she was here, if this was as real for her as it was for me. It was going to kill me if she walked out again. "What's up with the hardware, Red?"

The metal around her wrists was hard and cold around my neck.

"Well, I had this brilliant idea to show you that I trusted you, that I need you more than I need the truth. I figured getting naked and handcuffing myself to your bed would not only illustrate that I do trust you to do the right thing by me but also fulfill one of the fantasies you've been throwing around since the beginning. Only I forgot you don't have a headboard, let alone a headboard I could attach these to."

"No one has a headboard made for handcuffs in the real world."

She rolled her eyes and a smile tugged at her mouth. I was a goner. I wasn't going to let her go again even if she wanted me to, but I needed to know why she was suddenly here, so I told her, "We need to talk about your change of heart, Royal."

She lifted one of her burnished eyebrows at me and her dark eyes danced in merriment. "I know. But I'm naked. I have on handcuffs and I really missed you, Asa." She turned her head a little so that she could touch her lips to my own. "Plus you bought me a house. I think I need to say thank you in a way you'll always remember."

My better judgment told me to figure out where this was leading, to remind her that I had a major secret I was never going to be able to tell her, but she kissed me again. Every predatory instinct I had ever had roared to life with the need to claim, possess, mark, and own her forever as mine. Common sense had never been my strong suit anyway.

I tumbled her back on the bed with a growl.

CHAPTER 20

Royal

I spent weeks vacillating between the overwhelming amount of love I had for this man and the burning need to know what he was keeping from me. One day I was sure that whatever secret Asa was hiding didn't matter because I wanted to be with him more than I wanted anything. The next I would be eaten alive with curiosity about what he was hiding, and I knew I would never be able to let it go. It was like being caught in the middle of an emotional tug-of-war between my head and my heart, and neither one was winning.

My mom kept telling me to get over him. Dom kept telling me to go after him and I had no idea what the right thing to do was. I was lonely and I missed him, but it wasn't until Ayden called me today and told me that Asa had bought a house and that he never would have done that if it hadn't been for me, that I really understood that I did love him enough to let him lie to me. Ayden also hinted that if I really thought about it, I could probably figure out why he was adamant that he keep this particular thing from me and that got me bogged down and long-repressed instincts churning back to life. When some of the pieces started to click into place, I had to evaluate whether I really wanted to know the truth or not. I loved him and I loved my mother, and I had a feeling prying into that particular Pandora's box was going to change how I felt about one if not both of them forever. Plus, while Ayden wasn't about to let the proverbial cat out of the bag, she had given me enough hints and clues on top of my suspicions to know that certain lines that were unforgivable no matter how much I loved either of them hadn't been crossed. I knew whatever had happened between the two people I loved the most wasn't pretty, and I was resigned to leave it at that if it meant I got to keep them both.

One secret wasn't enough to give up a love that felt like it was going to come along only once in a lifetime. Ayden eased the remainder of my fears by reminding me that the only reason Asa was keeping something from me in the first place was because he was trying to protect me … just like he had done all those months ago when I was in a downward spiral and he stopped my fall. He wasn't lying to me to hurt me; in fact it was the opposite of that. Even when he was being secretive and cryptic he was always there to catch me.

I had to trust him and I had to show him that I did; thus I was handcuffed and naked while he crawled all over me. I was supposed to be vulnerable and open to him, only I didn't feel that way. I felt right. I felt like this was where I was supposed to be all along.

I knew he needed a grand gesture, something more than words to show him I needed him more than I needed the truth, and this was all I could come up with in a pinch. Besides, he'd had a thing for my handcuffs since the very beginning, so I called Dixie and asked her to text me when they were done for the night, parked around the corner, and then snuck into his place with a key Cora had snagged for me. There was something entirely exhilarating about stripping naked and binding your hands together in a symbolic gesture for a man like Asa. Handing myself over to him both body and soul should have been terrifying, but as soon as he opened his mouth and told me he had bought the house for me, I knew I had done the right thing. No secret was worth giving up a man that told you he needed you to be his home.

His heavy weight settled on top of me, and for the first time in two months I felt like I was grounded, not floating between what I was craving and common sense. This was where I needed to always be, with him, under him, inside of him. He made me feel real.

"How does it feel to be the one hooked up for a change?" He moved my arms from where they were looped around his neck and stretched them out as far as they would reach above my head. I drove the tips of my breasts into his chest and made every line of my body arch up into his. His eyes glowed hot enough to light up the entire room and his gaze made a warm flush work up under the surface of my skin.

"Under the circumstances not so bad." I gave the unforgiving metal a little tug and felt the response in Asa where our lower bodies were pressed together.

"They look way better on you than they ever did on me." The dry humor in his tone wasn't lost on me as he bent his head and sealed his mouth over mine.

It had been far too long since we had shared a real kiss. Not one filled with good-bye or regret. I missed it almost as much as I had missed him. His tongue twisted with mine while his hands swept down my naked sides and slipped around to grab on to the curve of my backside. He ravaged my mouth with his own. He ate up my response and I hardly noticed that he was moving us to the edge of the bed. He lifted his head and kissed each of my eyelids, the tip of my nose, and then moved on to the tip of each of my breasts, which were ridged and practically begging him for attention.

I nearly bolted upright at the first flick of his tongue across one turgid nipple. It felt like my entire body was electrified everywhere he touched. I lifted my hand to thread it through his hair and stopped short when both my arms jerked up over my head, forcing my eager flesh even farther into his waiting mouth. He laughed when I grumbled in frustration and lifted my eyebrows at him as he climbed off the edge of the bed so that he was on his knees between my legs.

He smirked at me, lifted one of my legs, and rested it on his shoulder. I squirmed a little bit because his delicious intent was clear all over his handsome face.

"Asa ..." I wasn't really sure what I wanted to say to him, but apparently his name was enough to convey all the emotion that was churning around inside of me.

"I know, Red. Believe me, I know." And then his head disappeared between my legs and all conscious thought ceased.

I couldn't stop myself from shoving my bound hands into his hair as the first swipe of his tongue across my sensitive folds had my entire body arching up off the bed. It made him chuckle, and the soft puff of air across my heated core sent every muscle in my body quaking. He let go of my backside with one of his hands and used it to tickle the delicate skin along my inner thigh. The double stimulation had my breath wheezing in and out and my blood running heavy and thick through my veins.

When he used the edge of his teeth on my clit and twisted so that he could sink his fingers inside the wet heat that he had stirred up, I almost came all the way off the bed. I yelled his name with a hoarse cry and let my head roll around on the bed because I felt like I was going out of my mind.

He stroked me with his tongue, he stroked me with his fingers, and he didn't stop even when I was yanking on his hair like a wild woman, the handcuffs rattling around between us. I told him I was close and that just seemed to urge him on even more. He tortured my center of pleasure, not letting up with his gentle ministrations even after I broke apart under him. I was panting, spent, and told him I wanted my turn, but he just slid his fingers out and lifted me up higher so that he could feast on me some more and started all over again.

If it was possible to die from pleasure, I was pretty sure I was looking death right in the face. It was only after two more spine-bending and voice-breaking orgasms, one with his mouth, the other with his clever fingers and his mouth on my nipples, that he finally let up on me. I was a boneless, worthless pile of satisfied goo when he climbed to his feet and started stripping off his own clothes. I wanted to touch, to pet all the rippling muscles that he revealed as his shirt hit the floor. That was hard to do with my hands locked together, but the way his eyes followed my palms as they skated over his abs and down lower so that I could help him with his belt made the awkwardness worthwhile.

"No one else does for me what you do, Royal." His voice was thick with passion and sweet with the South that still colored it. I looked up at him from under my lashes as I pulled his waiting erection free from the confines of denim that was keeping it from me. "You made this second chance I got at life worth living."

I blinked up at him and wrapped a hand around the base of his cock. I had to admit there was something extra sexy about the sight with the twin bands of silver around my wrists while I moved my hands up and down the thick shaft. I could feel the blood surge in the heavy veins underneath as he watched what I was doing with intent eyes.

"You cared about me when I was having a really hard time caring about myself. You have always challenged me and never once made me feel like a pretty showpiece and nothing more. You have always valued me, Asa, and I can't tell you how important that was for me." I grinned up at him and gave the rigid flesh that was throbbing in my hands a little tug. "And some of your games are fun, Asa, so don't ever change."

He sucked in a breath that made all his stomach muscles contract in a delightful way as I bent forward and ran the tip of my tongue all along every hot and hard ridge of his cock. He groaned and bent forward a little so that he could thread his fingers through my hair as I took him all the way into my mouth and hollowed out my cheeks. I sucked on him and swirled my tongue around the plump head. He grunted my name as I took him deep enough that the short, golden hairs of his happy trail tickled my nose. He tasted musky and strong on my tongue and all I wanted to do was undo him the way he had just done to me.

His fingers pulled harder and he started to move with less care as the tip of him hit the back of my throat. I used the edge of my teeth carefully and forced him to spread his legs just enough that I could get my hands between them and around his tightly drawn up sac. I tickled him on the outside in much the same way he had tickled me on the inside, which was apparently too much for him to take because he pulled away with a jerk and toppled me back onto the bed in an ungraceful heap.

He forced my legs up around his sides, looped my arms back around his neck, and sank into me with a satisfied sigh. He gazed down at me like I was the only girl in the world and then lowered his head so that his lips were resting right next to my ear as he started to move in and out of me at a furious pace.

"I was without this for too long. As much as I like that pretty mouth, I like being inside you a hell of a lot more." Well, that was good to know.

I gasped as he bit down on my earlobe and used the hand that wasn't holding his weight off of me to twist and tug at one of my overly sensitized nipples until it just hovered on the edge of being painful. The way he moved, the force with which he took me, made it clear this wasn't about makeup sex or even about reconnecting after months apart. No, Asa was marking me, making me his, and it was imprinted on every thrust of his hips, every sting of his teeth as they scraped across my neck. He was letting me know that this was it, and it made my heart and body so deliciously happy.

I felt my inner walls contract around him, trying to hold him inside as he moved within me. I could feel how wet I was around his hardness, could feel every little internal flutter along his shaft as he pounded into me. My hips automatically lifted up to his, trying to match the fervor with which he was loving me. He was filling me up with emotion and his impressive erection. All of it felt so good I wasn't sure I was going to survive any more of his attention. Not that I was ever going to ask him to stop or go easy on me. I liked that he was rough. Liked that along with all the pleasure there was the occasional bite of discomfort. It reminded me that Asa was never going to be like any other guy and that being with him was always going to mean I needed to stay on my toes. He wasn't an easy man to love, and frankly that was one of my favorite things about him.

No one would ever meet my needs the way he did, and he proved it by sinking one of his hands into the hair at the base of my neck and giving it a tug that wasn't at all gentle.

I couldn't do much with my hands, so I had to hold him to me with my eyes. I refused to look away. I watched everything. I watched the way desire and passion made his eyes go hazy. I watched the way he watched me. I watched the way it made him smug and satisfied when he could see that I was once again close to falling over that edge of completion only he had ever been able to bring me to. I watched the love that shone out of him for me when I broke, and then I watched him drown in the love I had for him as he followed me over a split second later. He collapsed on me with a groan and buried his face in the curve of my neck where it was tender from his nipping at the skin there.

I rattled the handcuffs over his head with a little laugh. "I'm ready to be able to touch you now."

He pulled out of me, which had us both gasping at the sexy glide, and rolled so that he was sitting next to me. He shoved his hands through his hair and grinned down at me. "Not sure I would have lasted for more than a minute if your hands had been free, Red. Where is the key?"

I had put it someplace where I absolutely wouldn't leave it behind or forget it. While playing around like this with Asa was fun, there was no way I wanted anyone outside of this room to know that my cuffs had been used for anything other than hooking up a criminal. I directed him to the pocket in my purse where I had stashed the key, and it only took him a minute to set me free. The skin underneath the cuffs immediately started to tingle as a rush of blood began to flow back to my hands, and Asa picked up each wrist and put a kiss on my pulse. It made my heart flutter and the way he smiled against the skin touching his lips made me think he could feel it.

"So this is us, Royal. Me and you from here on out, and I'm not letting you go again."

I reached out a finger and ran it across the arch of his eyebrow. "You get one secret, Asa. Everything else is mine. I'm not going to bring it up because I'm going to trust you and believe that you wouldn't keep something from me that I absolutely need to know in order to make this relationship between us work. I'm not going to ask about it, but this is the one and only thing you get. The rest is all mine."

He was a man with a past. He was a man with a promising future. He was a man that had a lot to give right now, and I needed to know that he was willing to share all of it with me. I didn't care if that made me seem greedy or unreasonable. I was asking for it all.

"You can have everything I have to give except for that."

I let my finger trace over the slope of his nose and down so I could outline his mouth with the tip of my fingernail. He didn't need to know that I had a pretty good guess what that big secret was. I didn't need all the details. I just needed him.

"Then this *is* it. Me and you from here on out."

He fell onto his back and pulled me over him so that I was draped across the hard planes of his chest. "The cop and the criminal. Who would have ever seen that coming?"

I traced a heart next to where his was steady and strong under my cheek. "I saw it from a mile away. It just took a little bit of time to get you to look in the same direction … and you're a *reformed* criminal."

He chuckled and twirled his fingers through the long ends of my hair where it wrapped around both of us.

"I stole your heart, didn't I?"

I rubbed my cheek on the rock-hard muscle that made a surprisingly good pillow. "I stole yours first, Asa." I let my eyes drift closed as he continued to pet me and rub his hand up and down my spine.

"Can't take something that was yours all along, Red." Oh my. That had a rush of tears rising up behind my eyelids.

"You're so smooth." My pillow moved as he laughed.

"I try. How do you feel about furniture shopping?"

I was almost asleep and feeling way better than I had in a long time. I gave his sides a little squeeze and turned my head so that I could put my lips right in the center of his chest.

"Whatever you want, Asa."

Because if he was going to give me everything he had to give, then I could only do the same thing.

EPILOGUE

Six Months Later …

Living with a police officer was an interesting experience. I'd gotten used to Kevlar mixed in with silk and cotton in the closet. The sight of guns around the house no longer made me jolt in surprise, and her odd hours no longer had me staying awake when she rolled out of bed at the crack of dawn or in the middle of the night. What I was still learning to navigate was the way her job affected her. There were nights I came home to find she was crawling out of her skin with leftover adrenaline, and I barely made it through the door before she was all over me looking for some kind of release for all that pent-up energy. Then there were days that she came home and could hardly look at me. Those were the days I found her curled up in the shower crying and had to pull her out and hold her until she came back into herself. I figured out pretty quickly those were the days the bad guys won. Luckily the days I got tackled and stripped naked were far more common, so I just learned to love her through both. I still thought her job sucked but she loved it so much that I kept my mouth shut … most of the time.

Dom had worked hard and had the help of a very skilled physical therapist that had become instrumental in more ways than one when he had returned to the force. Surprisingly, Royal had asked him if it was okay with him if she stayed partnered with Barrett upon his return. She felt like she had been leaning on Dom too hard thus far in her career, and with a different partner she was really forced to be the cop she was always meant to be. Plus, she told him there was no way her heart could handle seeing him with a gun pointed at him again, and Dom, being the outstanding friend and man that he was, took all of that in stride. All he had ever wanted was for Royal to reach her full potential and she was doing exactly that.

I tossed my keys in the fancy ceramic bowl she had picked out to set by the front door. Even with a designated place for all the keys to live I was still running across town intermittently to let her into her car because she was still locking herself out of things and places on a regular basis. It was cute and the way she said thank you always left me with a smile on my face. My sexy cop was a handful and I wouldn't have it any other way.

Tonight I was the one getting home late. I had so many irons in the fire sometimes it was hard to keep track of things anymore. The business that Rome was spearheading was going like gangbusters. Our initial investment had doubled in just a few months. I honestly took pride in taking businesses that needed a helping hand and breathing new life into them. I was still working a shift a week at the Bar, mostly because I just couldn't let it go. The place was like home to me when I really needed a place to feel welcome and I didn't have it in me to just walk away from that completely. Generally I worked a Wednesday or Thursday night mostly so I could watch the way Dixie and Church were still dancing around each other. It was like a reality TV show live and in color, only far more entertaining. Dixie had recently started Internet dating and Church had all kinds of grumbly and growly opinions about the fact. I couldn't figure out why he just didn't take her to bed and put them both out of their misery, but he wasn't explaining himself.

I had also found a tiny hole in the wall in LoDo that I was dying to turn into an old-fashioned cigar bar. The place sat maybe fifty people max and it was tucked away and hidden enough that I knew I could transform it into an exclusive spot that the trenderati would be dying to get into. Because he had been so good to me from the very start, I asked Rome if he wanted to buy in with me and was stunned when he told me no. When I told Royal his response she just smiled at me and told me the place was mine. Rome wanted me to have something all my own to either sink or swim with just in case the rest of it fell apart. He was trying to take care of me in his own gruff way. So tonight I had been talking with Zeb because I finally signed a lease on the place and wanted him to get in there to remodel the interior. The planning had gone longer than I expected, so I was quiet as I walked through the house just in case Royal was already in bed.

The lights in the house were off as I made my way through to that incredible kitchen and poured myself a scotch from my own private stash. The sliding glass door that led to the deck off the back of the house was cracked open and Tom Petty was playing softly from somewhere outside. Royal still liked her bubblegum pop, but when she was in a mellow mood and just needed to unwind after a long day, she tended to fall back on the classics, which I had to admit, I much preferred.

I took my drink and pulled the door open, my eyes automatically going to the set of Adirondack chairs that occupied the far corner of the deck opposite the hot tub. She was sitting in the dark outside in the cold; it was the first part of February, so there was still snow on the ground, and I wasn't at all surprised that all she had on was one of my long flannel shirts and a pair of Uggs. I swear she was antipants as soon as she hit the front door. Not that I would ever be stupid enough to complain about it. She had a beer in her hand and a soft smile on her face, which reminded me every time I saw her here that this house and these moments of making it a home meant nothing without her in them.

"Did you wait up for me?" I walked over to the chair she was curled up in and pulled her up to her feet so I could kiss her. She tasted like the outside and cold beer. She tasted like heaven and hell all mixed together. I snagged the seat she had been sitting in and pulled her back down so that she was sitting in my lap with her back pressed up against my chest.

She lifted the beer to her lips and snuggled into me. I sighed in pure contentment and wrapped an arm around her trim waist.

"Yeah. I didn't want to go to bed alone."

I rubbed my nose in her soft hair and told her, "You should've called me. I would have come home."

She put one of her hands over mine and I set my glass down on the ground because she was far more interesting to hold on to.

"I was actually talking to Ayden and lost track of time. I knew you couldn't be much longer, so I thought I would just sit out here and wait for you."

"Half naked."

She laughed and lifted an arm up to curl around my neck. "Of course."

"How's the drive from Austin going?" Ayden refused to get on a plane this far along into her pregnancy even if her doctor had informed her it was perfectly safe. She insisted she wasn't taking any unnecessary chances with her little girl, so she and Jet were driving in the unpredictable weather so they could be here next week for Rome and Cora's wedding.

"She sounds fine. Jet was the one suffering. He's doing that guy thing where he wants to drive straight through, and with a wife that's six months pregnant with a baby sitting on her bladder that just isn't happening. She told me he looks like he's going to shoot an embolism every time she tells him she needs to stop and use the bathroom.

Knowing your sister, she's doing it on purpose every fifty miles or so just to aggravate him."

"Probably. I'm excited for them to get here." I had Skyped with Ayden a few times, so I could see the way being an expectant mom was changing my little sister physically. I wanted to see how she was handling it up close and personal, with my own two eyes. And I wanted to put my hands on the baby bump that held my niece.

"Me, too." She fell quiet for a second and then asked softly, "Do you ever think about getting married and having kids?"

I took her beer out of her hand, set it down next to my scotch, and put my hands on her hips so that I could lift her and turn her around so that she was straddling me and we were face-to-face in the dark.

"Do I think about marriage and kids in general, or do I think about them with you, Red?"

She put her hands on my shoulders and shrugged, which sent her auburn hair slithering across my hands in a sexy, cool glide.

"Ayden's due in a few months, Rome and Cora are getting married in a week, Rule and Shaw are living in domestic bliss, Salem just told everyone she's expecting, and Saint couldn't tell Nash yes fast enough when he proposed over Christmas. There's just a lot of kids and forever-after going on around us and you never mention it. I just wondered if it was even in the cards for us."

I untangled one of my hands from her hair and put a finger under her chin so that she couldn't look away from me. "You want to get married, Royal?"

She rolled her eyes at me like that was the stupidest question I could ever ask. "Yeah. Eventually."

I nodded at her and leaned forward so I could kiss her lightly. "Then eventually we'll get married."

She gasped and her mouth fell open in a rather comical way. I pulled her closer so that I could whisper into her ear, "You wanna have my babies?"

She shivered against me as my hands drifted up along her bare thighs under the hem of my shirt. "Absolutely." She breathed the word into my neck as she fell forward to hold me closer.

"You let me know when you're ready for that to start and I'm on board." She would be an amazing mom, and while my skills and ability to parent were probably questionable at best, I would figure it out. Because having a family with this fascinating, fun, wonderful woman wasn't something I was ever going to miss out on.

My hands brushed up against warm, naked skin that was already damp and ready for whatever I wanted to do with her. She lifted a mischievous eyebrow at me and leaned back from where she was nuzzling on my neck so that she could get her hands between us in order to work on my belt.

"Were you planning on giving the neighbors a show?" I couldn't help the humor that laced my voice as she set my hardness free and ran her hand up and down the length.

"I left the lights off for a reason." She smiled at me, and my entire world was in that tiny gesture.

I grunted in response because she wiggled herself up over my straining erection and then slid down so that I was sheathed tightly inside her welcoming and pulsing body. At this angle I could feel the way her body had to stretch to accommodate me. It made my eyes twitch in pleasure. I used the hand that had been stroking her inner thigh and playing with the tender places that led to where we were joined to slip between her slippery folds and find her sensitive little spot of desire.

She said my name on a moan and started to move on top of me. We were still mostly clothed; all any nosy neighbor would see if they bothered to investigate was a flash of her spectacular rear end every time she lifted and fell as she rode me hard. She curled an arm around my shoulders and leaned forward so that our heads were pressed together. Every time she panted I tasted it across my lips. Every time I growled in satisfaction at her she breathed it in. I teased her clit ruthlessly as she ground into me, as her body sucked and pulled on mine with greedy motions. She was beautiful. The way she worked me over was beautiful, and when she came with my name on her lips and my hand coated in her passion, it was so fucking beautiful it pushed me over the edge and I followed right behind her.

We panted together and tried to catch our breath as I moved my hand to curl around her naked butt. She rubbed her cheek against mine and sighed as she told me, "I live for these moments with you, Asa."

I picked her up and carried her inside our house, our home, and thought that Ayden had been right. When you allowed yourself to love and be loved, that was when life really started. I might have come back from the dead once, but I hadn't started living until I let myself love Royal.

*

"Cora told me I have always been her hero, so I needed to look like one on our wedding day." Rome grumbled the response when I asked him how it felt to be in his dress uniform after being out of the army for so long.

We were all standing at the back of the church waiting for this shindig to get started. I think everyone had been a little surprised that Cora wanted to go such a traditional route with her wedding, but according to Rome, his little pixie had always wanted the fairy tale and he was more than willing to give it to her.

At first I had been stunned when he asked me to stand up with him. Of course Cora wanted Royal as a bridesmaid, so it made sense that I would be the one to walk her down the aisle. Rome had given me one of his somber looks and informed me that I belonged up there next to him just as much as Rule, Jet, Nash, and Rowdy did, and how could I argue with that?

Shaw and Ayden were trying to keep RJ entertained so that she didn't shove fistfuls of flower petals into her mouth while she waited for her very important duties as flower girl to start. The adorable, blond toddler was far more interested in making a mess with the rose petals than she was in whatever the women were doing to distract her. She kept looking up at Rome with a big toothy grin and asking him if it was time to get married. The big man just smiled back at his precious little girl and told her, "Almost."

Cora and Rome had welcomed a healthy baby boy only a few months prior. They had also broken the trend and skipped not only the letter *R* for the first name but also the *C*. Baby Zowen was sleeping soundly with Rome's mom and dad while his cousin watched over him carefully. Shaw and Rule's baby boy was just a little over a year old and he was fascinated by his infant cousin. Shaw insisted that the older the little boy got, the more and more his personality was making itself known. He wasn't wild and rebellious like Rule, nor was he mellow and introspective like her. She swore that each day that passed he reminded her more and more of Uncle Remy, and I think everyone in the Archer clan liked that assessment just fine. The baby was sweet, always had a smile or a giggle ready, and seemed content just to bask in his parents' love, and it made Shaw laugh every time she mentioned how much of a daddy's boy he was. Ry and Rule were the best of friends, and even now Rule was sticking his shaved head out of the back of the church to where all the guests were congregated to see how his son was doing.

Ayden groaned as she righted herself back up and walked over to me. My sister was always beautiful, but there was something about her being pregnant that made her out-of-this-world stunning. There was a softness about her that had never been present before and it looked really good on her. She walked over and looped her arm through mine. She just grinned at me when I put a hand on her protruding belly.

"Are you ready to do this?"

I lifted an eyebrow at her because she was looking at Royal where she had her head bent close to Saint's as the two of them chatted about something quietly. "Do you mean today or am I ready to do this with her?"

She put her free hand on top of mine on her belly and looked up at me. "Both."

I was walking her down the aisle as well as Royal since Jet was singing Madness's "It Must Be Love" while Cora walked to the altar.

"I'm ready for both."

She smiled at me and it made happiness bloom inside of me. For two kids from the wrong side of the tracks we really had managed to luck out and end up on the other side of things in a spectacular fashion.

"Is everyone ready?" Brite was officiating at the ceremony, so when he asked the question everyone snapped to attention like a bunch of good little soldiers as he and Rome headed to the front of the church.

When the music started up, Rule and Shaw clasped hands and started down the aisle toward his brother. No one was shocked when they only made it halfway down before he stopped and pulled his pretty blond wife in for a kiss. It made everyone sigh. Nash and Saint went next, the rock on her finger gleaming almost as bright as the smile on her face when she gazed up into those purple eyes, and the two of them glided elegantly down the aisle. Rowdy and Salem went next, both of them looking far too cool for the traditional black tuxes we wore and the simple off-the-shoulder black bridesmaid dresses Cora had picked out. Salem just laughed when, instead of holding her hand and walking down the aisle side by side, Rowdy pulled her in front of him, put his hands across her still-flat stomach, and walked her down the decorated church that way instead.

Royal appeared at my other side and hooked her arm through my free one. She winked at Ayden, then lifted up on her toes so that she could kiss me on the cheek.

"Our turn."

And here it was. This moment. A moment that would seem so simple, so insignificant and irrelevant to some, and yet it was everything to me. This moment was my life coming full circle, and if I hadn't been paying attention, I would've missed it and all the wonderful things that it was full of. Friends. Family. Love. Togetherness.

I took the two most important people in the world to me to the front of the church. I didn't miss the pride in Rome's eyes or the approval in Brite's when I took my place next to the men that had saved me from myself.

It was RJ's turn, and even with Sayer at the back of the church to give her a little nudge, the little girl didn't look like she wanted to move now that all eyes were on her. I saw her bottom lip start to tremble and Rome must have seen it, too. He took a few steps away from the altar so that she could see him. He held one of his hands out to her and Remy's eyes locked on her father and suddenly she was fine. A smile split her face and she marched down the aisle throwing the flowers like she had been born to be a flower girl. Rome tossed his head back in laughter as Remy stopped about halfway down and did a little ballet twirl just for dramatic effect. She forgot all about the flowers after that and ran the rest of the way to Rome, who hefted her up, making her squeal in delight. He put a smacking kiss on the little girl's cheek and walked back to his place in front of Brite.

Jet started to sing and Cora appeared at the back of the church with her father. Joe was also in his dress uniform from the navy, which made the fact that his daughter was in a flouncy, puffy, light pink wedding dress even more noticeable. Of course there would be no white wedding for the punk-rock pixie. It was like the entire church took a collective breath and let it out as the two of them made their way to the front of the church. Rome couldn't take his eyes off the woman that had helped him slay all his dragons. RJ kept clapping her hands and saying, "Mommy is pretty." She sure was. Cora's multicolored eyes gleamed with unshed tears as she slowly made her way toward her waiting family ... all of us.

When Joe handed Cora over to Rome, Rule broke the emotional silence with a loudly whispered, "It's about damn time," which had the entire church laughing. Jet stopped by to give Ayden a quick peck on the cheek and to pat her very round belly before taking his place next to me. We shared a look and I just nodded my head. I had had to do some serious work to earn my place up here next to these men, next to the man that loved my sister when I didn't know how. I would never forget it.

We all had marks, some physical, some emotional, some that would never leave us, and many of those marks were of our own making as we all tried to get to the place we were supposed to be. Our marks defined us, separated us, and made us the men we were today. One fact that none of us up here on this altar could dispute was that the most important mark, the most lasting marks we would all carry with us, came from falling in love with the remarkable women that stood across from us.

We were marked and had been marked in unforgettable and forever ways. We were all better men for it. Marked men. None of us would have it any other way.

AUTHOR'S NOTE

While the Marked Men series has come to a close, I do hope you'll continue on the journey with me into the new spin-off series. ***The Saints of Denver*** *will be based on many of the secondary characters we have grown to care about and love throughout the Marked Men's journey. (And maybe some that we don't like as much because I can't ever do things the easy way!) The new series takes place in the same world as the Marked Men, so I'm sure some of our favorites will be popping up every now and again. I'm so unbelievably excited to start this new adventure with this new crew of interesting, amazing, and definitely unique men and women ... It all begins with Sayer and Zeb's story ... talk about opposites attracting!*

Out October 2015

Asa and Royal's Playlist

So this was a tricky one. Asa is all over the map, so the musical choices that reflect his personality are, too, and I really pictured Royal as upbeat and bubbly, so I knew she needed a pop sound track—which I absolutely don't listen to. So the compromise was that I gave her all old pop songs that were popular when I was younger and can remember hearing on the radio. These choices are silly, catchy, and fun, which fits her personality, but definitely are not the fare that's on the radio today. (Though I do have a secret affinity for Eminem. Don't tell anyone!) This is an interesting one, but it fits and I think it's a good one to say good-bye on ...

Tom Petty, "You Got Lucky," "Even the Losers"
Shooter Jennings, "A Hard Lesson to Learn"
Diamond Rugs, "Blue Mountains"
Britney Spears, "Toxic"
Whiskeytown, "The Battle and the War"
U2, "With or Without You"
Jason Isbell, "Streetlights"

Raconteurs, "Salute Your Solution"

Funeral Party, "Finale"

Black Rebel Motorcycle Club, "Devil's Waitin'"

One Direction, "Better Than Words"

Justin Timberlake, "SexyBack"

P!nk, "Trouble"

Eagles of Death Metal, "I Want You So Hard"

George Thorogood, "Who Do You Love?"

Them Crooked Vultures, "No One Loves Me & Neither Do I"

The Killers, "All These Things That I've Done"

The Duke Spirit, "Love Is an Unfamiliar Name"

Christina Aguilera, "Dirrty"

Guns N' Roses, "Civil War"

Eminem, "Berzerk"

American Aquarium, "Northern Lights"

Band of Horses, "The Funeral"

Slobberbone, "To Love Somebody"

Black Angels, "You're Mine," "Love Me Forever"

Sea Wolf, "O Maria!"

Morningwood, "Best of Me"

Madness, "It Must Be Love"

AUTHOR ACKNOWLEDGMENTS

Before I get into my regular acknowledgments it occurred to me that I need to take a minute and holler at the other authors that have helped me navigate this crazy journey to get the Marked Men into the world. Writing is a joy and a passion but it is also a job, a job with the world's greatest perks and benefits no doubt. It's also a job that has some pretty crazy ups and downs and over the last few years there is a good chance I would have ended up quitting or in a strait jacket if it weren't for these wonderful and extremely talented ladies:

Jennifer Armentrout is my hero. I want to be her when I grow up and I'll make book babies with her any day.

Cora Carmack always makes me laugh. It's good to remember this is supposed to be fun and she never lets me forget it.

Sophie Jordan is the master of reinvention. She is genius and has so many voices and ideas. She is the prime example of how to always grow, always challenge yourself and to never be scared of something new.

Tiffany King is prolly the nicest human being alive. She showcases how easy and effortless it is to support instead of compete. I just love her and her entire outlook on life.

Kristen Proby is a class act. I love her to death and honestly she is the perfect author to showcase how to conduct yourself professionally and thoughtfully in this business and in life. We are an odd pair but I'm so glad she loves me back.

Lisa Desrochers was the first author to tell me that I had something special working for me. She was so kind and so excited for me it was infectious. She's brilliant and her take on romance is so fresh and different it's hard not to admire everything that sets her apart.

KA Tucker is an agency sister and an amazing author, seriously the woman gives me word envy all the time. Every time I read one of her books it makes me want to be a better writer. Plus she's just a doll and every time I'm in the same room with her I just want to hug her face off.

ACKNOWLEDGMENTS

Of course, since this is the end of the series, I have to thank, first and foremost, all the amazing readers who embraced it and loved it as much as I did. Would there have been more after *Rule* without you guys? I can't honestly answer that question with a yes. I love how my misfits found a place in your hearts and so did their misfit creator. I wouldn't push to do better without you guys. I wouldn't give of myself so fully with each book I write if I had never promised not to let you guys down. Being able to share my loves and my passions with so many people over and over again has really been a blessing.

Never doubt that the most important thing to authors is their readers. We want to thrill you. We want you to fall in love. We want to surprise you. We want to shock you. We want to make you angry. We want you to be blown away. We want you to stick with us while we try something new. But more than any of those things, we want to thank you for giving us a platform from which to let these stories shine.

So thank you and a million different thanks for a million different things.

The same goes for the bloggers who have had a hand in getting the boys out into the world. I appreciate those of you who have followed my career—through this series and, more importantly, beyond it. I know that being a blogger can be thankless, but please know that I am thankful for your support and promotion every step of the way. Hell, if it wasn't for bloggers, I wouldn't have had Karen, Michelle, and Rosette to help me navigate my first blog tour or promotional blitz. I wouldn't have had Denise to tell me, "Hey, you need to make a Facebook and a Twitter." I wouldn't have had Mel around to say, "You need a fan page and I'll help you run it," or Mich in all her Kiwi glory to be like "You're gonna be a star and I want to interview you even if no one knows who you are," and Lisa being all "Let's do a character interview—oh, you don't know what that is, I'll walk you through it." Plus, most of the events I come out to see you guys at are spearheaded by passionate bloggers. You are all so important to sharing the love of books with the world that I can't stress my gratitude for what you do enough. I always say I won't name-drop because I value all the bloggers who have been there for me along the way equally. But for those of you who have been on board from day one ... I especially thank you for believing in me and having faith in me being more than a flash in the pan. It matters so much to me.

Getting *Asa* wrapped up took a lot of work. He was a complicated guy with a difficult past, and getting him to a place where he understood that he deserved not only love but to be a better man took work. He really undid me and I wanted to make sure that he not only got the story he deserved but so did the rest of the gang. I absolutely couldn't have gotten him there without Vilma Gonzales (my book spirit animal) and Denise Tung (my story sensei). I needed both of them to make this the best story possible and guide me in the right direction when I was lost. Reaching the end of this series gives me goose bumps. Instead of feeling sad that it's over, I feel like I really did what needed to be done to have everyone be where they were supposed to be. Now all I am is excited to move on to the next thing. I've made many an important, valuable, interesting, and wonderful book friend along this journey. These two ladies rank at the top of that list. I have all the love in the world—and then more—for both of them.

I also wouldn't have nearly as much fun or be as connected to my reader base as I am without Melissa Shank. Man, is she just good people through and through. She manages my life when I can't do it, and she really is the bridge that makes it easy to travel out there and touch base with the people that it matters most to connect with … my readers. She works really hard to keep the minute details fun, and whenever I ask her to take on a task, I just assume it's handled and I think that's so rare to find in people these days. I'm grateful every day that she ended up in my corner. If you want to connect with me and my peeps … I'm talking the peeps that love all things Jay, please come on over and join the Crowd … we have a good time and always encourage everyone to play well with others.

www.facebook.com/groups/crownoverscrowd/

Since it's the end and I always go on and on about my usual suspects: my mom and dad; my Gma, who has read ALL my books and keeps them on a shelf, which just makes my heart happy; Mike, who manages all my heavy lifting for me (I never knew how important that was until I got divorced!); and my dogs … I feel like I can just sum it up and say no one is as lucky as I am. I have wonderful people in my life. I'm truly blessed to be surrounded by love and support on a daily basis. I would never ask for more and I will never accept less than all the wonderful things they have to give.

I do need to say that the idea of living in the moment, of being present and awake for all the wonderful things happening right now, is a constant battle I wage. Every single release day this struggle sends me into a tailspin, but I'm determined this time around to take the lessons this book is about and apply them to my actual life. I'm not only in the arena, I'm also in the moment.

Now on to business … oh yes, putting out a book is very much work and very much a business, so don't let anyone ever try and tell you otherwise.

I've been so fortunate that all the people that I work with in a professional and creative capacity are really wonderful … I mean really.

My editor, Amanda, is feisty and sweet. She only wants the best book possible to get into your hands, and she works really hard to make sure that happens. She hasn't ever tried to change what I do and I value her so much for that. With my books, what you see is what you get, just refined enough to make for an easier and more satisfying read. Amanda has also been willing to let me do different things and push boundaries, and has embraced all my crazy … hell, half the time she encourages it. I really feel lucky she is the one that opened the door for me to be able to tell my stories my way, and hearing her feedback as we work together has not only made me a better writer but a better person along the way.

There is an army of women behind the scenes at a big publishing house that works tirelessly to bring romance and books in general out into the wild. When I was younger I could only dream of a job like that, so to see the girls that do it and do it so well really makes my soul happy.

Jessie and Alaina really do an excellent job not only of managing the business of Jay but also of managing Jay. I'm not always the easiest person in the world to navigate around, but they do it flawlessly and they make the business part of what I do fun. Even though publishing is a business and sales and numbers really do matter, all of the team at HarperCollins make me feel like it's just as much about me. I've said it before and I'll say it again: I ended up in the place I was supposed to be and now I can't imagine being anywhere else.

So thanks, ladies, for giving me this opportunity and working as hard as you do.

KP … oh, where do I start to sing the praises of this lady and her tireless dedication to her clients? She's amazing. The end! Seriously, I loved her before I needed her, but now I love her even more. My admiration for this woman borders on obsessive and I tell her all the time she better hold a spot on the InkSlinger team because if this writing thing doesn't pan out I'm going to work for her. I'm so honored to be part of the InkSlinger roster of talented and groundbreaking authors … know it!

Somehow I've ended up with this ridiculously cool group of people in Texas I get to call my homies. They are funny, kind, and all of them have hearts as big as the state they live in. So this is my special shout-out to the Lone Star peeps that always make me smile: Heather and Brad Self, Stephanie Higgins, KP Simmon, Vilma Gonzales, the entire Shank family (Jake is the best books husband in the land and Lizzy gives me hope for the future), Danielle Sanchez, Yesi Cavazos and Trini Contreras and Damaris Cardinali (okay, Damaris is an East Coast girl, but I always think of her and Trini hand in hand, so she ends up here ☺).

Okay, so this a big one … a major one … the person who deserves more thanks than I can even begin to try to explain and that's my agent, Stacey. She is all the things. She's my support system. My business partner. My priest. My mom. My fashion consultant. My cheerleader. My voice of reason. My sparring partner. She plays so many roles really that I can't thank her or give her enough credit for all the ways she helps me out in my life and my career. I owe my having more books beyond *Rule* and even more series beyond the Marked Men to her. She believed in the boys when others were all "That girl can't spell and I don't think she's ever seen a comma." She always had more belief in me than anyone else and she has never wavered in her assertion that I am supposed to be writing books for a living.

She always tells me she's a fan first and my agent second. I'm her fan first and her client second. I owe pretty much every great opportunity that has come my way since all of this started to Stacey and I don't think there will ever be enough time or words to thank her for that.

So here we are at the end of what really has been an epic journey. I've loved every second of it, even the seconds I hated. I'm really looking at things as if one door has closed and now I'm hurtling myself out an open window and just seeing where I'll land. I have so many fun ideas that I really, really hope you guys want to jump with me.

As always I'm easy to find if you want to holler at me and have me holler back:

- www.facebook.com/jay.crownover
- www.facebook.com/AuthorJayCrownover
- @jaycrownover
- www.jaycrownover.com
- http://jaycrownover.blogspot.com/
- www.goodreads.com/Crownover
- www.donaghyliterary.com/jay-crownover.html
- www.avonromance.com/author/jay-crownover

Thank you for everything.

Love & Ink
Jay

The first step toward getting somewhere is to decide that you are not going to stay where you are.

—*J. P. Morgan*

Rule

JAY CROWNOVER

Sometimes opposites do more than just attract... They catch fire and burn the city down

Shaw Landon is a good girl from a nice family. She knows what she should want: top grades, then a steady job, and, some day, a nice guy to take home to her parents. She also knows what she shouldn't want... but it's hard to stay away from a guy like Rule.

Rule Archer is the guy your mother always warned you about: a tattoo artist with a cocky swagger, a heart-melting smile and a wicked glint in his eye. With his terrible reputation, he's used to getting everything and everyone that he wants. But even he knows that beautiful Shaw is strictly off limits.

... But what if everything you want is exactly what you need?

Turn over to read the first chapter

CHAPTER 1

Rule

At first I thought the pounding in my head was my brain trying to fight its way out of my skull after the ten or so shots of Crown Royal I had downed last night, but then I realized the noise was someone storming around in my apartment. *She* was here, and with dread I remembered that it was Sunday. No matter how many times I told her, or how rude I was to her, or whatever kind of debauched and unsavory condition she found me in, she showed up every Sunday morning to drag me home for brunch.

A soft moan from the other side of the bed reminded me that I hadn't come home alone from the bar last night. Not that I remembered the girl's name or what she looked like, or if it had even been worth her while to stumble into my apartment with me. I ran a hand over my face and swung my legs over the edge of the bed just as the bedroom door swung open. I never should have given the little brat a key. I didn't bother to cover up; she was used to walking in and finding me hungover and naked—I didn't see why today should be any different. The girl on the other side of the bed rolled over and narrowed her eyes at the new addition to our awkward little party.

"I thought you said you were single?" The accusation in her tone lifted the hair on the back of my neck. Any chick who was willing to come home with a stranger for a night of no-strings-attached sex didn't get the right to pass judgment, especially while she was still naked and rumpled in my bed.

"Give me twenty," I said, my eyes shifting to the blonde in the doorway as I ran a hand through my messy hair.

She lifted an eyebrow. "You have ten."

I would have lifted an eyebrow back at her tone and attitude but my head was killing me, and the gesture would have been wasted on her anyway; she was way past immune to my shit.

"I'll make coffee. I already invited Nash but he said he has to go to the shop for an appointment. I'll be in the car." She spun on her heel, and, just like that, the doorway was empty. I was struggling to my feet, searching the floor for the pair of pants I might have tossed down there last night.

"What's going on?"

I had temporarily forgotten about the girl in my bed. I swore softly under my breath and tugged a black T-shirt that looked reasonably clean over my head. "I have to go."

"What?"

I frowned at her as she lifted herself up in the bed and clutched the sheet to her chest. She was pretty and had a nice body from what I could see. I wondered what kind of game I had thrown at her in order to get her to come home with me. She was one I didn't mind waking up to this morning.

"I have somewhere I need to be, so that means you need to get up and get going. Normally my roommate would be around, so you could hang out for a minute, but he had to go to work, so that means you need to get that fine ass in gear and get out."

She sputtered a little at me. "Are you kidding me?"

I looked over my shoulder as I dug my boots out from under a pile of laundry and shoved my feet into them. "No."

"What kind of asshole does that? Not even a 'thanks for last night, you were great, how about lunch?' Just 'get the fuck out'?" She threw the sheet aside and I noticed she had a nice tattoo scrawled along her ribs that curled across her shoulder and along her collarbone. That was probably what had attracted me to her in my drunken stupor in the first place. "You're a real piece of work, you know that?"

I was a whole lot more than just a piece of work, but this chick, who was just one of oh so many, didn't need to know that. I silently cursed my roommate, Nash, who was the real shit here. We had been best friends since elementary school, and I could normally rely on him to run interference for me on Sunday mornings when I had to bail, but I had forgotten about the piece he was supposed to be finishing up today. That meant I was on my own when it came to hustling last night's tail out the door and getting a move on before the brat left without me, which was a bigger headache than I needed in my current state.

"Hey, what's your name anyway?"

If she wasn't pissed before, she was downright infuriated now. She climbed back into a supershort black skirt and a barely there tank top. She fluffed up her mound of dyed blond hair and glared at me out of eyes now smudged with old mascara. "Lucy. You don't remember?"

I slimed some crap in my hair to make it stand up in a bunch of different directions and sprayed on cologne to help mask the scent of sex and booze that I was sure still clung to my skin. I shrugged a shoulder at her and waited as she hopped by me on one foot putting on heels that just screamed *dirty sex*.

"I'm Rule." I would have offered to shake her hand but that seemed silly so I just pointed to the front door of the apartment and stepped in the bathroom to brush the stale taste of whiskey out of my mouth. "There's coffee in the kitchen. Maybe you should write your number down and I can give you a call another time. Sundays aren't good days for me." She would never know how true that statement was.

She glared at me and tapped the toe of one of those awesome shoes. "You really have no idea who I am, do you?"

This time, even against my throbbing brain's wishes, my eyebrow went up and I looked at her with a mouthful of toothpaste foam. I just stared at her until she screeched at me and pointed at her side. "You have to at least remember this!"

No wonder I liked her ink so much; it was one of mine. I spit the toothpaste in the sink and gave myself a once-over in the mirror. I looked like hell. My eyes were watery and rimmed in red, my skin looked gray, and there was a hickey the size of Rhode Island on the side of my neck—Mom was going to love that. Just like she was going to fall all over herself about the current state of my hair. It was normally thick and dark, but I had shaved the sides and dyed the front a nice, bright purple, so now it stuck up straight like a Weedwacker had been used to cut it. Both my folks already had an issue with the scrolling ink that wound around both my arms and up the side of my neck, so the hair was just going to be icing on the cake. Since there was nothing I could do to fix the current shit show looking back at me in the mirror I prowled out of the bathroom and unceremoniously grabbed the girl by the elbow and towed her to the front door. I needed to remember to go home with them instead of letting them come home with me; it was so much easier that way.

"Look, I have somewhere I have to be, and I don't particularly love that I have to go, but you freaking out and making a scene is not going to do anything other than piss me off. I hope you had a good time last night and you can leave your number, but we both know the chances of me calling you are slim to none. If you don't want to be treated like crap, maybe you should stop going home with drunken dudes you don't know. Trust me, we're really after only one thing and the next morning all we really want is for you to go quietly away. I have a headache and I feel like I'm going to hurl, plus I have to spend the next hour in a car with someone who will be silently loathing me and joyously plotting my death, so really, can we just save the histrionics and get a move on it?"

By now I had maneuvered Lucy to the entryway of the building, and I saw my blond tormentor in the BMW idling in the spot next to my truck. She was impatient and would take off if I wasted any more time. I gave Lucy a half grin and shrugged a shoulder—after all it wasn't her fault I was an asshole, and even I knew she deserved better than such a callous brush-off.

"Look, don't feel bad. I can be a charming bastard when I put my mind to it. You are far from the first and won't be the last to see this little show. I'm glad your tat turned out badass, and I'd prefer you remember me for that rather than last night."

I jogged down the front steps without looking back and yanked open the door to the fancy black BMW. I hated this car and hated that it suited the driver as well as it did. *Classy, sleek,* and *expensive* were definitely words that could be used to describe my traveling companion. As we pulled out of the parking lot, Lucy yelled at me and flipped me off. My driver rolled her eyes and muttered, "Classy" under her breath. She was used to the little scenes chicks liked to throw when I bailed on them the morning after. I even had to replace her windshield once when one of them had chucked a rock at me and missed while I was walking away.

I adjusted the seat to accommodate my long legs and settled in to rest my head against the window. It was always a long and achingly silent drive. Sometimes, like today, I was grateful for it; other times it grated on my very last nerve. We had been a fixture in each other's lives since middle school, and she knew every strength and fault I had. My parents loved her like their own daughter and made no bones about the fact that they more often than not preferred her company over mine. One would think with all the history, both good and bad, between us, that we could make simple small talk for a few hours without it being difficult.

"You're going to get all that junk that's in your hair all over my window." Her voice—all cigarettes and whiskey—didn't match the rest of her, which was all champagne and silk. I had always liked her voice; when we got along I could listen to her talk for hours.

"I'll get it detailed."

She snorted. I closed my eyes and crossed my arms over my chest. I was all set for a silent ride, but apparently she had things to say today, because as soon as she pulled the car onto the highway she turned the radio down and said my name. "Rule."

I turned my head slightly to the side and cracked open an eye. "Shaw." Her name was just as fancy as the rest of her. She was pale, had snowy white-blond hair, and big green eyes that looked like Granny Smith apples. She was tiny, an easy foot shorter than my own six three, but had curves that went on for days. She was the kind of girl that guys looked at, because they just couldn't help themselves, but as soon as she turned those frosty green eyes in their direction they knew they wouldn't stand a chance. She exuded unattainability the way some other girls oozed "come and get me."

She blew out a breath and I watched a strand of hair twirl around her forehead. She looked at me out of the corner of her eye and I stiffened when I saw how tight her hands were on the steering wheel.

"What is it, Shaw?"

She bit her bottom lip, a sure sign she was nervous. "I don't suppose you answered any of your mom's calls this week?"

I wasn't exactly tight with my folks. In fact, our relationship hovered somewhere around the mutually tolerable area, which is why my mom sent Shaw to drag me home each weekend. We were both from a small town called Brookside, in an affluent part of Colorado. I'd moved to Denver as soon as I had my diploma in hand, and Shaw had moved there a few years later. She was a few years younger than me, and she had wanted nothing more than to get into the University of Denver. Not only did the girl look like a fairy-tale princess, but she was also on track to be a freaking doctor. My mom knew there was no way I would make the two-hour drive there and back to see them on the weekends, but if Shaw came to get me, I would have to go, not only because I would feel guilty that she'd taken time out of her busy schedule, but also because she paid for the gas, waited for me to stumble out of bed, and dragged my sorry ass home every single Sunday and not once in going on two years had she complained about it.

"No, I was busy all week." I *was* busy, but I also just didn't like talking to my mom, so I had ignored her all three times she had called me this week.

Shaw sighed and her hands twisted even tighter on the

steering wheel. "She was calling to tell you that Rome got hurt and the army is sending him home for six weeks of R and R. Your dad went down to the base in the Springs yesterday to pick him up."

I bolted up in the seat so fast that I smacked my head on the roof of the car. I swore and rubbed the spot, which made my head throb even more. "What? What do you mean he got hurt?" Rome was my older brother. He had three years on me and had been overseas for a good portion of the last six. We were still tight and, even though he didn't like all the distance I'd put between me and my parents over the years, I was sure that if he was injured I would have heard it from him.

"I'm not sure. Margot said something happened to the convoy he was in when they were out on patrol. He was in a pretty bad accident I guess. She said his arm was broken and he had a few cracked ribs. She was pretty upset so I had a hard time understanding her when she called."

"Rome would have called me."

"Rome was doped up and spent the last two days being debriefed. He asked your mom to call because you Archer boys are nothing if not persistent. Margot told him that you wouldn't answer, but he told her to keep trying."

My brother was hurt and was home, but I hadn't known about it. I closed my eyes again and let my head drop back against the headrest. "Well, hell, that's good news I guess. Are you going to go by and see your mom?" I asked her. I didn't have to look at her to know that she had stiffened even more. I could practically feel the tension rolling off her in icy waves.

"No." She didn't say more and I didn't expect her to. The Archers may not be the closest, warmest bunch, but we didn't have anything on the Landons. Shaw's family crapped gold and breathed money. They also cheated and lied, had been divorced and remarried. From what I had seen over the years, they had little need or interest in their biological daughter, who, it seemed, was conceived in order to get a tax deduction rather than time spent in a bedroom. I knew Shaw loved my house and loved my parents, because it was the only semblance of normalcy she had ever experienced. I didn't begrudge her that; in fact I appreciated that she took most of the heat off me. If Shaw was doing well in school, dating an affluent undergrad, living the life my parents had always wanted for their sons but had been denied, they stayed off my case. Since Rome was usually a continent away, I was the only one they could get to so I took no shame in using Shaw as a buffer.

"Man, I haven't talked to Rome in three months. It'll be awesome to see him. I wonder if I can convince him to come spend some time in D-town with me and Nash. He's probably more than ready for a little bit of fun."

She sighed again and moved to turn the radio back up a little bit. "You're twenty-two, Rule. When are you going to stop acting like an indulgent teenager? Did you even ask this one her name? In case you were wondering, you smell like a mix between a distillery and a strip club."

I snorted and let my eyes drift back shut. "You're nineteen, Shaw. When are you going to stop living your life by everyone else's standards? My eighty-two-year-old grandma has more of a social calendar than you, and I think she's less uptight." I wasn't going to tell her what she smelled like because it was sweet and lovely and I had no desire to be nice at the moment.

I could feel her glaring at me and I hid a grin. "I like Ethel." Her tone was surly.

"Everybody likes Ethel. She's feisty and won't take crap from anyone. You could learn a thing or two from her."

"Oh, maybe I should just dye my hair pink, tattoo every

visible surface of my body, shove a bunch of metal in my face, and sleep with everything that moves. Isn't that your philosophy on how to live a rich and fulfilling life?"

That made me crank my eyes back open and the marching band in my head decide to go for round two.

"At least I'm doing what I want. I know who and what I am, Shaw, and I don't make any apologies for it. I hear plenty of Margot Archer coming out of your pretty mouth right now."

Her mouth twisted down into a frown. "Whatever. Let's just go back to ignoring each other, okay? I just thought you should know about Rome. The Archer boys have never been big on surprises."

She was right. In my experience surprises were never a good thing. They usually resulted in someone getting pissed and me ending up in some kind of fight. I loved my brother, but I had to admit I was kind of irritated he hadn't, one, bothered to let me know he was hurt, and, two, was still trying to force me to play nice with my folks. I figured Shaw's plan for us to ignore each other the rest of the way was a winner, so I slumped down as far as the sporty little car would allow and started to doze off. I was only out for twenty minutes or so when her Civil Wars ringtone jarred me awake. I blinked my gritty eyes and rubbed a hand over the scruff on my face. If the hair and the hickey didn't piss Mom off, the fact I was too busy to shave for her precious brunch might just send her into hysterics.

"No, I told you I was going to Brookside and won't be back until late." When I looked across the car at her she must have felt my gaze because she looked at me quickly and I saw a little bit of pink work its way onto her high cheekbones. "No, Gabe, I told you I won't have time and that I have a lab due." I couldn't make out the words on the other end but the person sounded angry at her brush-off, and I saw her fingers tighten on the phone. "It's none of your business. I have to go now, so I'll talk to you later." She swiped a finger across the screen and tossed the fancy device into the cup holder by my knee.

"Trouble in paradise?" I didn't really care about Shaw and her richer-than-God, future-ruler-of-the-known-universe boyfriend, but it was polite to ask when she was obviously upset. I hadn't ever met Gabe, but what I'd heard from Mom when I bothered to listen was that he was custom-made for Shaw's future doctor persona. His family was as loaded as hers; his dad was a judge, or lawyer, or some other political nonsense I had no use for. I was sure, beyond a shadow of a doubt, that the dude wore pleated slacks and pink polo shirts with white loafers. For a long moment I didn't think she was going to respond, but then she cleared her throat and started tapping out a beat on the steering wheel with her manicured fingers.

"Not really, we broke up but I don't think Gabe really gets it."

"Really?"

"Yeah, a couple weeks ago, actually. I had been thinking about doing it for a while. I'm just too busy with school and work to have a boyfriend."

"If he was the right guy you wouldn't have felt that way. You would have made the time because you wanted to be with him."

She looked at me with both blond brows raised to her hairline. "Are you, Mr. Manwhore of the Century, seriously trying to give me relationship advice?"

I rolled my eyes, which made my head scream in protest. "Just because there hasn't been one girl I wanted to hang out with exclusively doesn't mean I don't know the difference between quality and quantity."

"Could have fooled me. Gabe just wanted more than I

was willing to give him. It's going to be a pain because my mom and dad both loved him."

"True that; from what I've heard he was pretty much custom-made to make your folks happy. What do you mean he wanted more than you were willing to give? Did he try to put a rock on your finger after only six months?"

She gave me a look and curled her lip in a sneer. "Not even close, he just wanted things to be more serious than I wanted them to be."

I laughed a little and rubbed between my eyebrows. My headache had turned into a dull throb but was starting to be manageable. I needed to ask her to swing by a Starbucks or something if I was going to get through this afternoon.

"Is that your prissy way of telling me that he was trying to get in your pants and you weren't having it?"

She narrowed her eyes at me and pulled off the freeway at the exit that took us toward Brookside.

"I need you to stop by Starbucks before going to my parents' house, and don't think I didn't notice you aren't answering my question."

"If we stop we're going to be late. And not every boy thinks with what's in their pants."

"The sky isn't going to fall on us if we show up five minutes behind Margot's schedule. And you have got to be kidding me—you strung that loser along for six months without giving it up? What a joke."

That made me flat-out laugh at her. I laughed so hard that I had to hold my head in both hands as my whiskey-logged brain started screaming at me again. I gasped a little and looked at her with watery eyes. "If you really believe that he wasn't interested in getting in your pants, you aren't nearly as smart as I always thought you were. Every single dude under the age of ninety is trying to get in your pants,

Shaw—especially if he's thinking that he's your boy. I'm a guy, I know this shit."

She bit her lip again, conceding I probably had a valid point as she pulled the car into the coffee shop's parking lot. I practically bolted out of the car, eager to stretch my legs and get a little distance from her typical haughty attitude.

There was a line when I got inside, and I took a quick look around to see if I recognized anyone. Brookside is a pretty small town and usually when I stopped by on the weekends I inevitably ran into someone I used to go to school with. I hadn't bothered to ask Shaw if she wanted me to grab her anything because she was being all uppity about having to stop in the first place. It was almost my turn to order when my phone started blasting a Social Distortion song in my pocket. I dug it out after ordering a big-ass black coffee and took a spot by the counter next to a cute brunette who was trying her hardest to not get caught checking me out.

"What up?"

I could hear the music in the shop blaring behind Nash when he asked, "How did this morning go?"

Nash knew my faults and bad habits better than anyone, and the reason we had maintained our friendship as long as we had was because he never judged me.

"Sucked. I'm hungover, grumpy, and about to sit through yet another forced family function. Plus, Shaw is in rare form today."

"How was the chick from last night?"

"No clue. I don't even remember leaving the bar with her. Apparently I did a huge piece on her side so she was a little pissed that I didn't remember who she was, so ouch."

He chuckled on the other end of the line. "She told you that, like, six times last night. She even tried to pull her top off to show you. And I drove your dumb ass home last night, drunko. I tried to get you to leave at, like, midnight but you weren't having any of it, as usual. I had to drive your truck home and then take a cab back to get my car."

I snorted and reached for the coffee when the guy behind the counter called my name. I noticed the brunette's eyes follow the hand that wrapped around the cardboard cup. It was the hand that had the flared head of a king cobra on it, the snake's forked tongue making the *L* in my name that was inked across my four knuckles. The rest of the snake wound its way up my forearm and around my elbow. The brunette's mouth made a little O of surprise so I flashed her a wink and walked back to the BMW.

"Sorry, dude. How did your appointment go?"

Nash's uncle Phil had opened the tattoo shop years ago on Capitol Hill when it mainly catered to gangbangers and bikers. Now with the influx of young urbanites and hipsters populating the area, the Marked was one of the busiest tattoo parlors in town. Nash and I met in art class in the fifth grade and have been inseparable since. In fact, ever since we were twelve our plan was to move to the city and work for Phil. We both had mad skills and the personality to make the shop bump with business so Phil had no qualms apprenticing us and putting us to work before we were both in our twenties. It was killer to have a friend in the same field; I had a plethora of ink on my skin that ranged from not-so-great to great that chronicled Nash's evolution as a tattoo artist, and he could state the same thing about me.

"I finished that back piece that I've been working on since July. It turned out better than I thought and the dude is talking about doing the front. I'll take it, because he's a fat tipper."

"Nice." I was juggling the phone and the coffee, trying to open the door to the car when a female voice stopped me in my tracks.

"Hey." I looked over my shoulder and the brunette was standing a car over with a smile on her face. "I really like your tattoos."

I smiled back at her and then jumped, nearly spilling scalding hot coffee down my crotch as Shaw shoved the door open from the inside.

"Thanks." If we had been closer to home and Shaw wasn't already putting the car in reverse I probably would have taken a second to ask the girl for her number. Shaw shot me a look of contempt that I promptly ignored, and I went back to my conversation with Nash. "Rome is home. He got in an accident and Shaw said he's got a few weeks of R and R coming to him. I guess that's why Mom was blowing my phone up all week."

"Kick ass. Ask him if he wants to roll with us for a few days. I miss that surly bastard."

I sipped on the coffee and my head finally started to calm down. "That's the plan. I'll hit you up on my way home and let you know what the story is."

I flicked my thumb across the screen to end the call and settled back into the seat. Shaw scowled angrily at me and I swore her eyes glowed. Really. I have never seen anything that green, even in nature, and when she gets mad they are just otherworldly.

"Your mom called while you were busy flirting. She's mad that we're late."

I sucked on more of the black nectar of the gods and started tapping out a beat on my knee with my free hand. I was always kind of a fidgety guy and the closer we got to my parents' house, the worse it usually got. Brunch was always stilted and forced. I couldn't figure out why they insisted on going through with it every single week and couldn't figure out why Shaw enabled the farce, but I went, even when I knew nothing would ever change.

"She's mad that *you're* late. We both know she couldn't care less if I'm there or not." My fingers moved faster and faster as she wheeled the car into a gated community and passed rows and rows of cookie-cutter minimansions that were built back into the mountains.

"That's not true and you know it, Rule. I do not suffer through these car rides every weekend, subject myself to the delight of your morning-after nastiness because your parents want *me* to have eggs and pancakes every Sunday. I do it because they want to see *you*, want to try to have a relationship with you no matter how many times you hurt them or push them away. I owe it to your parents and, more important, I owe it to Remy to try to make you act right even though lord knows that's almost a full-time job."

I sucked in a breath as the blinding pain that always came when someone mentioned Remy's name barreled through my chest. My fingers involuntarily opened and closed around the coffee cup and I whipped my head around to glare at her.

"Remy wouldn't be all over my ass to try and be something to them I'm not. I was never good enough for them, and never will be. He understood that better than anyone and worked overtime to try and be everything to them I never could be."

She sighed and pulled the car to a stop in the driveway behind my dad's SUV. "The only difference between you and Remy is that he let people love him, and you"—she yanked open the driver's door and glared at me across the space that separated us—"you have always been determined to make everyone who cares about you prove it beyond a shadow of a doubt. You've never wanted to be easy to love, Rule, and you make damn sure that nobody can ever forget it." She slammed the door with enough force that it rattled my back teeth and made my head start to throb again.

It has been three years. Three lonely, three empty, three

sorrow-filled years since the Archer brothers went from a trio to a duo. I am close to Rome—he's awesome and has always been my role model when it comes to being a badass—but Remy was my other half, both figuratively and literally. He was my identical twin, the light to my dark, the easy to my hard, the joy to my angst, the perfect to my oh-so-totally fucked up, and without him I was only half the person I would ever be. It has been three years since I called him in the middle of the night to come pick me up from some lame-ass party because I had been too drunk to drive. Three years since he left the apartment we shared to come get me—zero questions asked—because that's just what he did.

It's been three years since he lost control of his car on a rainy and slick I-25 and slammed into the back of a semi truck going well over eighty. Three years since we put my twin in the ground and my mother looked at me with tears in her eyes and stated point-blank, "It should have been you" as they lowered Remy into the ground.

It's been three years and his name alone is still enough to drop me to my knees, especially coming from the one person in the world Remy had loved as much as he loved me.

Remy was everything I wasn't—clean-cut, well dressed, and interested in getting an education and building a secure future. The only person on the planet who was good enough and classy enough to match all the magnificence that he possessed was Shaw Landon. The two of them had been inseparable since the first time he brought her home when she was fourteen and trying to escape the fortress of the Landon compound. He insisted they were just friends, that he loved Shaw like a sister, that he just wanted to protect her from her awful, sterile family, but the way he was with her was full of reverence and care. I knew he loved her, and since Remy could do no wrong, Shaw had quickly become an honorary member of my family. As much as it galled me, she was the only one who really, truly understood the depth of my pain when it came to losing him.

I had to take a few extra minutes to get my feet back under me so I sucked back the rest of the coffee and shoved open the door. I wasn't surprised to see a tall figure coming around the SUV as I labored out of the sports car. My brother was an inch or so taller than me and built more along the lines of a warrior. His dark-brown hair was buzzed in a typical military cut and his pale-blue eyes, the same icy shade as mine, looked tired as he forced a smile at me. I let out a whistle because his left arm was in a cast and sling, he had a walking boot on one foot, and there was a nasty line of black stitches running through one of his eyebrows and across his forehead. The Weedwacker that had attacked my hair had clearly gotten a good shot at my big bro, too.

"Looking good, soldier."

He pulled me to him in a one-armed hug and I winced for him when I felt the taped-up side of his body clearly indicating some injury beyond the busted ribs. "I look about as good as I feel. You look like a clown getting out of that car."

"I look like a clown no matter what when I'm around that girl." He barked out a laugh and rubbed a rough hand through my spiky hair.

"You and Shaw are still acting like mortal enemies?"

"More like uneasy acquaintances. She's just as prissy and judgmental as always. Why didn't you call or email me that you were hurt? I had to hear it from Shaw on the way over."

He swore as we started to slowly make our way toward the house. It upset me to see how deliberate he was moving and I wondered if the damage was more serious than what was visible.

"I was unconscious after the Hummer flipped. We drove

over an IED and it was bad. I was in the hospital for a week with a scrambled noggin, and when I woke up they had to do surgery on my shoulder so I was all drugged up. I called Mom and figured she would let you know what the deal was, but I heard that, as usual, you were unavailable when she called."

I shrugged a shoulder and reached out a hand to steady him as he faltered a little on the stairs to the front door. "I was busy."

"You're stubborn."

"Not too stubborn. I'm here aren't I? I didn't even know you were home until this morning."

"The only reason you're here is because that little girl in there is bound and determined to keep this family together regardless if we're her own or not. You go in there and play nice; otherwise, I'll kick your ass, broken arm and all."

I muttered a few choice words and followed my battered sibling into the house. Sundays really were my least favorite day.

What do you do when
the one who defined your past
becomes your future?

'His kiss was like the past and like the future; the then and the now.'

Nash Donovan, tattooist and good-time guy, never knew his father. But when his Uncle Phil reveals a terminal illness, he wants Nash to know a family secret. Reeling from the truth, Nash needs something to hold on to – and the nurse with the beautiful grey eyes seems somehow familiar…

Saint Ford doesn't know what to think when Nash crashes back into her life. They knew each other way back when, and although she feels – and looks – different, she can't tell if Nash is still the same guy: the one who made her life hell and who she vowed never to forgive. Trouble is, Nash is impossible to stay away from…

Can she forgive the first man to steal her heart – and herself – for the mistakes of the past?